Passionate Jade

GEORGIANNA BELL is a well-known author under another name. She lives in Scotland, loves Scottish history, and will be writing more novels under this name.

GEORGIANNA BELL

Passionate Jade

Collins

FONTANA BOOKS

First published in 1979 by Fontana Paperbacks

© Georgianna Bell 1979

Made and printed in Great Britain by
William Collins Sons & Co Ltd, Glasgow

For Netta Martin
who is also Lucy Ashton,
For Claire Carlton
and Susan Watt
with thanks for
their generous assistance.

PART ONE

CHAPTER ONE

The old house lay serene and beautiful in the clear winter light, surrounded by the clusters of great trees which were such a feature of Ayas Bywaters. Jade looked back at it for as long as possible until the carriage turned the corner of the road.

London, Mama had told Jade, was filled with diversions. There would be elegant clothes to buy, new people to meet, entertainments to sample. The London house, in Allamond Road, was spacious and central, and she, Jade, was to be introduced to the fashionable world.

Jade doubted if she would like anything as much as Ayas Bywaters, and her country life. She thought of the house on a summer day with tea on the lawn and the smell of roses warm and sweet. Still, her curiosity was aroused at the thought of London, of new clothes and new people in place of the neighbours she had always known. She knew what Mama's plans were for her, and felt a tingle of pleasure and fear.

Vera Benedict watched her changeling daughter with wary pride. She had never wished to call her by the name her husband had insisted on in a rare moment of dominance, but even Vera found her stunning, beautiful green eyes and her almost Chinese delicacy of form suited the name. Among the country gentry and their fair daughters, Jade stood out with a disturbing individuality.

But she had kept Jade isolated far too long and the child would soon be sixteen. She owed it to her daughter to arrange a good marriage. Where they had come from, pleasures were all bucolic and the men were the same. Jade would have been wasted on one of them. London was the proper place for an heiress who was witty and intelligent as well as beautiful. Miss Jardine Benedict would catch a baronet or perhaps even an earl. By the time she had her birthday, if Vera had anything to do with it, she'd be betrothed. Jade was an only child. She'd be a remarkable enough catch to attract almost any eligible man. Vera's fingers curled sensuously inside the muff and her face relaxed into lines of satisfaction.

A new life could not fail to hold adventure for the whole family.

When Jade awoke that first morning at Allamond Road, she could hardly believe she was not in yet another inn on the long journey. It was strange to wake up in changed surroundings, and to think of them as home.

Jade wanted to know more of London than the elegant houses across the street, but her mother's first preoccupation was to find a housemaid who would also help Jade. Jade had been upset when her old maid from Ayas Bywaters had refused to accompany them to London, but she knew of the young man with whom her maid was walking out. Jade felt both excitement and curiosity watching her companion of almost her own age being already in love with a man. Would she ever feel this?

Her father took her out in the carriage to have her first look at London. Handsome and charming, Mark Benedict was almost as delighted as Jade to see London again. He had been kept from it for so long by Vera. They looked at the Thames and the Tower and Somerset House and marvelled at the constant procession of horses and conveyances, the crowds thronging the narrow pavements, the urchins and journeymen, bakers and costermongers. The strangest things they saw sold were birds' nests in a big shallow basket. Jade could not imagine what they were for but Mark asked and was told that a canary was sat on the nest to hatch out the eggs.

The glass globes containing gold and silver fish were prettier by far. 'We'll make a pond,' Mark said, 'and come to buy some.' There were flowers and hot chestnuts and pastries and oranges, bow-fronted shops glowing with light so that one didn't notice the winter greyness.

Mama succeeded in hiring her maid so the stolen pleasures of exploration were over. There was not the same freedom when Vera was with them, insisting that Jade have interminable fittings for new, smart clothes and fashionable shoes.

However boring the fittings were, Jade could not help but enjoy the results. She was feminine enough to obtain a sensuous pleasure from the feel and colour of the beautiful materials she was to wear. Silks, velvets and fur, lace and ribbons, little green leather shoes, satin pumps, high-heeled boots, cambric undergarments, Jade thought them vastly pretty without ever having the conviction she would really wear them all.

Her conscience was stirred whenever she saw the street children, hunched and grimy, the pale faces and threadbare garments of the poor. She thought it terrible that there was no benevolent hand and pocket to pay for plenty for them and Vera was impatient that her daughter seemed not as grateful as she'd have wished when the packages arrived from the dressmakers.

Vera had not wasted her time. She had left cards at several houses and had had others returned. People were curious and the Benedicts were known to be affluent. The servants gossiped. Already, she had arranged a ball for the end of the month and a large number of guests were expected. Allamond Road was a good address and Vera and Mark presentable even if from the country. An only child could expect a generous dowry and eventually to inherit all there was. Parents of second and third sons would take care they were introduced to Miss Jardine. A patrimony stretched only so far.

Marriage was a state Jade found difficult to envisage. Mama was so much the dominant partner in her parents' relationship, but Papa was more fun. He loved her in spite of all her faults. They laughed together. Mama had little sense of humour and, regrettably, her social position had come to mean more than real happiness.

There was no point in worrying about it. Perhaps she would meet someone like her father, though Jade thought she'd prefer someone stronger.

The weather grew colder. Vera decided it would be pleasant to go to the theatre. She chose the Haymarket though Mark expressed a preference for Drury Lane.

'We can go there another time,' Jade said. The future stretched out, prolonged and mysterious. They could visit every theatre in London. Bubbles of anticipation rose inside her, headier than champagne. She was told to wear the cream-coloured gown, with the edging of marmot. It was a very pretty garment, falling in folds from just under the high bodice. The Empress of France had favoured the fashion and it was charming. Over it, Jade wore a cape of brown velvet with a turquoise lining and a turquoise velvet ribbon in her hair. Her muff was of fur to match the narrow edging on the gown.

People stared into the carriage as they drove through the faintly misty streets, the gaslights diffused into yellow circles, each smaller than the one before. The effect was enchanting. Jade had always been influenced by visual beauty.

They had a box at the Haymarket. Vera's idea had been that they should be seen and noted but Mark and Jade wanted only to see everyone else. The little gilt chairs shone in the curtained dimness but there was sufficient light to make out the entire auditorium. White necks and bosoms were illuminated, soft and ethereal as pearl. Eyes gleamed in smoky sockets. Jewels glittered in piled-up hair. A red-head wore a green gown cut almost as low as her nipples which stood out against the stiff satin a little defiantly as though she knew she would be censured. Plumes nodded.

Men were either elegant in dark colours or showy in embroidered splendour and fancy waistcoats. They stared from behind quizzing-glasses.

There were thumps from behind the stage curtains and Jade could not help laughing. The sound of her amusement brought some of the glasses to bear on the Benedict box. Vera preened herself, resplendent in blue velvet and pearls. Her fair hair hung down the back of her neck in fat curls. Everything about her was a little over-stated just as Jade was naturally subtle.

It was then that Jade saw the occupants of the box directly opposite. The deep well of the theatre lay between them like an obstacle but she knew she would not easily forget them. The woman was tall and slim with high cheekbones and well-set eyes that could be any colour between grey and black. Her hair was drawn back into a dark chignon that was so much more attractive than the curls most of the women affected. The pewter-coloured gown with the soft sheen was in far better taste than Mama's blue or the peacock colours that filled the stalls and balconies.

The man beside her was quite arresting. There was little colour about him but black and white, his skin paler than was usual and his shirt snowy clean and ruffled; the rest of him, eyes, brows, hair and clothing dark as night. His nose and lips were well cut, the ends of his mouth blunted in a way Jade found fascinating. The couple seemed detached from the rest of the audience, even, strangely, separate one from the other, though, now and again, the man turned a look on the woman that she could only call possessive.

He lit up a cigar and Jade watched the way his strong, lean fingers held it, the way the end reddened into life as he drew on it. It was the only spark of colour about him. He was fire-fly and dusk, ivory and ebony, sable and alabaster.

She envied the woman who sat next to him with such calm detachment. If she were asked to choose what manner of man she most admired, Jade supposed she would describe him. The sight of him gave her the strangest pleasure and yet the indulgence was mixed with a restraint that was foreign to her nature; almost as though she knew that he was out of reach and that it could only hurt her to think of him without caution.

She was to remember him often in the ensuing days, to see the box in which he sat hazed ever so slightly with smoke from the cigar, the glitter of his black eyes as he bent towards his partner – was she his wife, his lover, his sweetheart? The thought had the power to disturb her.

The fog had come right up to the windows, shrouding the house in mystery. Outside, the new gaslights showed through the vapour, soft and yellow and not quite real. To a girl who had lived her life until recently outside a small country town, the gas was a miracle. People, her father told Jade, were afraid that the flame would go back down the pipe, but of course it was not true. It was like stories of Bonaparte eating babies for breakfast. Papa, for all that he seemed indolent and sybaritic, knew a great deal that was practical.

Jade, still unused to the splendour of the London house, stretched herself luxuriously against the silk-sheeted pillow. The candlelight gilded the white silk and turned what portions of her skin were visible to ivory. The touch of the soft, smooth materials against her breast and loins was unexpectedly sensual.

She had a sudden need to look at herself without clothes. The room was warm as Eliza had recently made up the fire. It was the sound of the coals being thrown into the grate that had awakened Jade. Her mother had sent her to have a rest before getting ready for the ball they were giving this evening. Jade, struggling out of sleep, saw Eliza rise from her poking and arranging to stare at the bed and her expression had been odd and a little frightening as though the thoughts she normally kept hidden had struggled to the surface. She had not been able to see that Jade had her eyes open for the hangings had darkened that part of the bed and Eliza had shown, in that unguarded moment, that she resented the fact that Miss Benedict was comfortably at rest while she laboured up the stairs with a heavy bucket.

Jade could not blame her, but now she had become uncomfortably aware of the girl as a person instead of a comforting part of the new background. And then Eliza had done something quite extraordinary. She had gone up to the cheval mirror that reflected the candleglow and stared at herself challengingly, her hands closing over her breasts and travelling down over the rest of her body as though she experienced some great pleasure from the contact. Her face had changed, all the censure wiped out in a blurred softness. Her tongue came out and ran itself over the parted lips. She gave a tiny, stifled moan.

Then, there was some small sound on the stair and Eliza rushed back to the hearth, picked up the brass bucket and was gone.

Getting out of bed, Jade took off her nightgown and went to the mirror. She was much slimmer than Eliza but she was not yet sixteen. How pale bodies were! Her breasts were small and hard like white lemons. Everything about her was white except for the triangle of hair between her thighs and that was the same light, glossy brown as the long hair that fell straight and silky over her shoulder blades and tickled the indentation of her waist as though, for a moment, ghostly fingers touched her.

She wondered why she had pelvic hair. Perhaps it was nature's way of hiding a part of her Mama always insisted was private and never to be spoken about. Jane thought the soft brown pelt only drew attention to it. Men, she was sure, were fashioned differently, though the marble statues in the art galleries wore leaves over that area and that only confused the issue.

The remembrance of Eliza's fondling of herself and the thought of the statues that hid their secrets sent a queer little tingle deep inside her body. She wished she were not so untutored. But it would not be for long! Tonight's festivities were mostly on her own behalf. It was her introduction to a society from which she would be expected to choose a husband. Or have one chosen for her. That was far more likely.

If it had not been that Mama had recognized Jade's struggle

to understand her own evolving personality, she'd have stayed in the lovely, safe house in the country where she could keep an eye on the husband she adored but did not trust. In so small a circle of acquaintances, everyone knew everyone else and it was difficult for Papa to do anything that was not noted. He had married an heiress, the daughter of Ben Jardine, one of the merchants who had prospered out of the East India Company and the spice trade. Mama had fallen wildly in love with Papa who had no money but was handsome, charming – and weak. She insisted on having him and in the end Grandfather had given way on condition he doled out the allowance as he thought fit and that the first child bore the family name.

There must be no other girl in the world who was called Jardine! But Mama had suffered complications at the birth and could have no more babies, so Jade had been christened after the old man. It was Papa, who for once had asserted himself, and took one look at his daughter's long, slightly slanting green eyes and said that she would be known as Jade for her eyes were the very colour of the valuable Chinese stone that was carved into such beautiful intricacies. He had given her what must surely be the tiniest piece of jade in the world, no bigger than the top of her thumb and depicting a sea-horse. She kept it usually in a secret pocket of her girdle for she was superstitious about being separated from it. The hooting of an owl brought her back to the present. An owl, in London!

It was too early to get ready for the ball. She would be put into bodice, stays and embroidered drawers, petticoats and stockings, then fastened into the gown she had not yet worn, the white satin in the French style with tiny puffed sleeves, wide square neck, the skirt hanging slim and almost straight from just below the bosom, just long enough to give a glimpse of the jade-green slippers that matched the fan, the two plumes in her head-dress and the embroidery on sleeves and hem.

She pulled open the door of the press and watched the gown sway ever so gently on the hanger, loving the soft sheen on the material, then shivered as she realized she was still naked and the heat of the fire did not penetrate the corners of the room.

Pulling a house-robe around her she went towards the window, drawn by the soft moons of the gas-lamps, each one paler than the last, dying away in a pall of soft grey. There were a few trees down the street and they too were mere ghosts stretching out dim claws to touch at window-panes. The effect was so magical that Jade opened the window and leaned out, revelling in the sense of doing something that would be forbidden. Mama and Mrs Baker, the housekeeper, would say that the fog would very quickly leave a covering of soot and smuts over the walls and furnishings but the touch of the opaque curtain was unexpectedly exciting, smelling of autumn and sulphur, catching at her throat.

The wind was rising. Jade could hear it whining in the chimney, striking a scatter of sparks from the burning logs in the fireplace. She had a sudden glimpse of the sky, the moon scudding behind the roofs and chimney pots, the veils of grey torn from the arms of the trees like wisps of georgette or dirty muslin, and then she was looking down into the deep basement in front of the house. Her breath caught in her throat. The greenish light from the small window lay upon two faces. The woman was surely Eliza! She obviously thought herself safe from discovery under cover of the fog, seeming not to realize that the wind had created a pocket in the obscurity.

The man lifted his head briefly and Jade saw that he was young and reddish-haired. He was smiling broadly as though he and Eliza exchanged some private joke. Jade stiffened, recognizing his features, yet not quite sure when or where she had seen him before. Then she remembered. It had been two days ago, when she and Mama had been getting into the coach to visit the dressmaker for the last time before the ball. He'd stood at the corner, the sunlight on his face and the bottle-green coat, lighting up a pipe as though he had all the time in the world.

Jade had a good memory for faces and events. Her mind stored up everything as a squirrel hoards nuts. She remembered then that Mrs Baker had told Mama Eliza seemed very satisfactory and was walking out with a respectable young man. She worked hard and was no trouble in the weeks she'd been with the household. She thought the girl would 'do'.

Jade wondered what Mrs Baker would say if she could see Eliza now. The man was running his hands down her body, just as the girl had done in this room half an hour ago. Eliza had known he was coming. That owl call! There were no owls so near the city centre. It was because Jade heard them constantly at Ayas Bywaters that she had not reacted more positively to the sound.

Eliza lifted a waxen-pale face made eerie by the reflected scullery light and began to shift her head from side to side, her closed eyes giving the impression that her features were those of a death-mask brought weirdly back to life. The man's hands lifted Eliza's skirts up to the waist and he seemed to thrust himself forward though Jade couldn't see properly because of the shielding folds of material. There was just this strange rhythmic dance with its own regular pattern, Eliza's head jerking from side to side, her knuckles white on the man's thrusting shoulders. Then she opened her lips on a long-drawn-out cry that was snatched away by the force of the breeze. The two figures lurched into a tight embrace that seemed to go on for ever, then they fell apart. Jade saw the man fumble with his breeches, Eliza drop her skirt and lean for a moment against the wall. They seemed to become aware of the fact that the fog had begun to disperse. Eliza looked nervously over her shoulder and held out a hand in parting. Another moment and she had opened the scullery door, releasing a flood of yellow light. The man laughed softly, made his way slowly up the steps as the scullery door closed, then stepped out into the thinning haze. He stood there, a dark shadow against the drifting vapour, then was swallowed up as the breeze was stilled and the stealthy fog crept slowly back, obliterating the basement and the steps.

Jade drew back and shut the window. She was not sure what she had seen. A glance at the clock on the mantel showed her that it had all happened very quickly. The remembrance of the short encounter had excited her more than she cared to admit. She had once overheard Cook at Ayas Bywaters say, 'You must never let 'is 'and go above yer knee. 'Tis where all the trouble do start!'

The stranger's hand had been well above Eliza's knee. She knew in that instant where trouble began and the same itchy tingle ran into the hollow between her thighs, tantalizing, disturbing. She flung herself about the room, restless, longing for the moment to have her bath and to put on the new gown for the first time. White and jade. Jade and white. The words became a refrain, a new nursery jingle like 'oranges and lemons'. 'Here comes the chopper to chop off your head.' She had never liked the ending. Images of her white skin, her white gown with the narrow jade trimming, the brown pelt that hid the entrance to her body, crowded her mind. If only

15

she knew what it all meant. And how could she ever look Eliza in the face knowing what she'd just witnessed? She should have drawn back from the window at once only she'd felt hypnotized. But it was the most intriguing thing that had ever happened and the body she had always regarded as something to be fed and always covered had taken on a new dimension. Her childhood had receded as the fog was now retreating to show the lumped shapes of the houses opposite, the crooked branches of the trees, the diffused circle of the moon beyond the chimneys.

Mama's voice was carried up the stairs, a little sharp with tension and relief that now her guests' carriages would be able to find their way, ordering Kate upstairs to supervise Miss Jade's bath and dressing and hurry, do!

Altogether, it promised to be the most interesting evening of her life.

She did not know any of her mother's guests. Mama and Papa stood at the door while a number of strange, well-dressed people were announced, said a few words then passed into the ballroom where they were reflected briefly in the shining floor then moved on to sit in one of the little gilt chairs or to hold conversations in bright, small groups.

Jade stood beside her parents, swishing the little green fan to and fro because of the heat of the hundreds of candles added to the fire's warmth. The chandeliers looked very fine, the little flames catching glints from the carved glass pendants. She was unaware of how young and striking she looked in the simple gown and the short string of pearls that encircled her neck, the tiny sea-horse dangling from it to nestle in the hollow of her throat. Her hair had been swathed on top of her head and held in place by the band that supported the two green plumes. A ring with a jade stone encircled the third finger of her right hand. Papa had placed it there just before they took up their positions. It was exactly right for her.

The musicians were playing but nobody would dance until Mama and Papa chose their partners. She felt so cool and detached now in the current of air engendered by the movements of the fan, the agitation of her senses schooled to calmness.

'Sir Piers Mandrake and Lady Elizabeth Mandrake. Mr Rupert Mandrake.'

Jade found herself staring into a pair of dark and lively

eyes. Rupert Mandrake looked a great deal more interesting than any of the other young men who had so far gone into the ballroom. His dark brown coat was very well fitting as were his cream-coloured breeches. His stockings and cravat were impeccably white and his satin waistcoat, embroidered in self colour, gleamed as pearly white as her own dress. She hardly saw his parents apart from noting that Sir Piers had a florid face, hawk-nosed and a little cruel, and that Lady Elizabeth was fair and a trifle nervous. Rupert immediately engaged her attention and Jade could not decide whether it was on her own account or because his forceful father had insisted that he made a good impression on the Benedicts' only child. It was one of the drawbacks of being wealthy, she thought, not without regret, then caught her mother's eyes on her, knowing that Mama looked for any flaw in her appearance. Mama was such a perfectionist, unable to bear anything that was soiled or disordered, rejecting anything that she suspected to be unclean. There was something obsessive, Jade decided, in such a necessity for cleanliness. It was fortunate Papa was not so strict. Dear, handsome Papa –

'There's no need for you to wait with us,' Mama said, and Jade realized that it was the Mandrakes who had been invited specially and that it was Rupert who had been singled out as the prize catch, the others so much camouflage, or as second-best should the bigger fish not nibble the bait. She smiled and allowed Rupert to take her arm and direct her through the opened double-doors, so shining white and gold, towards the nearest of the potted palms that cast their spiky shadows on the green silk wall-covering. Since Grandfather Jardine had died, there had been so much more money for extravagances.

Rupert leaned over her protectively, projecting a scent of sandalwood, his white teeth gleaming. Jade was obscurely conscious that this was both pleasurable yet a little effeminate. He was such a splendid young man, yet he seemed not quite real. His father, however, was real enough for both of them. Jade became conscious of his hawklike regard, the cold appraisal of his eyes. 'Why, he looks as though he measures me up for himself!' she thought indignantly and experienced a swift flicker of fear she pushed aside immediately as a ridiculous fancy.

'How very well your gown becomes you,' Rupert said

smoothly with never so much as a glance in his father's direction.

'Thank you.' She wished she knew more of the art of flirtation but there had been no chance to learn before they came to London. The young men who previously came into her orbit were shy and bucolic and she was considered too young for dalliance. But tonight the Empire-styled gown emphasized her tiny firm breasts and clung gently to her hips. The upswept hair left her little neck exposed and graceful.

'How strange your eyes are. I have never seen such an unusual colour. Jade green, I should say, Miss Jardine.'

'So my father says. Do you live in London, Mr Mandrake?'

'Rupert.' The dark eyes seemed to caress her, so smiling and agreeable that she almost overcame her resistance to the perfume of sandalwood on a man.

The music became more urgent and Mama and Papa were there, Papa leading out Lady Elizabeth and Mama on Sir Piers's arm looking very beautiful in her pink gown which was trimmed with lace and some seed pearls in an imitation of a picture she'd seen of the Empress Josephine's at her coronation. Sir Piers was smiling wolfishly, the light from the chandelier snaking down the sides of his magnificent coat. Beside her husband, Lady Elizabeth cut no very dramatic figure and Jade felt sorry for her.

Rupert had to give up Jade to other partners who had asked for dances but again and again he came for her, dancing very exquisitely, altogether so personable that almost any girl would have considered herself fortunate to be singled out as a prospective wife. The purpose of the entire evening was narrowed down to the necessity of responding to the wishes of Mama and Sir Piers.

They drank two glasses of champagne in quick succession and somehow, without quite knowing exactly how she had got there, Jade was in the conservatory, surrounded by the sweet humid scents of tropical growth and with the fuzzed ring of the moon seen through the remnants of fog that breathed on the greenish glass.

'I find you altogether too distracting, Miss Jardine,' Rupert said just a little thickly as though his tongue had become a fraction large for his mouth.

'Mama —'

'Will not worry too much if she knows we are together. After all, isn't that the purpose of this rout?' His hand touched

18

her arm and slid up towards her shoulder.

'I suppose it is. But I hadn't imagined you'd progress so fast.'

'What d'you know of it, eh?' His tone had sharpened a little. 'You're not spoiled goods, are you?'

'Spoiled goods? I only meant that I shouldn't have left the ballroom. And you shouldn't have asked me.' Jade was a little dizzy from the effects of the champagne and the unaccustomed languor that was creeping over her limbs. Rupert had placed a hand on her thigh and she was again reminded of Cook. 'You must never let 'is 'and go above yer knee. 'Tis where all trouble do start.' She repeated the admonition in a breathless, laughing whisper and Rupert was suddenly still and silent.

'You're a baggage, young miss,' he said at last. 'I never know how I am supposed to treat you. My father says you are an inexperienced fifteen, then you come out with damned titillating remarks that make me wonder just how innocent you really are.'

'I am fifteen. It was Cook I heard say what I repeated. You had your hand on me, or had you forgotten? It seemed best to make a joke of it.'

His laughter was a little forced. 'I still think –'

'I've had no – personal experience of men.' The champagne bubbles were tickling her nose, making her want to sneeze, yet the insidious effect of the wine was far from having dissipated. 'But I am not blind, or stupid.'

The lights from the house had found their way through the thicknesses of glass and the resulting greenness lay on Jade so that she looked strange and alien as a figure from the sea.

'I'm inclined,' Rupert said softly, 'to have you, my girl. That gown leaves little to the imagination for all its plain cut. And there's something about your mouth tells me it's for the taking.'

'Only you'd spoil everything, wouldn't you, if you were to –' She stopped, not knowing how to go on, wondering what the next step would be.

'You tantalizing little jade,' he whispered and moved close. 'I was not enamoured of my father's insistence that I take a wife. I confess I was happy enough with gambling and mistresses, but damn me if you aren't more full of promise than any I've had so far.'

'I should not have had the champagne –'

But Rupert would not let her speak. He had pressed her

against one of the twisted metal pillars and forced his mouth over hers. And then, he had opened her lips with his tongue and had darted it inside, between her teeth, like the head of a snake.

She tried to push him away but he was stronger than one would imagine from his dandyish appearance and her body was far more relaxed than she'd believe was safe. It was as though she melted against him, her own body seeming to fit into Rupert's like matching pieces of a puzzle. And the strangest thing was happening to him. It was incredible, but something moved between their tightly locked forms, a part of him that had grown hard and seeking, that meant to probe –

Gasping, she thrust at him. 'Don't! Please – '

'Damn you, my dear,' Rupert said with a trace of viciousness.

'Don't be a fool,' Sir Piers snapped harshly and Jade saw him outlined in green, the hawk-nose jutting. 'I saw you slip away. You gave her two glasses and don't think I was the only one to see. That mother of hers ain't a fool, my boy. You play this cool, d'ye understand? It's not a mistress you're panting after like a rutting dog. Now, apologize to the girl. Your intentions are honourable. She do understand, don't she? That it's marriage, not seduction?'

'Of course she understands. More than you or her mama think – '

'She's – she's not – ?' The cruel voice had grown sharp with interest.

'She's a tease.' Rupert's face was angry in the gloom. 'That's all I'm certain about.'

'Any pretty girl of that age is a tease. Ain't ye discovered that yet? My son begs your pardon, Miss Benedict, but he found you irresistible and none could blame him.'

'I do not. I blame myself. I'm not used to wine, well, not so much so fast.'

'He should not have encouraged you.' A cold hand touched her shoulder, arousing acutest repugnance. Jade was suddenly almost sober again and thankful that it was not Sir Piers for whom she was intended. Her flesh crept, goose-pimpled.

'There's no harm done. He did nothing but kiss me.'

'He should have treated you more gallantly.' The chill finger moved from her shoulder to tickle her under the chin. 'A pretty puss you've turned out to be. Saw you in the coach with your mama but I could not have looked closely enough. You know your mother thinks my son a good match, eh?'

'Yes. But Papa would want me to be in love, I think, as well, and so would I.'

'We'd look after ye well at Wood Park.'

'Wood Park?'

'That's where ye'd live with all of us.'

'Wouldn't Rupert have his own house?'

The cold finger was removed at last. 'No need, my pretty dear. Plenty of room for all.' There was a warning note in Sir Piers's voice that made Jade see a life that would not be quite the paradise she had always imagined. An agreeable young man and a handful of servants of one's own were not the same as living in the house of one's in-laws. She remembered Sir Piers's look of appraisal that had not seemed to be on his son's behalf and it was as though his cold touch was still on her body.

She had never been so glad to hear her mother's voice, the quick tap of her footsteps hurrying towards them. 'Oh, there you are!'

'She was showing us the hot-house, ma'am. 'Tis most pleasantly warm, and the palms are very fine,' Sir Piers said as though the strange episode had never taken place. Rupert shifted uncomfortably. He seemed much in awe of his father but who would not be? Perhaps he was too angry to speak.

'The gardener remained with us, I'm glad to say, not that there's much outside, but this needs a great deal of attention. Why, you're shivering, child. Perhaps I should send for a light shawl.'

'There's really no need,' Jade replied. 'I'll go myself. The servants must be very busy. Anyway, I would like to go upstairs for a moment.'

'Take the hare's foot to your nose while you're about it. The heat of the ballroom has made it shine.' Trust Mama to notice imperfections.

Sir Piers and Rupert bowed politely though their expressions were not so decorous. It was lucky Mama was more concerned with Jade's appearance and that she supposed her daughter meant to visit the stool-room.

'I will not be long, Mama,' Jade said, and it must have been the last lingering effects of the champagne that made her see her mother, for an instant, as a distant figure in shining pink, a spun sugar doll getting smaller and smaller. She wanted to reach out and bring her back but the moment passed.

She went upstairs slowly, glad to be alone, to assemble her thoughts.

Jade paused at the door of her bed-chamber, experiencing a curious reluctance to go inside. She wished she had not drunk the champagne so recklessly. The glasses had been very full and the sparkling liquid looked so pale and innocent. But the effects she'd imagined gone when Sir Piers had touched her, awakening such intense dislike, had returned and her head felt light and her stomach unsettled.

It was no use to skulk upstairs wishing that this or that had not happened. Life was full of happenings and she must face up to them. Part of her had enjoyed the encounter with Rupert, she realized in retrospect. It had been amusing to see his inability to gauge her responses, and she must confess to having been excited by that strange, searching kiss that probed her mouth as she'd imagined that other part of him meant to probe –

Her mind was jerked away from thoughts of Rupert as she heard a small sound close by. One of the servants? But no one came. Jade shivered again. The staircase was not warm and the white velvet spencer would be welcome and less cumbersome than a shawl. She could always take it off when the heat became too great.

Pushing open the door that stood slightly ajar she was aware of the reflected light from the passageway shivering in the surface of the lacquered cabinets that furnished her room. Grandfather Jardine's East Indian travels had embraced other countries besides the Indies and the beautiful Chinese pieces he'd brought back had come to Jade on her father's insistence. The candleglow picked out writhing dragons and exotic water birds surrounded by flowers and Oriental trees, the gilded splendour of the throne-like chair that was cushioned with jade-coloured silk.

She lifted the candlestick from the small table and went into the bedroom, seeing, with a return of sensuous pleasure, the colours rush out of the former gloom, all the richness of gold and green and ivory she loved so much.

Removing the spencer from the appropriate wardrobe, she put it on, warmed her fingers briefly at the pink glow of the fire and returned to the staircase. It was only fancy that made her imagine someone had been in her room, some person who had no right to be there. The house was full of strangers anyway, and someone might have mistaken her door for the entrance to the room that was set aside for cloaks and wraps.

Reaching the foot of the stair, Jade was aware of a current of air proceeding from the morning-room. The cold licked round her ankles as though a window had been left open, and here again, the door was ajar, disclosing a small movement of flickering light.

'Eliza! Is that you?' Jade asked, though why the girl should be attending to fires in a room not normally used after midday she could not imagine. There was no answer but she heard, quite distinctly, a faint foot fall. Impulsively, she went into the room and stood still. The window was open, disclosing tendrils of shifting mist, and there in the middle of the floor stood the red-haired young man in the green coat.

She could never explain why she did not call out. The whole course of her life would have been altered if she had. But, for the moment, curiosity was predominant. This was Eliza's respectable young man, the lover who had so recently done such disturbing things to Mama's housemaid under cover of the fog.

'I suppose you want to see Eliza again,' Jade said, and watched an expression of wariness come over the good-looking young face.

'Eliza? Why should I want to see 'er? And who's she, anyway?' He sounded nervous and uncomfortable, exactly as anyone would who had been caught in a compromising position that was not too serious.

'Oh, come now,' Jade said. 'I've seen you near the house and I've seen you with Eliza. Mrs Baker knows about you. But you know what will happen now that you've forced your way inside, or did Eliza let you in?'

So hunted did he look that she was almost sorry for him. His features were captivating and the set of his mouth betrayed the promise of good humour under other circumstances. Jade noticed that his coat was shabbier than it had appeared earlier on the sunlit street and that the black beaver hat needed brushing. His boots, too, were neglected.

There was something else that she noticed. The drawers of the bureau where Mama did the accounts and wrote her letters were open and there was a rather dirty sack lying beside it, its shape divulging the fact that it contained a variety of articles whose outlines were disturbingly those of clocks and goblets, candlesticks.

'Why, you're a thief!' she said softly, and stepped back a pace or two. 'And Eliza must have helped you. Those windows are never left unfastened. And to think I was going to let you go without calling my father!'

The man's face had changed. It was almost as though he saw someone behind her but she had heard nothing. Jade half-turned her head and became aware of a figure on the edge of vision, someone standing quite close, their arm upraised. She moved instinctively but it was too late. Something crashed on to the back of her head and for a moment it was engulfed in sharp pain. And then the lights and zigzags of colour tailed away like shooting stars and were lost in infinity.

She did not know where she was. It was dark and cold and something sour and heavy pressed down on her. Her body appeared to lie on varying degrees of hardness so that her shoulders and back and thighs hurt a good deal, and one of her feet seemed wedged though she had not the strength to try to release it.

Iron wheels ground over cobbles, and she moved with them, each painful protuberance below her biting into another place, the round of her shoulder, her calf, her left buttock.

The nausea kept her where she was. It was agony to move her head even slightly and she'd probably faint if she tried to sit up. But she managed to lift one hand under the folds of greasy material so that it no longer lay on her face.

She remembered what had happened before the period of darkness. The young man in the morning-room. The person who had come behind her unheard. It was unbelievable but her present position meant that it was no nightmare but reality. She had disturbed thieves and was struck on the head so that she could not raise the alarm. The hard objects upon which she lay were the plunder from the robbery.

Other sounds began to penetrate the folds of the frowsty blanket that covered her. More than one pair of footsteps that kept pace with the barrow on which she had been placed. She knew it must be a barrow because of its shape, and the other hand, investigating, had come upon the edge. A dog barked in the distance and a cat had spat and howled as one of her captors kicked out at it in passing.

Jade lifted the edge of the blanket cautiously and was rewarded with a taste of the fog that seemed to have descended again, obliterating everything but the diffused shapes of distant lights. She dropped the blanket quickly as one of the men spoke.

''E's not goin' to like it, Paddy.'

'Wot could we do?' She could almost see the man in the green coat shrug. He had had an Irish look about him even if his accent was gutter London.

'He's goin' ter want yer guts for bringin' that little package of trouble.'

'She knew about Eliza. The Runners'd know she was a plant and we couldn't use 'er no more, and she's good is Eliza. Best house-maid we'd ever get and some of them houses is fortresses without a wench inside. Molly'd be no use. Stickin' a chiv in the mistress as soon as look at 'er if there was any trouble.'

'You must have been careless, then.'

'How'd I know she'd come to the blasted morning-room? So far as I knew, all the family an' guests were to be in the ballroom an' the servants too busy to wander about. Then, there the silly young bitch was an' I knew as she'd see them things in the sack.'

Jade tried to raise her head but was rewarded with a blinding pain across her eyes and a grinding throb in her skull. A flicker of panic ran along her nerves. If she'd been able to sit up and scream they might run away for fear of discovery. But she could still scream. All she had to do was to wait for someone to come by, only it was obviously late and they might pass no one else.

'Should have killed 'er instead of bashing 'er head,' the unknown man was saying as the pain subsided to a dull, unpleasant gnawing at the back of her skull.

'No,' the man called Paddy said. 'If she saw me, someone else could 'ave and I don't get topped for nobody. Guv-nor Jack'll think of something. Saw me more than once, according to wot she said, an' I *was* careful.'

'Allus most noticin' at that age.'

'Little beauty, ain't she, though?' Paddy replied with satisfaction. 'A sin to have cut 'er off in 'er prime. The Guv'nor might put 'er to Rosie's. That'll teach 'er to poke 'er nose into fings wot don't concern no one else. But more likely he'll just get rid of 'er. Got a tongue, she has, and it's not likely she'll keep it atween 'er pretty little lips.'

'Like to put something there myself,' the other man said softly. 'Hope the Guv don't get rid of 'er too quickly. A lot tastier than Eliza, I'll bet. Not that we'll ever know, not with Nick about. Unless – unless we pushes this barrer up a lane an' as a go 'afore we gets back? Come on, what d'yer say? I'm more than game. Got a pair o' green feathers in 'er hair that need takin' off. Along wi' a lot of other things –'

The barrow had ground to a halt. Paddy was half-laughing and the other man insisted, 'Me first, then. You 'ad your share already.'

'Can't rightly count our Liza. Where's the thrill?'

'I ain't had nobody fer days.'

Jade pressed herself farther on to the barrow, hardly noticing the pain from the sharp-edged objects around and under her. She had not understood what the conversation meant but she felt threatened and too ill to defend herself against one man, never mind two. Desperately, only half aware of the argument that went on between Paddy and his accomplice, she tried to turn herself over in order to slip off the side of the barrow but the blow had been severe and she could not manage it. Although she felt it to be useless, she screamed as loudly as she could, following the first cry with another louder still.

'Gawd! Yer shouldn't have stopped. Put yer hand over her trap fer Jesus' sake. Go on, Paddy! Want ter be caught wi' all this? It's a hanging lot.'

A hand groped over the blanket and Jade's mouth was compressed cruelly hard.

'We'd best get 'er back to the Guv.'

'What's that? Gawd, it's a bleedin' Charley!'

'What's goin' on then? Who was that a-yellin'?'

'Nobody 'ere, Officer. Up there on that waste ground it were. Some wenches take their pleasures a bit noisy like.'

'It was 'ere,' the Charley said obstinately. 'What's on the barrer, then? Let's 'ave a look.' Through the thick, smelly folds of the covering, Jade could see the muted light of the night-watchman's lamp. She squirmed.

'Bits o' scrap,' Paddy said quietly, pressing harder on the girl's mouth.

'Want ter see it.' The Charley bent lower over the barrow.

Paddy, his attention diverted for a moment, relaxed his hold and Jade let out a muffled shout and kicked out with the foot that was free.

''Ere! You got someone there. Wot's the game?'

'For Christ's sake!' Paddy said urgently. 'Give 'im a tap

on his nob and be on our way. Afore anyone gets woke up.'

There was a succession of thuds and the lantern crashed to the cobbles in a sudden upsurge of flame. The Charley cried out, gurgled and sank to the ground without another sound. Jade moaned as the barrow began to move, faster and faster, jolting and grating, throwing her from side to side. Her head struck one of the candlesticks and she could feel her senses swim away on a tide of pain.

Jade had no way of telling how long it was before she came to herself. But she was no longer on the barrow. She was being propelled between two men, her toes scraping the cobbles of an alley lit only by the dim light from a window across which some dingy material had been pulled, leaving a corner through which she could see the cracked cornice of what had once been a fine plaster ceiling.

A few dim figures stood in the shadows, silent and hostile. The strength of their dislike crept towards her like the fog which, once again, had receded into the middle distance. A sickening stench came from the dark piles of refuse against which her once white skirts brushed. She cried out but no one moved. She was forced through a doorway into total blackness.

The man with Paddy suddenly stopped and thrust her against the wall.

''Ere!' Paddy said. 'We'd given up that idea. Never was too keen on it.'

'Shut yer gob.'

Paddy seemed to be going away and with him her faint chance of reprieve.

'Don't leave me!'

She was aware that the man clamped his legs around hers. He pulled impatiently at the bodice of her dress and prised free one of her breasts. The dark was not so intense and she could see the shape of him, smell the foul odour of his clothes. She tried to push against him but he was powerful and seemed not to notice her puny struggles. His mouth came down upon her nipple and he sucked at her breast as though he were a baby. Then he was pulling up her gown just as Paddy had done with Eliza's skirts, fumbling with the fastenings at her waist, dragging down the embroidered drawers, his fingers thrusting inside the little curtain of hair and hurting the soft flesh inside her body.

'No – No!'

She might never have spoken. It was all horrible and degrading and yet the tugging on her nipple was arousing a feeling that was not entirely one of disgust. The warm tingle ran right down her body and lodged between her thighs as though it were the prelude to pleasure instead of intolerable indignity. Her foot had gone to sleep and she could not raise her leg to kick at him as he parted her thighs.

Grunting and excited, the man was exposing his own body, pushing it against hers so that the heat burned against her cool skin. She cried out.

Then there were running footsteps on the stairs, Paddy's voice saying, ''E's got 'er down there, poor little bugger. Tried to get 'er here all in one piece, I did.'

'Tom! Leave off. Guv'nor wants to see 'er.'

Tom continued to thrust himself against her and Jade thought her body would split. She gave a great scream. The two figures hurtled towards them and Tom was pulled away, cursing and struggling. She slid to her knees, pulling her undergarments to respectability before anyone could bring a light. Her breast pounded as though she'd run some punishing race.

'Didn't get nowheres,' Tom was grumbling ill-temperedly. 'Tight as a bleeding clam that one is.'

Paddy's arm came around her waist and lifted her to her feet. 'Seems yer was lucky,' he whispered. 'Brute, Tom is. Sorry I encouraged 'im, back along the road.'

Jade said nothing. She was breathless and distressed and the green plumes had come off her head, allowing the coils of brown hair to fall around her shoulders. She told herself she would not cry or let them see that she was afraid. All the terrible stories she'd heard of Bluegate Fields and the Devil's Acre rose up to haunt her. House after house and street after street of decayed property given over to London's Underworld. Papa had discussed them with a politician he'd had to dinner one evening and somehow Jade had been forgotten while the talk had gone on, filled with unsavoury details that had half-thrilled and half-repelled her. She'd never have been allowed to stay if Mama had been there but she'd had a migraine that evening and was compelled to go to bed at the last moment.

Her parents seemed suddenly to be at the other side of the world. But they'd know by now that she was not in the house and that treasures had been stolen. The Bow Street Runners would know where to look, Jade reasoned.

Paddy pushed her towards the stairs. She stumbled, aware

that her body hurt between her legs as though she had cut herself, the sore place chafing against her drawers. A faint light filtering down the upper part of the noisome stair showed her the breast still exposed. Quickly, she pulled up the neck of the gown, realizing that the nipple burned as though Tom still had his mouth on it.

Shivering and heated in turn, she was made to enter a large room that was filled with men and women who said nothing, only watched her being forced across the floor, having to evade outstretched legs and crouched bodies, her gaze refusing to believe such people existed. An enormous man dwarfed the area near the sulky fire. He was quite bald and his skin was white and shiny as lard as though he never saw the light of day. Black eyes were enclosed in smudges of darkness that contrasted horribly with the remaining pallor. His body was gross, each thigh and leg far vaster than her own body. His eyes fastened on her like leeches. It was a nightmare from which she would surely awake!

An old woman leered at her from the other side of the room. Her open mouth was toothless apart from a blackened stump and she clutched a grey shawl around her shoulders with spider-like fingers. A dwarf leaned against one corner, his head human-sized but his arms and legs thickened stumps. Jade tried to repudiate the room and everything in it but it would not go away, the bruises she'd received during the wild race with the barrow reminded her that she *was* here, that she was a danger to each person who scrutinized her. But she would not crumple or beg, and if there was the slightest opportunity to escape she would take it, however precarious.

Seeing Tom for the first time, she was ashamed that she had experienced that hateful flicker of sensuality. He had coarse good looks, it was true, but there was a depravity stamped on his features that no one could miss. He was still angry with Paddy and the other man who held her by the left arm, a nondescript little person with bowed legs, as if he might once have been a sailor, and surprisingly strong hands.

A woman with dyed red hair laughed as Jade was hurried past her, the dull glow of the fire reflected in a dress of shoddy yellow satin trimmed with soiled lace. The smell in the room, though not as bad as in the alley or on the stair, was still unpleasant and this was cold November. Jade, trying to envisage what it must be like in summer, was appalled.

Another room lay beyond the large one and into this Jade

was impelled so forcibly that she fell into the empty space in the middle of the floor, the breath driven from her so that she had to lie for a minute or more before pulling herself up on to her knees. Behind her, the door was banged shut.

A tall man, leaning back in a chair, faced her. Something in his expression brought a small comfort; indeed, if she had been confronted by both this man and Sir Piers Mandrake she would have turned to him had she felt herself threatened. Jade became conscious of the dirt that marred the white satin and the velvet spencer, the wild tangle of hair that tumbled around her shoulders. Lifting a hand to push it away she saw that her fingers were smeared with black.

'So this is the girl,' the man said in a voice that was more like a superior clerk's than that of a criminal.

'Had to bring 'er, Guv'nor,' Paddy said, shrugging. 'Hadn't no choice.'

'Eliza should have hit 'er harder,' Tom said sourly. 'Then there wouldn't have been no need.'

'Eliza struck me?' Jade could neither restrain the question nor her surprise. She had imagined Tom to have been her assailant.

Someone laughed mockingly and Jade found herself being stared at by a girl who sat in the shadows. She gave an impression of a beauty, a peachy complexion, a riot of smoky black hair and brown eyes in which the firelight left red sparks. 'Quite the little lady, ain't she! Eliza struck me? All la-di-da and hoity-toity as if we was 'er servants. Well, we ain't, your little ladyship!' The mockery turned to ugliness.

'Yes,' the quiet man said as though there had been no interruption. 'Eliza did hit you because there was no other choice. Tom is despicable because he did have a choice of conduct. He, as you may have realized, was outside the house, keeping watch for Robin Redbreasts. You know what they are?'

'Bow Street Runners,' Jade answered and saw the dark girl's malicious smile.

'What to do with you,' the Guv'nor murmured, taking a handkerchief from his pocket to cover a fit of coughing. 'It's difficult. If we let you go it means we can't use Eliza any more, and she's indispensable. You, on the other hand, are not, which is your bad fortune.'

'Let me do it,' the dark girl whispered, and the little red lights seemed to consume the pupils of her eyes.

'Be quiet, Molly. It's my decision.'

Jade, who had grown rigid with unease, relaxed sufficiently to look around the room. So far she had seen only the small group before her. In a chair by the curtained window, a girl of her own age sat quietly, shrouded in the gloom. She looked pretty and gentle and curiously innocent though of course she could not be. It was some trick of the firelight or candle-glow. Her hair curled around her delicate face as in some painting of an angel or a cherub, and her eyes were blue. Unlike Molly who looked flashy and gypsy-like, her gown was simple and fairly clean. She can't be one of them, Jade thought, knowing she was wrong.

The girl stared at Jade and smiled unexpectedly. It was a very sweet smile and Jade was inexplicably drawn to her.

The Guv'nor noticed the interchange and his own expression softened. 'Are you all right, Nan? You aren't too cold sitting over there?'

The girl's eyes grew lambent. 'I'm all right.' Her voice was curiously lifeless in spite of the obvious affection she had for the Guv'nor and she spoke slowly as though she had difficulty in assembling her thoughts.

The Guv'nor looked fiercely angry and got up from the battered chair. 'Some of your friends,' he told Jade coldly, 'were responsible for Nan's disability. I see you recognized her limitations. Two splendid young bucks in their new carriages, racing for a wager down a narrow street. My daughter came out of a shop and was struck on the head. They did not wait to find out if she was still alive. I never saw their faces, which is just as well or I'd have swung for them. I picked up Nan. She was not dead but her mind, as you see, was affected. And that is why I turned against the rich and rob them. Or, I should say, I plan the thefts and my friends carry them out for me. They carry out *all* my orders. There must always, you see, be a brain behind an enterprise. Here, I am the brain. I still cannot decide what to do with you –'

''Tis foolish to keep 'er,' Molly said, and her tongue crept along her upper lip. She looked for all the world like a beautiful cat.

'Shouldn't you be going about your business?' the Guv'nor observed with a trace of sharpness. 'It's time.'

'They'll keep,' Molly said, yawning, but she rose to her feet and picked up a handsome cloak that was edged with narrow

31

fur and slung it over her shoulder. In spite of the fact that the cloak was of good quality, Molly still contrived to look, if not vulgar, quite definitely garish. Intercepting Jade's silent condemnation, the girl narrowed her hot brown eyes and shouted, 'What yer lookin' at, eh? You ain't nobody now, little miss. End up in a whorehouse you will, like all the rest. Won't be so hoity when you serves fifty men a day and 'as your clothes taken away so you can't run 'off nowheres! A few years of that an' your own ma won't know yer. Send the little bitch to Rosie's if you don't want to knock her off.'

'Molly, you have clients waiting,' the Guv'nor said quietly, but it was plain that his patience was stretched to the limit. 'Clients who pay well.'

'You get yer share!'

'I know that, but neither of us will should they tire of waiting.'

'Won't go, not till I turns up! Worth waiting for, I am. Variety's what they likes an' what they gets. Tell Nick I'll see him later, at Fred's.'

'Very well.'

Molly darted a last unfriendly look at Jade. 'I want that gown. Ma Lee will know how to clean it, an' I like them pearls too.' She came towards Jade on a strong whiff of patchouli and body odour and snatched at the necklace. Jade gasped, remembering the tiny sea-horse that was her luck. She couldn't let this dreadful woman take it. She put up her hand to save it but the string snapped under Molly's strong grasp and all the little milky spheres tumbled to the floor, rolling away under chairs and the fringes of tattered carpets. In a trice, everyone except Guv'nor Jack and Nan were down on their knees, scrabbling and pushing. 'Leggo that!' Paddy shouted.

'Yer thievin' hag!'

But the hand that was pressed against the hollow of Jade's throat still held the tiny hardness of the jade carving. It had not fallen with the pearls but remained with a portion of the string. Without drawing attention to herself, Jade lowered her hand, retaining her grip on her father's gift. They would take the matching ring, she realized that, but she'd never give up the sea-horse. It was tiny enough to be concealed in a very small hiding-place and it was also doubtful if anyone would recognize its worth even if it were seen.

Molly, panting, her cheeks red with exertion and excitement, got up and slipped her trophies into the bag over her arm, then sauntered out of the room. Some of the tension went with her departure.

The Guv'nor dispatched Paddy and Tom on some errand Jade did not hear. Alone with Nan and her father, the girl became aware of all her hurts and stiffness. She remembered the assault on her by Tom. The confusion of voices from the next room emphasized the realization that she could not escape. Molly's words haunted her. Papa and his politician had mentioned whorehouses though they had not been as specific as Molly as to what went on there. But she knew now that it was concerned with what Paddy had done with Eliza and Tom had almost done with herself. Mama would be disgusted if she knew what had happened downstairs in the dark. Mama –

'The Runners will find me,' Jade made herself say and her voice did not break. 'My father will never rest until he gets me back. He has friends in Parliament – '

The Guv'nor laughed not unkindly. 'There's not a Redbreast alive who'd come within a mile of this place, so you can save your breath, child. They know they'd have their gizzards slit. No, not by me, so you needn't look so reproachful, but you've seen enough of the others to know that what I say's true. Isn't that so?'

His hand moved towards Nan's head, his fingers twisting the little curls and letting them spring back again as though he enjoyed their golden glitter. And then the softness vanished. 'You must get out of these clothes. You heard what Molly said. She's not above stripping you naked in front of the others. I'd spare you that.'

Jade reached out and grasped the arm of the nearest chair. She was very tired.

'I hope Tom was not too unkind?'

'He was – a perfect gentleman.'

'You've not lost your sense of humour,' the Guv'nor said, and Jade knew that he respected her for refusing to be a coward. He went to the door and shouted, 'Ma! Ma Lee. Come here.'

Nan had come forward to touch Jade's long, glossy hair. 'Pretty,' she said softly.

'She likes you,' the Guv'nor said with a trace of bitterness. 'Doesn't like many folk. How could she, though, living as we do?'

'You don't have to,' Jade answered. 'You are educated –'

'And work for the likes of those who took away my daughter's wits? The bile would rise in my throat. Better by far to take from them – Oh, there you are. Could you find some gown to cover this child? She'd be safer without these garments she's wearing. See they're cleaned and taken round to the usual place. They'll fetch a good price.'

Ma Lee tossed her red head and grinned. The large, soft bosoms were all too clearly defined under the dirty yellow satin. As she advanced towards Jade, they shook with each bouncing step. Her nipples stood out obscenely against the shiny stuff, but she seemed unaware of her appearance.

'Won't need anything very big for that little sparrer, nor too good, neither.'

'Clean, if possible,' the Guv'nor said wearily and coughed into his 'kerchief.

The big room outside was not quiet now. Voices rose and fell, laughing, quarrelling. Whispering. The night stretched ahead, endless and terrifying. Jade longed to relieve herself but could not bring herself to ask where she should go.

Ma Lee lumbered away, her hips jiggling.

'Pretty,' Nan said slowly but clearly.

'By God,' the Guv'nor said huskily, 'but she does fancy you, poor little wench.' He was very pale now that the coughing bout was over and Jade noticed for the first time how thin he was and how finely-drawn his face. She thought for a second that there was a stain on the handkerchief but he pushed it back into his pocket so quickly that she could not be certain.

'It's dreadful,' Jade said, 'that anyone could run down a human being and go on as though nothing untoward had happened. Is she – happy, do you think '

The Guv'nor said nothing for a moment or two. 'I don't know. She was so quick and sparkly – Look here. God knows what'd happen to you if I sent you out there. Nan sleeps in that little cupboard of a place off the corner there. There's a skylight and a mattress big enough. You'd best stay with her since she seems to like you. There's no way out so you needn't get hopeful.'

'Thank you.' Jade's fingers pressed into the hard outlines of the sea-horse. She knew it was lucky. 'You couldn't – send a letter to my home – ?'

The Guv'nor's expression became bleak and closed. 'They'll

not see you again. I thought you knew that.'

She closed her eyes. Someone was walking through the outer room. The footfalls were heavy and determined and Jade knew they were made by somebody big and arrogant. Sure of themselves. The door swung, creaking on its hinges, then was slammed shut, the reverberation rocking the sparse furniture.

'What's this?' She was pulled round with enormous force to face a tall, strongly built man who reminded her of Sir Piers as he might have looked twenty years ago. Wide shoulders, large though well-shaped nose, a hard mouth that would not smile easily, eyes that bored into hers. Hair of a dark red that was uncommon. The Guv'nor, for some reason, had not frightened her but this man did.

She raised her head, giving him back stare for stare, swallowing her fear.

'Leave her alone, Nick. She's only a child.'

The big hands released her slowly. The cruel lips smiled. 'The right age for tuition.'

'Molly is expecting you at Fred's. See she doesn't lose all her earnings at roulette. She's grown too fond of gambling.'

'And her?' Nick continued to watch Jade. 'Heard all about it from Paddy.'

'She'll be with Nan.'

'Special treatment? Fancy her yourself, Jack? That's not like you.'

'You should go to Fred's,' the Guv'nor repeated steadily.

For a moment Jack and the man called Nick stood eye to eye, anger in both set faces. Then, as if by magic, a pistol appeared in the Guvnor's thin hands. He turned it over idly. 'I must clean this. It's been neglected of late.'

Nan made a little distressed sound and Jade went to her, putting an arm around her shoulder. 'It's all right. No one will hurt you.'

'Quite the little nursemaid,' Nick said nastily, his face white with rage. The furious gaze travelled over Jade's body from throat to ankles, arousing a hot discomfort.

'Someone must be kind,' she told him. 'There's much that must be made up for –'

He stepped closer, his expression changed to one of surprise. 'I'd like the teaching of you, young miss,' he whispered. 'And I'll have it, just wait and see.' Then he swung round and was gone in three great strides, ignoring the Guv'nor and the weapon he examined with such studied care. The room shook a second time.

'You have great presence of mind,' Jack said to Jade. 'And I like your championship of the underdog. Ma! Ma?'

Ma Lee came lumbering back, a brown-striped gown hanging over her ample forearm. ''Tis all I can find. Now, miss. Off wi' them things.'

Jade flushed.

'I'll leave you for a while,' Jack told Ma Lee. 'But don't be long.'

As soon as he had gone, the red-haired woman told Jade to hurry. 'Won't see nothink I haven't seen before.' She cackled as if she'd made a great joke.

Rather than have the fat, grimy hands on her, Jade began to take off the white gown, afraid that she might let go of the jade piece by mistake. Ma Lee snatched up the dress greedily as soon as it slid to the floor.

'Come on! Heverythink!' she shouted.

'But you've only brought –'

'That's right, dearie. We don't bother with nothing else 'ere. If you don't take off them underthings I'll call one of the men in to do it. Tom, for instance.'

Jade removed the chemise, stays and drawers, then pulled off her stockings.

'Coo! Not enough on yer to feed a cat.' The woman gathered up the discarded clothing. 'Good stuff this is. And what about that ring? Hand it over. That's the way.'

Jade said nothing but, as she pulled the gown over her head noticing that it still smelt very faintly of a mingling of sweat and perfume, a hard lump found its way into her throat and lodged there. Her head had begun to ache again and her crotch stung painfully. She slid the sea-horse into the small pocket in the skirt.

The woman had gone and Nan had come back, her huge blue eyes full of sympathy. Jack, re-entering the room, saw them stand together as though giving one another comfort. He picked up the stub of a candle in a greasy stick and led the way to the door to Nan's 'cupboard'. It was long and narrow and the candle-light danced against the skylight beyond which there was only a vague dimness unrelieved by moon or stars. There were blankets on the mattress and a bucket in the corner. At least she would not have to go through that awful room a second time.

'Good night, Nan, love.'

Nan turned to kiss her father, her hair turned to magic by the bright yellow nimbus.

'You'll be safe enough tonight,' the Guv'nor told Jade. 'I'll be in the next room.'

It was dark when he closed the door. Nan lay down almost immediately and pulled up the covers. Jade rushed for the bucket, then stood up on a spindly chair at the end of the cubby-hole to press against the skylight. But it had been nailed down and she made no impression on it. The glass was very thick and would be difficult to break. Even if she did get on to the roof where would she come down but into another world just as bad as this?

Lying beside Nan who was already asleep, Jade's thoughts would not let her drowse. Eliza, Paddy, the Chinese cabinets in her room, Sir Piers and Rupert Mandrake, the Charley struck down in the street, Jack, Tom, Molly, Ma Lee, Nan, Nick. Her thoughts stuck there and refused to let his image go. She heard, in the dark, his whispering voice. 'I'll have the teaching of you, just wait and see,' and in spite of herself that treacherous little flame sparked inside her body as though his threat was more a promise.

CHAPTER TWO

Jade woke out of a dream she could not remember but which had oppressed her. For a moment she could not think where she was. There was a smell composed of stale air and sweat, of cheap scent and other, less pleasant things. There was a warmth at her back that sent her rigid with fear, reminding her of – what did it remind her of? She could not, at first, decide. And then, all the events of yesterday rushed back, each worse than the one before.

Mama would be mad with fear by this time. And Papa – Jade dug her fingers into her pocket and took out the sea-horse. Enough light came through the heavy glass of the skylight to show her the tiny, delicate lines of the carving. She raised it to her lips and kissed it.

Nan, disturbed by the movement, began to sit up and Jade returned the carving to the pocket. She still had her luck, incredible though it seemed. Tom had not brutalized her, the Guv'nor had not had her killed. She had been left alone all night. The Runners must have been searching for her for hours and Papa's friend would see that they found her. Jade would not think of Guv'nor Jack's cruel words. She must see her parents again.

'What – do – they call – you?' Nan's thoughts took even longer to formulate first thing in the morning and Jade was conscious of a fierce protectiveness towards the tragic girl. If she were fortunate enough to be restored to her home she would want to help Nan in some way.

'Jade,' she answered and sat up so that she could see Nan the better. Even rumpled after sleep, she looked pretty and angelic and the little round curls kept their shape. Looking closer, Jade saw the end of the scar that must run across her head from the left temple.

'Jade?' Nan frowned.

'It's not my real name. That's rather ugly and more like a man's.'

'You are – pretty.'

'Thank you.' Jade rose stiffly, aware of her bruised back and hips and the pain at the back of her head. Standing on the wobbling chair, she tried again to shift the skylight but it remained obdurate. The fog seemed to have gone and there was an impression of clear sky, the lowering shapes of chimney-pots.

The door opened suddenly and she almost lost her balance. Recovering herself, she found herself looking down at the dwarf who grinned cheerfully and shook his head. He had a plate of bread in one hand and a jug of ale in the other.

'Never get out there! No one get in either. Guv'nor won't let anyone hurt Nan. Here. Breakfast.' The little man set down the food and drink on the floor and went out again, still smirking.

Jade realized that she was ravenously hungry. She'd been too excited to eat yesterday and that was probably why the champagne had affected her so strongly. They would not bother to feed her if she was to die. Rosie's. That was where she was going to go. Guv'nor Jack detested the well-born and wealthy because his quick and sparkling child had, because of them, become close to imbecility. He stole from the rich and would have no compunction about sending her to a brothel. She must not deceive herself. But she was not there yet!

Nan was offering her a piece of bread and the ale-jug. Together, they sat on the edge of the mattress, sharing the repast scrupulously, Jade drinking from one side of the jug, the girl from the other, Nan laughing as though she were pleased. The sense of companionship was unexpectedly sweet. Jade had always wanted a brother or a sister. But Mama had explained why there were none and never would be. She must not think of home if she were to remain brave.

Jade looked up, aware that she was being watched, and saw Nan's father leaning against the jamb. His face was quite grey and he looked very tired. He could not have failed to see his daughter's pleasure in Jade's company. Not that she wanted to trade on the poor child's affection but hope dies hard and Jade was still optimistic. If Nan's penchant for her swayed the Guv'nor, she'd not object in the least. But neither would she wish it construed as opportunism.

'Nan, love. I want you.'

'What about me?' Jade asked.

The Guv'nor grimaced. 'Best stay here for a bit. And don't get any fancy ideas about sloping off. The Maul has orders to keep you here.'

'Maul?' Her skin crept.

'The large man you saw last night.'

Images of gargantuan whiteness rushed back at her. Dark eyes ringed with blackness. Unhealthy. Gross – She shuddered.

'I see you do remember. He has a liking for disobedient children, though he'll not put a foot out of place if you stay here.'

'You didn't mean it? About not seeing my parents again?'

'I'm afraid I did.'

'They've done nothing to you. You can't punish us for what someone else has done.'

The tired eyes grew remote. 'Now you are naïve. I call the tune here.'

'Then what are you going to do with me? I'd rather know than – imagine.'

'I think you would.'

She thought for a moment that he would relent and went up to him to put a small hand on his sleeve. But he shook it off brusquely. 'No you don't, young miss! I want none of your feminine tricks here. Think I don't know women, eh? Since I took to crime I've seen every type of woman there is under the sun. And yours is the most dangerous. The bravery, the small, intimate pleas. The beauty – Promises.'

'I promised nothing!'

'You *thought* you didn't! A different matter altogether. Now come, Nan. We must be off.' He held out his arm and Nan took it obediently as she would do everything else that was suggested to her with a modicum of kindness. No wonder he kept her in this 'cupboard'. Someone like Paddy would easily get around Nan and the Guv'nor could not always be there. For an instant, Jade was sorry for them both. Then, anger took over. He had made her out to be devious and she was sure she was not. And then she recalled her thoughts of a few minutes ago, how she hoped Nan's affection for her might bring privileges. It annoyed her that he was right and then she saw that in another way it was amusing.

But, after they had gone and the door was shut, she became prey to a fever of anxiety. She hated the ill-fitting gown that had belonged to another woman not too particular about personal fastidiousness, and the dislike led her thoughts back to her mother and the episode with Tom in the downstairs darkness. She must try to escape while the Guv'nor was out. Her hair was unremarkable in its present state of untidiness and the brown dress was dowdy. If she kept her face down – Jade opened the door to Jack's room. It was empty apart from the pallid intrusion of lances of sunlight that showed up the shabbiness of furniture and carpets that had once been beautiful. Her toe caught in the threads and she was almost pitched forward on to her face. Trembling, she stepped on to the dusty floorboards. The other door was slightly ajar and there was, surprisingly, no sound from the outer room. Last evening it had been so full. But the people who crowded it had other matters to occupy them in the daylight. The politician Papa knew had enumerated those occupations. Magsmen, shofulmen, macers, sweeteners, jolliers, nobblers, fancymen, prostitutes, bully-boys, coiners, child-beggars, sweep-boys who got into windows too small for an adult thief and opened doors – cracksmen and fences – the names came pouring back from her subconscious.

Rosie's. The name conjured up a succession of encounters like the one with Tom. Forget that flicker of response! Remember only that she'd been placed on the same level as a housemaid. Put against a wall and exposed –

But Rupert had not been much better for all the scent of sandalwood and his fine family. A pillar was not so different from the wall, but the real difference lay in the fact that she could have stopped him with a word or a slap. Here, men got what they wanted by force. At Rosie's there would be countless men all wanting that same thing and she could not refuse them. She felt sick and excited in turns, unable to understand herself.

Faint sounds of voices rose from the streets and alleys outside. If she did not look at anyone, no one would challenge her. She clenched her hands to stop their shaking. It might be her last chance to get away.

Cautiously, she put her head around the door. The room smelt of bodies and refuse but she saw no one. A number of palliasses and blankets lay about the floor. There were sacks and bundles, rolled cloaks and capes, cracked boots and down-at-heel shoes lying where their owners had kicked them off. In a corner lay a heap of what looked like old lead and piping, the glimmer of copper.

She took a step and another. Unchallenged, she became bolder. She'd make for the first Charley or respectable passer-by. Another hour and she could be at home, denouncing Eliza before she had time to give in her notice and have references forged so that she could take up another post in a wealthy household.

Jade was half-way to the staircase door when the shadow appeared. The shadow grew longer and wider, engulfing her like a chill, dark sea. She wanted to run away but her legs would not carry her. The floorboards creaked and the bald, white head appeared in the black well of the staircase. Black raisin eyes glittered in their dark sockets. His shoulders became visible, straining against the soiled white shirt, his stupendous thighs encased in light breeches stained with urine.

Her throat dried.

The Maul smiled and came on. Jade forced herself to move, conscious that there were other footsteps behind the big man. She ran, stumbling over the hem of the too large gown, to fall a yard away from safety. Gasping, she turned herself over, seeing the Maul's immense tree-trunk legs spread above her, the white-shirted paunch hanging over them, then his chest, neck and head dwindling to comparative smallness in the obscurity under the cracked plaster ceiling. His red lips were wet.

There was no moisture at all in her mouth. She closed her eyes against the inevitable, then heard Nick's voice shouting,

'Get back to your cage, you great ape. I'll let the Guv'nor know what you've been at! You know she's to be his little dolly mop, don't you? Don't be such a fool.'

She sensed that the preposterous legs were creaking away and was taken with a fit of uncontrollable shivering. Dimly, she felt herself lifted up from the floor and crushed against a chest that was as hard as the boards she had just lain upon. The ceiling of Jack's room swirled and danced above her and then she was in the safety of Nan's cupboard, lying on top of the disturbed blankets, her heart thudding against her ribcage as though it would never quieten.

'Doesn't suit you like the white gown,' Nick said, his smile mocking. His face took shape gradually, the nose proud, his mouth more like Sir Piers's than she could bear. The glow from the skylight turned his hair to the colour of garnets. He pushed the door to behind him and leaned against it.

She could not get up.

'Dowdy, that gown is,' Nick went on, 'but the shape underneath's the same. Like my women neat and small. Not used –' His voice was getting softer and softer and he was dropping to his knees beside the mattress, his bulk seeming to fill the narrow place. His hand covered a breast and she had no strength to push it away. Strong fingers teased at the nipple arousing only the faintest pleasure. If a charging lion had burst in she would have let it eat her rather than have tried to move a muscle.

His other hand was sliding from the arch of her foot and over her ankle, up the rounded calf and over the knee. Up the soft, bare inner portion of her thigh. Inside her body, his finger caressing very gently, yet still disturbing the place where Tom had hurt her. She flinched involuntarily. 'Tom hurt you, did he? Didn't damage you altogether, I'm glad to say.' The exploring finger had dipped deep inside, inducing a spasm of almost intolerable need.

Jade found her reaction incomprehensible. She hated him, detested everything about him, yet what he did made her want him to go on with his stroking and petting until there was an end to the pleasure. But still more, she hated herself.

The sound of Jack's voice from the outer room made Nick turn his head with a scowl. Then he stared down at her, pulling back the gown until she was covered. 'A pity,' he whispered, 'but there'll be lots more times. Lots of them.' Then he was up and out of the door, closing it very softly. She heard him throw himself into one of Jack's chairs, the back creaking under his weight, his boot heels scrape across the floor.

She thought she would never be able to get up again.

It seemed hours before she recovered from the fright Maul had given her. She had not been able to overhear the conversation between Jack and Nick Caspar. Their voices had been lowered, obviously for her benefit, and she had only known it had ended when she heard the sounds of Nick's departure.

Soon after, the old woman with the black tooth flip-flopped in to remove the bucket. Jade heard her go to one of the windows in Jack's room, open it and toss out the contents into the alley below. Someone shouted. The old woman screeched an answer.

'For God's sake be quiet!' the Guv'nor growled and rustled papers.

The bucket was replaced and the old hag went about her business. Nan came back, her cheeks flushed with the fresh air, her childish curls gleaming, and Jade, looking at her closely, saw what she had noticed yesterday, that Nan's eyes were eminently expressive. It was her speech that seemed most affected.

'Jade!'

It was poignantly sweet to be hugged so wholeheartedly. Tears pricked at the backs of her eyes but she would never let anyone see them. Nan, in her halting way, told Jade that she and her father had called on Mr Isaac.

'Nan!' the Guv'nor shouted. 'I told you never to mention him!'

Nan looked confused, then pulled some sweetmeats from her pocket and offered them to Jade who stored the name of Isaac in her mind. She would be free of these people one day and she intended to forget nothing. The image of Nick, his hair garnet-red, came back to prick at her senses. She chewed at a sugared comfit and tried to dispel the disturbing responses he evoked but her traitorous body would not allow it. Mama, she thought with the onset of panic, would never understand, not with her hatred of anything she considered defiled. How could she ever confide in her mother? Pits of inadequacy opened in front of her. Her parents would find difficulty in marrying her into a respectable family after this unsavoury episode. It was odd how both Sir Piers and Rupert Mandrake had insisted upon chastity while coveting her in much the same way as the Guv'nor's mob. She found it hard to visualize Rupert now apart from an inadequate memory of white teeth and sparkling eyes. But she remembered the vicious edge to his voice when he said, 'Damn you, my dear.' 'She's a tease,' he had told Sir Piers, enraged by the fact that his son had been made indiscreet by wine and proximity.

I have been cured of that fault, Jade thought bitterly, detesting the old, brown dress, longing to bathe and wash her hair. The comfits were making her feel sick but she would have disappointed Nan had she refused them.

The voice she feared most impinged on her consciousness. Molly had come back and was airing her views in Jack's room. 'There's yer rhino, Guv'nor. You needn't 'a worried. They'd have waited all night. Allus in a generous mood after a turn or two at Faro and such like. An' Fred do keep a good class o' rooms. They like all them cupids and red paper. Nice, lusty colour is red with gold. An' where's 'er ladyship?'

'With Nan.'

'Oh. We ain't good enough, then? Prissy little bitch! Should have sent her straight to Rosie's. What's the use of puttin' it off?'

'She's a determined wench. We have to make sure she can't talk even if she wants to.'

'Going to kill 'er then?' Jade could almost see Molly lick her lips. 'Paddy shouldn't have been so soft. If it had been some little drab—'

'He explained. If the girl had noticed him on at least two occasions, who's to say no one else did? Now that she's disappeared, someone else could remember him. And if she's dead—'

'Topped anyway if she's still here,' Molly reasoned, 'when they comes.'

'But she won't be. At least—'

'Going soft, Guv'nor?' Molly derided.

'Not at all. Nick had a suggestion for quietening the Benedict child—'

'Not so much of the child! Knows 'er onions, I suspects.'

'She's only fifteen.'

'Nearly sixteen, Paddy said. Eliza told him. There was plans for 'er birthday. Goin' to be spliced to one of them young spigs of nobility yer loves so much. She heard all about it by putting 'er ear to the bedroom door. Married folks allus talks in bed. I'd been tumbled when I was thirteen— More'n once.'

'Girls of that sort take longer to –'

'Grow up? I can tell you something about that little madam. Got the makin's of a prize whore. I could see it in 'er face, the way she was standin'. Take to Rosie's like a duck to water. Open 'er legs for anybody an' enjoy it. Tom said she didn't try too hard to push 'im off. Often worse, them women.'

'Tom would have to say that,' the Guv'nor said drily. 'Nick's idea was better.'

'An' what's that?' Something had crept into Molly's voice, something Jade defined as jealousy.

'Little pitchers have big ears,' Jack observed. Their voices descended to a whisper.

Nan continued to nibble tranquilly at her treat, offering Jade the depleted bag. She refused as firmly as she could, straining her ears to catch an incautious word from the other side of the door.

'How will you keep 'er quiet?' Molly said at last.

'The usual way. Tom visited the apothecary last night.'

'Oh. That way.' Molly was satisfied. She yawned. 'Got to lay me 'ead down for a bit.'

'Very well, Molly. We'll need you tonight. Not that it'll interfere with your usual arrangements. There'll be plenty of time for both.'

'Ooh!' Molly yawned again. 'I'm bleedin' tired.' Her high heels made little stabbing noises against the floor and her skirts trailed in the dust.

Jade heard Jack sigh. He riffled the papers and threw them aside, then got up and came towards Nan's cubby-hole. A moment later he was standing, white-faced, looking at them both with an expression of what Jade took to be self-detestation.

'Are you happy, my Nan?'

Nan said that she was but the Guv'nor looked no more pleased.

'Who usually looked after her? When I was not here?' Jade asked.

'Ma Lee. Sometimes one of the other women.' Jack looked at her angrily as though she had touched some sore spot.

'Not a very good arrangement. If one treats Nan kindly she will do – anything.'

'I don't need your opinion!' Jack snapped, but Jade could see that he had already thought of this for himself.

'You cannot take her everywhere you go. She must be

sixteen or thereabouts, and she's one of the prettiest girls I've seen. Bursting out of that gown.'

The Guv'nor turned whiter than ever.

'Where did you learn to shoot? It seems a strange accomplishment for a former clerk.' Jade pressed her advantage.

'Did you imagine I could walk into this warren just because I wanted revenge? I took lessons from a footpad up on the heath. Helped him to rob coaches and he repaid me with lessons in marksmanship. I showed a natural aptitude for it. We were partners for a time until he was taken one night when I was nursing Nan through a fever in the hovel we lived in. They hanged him but I had our plunder, or most of it. It was hid in a hollow tree on the heath, what we hadn't fenced already. Then I discovered, at the hanging, that I'd earned a reputation that kept men wary of me. So there's my rise to power, young miss. I've the added advantage of penning the most convincing references, forgeries and the like. There's no one else but Nick Caspar can write.'

His face darkened as he spoke Nick's name. Jade saw there was indeed no love lost between them, yet they appeared to be partners.

'Don't send me to – that place,' she said, knowing better than to try any feminine wiles. 'Please, don't.'

'Rosie's? You never get away from there! She hasn't lost a girl in years.'

'Nan likes me. I could – look after her when you aren't here.'

He hesitated and Jade realized the thought had already crossed his mind.

'I'm sorry for her. But she's not as bad as you imagine. It's her speech that's difficult, not so much her thinking. Her eyes show she knows what you're saying.'

'She – doesn't act like a girl almost a woman.'

'You've treated her for so long as a child – no one talks to her as if she'd any sort of mind. You ask her if she's hot or cold or happy, then go away before she can get out the words she's probably looking for. You don't want her to grow up, though, do you? It's easier to keep her as a child, think of her as one. But men aren't going to –'

'Damn you! Keep your opinions to yourself! You'll soon have a lot more to think about than Nan. Do you understand? People don't think at Rosie's. There isn't time to.'

He was gone before she could think of any rejoinder.

The dwarf brought their dinner, piping hot pies filled with meat and gravy. Jade seized hers ecstatically and took a big bite out of it so that the juice ran down her chin. The little creature hopped up and down, grinning and cackling. He set Nan off laughing too and Jack came back for a moment to watch her moodily, then went before Jade could continue her subversive tactics.

It's afternoon, she thought, and I'm still alive. Jack is finding it hard to punish me and Nan would not forgive him if he did. The Runners must be coming closer. I don't believe that if there were enough of them they couldn't break in. She tried to recall the name of Papa's friend at Westminster but it evaded her. Then the delightful pleasure of warm, tasty food in her mouth drove everything else from her mind.

Wiping her mouth on the hem of the brown dress in the absence of anything else suitable, she was shocked to hear Eliza's voice.

'What's going on in the Benedict house?' Jack asked sharply.

'Just what yer'd expect. The missus in screaming tantrums. Pa very quiet and seeing all 'is friends. Says he'll be asking questions in Parliament if someone don't find Miss Jardine. Where is she?'

Jack must have gestured towards the door.

'Oh. I was goin' to spin that tale about leavin' to marry my intended but I daresn't in case they smells a rat. Got to stay a week or two till things blow over. Mistress thinks she's dead. Given up, she has, and the master's finding it hard to deal with her. Thought he'd be more likely to crumble but 'e seems to be takin' charge. Never thought he had it in him.'

Jade came to the doorway and stared at Eliza. She looked just the same, her round, rosy face shining and innocent, her clothes quiet and restrained. The girl's expression altered subtly as she took in Jade's tangled hair and grimed face and hands, the drab, brown garment that hung loosely on her slim body. For a moment Jade wanted to strike her for the triumph she had not taken the trouble to hide.

'Doesn't it worry, you, Eliza, that you've caused my parents terrible pain – They have only one child –'

'Had, Miss Jardine. Had.'

'I'll get back to them somehow.' The words were out before Jade could stop them.

'Will you, Miss? Will they really want you when we've finished with you? A lady like your mother who hates anything that isn't just so. She'd rather you was dead, wouldn't she!'

There was a terrible truth in the observation. Jade had thought of it herself, more than once. But Papa, surely he would think differently? He must.

'And your papa,' Eliza went on inexorably, 'has you on a pedestal. 'E won't feel the same about you once you've been to Rosie's or had the Guv'nor's bucks sniffin' around you. Tom fancies you a lot, so I hear.'

Impossible to believe that this girl had blackleaded ranges and coaxed reluctant fires to a blaze, obeyed Mrs Baker in her every whim or requirement. Jade wondered how many other households in London were infiltrated with such deathly cuckoos in the nest. Nothing seemed secure.

'My father would pay –'

'Not as much as I'd hope to get lettin' in Paddy and Tom over the months and years. Did you get a good price from Ikey?' Eliza asked Jack.

'More than I expected.'

'That's good, then. She ain't worth botherin' about.'

'She'll not cause you any trouble.'

'Best be goin' back, then. It's only an 'alf day. Mustn't draw attention to myself by being late.'

Jade could not restrain her feelings any longer. She rushed at Eliza, crying out, seizing her by the shoulders and shaking her until the bonnet slipped back on to her shoulders and the deceptively neat hair began to fall into dishevelment.

'Why, you little – !' Eliza, unable to think of a term that was bad enough, began to fight back and the next moment they were rolling on the floor, ignoring Jack who tried to restrain them, Jade scratching and pulling at Eliza's hair and tugging at the buttons on the neat bodice, Eliza more cruel in her tactics, pinching and tearing until the brown dress ripped from neck to waist and her nails scored a red trail down Jade's white skin. Gasping with pain, Jade tried to break away but could not. The red, polished cheeks came close and strong teeth were bared close to her neck. Then Eliza seemed to retreat like magic, her face still working with rage, strong hands linked around her waist. She was set aside, cursing and whimpering with impotent fury while Nick Caspar bent down, his grey eyes flicking over the torn dress that revealed portions of white flesh Jade had not had time to hide. The cruel smile encompassed her, reminding her of their last meet-

48

ing this morning. She became aware of his animal warmth, the breadth of his chest under the fine shirt and the mole-grey coat that set off the dark red hair as a more brilliant colour would not.

'There'll be lots more times. Lots of them.' The memory of his words penetrated the fog of fear and anger like a scythe through long grass. Her fingers scrabbled uselessly at the edges of the torn material. She became conscious of Nan's terror-filled eyes: coming nearer, the touch of the girl's small hands.

Eliza, her fingers prodding the disturbed hair into order, jammed the bonnet on her head. 'Just keep her out of my way, that's all!' she screamed.

'What could you expect?' the Guv'nor reasoned, not seeming as angry as Jade had expected.

Nick Caspar lifted her to her feet, his glance telling Jade that it made no difference to him that she was dirty and ill-dressed. He wanted her and meant to have her.

Eliza, ready to go and pale with fury, shouted, 'Molly'll have something to say if you mean to tumble that little bitch!' and ran from the room.

Molly. Jade thought of Molly's hatred of her and her kind.

'Go back to your sty!' she shouted, tearing herself away from Nick's hold.

He began to laugh, the cruel face relaxing into an unaccustomed amusement.

'Poor – Jade,' Nan said and hurried after her as she ran back to the dubious safety of the cubby-hole.

'Jade,' Nick called after her. 'Is that your name? I did wonder.'

'Leave the girl alone,' the Guv'nor said. 'At least the child has spirit. Most would have given up long ago and become tiresome encumbrances. Not that it will do her any good.'

Jade did not wait to hear any more. She banged the door and stood there, her body shaken with a passion that was only half rage. She became aware, minutes later, that Nan waited patiently for the paroxysm of feeling to pass.

Jade sighed and controlled herself for Nan's sake. If it had not been for two reckless young lordlings without scruple, the Guv'nor would not have turned rogue and Nan would be as quick-witted and lovely as any respectable girl looking for love and marriage. It would be a big-hearted man who would overlook her apparent slowness and put a ring on her finger. Jade, unable to bear the thought of someone like Tom or Nick taking advantage of the girl, smiled and drew her back to the mattress where they could converse until something else encroached upon their tight little world. She was in no hurry. There was nowhere to go.

At least the disorderly scene with Eliza had rid Jade of the brown dress. Ma Lee came later with a smaller one in a shade that matched her strange eyes. The silvery green was to her liking and had a pocket concealed down the side where the sea-horse could be hidden. Dear Papa. She choked as she thought of him.

'Pretty,' Nan said approvingly and touched Jade's eyelids as though to show her she had noticed the similarity between the colour of the dress and Jade's irises.

It was then that Jade knew she was right in her assumption that Nan was not entirely the half-wit everyone had assumed her to be since her lively chatter had turned to more tortuous conversation. If one had sufficient patience, Nan could communicate reasonably adequately – and Jade had all the time in the world.

She pushed aside the panic the thought evoked and continued to talk with Nan, her gaze rejoicing in the greyish-green of the material that covered her and clung to her breasts and thighs as the detested brown stripes had not.

Molly's words kept breaking into her closeness with Jack's daughter. 'Open her legs for anybody an' enjoy it!' It was like an epitaph on a tombstone. That flicker of enjoyment when Tom nuzzled her breast. The exquisite pleasure when Nick explored her body during that traumatic lethargy after the encounter with Maul. She should have hated it, fought against them both, but Tom had been right. She had not been wholehearted. It seemed that she was meant to enjoy sexual relations. The thought was uncomfortable but she was as God had made her. If indeed he had! Would God have subjected her to this ordeal if he were all goodness as Christians imagined?

The door opened to disclose the stunted body of the dwarf and Jade knew that there was some great unfairness about the disposition of the human race. Why should this poor little creature be singled out for heartache and mockery? Would he be more fortunate in another life? She liked to imagine that this might be so.

Eliza's savage scratches took her mind away from philosophy. The dwarf had brought food and drink, this time in separate pewter pots. He thrust one of them into Jade's hands and waited, so trustingly, for her to drink that she could not disappoint him. The dark brew was faintly bitter but she was thirsty and it could be hours before she was offered anything else.

'Who are you?' Jade asked, draining the pot to the dregs.

'Drogo. Drogo.' He smiled his incessant wide-mouthed grin. There was something Italianate in the shape of his head and the large nose. She pictured him taken from a distraught and screaming mother who could not bear to look at what she had spawned. Pity tugged at her, making her respond to the little man. His dark eyes were quite handsome and long-lashed.

The eyes suddenly became very large and lustrous, the lashes brushing his cheeks like fans. His nose seemed so close, yet the rest of his face receded in the oddest way so that his head was elongated and his body dwindled into shadow. His smile gobbled her up.

Jade fell back on to the mattress, the food falling from her hands, while Nan stared at her incomprehendingly. The dwarf's shadow scampered across the floor like a rat and was gone.

It was dusk when she awoke. Jade could barely raise her head. She was enmeshed in a drowsy numbness that kept her still and quiet. There were strange colours in the dimness of the cubicle, glimpses of peacock and crimson and dingy gold. They were not there, yet she was conscious of them in a disembodied way. Her hands seemed too large for her body and would not do what she wished. Jack came to look down at her, his face, like Drogo's, all nose and mouth and heavy eyelids. Nan's blue eyes, lovely as cornflowers and crystal clear, were coming down almost to her face, her lips saying guttural, spasmodic words that made no sense. Ma Lee, her red hair flaming, her enormous bosom with the risen nipples embarrassingly prominent, leant over her like some monstrous sulphurous cloud.

Molly with her bitter, vituperative mouth and her hair dark and wild, the glint of gold in her ears. Drogo again, all head and snigger, scarcely any body at all.

Jade screamed, or thought she did. She had not heard anything but the whisper of continuous sound that had enveloped her ever since she came out of her sudden and inexplicable sleep. Then her languorous gaze rested on the pewter cup that had fallen to the floor and remained there. A dreamy peace took place of the stirrings of rebellion and distrust. The candle-flame mesmerized her with its rising and falling, its piercing golden beauty.

She was alone, the candle-light gleaming against the sky-light in shifting patterns of yellow, now a gilded cockerel, then a flower or a sea-anemone, feathers and leaves and moving lace. Her solitude seemed of inordinate length.

A shadow fell across the mattress and she turned her gaze slowly to see a man's dark silhouette, a half-inch of dark red hair outlined against light from the Guv'nor's room. He was beside her, pushing her back against the covers. She did not really feel them. It was as though she floated on warm, soft water. The touch of his mouth on her throat made her sigh. His body had no weight for all that it lay over her own.

And then, she never knew why he rose from her, but he was standing, the upper portion of his body receded into the pall of crimson and blue and green. He was gone.

Aeons later, Ma Lee returned to drag her from her coma, pulling a rough, dark cloak around her, pushing her into Jack's room where Molly, Nick, Tom and Paddy stood waiting. Dizzily, she tried to catch and keep the outlines of each face and figure but she saw only an eye here, a smiling mouth there, a curl or an ear-ring, a hand caught at the neck of a coat, strong thighs, a shabby boot.

She was walking yet her feet hardly felt the stairs. Maul was coming up the steps and even through the dreamy passive-ness she was afraid, cowering away from the preposterous figure, clutching at Paddy's arm. Paddy would be kind –

She was dimly aware of Molly's harsh laughter, of Nick grasping her wrist, his arm around her waist. Another fear began to penetrate the lethargy. Had she drifted off to sleep after Nick had kissed her throat? Had something happened to her between the kiss and the time he rose from her? How would she know? Threads of panic began to course through her and she knew that the effects of the drug that had been put into the drink in the pewter mug were wearing off a little.

They pushed their way through a thick mass of people in a yard where the light from a lantern showed her a kind of pit where a dog ran snarling and tearing at shadows. Then she saw that they were not shadows. Each flittering blackness had eyes, tiny specks of garnet that flashed as the light caught them. And there were shrill little screams that were cut off sharply as the dog's jaws closed, crunching and chewing.

She tried to protest, but was shoved on, the stench of closely packed bodies sour in her throat. Candle-light glimmered greenly on to a cobbled corner were two bodies lay entwined. Then she was prodded into a black archway where their footsteps rang hollowly and they emerged into an ill-lit street where still shapes sat against damp walls. A baby cried. Someone coughed and the sound was like Guv'nor Jack's racking attacks. A man reeled towards them, then fell like a stone –

The smells and the crouched figures grew less. Tumbledown slums gave way to more respectable streets. Curtains glowed in soft, pretty colours, concealing what must be rooms like the ones in her parents' home, filled with fine polished furniture and precious objects.

The conviction grew that the Guv'nor must be sending her back home after all. A violence of feeling overcame her. 'Home,' she said, 'my father will pay – '

'Don't be a fool!' Molly mocked. 'You ain't goin' home, dearie.'

'Where, then? Where?' The hope died hard. Jade wanted to strike out, to run, but her limbs were still bound with drowsiness. It was because she had attacked Eliza that they'd given her the drug. The Guv'nor had mentioned the visit to an apothecary the previous night.

'Not far now.' That was Paddy, his tone infused with a kindness that was in none of the others. What circumstances had forced him into crime? He was not vicious as all the others were, apart from Jack who had a real motive for revenge. But she knew nothing about them except that Nick had been at least partially educated. And she must not think of Nick with his whispered threats that seemed more a committal. Had he forced himself upon her while her body and mind were helpless? Or had he been disturbed? If it has happened, it cannot be undone, she reasoned. I could not have prevented it. But it would have been better had I known, if I'd been able to fight against him.

Jade became aware of a familiar figure on the other side of the street. It was Ma Lee, dressed incongruously quietly, who passed slowly under the greenish light of a gas lamp. She looked unexpectedly respectable, all her lip paint and powder removed, the cape and bonnet as innocent-seeming as Eliza's. She carried a carpet-bag that appeared to be heavy for she stopped for a moment to transfer the bag to the other arm before going on for a few more steps.

Molly, seeing the direction of Jade's gaze, produced a small, very sharp knife and held it close to her neck. 'Don't you say nothing or you'll find your gizzard lettin' in a whole lot of fresh air. On the other hand, I don't care if you opens yer mouth for it'd be a real pleasure to cut yer throat. Understand?'

'Yes. I understand.'

'Real quick on the uptake, ain't she!' Molly sneered, looking more beautiful than ever in the diffused glow. They passed a great hedge of rhododendron at a leisurely pace, then Nick halted and looked quickly to right and to left. Ma Lee crossed the road, set down the bag unobtrusively just beside the first of the pillars that marked the gateway to a drive and walked on sedately without a word or a look.

Tom lifted the bag, and somehow they were all in the darkness beyond the gateposts, the pale ghostly light filtering through the leaves.

'How long afore Ma comes back to pick up the carpetbag?' Paddy whispered.

'Fifteen minutes. You can take everything back to the pillar an' she'll be miles away with all the tools if anything goes wrong, which it won't. Good canary is Ma Lee. Butter wouldn't melt in her mouth,' Nick said softly. 'But we must hurry. Molly has her usual appointments. Can't keep her gentlemen waiting.'

'Gentlemen!' Molly spat viciously on to the path. Jade could no longer see the glint of the knife but she knew it was still there in the pretty, brown hand. Molly had some foreign blood in her veins to be so golden-brown in an English winter.

'Pays for your livelihood, though,' Paddy reminded, then there was nothing but the soft sounds of their footfalls in the drifted leaves, the acrid scent of autumns past.

They came to a door in a rampart of stone wall that must be the back of a mansion and Nick opened the bag after telling Tom to go hide himself in the hedge and make the usual noise if anyone else entered this way once they'd effected an entry. Tom vanished and Paddy lit a lantern that shed a light no bigger than the size of a shilling on to the assortment of strangely shaped keys, chisels, jemmies, augers, ropes and jacks. Jade had seen most of these articles before at Ayas Bywaters when watching repairs being done to french windows and other parts of the house and stables. It had never occurred to her that they might have had a destructive as well as a constructive purpose. There were some hooked steel implements she did not recognize and a strange drill which looked as though meant to be clamped to something else, a sack whose use seemed obvious.

Jade, terribly conscious of Molly's threatening proximity, began to see the benefit of a decoy like Ma Lee. Once the tools had been removed, it could be extremely difficult to lay a charge against anyone found in the vicinity even if the stolen goods were discovered close by. Runners would require to prove breaking-in and entering and the lack of house-breaking kit could prove an insurmountable obstacle.

A hot discomfort overcame her as she thought of what discovery could entail. Even if she were allowed to tell the story of her capture, she realized what terrible disgrace she would bring to her mother and father. Ben Jardine's grand-daughter a thief, living in a rookery with the filth of the city! Mama would never recover from the shock and the shame. If only she could take advantage of some unguarded moment.

'An' don't get no ideas,' Molly whispered and allowed the tip of the knife to press lightly against Jade's skin. It was so sharp that even that gentle pressure drew blood and left a biting pain that made Jade gasp.

Paddy's bulk was between Jade and Nick so she saw nothing of the process of defeating the lock but her heart leapt as the door yawned open on to obscurity.

The two men waited, listening. Jade became intensely conscious of the smell of Molly's body and the cheap scent that could not disguise the odour of sweat and infrequent washing. Those men who slept with her, did they not notice, or did they enjoy the earthy thrill?

Nick and Paddy were no longer on the back step and Molly was prodding Jade in the bruised small of her back. The girl stumbled forward, wincing, into the still-warm kitchen, lit faintly with pink from the dying embers of sea-coal. Black leading glimmered, copper pans gave off a dim rosy glow. Inside the high-backed settle that surrounded the ovens there was utter blackness.

'Here!' Nick pushed the bag towards Molly and grasped Jade's arm hurtfully. 'Go to the gate and look out for Ma Lee. As soon as you see her, set it down where she left it. It's dark there and no one will see it till she picks it up again.

Then, come back as far as the door. Don't want too many of us inside.'

Molly obviously wanted to argue but had sufficient respect for Nick's rages to obey. Paddy moved forward softly and opened the door to the house stair. He moved the lantern carefully, allowing the pencil-thin beam to explore the dimness. 'All right,' he whispered.

Between them, Jade was impelled up the narrow staircase. Another door opened on to a wide, marble-floored hall lit by the beams of the gas-lamp outside filtering through the glass fanlight. Silently they progressed, she dry-mouthed and soft footed as her companions. A room opened up before them, Paddy's light-beam playing on glass cabinets containing a multitude of small carved figurines. On each shelf was set out a treasure in jade, ivory, onyx and soapstone. The jade was in several shades of green, white and glowing paleness. She wanted to explore the pocket of her dress, to touch the sea-horse, but Nick watched her too closely and would take it from her.

The first cabinet was open and Paddy held open the neck of the sack. The little horses and riders, the carved Chinese emperors and their bodyguards, pagodas and ships slid into the soiled hessian receptacle.

Paddy grabbed at two heavily maned lions, substantial pieces that must have weighed a great deal, but before he had time to slip them into the sack, a light showed at the bend of the upper staircase and a robed figure appeared, carrying a branch of candles.

'Who's there?'

Jade imagined, after the first shock of horror, that Nick and Paddy would run, taking her with them, but they did not. It was almost as though they wanted her caught. And then she realized that this was to be Jack's hold on her. For the first time she saw that Nick and Paddy had their faces smeared with a dark stain and had concealed their hair under beaver hats. Nick tugged swiftly at the back of Jade's hood which slipped back leaving her pale face in full view. The candlelight beat against it, revealing the strange, memorable green of her eyes.

'Don't think to get away with this,' the man on the stair growled angrily. 'I'd know you anywhere, you thieving guttersnipe! Hurry, Benson, man!' A second man arrived behind the first, a tough, broad-shouldered person who looked well able to take care of himself.

Jade struggled to pull on the hood of the cloak but Nick and Paddy held an arm apiece so that once again she could be clearly seen. She opened her mouth to beg for help but Nick, divining her purpose, gave her a ferocious swipe that sent her crashing to the floor. One of the cabinets rattled precariously.

A fight was taking place between the householder and his butler and Paddy and Nick Caspar. The branched candlestick had fallen to the polished floor, extinguishing the light most effectively. She tried to crawl away while the attention of the men was diverted. For a time it seemed that she had succeeded. She groped her way to the top of the servants' stair, aware that other people were moving in the upstairs rooms, awakened by the bangs and shouts. Half-crawling and half-tumbling, she reached the foot of the stair and lurched unsteadily across the kitchen floor, guided by the faint glow on the stone flags. It was as she reached the deep shadow of the settle that an arm snaked out and fastened itself around her throat. Jade felt the wicked point of the knife blade nick her breastbone.

'Goin' somewhere?' Molly hissed.

There was a great clatter on the stair. 'For Christ's sake, scarper!' Nick ordered roughly. 'They both got a real look at her ladyship. Now we got to get away.'

She was manhandled, sobbing and struggling, down the short drive to the street, Tom coming after like a shadow. There Nick grabbed her and slung her over his shoulder as she was impeding their progress. Jade was swung dizzily, aware of distant shouts that grew fainter, of the thudding footfalls and heavy breathing of her captors. She let out a scream and then another.

Nick stepped behind a wall while Paddy tied a handkerchief around her mouth.

'Should have croaked the little bitch,' Molly said vengefully. 'Unlucky, she'll be.'

'Shut up,' Nick advised briefly and loped away again towards the warren of dark, depressing streets, Paddy swinging the sackful of collectors' pieces and Molly's heels making 'clacks' on the cobbles.

They stopped at an entrance to a narrow, filthy yard and went to the end of it. A cat, all green eyes and bared teeth in the narrow glow of Paddy's lantern, rushed away over heaps of refuse. Jade was set upon her feet and the 'kerchief removed. Molly's knife glinted.

'You can shout till Doomsday,' Nick said softly, 'and no one'll raise a finger. Not here.'

It was true. This was a terrible place, worse almost than Jack's unsavoury refuge. Someone lay against a sweating wall, more dead than alive. There was a suggestion of movement inside one of the rotting doors.

The last door was in better condition. Paddy knocked four times and there was sound of dragging footsteps, a crack of light spilling on to the broken step. 'Open up, Ikey,' Paddy said softly. 'It's Nick and me. And Molly.' There was a rattle of a chain and the door was opened slowly and creakingly.

A thin man in a long black robe stood there, only his outline and the sparse fronds of his grey hair visible. 'You'd better come in. Hurry.'

Jade found herself in a narrow passage beyond which a meagre light played on a smallish room that was better furnished than she had expected. While the chain was being replaced on the door, Molly hustled her into the room and stood close beside her.

There was a big old desk, some scratched cabinets with old books and scrolls of papers tied with dingy tapes. The window had been boarded up so that it would be difficult to break into. Above the mantel-shelf was an old-fashioned flint-lock and a powder horn. A thick layer of dust coated the place, drifting into the corners with a settling of fluff to make a carpet of sorts. Jade sneezed.

'Who is she?' a thin old voice asked peevishly.

He was a Jew, Jade realized, seeing the skull cap set on the back of his head and the once fine dark eyes pouched in bags of wrinkled flesh. His long face was pale and lined and into the lines was engrained a deposit of dirt that made the skin resemble old tallow. The hooked nose gave him a presence of which she was instantly aware, an aura almost of nobility at variance with his self-neglect.

'A new girl. Look at her well,' Nick said. 'She'll be back. This, Miss Jade, is the fence who'll dispose of the things you helped us steal this evening.'

She opened her mouth to repudiate the suggestion but Molly scratched her between the shoulder-blades with the knife she was itching to use. It was foolish to argue.

'Where's the stuff?' Saul Isaac asked, having inspected the

girl thoroughly. Paddy lifted the sack and tipped the contents on to the desk top. Isaac drew a deep breath and bent his long nose over the jumble of carvings. The lions were there, Jade noticed. Paddy must have had time to take those in spite of the appearance of the two men on the staircase.

Jade was overcome by a sensation of faintness that she knew must have its source in the drug she had been given. The dirty room and the old man took on an appearance of unreality. Nick and Paddy, their faces blackened, were like troglodytes or chimney-sweeps. She could not see Molly but she sensed her brooding presence even through the fog of numbness.

The conversation with Isaac became a meaningless jumble. She swayed on her feet and was vaguely conscious of reaching the foetid air of the narrow yard. Then there was nothing more.

She woke early feeling very much better apart from having a dry mouth. Nan lay beside her, her hair bright under the cold blue of the skylight.

Remembering last night, Jade was suddenly frightened. She had been seen apparently robbing a house and the value of the objects taken was great. There would be a severe penalty. It was not as though she had fought against her companions. She had said nothing, made no attempt to run from them. The man in the robe and the broad-shouldered butler would swear that she was helping Nick and Paddy who, because of their precautions, would never be identified.

There was also her own private dread of having been used by Nick. She was not sure how one would know but could not reconcile herself to remaining in ignorance and making herself needlessly unhappy.

It was Ma Lee who brought in breakfast, her double chin shaking as she walked and her bosom less restrained than ever in a puce-coloured gown that must once have been striking. Ma would know. It couldn't be helped if she laughed at her.

'Thank you.' Jade accepted the bread and milk and nudged Nan.

'Wot's wrong?' Ma Lee asked, noting Jade's strained expression.

'How – how do you know if a man has – has been with you?'

Ma Lee guffawed as Jade had expected, then looked shrewd.

'Oh, you're thinkin' of yesterday when the Guv' had to dope you. Funny effect it has.' The sharp little eyes softened. 'What makes you think – ?'

'I thought someone was here with me. Lying on the mattress.'

'You'd bleed and hurt something cruel. There.'

The girl relaxed. It had not happened and she could hardly contain her sense of release. Then she frowned. 'Always? Does that always happen?'

'Lor' love yer, no! Wouldn't be no human race if it did. No, 'tis yer maidenhead breaking. Happens to everyone, once. Who was it who lay down wi' yer?' She was unashamedly curious.

Jade flushed and did not answer.

'Nick Caspar. Was it him?' Ma's voice dropped.

Jade stared at the dirty floor.

'You'd best be careful,' Ma whispered, all trace of amusement vanished. 'When I tells yer Molly's his woman, you'll understand what I means.'

Eliza had delivered the same warning. Jade's stomach muscles clamped tight.

'Why should he want me when Molly's so good-looking?'

'Ah, but she's from the gutter and Nick finds it extra exciting to tumble a lady. An' you got a good little figger on yer for the wrong side o' sixteen. Not that I goes much for looking like a lamp-post with a couple of knobs on, but, then, I ain't no man.'

Jade almost smiled as Ma's mammary glands joggled under the puce satin.

'Can't stay 'ere talking. Guv'nor wants you to 'urry with breakfast.'

'Why?'

Ma Lee looked evasive. 'Don't rightly know.' But she did know and all of Jade's forebodings returned. Last night she had become an accomplice to theft. The Jew would swear that she had accompanied the two men with whom he'd obviously had previous dealings. She wondered where Isaac would sell the collector's pieces, then realized that another collector might have coveted the jade and alabaster for long enough. Papa said men became fanatical about such things. He'd known a collector of paintings who was none too particular where he bought additions to his secret gallery.

Jade finished her breakfast, wishing that sugar had not been added to the milk, then wondering if the sugar had covered up the taste of something else. But she had been thirsty and there was nothing else to drink.

Nan was merely stirring when the Guv'nor called to Jade. 'Come on, girl. Ma told you to be quick.'

She smoothed down the crumpled skirts and dragged her fingers through her hair but made little impression on either. And nobody knew how she longed to wash!

It was disconcerting to find Nick and Paddy in Jack's room. A good deal of light came in and the sky looked clear. A subdued roar came from the streets as though something momentous was about to happen. Members of the Royal Family rode in their carriages on the occasions of their birthdays. But would people who detested nobility and everything it stood for show such pleasure in the Regent taking a turn in his coach? She decided they would not.

A curious calmness settled upon her spirits. It was as though nothing really mattered. It was immaterial that she was soiled and slatternly, that she was a thief, that as surely as the sun would rise tomorrow, Nick Caspar would not be disturbed next time he visited her.

'The milk,' she whispered but no one heard. 'I knew – '

'We are going out, Miss Jardine.'

'Out?' The thought did not elate her. There was only a flicker of mild surprise. It crossed her mind, without any repugnance, that Nick's hair was the colour of the rats' eyes she saw in the pit last night.

'She'll be as mild as a lamb till we get there,' Nick said, smiling lazily.

'Ma!' Guv'nor Jack shouted. 'Stay with Nan till we're back and give me that cloak. It's cold outside.'

Ma did not look so grotesque. Perhaps it was because she had a look of real pity. Jade could not imagine why she should need compassion. The sky was blue and it would be pleasant to walk in the fresh air. She would be all right with Jack and Paddy.

Ma fastened the neck of the cloak. 'Do yer 'ave to?' she muttered gruffly. 'Haven't yer done enough?' Her hand lingered for a moment on Jade's shoulder. 'Poor little sod.'

'It's your neck too. Besides, once she knows what can happen, we can get her ready for more pleasant work than thieving.'

'You won't really send 'er ter Rosie's? Not a game little sprig like 'er?'

'More specialized work,' Nick said dangerously softly. 'Like

Molly's. Something for every taste. Only she'll have to be broken in.'

Ma's face showed real anger. Jade wished apathetically that she could follow all the cross-currents of the conversation but it was of no importance. She would enjoy being out of this house for a while and at least Molly was not there.

'Someone'll kill you one day, Nick,' Ma ground out and bludgeoned her way into Nan's cubicle, slamming the door.

'Come on. Don't want ter miss nothing,' Paddy said. 'It's not long till eight.'

Jade, supported by Jack's arm, glided down the stairs. The stench was still there around house and alley but she hardly noticed it, any more than she did the beggars and tattered children, the grey-faced women with babies wrapped in shawls. The moving figures were part of a dingy background where shadow fought with shadow and nothing was real.

She felt no stab of apprehension until the cold air revived her in a great, wide street with good houses down one side and a huge new building dominating the other. There was a sound of hammering from in front of this enormous place and a long, sinister platform covered with black above which soared the massive crossbars of three gibbets. She tried to repudiate the sight but could not.

To come to her senses in a press of gabbling, laughing and unheeding men, women, journeymen, pastrycooks and butchers who had decided to open their premises an hour or so late rather than miss the spectacle, revolted her. There were smells of fried fish and ginger beer, pies and oranges. A dirty hand flourished ballad sheets above the heads of the crowd. A chestnut vendor had difficulty in protecting the brazier filled with red charcoal that was his trade.

'Jellied eels! Eels!'

The crowd was so thick that there was no chance of moving. With the stripping away of her false sense of peace, Jade found the situation doubly horrible. She was tied to Jack and his gang for it would be impossible to shift without being trodden upon. On every side she was hemmed in by lusty, sweating, vociferous humanity in a holiday mood. She could no more appeal to anyone there with tales of kidnap than she could find herself in a ship bound for China.

It would be a different matter when the mass thinned after the hanging. This was to be her lesson. She was to see what happened to persons who stole valuables. They'd not have hanged her for a loaf, but the carvings had been a topping job.

'It's Mayberry's mob gettin' scragged this morning,' Paddy told her, not noticing her wide-eyed pallor. 'Well, three of 'em. Father and two sons.'

Nick had made the most of the enforced proximity and had an arm around her body and a hand under the cloak. His fingers kneaded at her right breast, pulling at the nipple so that she again experienced that warm flicker in her loins. The touch worked upon his senses equally strongly for she felt his flesh quicken and rise to push against her buttocks desirously. A deep shame made her kick out at his ankle. It was bad enough to be forced to watch this debauched drama without being expected to allow Nick Caspar his furtive titillations. Bending her head just as he took away his hand, she fastened her teeth in his wrist and bit it, drawing several drops of blood that stained his lace cuff.

'Bitch!' he whispered into her ear. 'You'll pay for that later. Blood for blood.' But he did not sound as angry as she'd expected.

She tried to move nearer to Jack who she knew would never touch her but she only succeeded in turning in another direction so that not only the grim sable platform was in her line of vision, but the balconies of the tall houses opposite. Each was crowded with men and women of superior dress to the ones surrounding her. She saw a tall slender woman in a fur-edged cloak and a turban-shaped hat in which two green plumes were fastened. Her face was oval and her eyes large and of a very deep grey. She spoke to a distinguished-looking man in a dark red redingote and tall beaver hat who looked much older than she and who managed to keep both an eye on her and one on the scaffold. The woman appeared unmoved by the sight.

Jade found it impossible to believe that only two nights ago she had moved in such company and had expected never to do anything else. A great homesickness took possession of her and then she felt bitterness that educated and sophisticated people could find diversion in the deaths of three criminals.

They were joined by a young man whose face she could not see, only a broad and well-shaped back covered in a black coat, a wrist half-disguised in a flounce of lace and strong, shapely thighs encased in the tightest of light-coloured breeches. Then he turned to smile at the grey-eyed woman and for the space of a heart-beat Jade felt as though she had been struck a blow under the ribs. His face was the colours of moonlight, all white and black, distractingly handsome. Although she had not recognized the woman in the cloak and turban as the one in the box at the Haymarket, she knew the man immediately. The dreams she had woven around him seemed ridiculous in this harsh, all too real place. She'd been a child when she saw him first. Now, she was a woman, soiled and degraded. But nothing of her feelings towards him had changed. The dreams were foolish but the attraction remained, the indefinable conviction that they were to mean something to one another. And, as though he were aware of the brief violence of her reaction he glanced down, returning her regard with a trace of contempt she found intolerable. But what could she expect? She had not washed or combed her hair for days and the cape was old. His gaze lingered for a moment on her eyes. He'd remember them, Jade thought, then was pushed boisterously while a man from the nearby coffee-house attempted to carry a large tray on which three breakfasts were laid. The crowds sent it good-humouredly over their heads.

Jade ventured another look at the balcony. The man with the black eyes and hair was taken with the beautiful woman. That was perfectly clear. But she glanced at the other man from under drooped lids, her lips twisted into the strangest smile, and he smiled back as though they had some secret of which the dark man had, as yet, no knowledge. On the next balcony a group of drunken young men laughed foolishly.

Her attention was distracted by the noisy approach, inside the low barrier around the scaffold, of constables armed with truncheons who took up their positions beside the black platform. Coiled ropes appeared at the back and were set quickly under the three crossbars. The inebriated bucks crowded to the rail for a better view.

She thought no more of society folk gawping from balconies but of the men who would, at this moment, be eating their breakfasts which would lie heavy in their stomachs, if they lay there at all.

Jade wondered, for a moment, which morning this was and was surprised to find out it was Monday. She wanted to ask Jack what those men had done but the words choked her, and the constables were too far off to cry out to for help.

That was why the Guv'nor had come late, so that they'd be crushed at the back with no way of escape.

Desperately, she looked for a friendly or refined face but saw none.

'Don't raise your voice, my dear,' Nick advised with chilling precision. 'I'd maze your thoughts for you and everyone'd think you'd just fainted.'

'Whole of Snow Hill's jammed,' Paddy said cheerfully. 'Gettin' a good send-off.'

His macabre humour sickened her afresh. Some people were singing hymns and others took up bawdy songs in opposition. A clock bell began to chime the hour.

'Good old St Sepulchre,' Paddy breathed.

A great sigh went up from the crowd. There was a jingle of a second bell and a door opened in the massive wall of Newgate. Jade swallowed convulsively as a party of people climbed up and on to the scaffold. She had expected to see three men but the figures she saw were of a man, a youth and a boy younger than herself. His face was blind with fear and the colour of old bones. All three had on open-necked shirts and their hands were pinioned with wide straps of leather. A chaplain droned in the background, his eyes never leaving the page of the prayer book he carried. No one listened.

She could not bear to look at the executioner.

'Hats off!'

The crowd rustled monstrously to display a multitude of unkempt and greasy heads.

Jade saw only the boy who could not move for terror. 'Jesus,' she whispered over and over again. The hangman had strapped Mayberry's legs together and pulled a nightcap over his face, then passed to the youth whose mouth worked right until the cap was drawn over it.

'Jesus,' she muttered and found herself praying as she had never done before. Her legs felt as though they did not belong to her and she was suddenly afraid of being trampled by the milling crowd. Jack was supporting her, seeing her loss of colour. A small tight scream passed the boy's lips and then his face was gone.

Half-blinded with tears, she moved her head and caught a swift glimpse of the dark young man on the balcony. He stared almost unseeingly at the gallows and she could have sworn his own eyes were as filled with anger as her own. Then he passed inside the french window, leaving the woman and the man in the redingote to their masochistic pleasure. A great, expectant hush fell, there was a sharp crash, a multitude of sighs.

'Hang on his legs!' someone shouted and a woman screamed with excitement.

Jade saw nothing more, only stood in the tight circle of Jack's arm until the gradual moving away of the crowds, dispersing to shops and offices and homes, freed her from the crush. She opened her eyes then. The bodies swung slowly and something dark and shiny ran out of the child's breeches-leg to drop on to the scaffold.

White and rigid she asked, 'What had they done?'

'Stolen things. Like you did last night. Fenced other people's valuables,' Jack said coldly and quietly. 'It's what we can all expect if we make a mistake.'

The balcony was empty.

It wouldn't happen to her if she could only get away, Jade thought. If only she could get home before anything really bad happened. But she was too drained and stricken by what she had seen to do anything at this moment. Later, when she was feeling better.

Later.

Jade had intended to take a note of each street on the way back, but instead of trying to read half-obscured name-plates, her mind alternated between the bone-white terror of the boy's face and the memory of the man with the black and white colouring that made her think of moonlight.

She grew very cold, having on only the green dress and the cloak, the thin shoes she'd worn for the party. Where was her white gown now? Being cleaned up for a woman like Molly! And then the griping stomach fear overcame her attempt at normality. Soon she would be a woman like Nick's girl.

Seeing a narrow alley on her left, she slipped into it almost without thinking and began to run until her breath laboured. Paddy had shouted a warning and their footsteps clattered some distance behind, interspersed with angry accusations. A drunk man reached out, smiling, to grab at her ankle, but she evaded him. A woman entirely grey, skin, hair, clothes, stared at her blankly, then stepped out into the alley to watch her distracted flight.

She got in the way of Jade's pursuers for the girl heard the clamour and the acrimonious exchanges, then the resumed pounding of their feet. The end of the alley loomed up, enclosed in a mesh of dirty shadow. There was a smell of rotten wood and ordure that caught in her throat, making her retch. But there was no way out.

She hammered at the nearest door and it was opened by a child with a wizened face who frightened her because he looked like a little old man. Taking one look at the oncoming figures of Nick and Paddy, he gave her one half-sympathetic, half-cynical look and slammed the door. She heard the bolt being shot home and leaned against the rough wood from which the old paint hung in leprous strips.

Nick was furious. He pulled her round towards him and slapped at her face and head so that the pain of the earlier blow from Eliza awoke making her cry out and stagger back.

'You'll kill the girl,' Jack said icily. 'She's learnt her lesson.'

'A few words from her and you'd be dangling alongside Mayberry and his whelps.'

There was a hostile silence in which Jade slid to the ground, her back still against the peeling door.

'Made a mess of her face,' Paddy said, and that was the last Jade remembered until she found herself back in Nan's cubby-hole, Nan and Ma Lee bending over her solicitously. Ma had even brought a pannikin of water and was bathing her cheeks and brow. Jade wanted, ridiculously, to hug the woman. She had more warmth than Mama. And then she hated herself for the disloyalty.

She tried to sit up but fell back, moaning. There was a last impression of Nan's blue eyes filled with tears, then Jade slid backwards into a dark river that carried her away from slums and gallows and hanged children, into the dubious safety of unconsciousness.

It was several days before she recovered from Nick's beating. She had lain, very quiet, in the narrow room with the skylight conscious of Nan's presence, of the regular visits from Drogo who continued to grin even though his limpid eyes were concerned. Ma Lee came often, bosoms more extravagantly bountiful than ever, and if she smelt a little what did it matter when she was kind.

The second visit from Eliza roused Jade from apathy. The sound of Eliza's voice stimulated the first healthy anger she'd experienced since they fought one another on the floor of Jack's room. Unsteadily, Jade forced herself to pull open the door and lean against the jamb.

'My Gawd!' Eliza mocked. 'Who's the scarecrow, then?'

'How are they?'

'You mean the Benedicts?' Eliza played out the charade spitefully.

'You know who I mean. It's little enough to ask.'

'Tell her,' the Guv'nor said sharply and was taken with another fit of coughing.

'Mama's worse. Sure 'er little girl's dead by this time and Pa in much the same mind. Them Mandrakes called, very smooth and slimy, askin' about Miss Jardine. Won't be coming no more 'cos they thinks the same. Heard that Sir Piers say the criminal classes don't take no prisoners. Pa seems to know what happens to the girls first. There was some Runners in at Rosie's, by the way, lookin' fer new girls so it's lucky yer didn't send 'er there. Caught Rosie without 'er protection. Pip and Cally was out fer a pie. Only away five minutes so the Redbreasts 'ad been watchin'. But it was lucky in a way 'cos they won't be back there lookin' for 'er little ladyship.'

Eliza yawned and ugliness seeped through the picture of conventional respectability she projected so effortlessly.

'What do you mean, Mama's worse?' Jade asked.

'Got stupid all of a sudden, ain't you, dearie. Must have been that roughing up you had from somebody. Coo, all the colours of the rainbow, yer are! I mean your mama's bound for the loony house. Out of her mind. Says she can't stand the house any more an' they must get away. Your pa's thinkin' of taking her abroad. But he'll wait a little time yet. Knows someone who wants to buy the house, though.'

'It's your fault, all of you. Poor Mama.'

'Poor Mama with her pearls an' her silk dresses an' furs!' Eliza ridiculed viciously. 'Poor thing. Won't be able to wear 'em in Bedlam.'

'I hate you.'

Eliza stood up, her eyes hard as flint. 'Best be careful, Miss Jardine. Could get that pretty face o' yours cut up something cruel if I let on to Molly that 'er precious Nick's sniffin' around. She'd enjoy takin' the point of that chiv of hers to yer cheeks. Mebbe yer eyes if she's feelin' spiteful enough. You'd best sing very small, me dearie.'

'You'll say nothing of the sort,' Jack said roughly and Jade had a glimpse of the 'kerchief he thrust into his pocket. An ugly red blotch marred the white material. He was ill and he was her chief protection, hers and Nan's. The unpleasant knowledge diverted her from her anger against Eliza.

'It's shut 'er up, anyway.'

'You'll find Paddy at the Lamb,' the Guv'nor told her, 'and don't let me find you stirring up trouble with Molly.' He opened his drawer and took out the pistol, examining minutely the chasing on the stock. It seemed his favourite show of authority.

'Be glad when I can get away from the Benedict house. Gives me the creeps, her mama does. Wanders around at night with a candle and the Master has to follow 'er in case she sets fire to the drapes.'

'You've given the child a graphic picture. Now be on your way, Eliza. Wouldn't do to be back late from your half-day.'

'No. No, it wouldn't.' Eliza's cold gaze flicked over her victim's disreputable figure and matted hair. Then she smiled slyly and Jade longed to strike the smirk from her lips.

Instead, she ran back into Nan's retreat and crouched in the farthermost corner under the skylight. Mama deranged and Papa accepting the fact of her death. Eliza and Molly her bitter enemies. Nick biding his time. The Maul. The theft and the hangings.

But there was Nan, Ma Lee and Paddy. Guv'nor Jack who respected her. Slowly she uncurled her body and stood up on the rickety chair. The skylight still did not budge but at least she still tried to escape. She had not given up.

Lying down on the mattress, Jade tried to fill her thoughts with pleasant things but each one seemed to hold some rot or worm at the centre. And then the face of the man on the balcony came into her mind and refused to be ejected. He was the only man she would ever have described as beautiful. Yet he was not effeminate.

She felt that she would see him again and the thought brought a strange comfort.

It was another week before Jade's bruises faded, not entirely, but enough to make her look pretty again. Ma Lee had produced hot water from some unknown source and Jade had washed her hair in an ecstasy of pleasure, then taken off the gown to clean herself from top to toe. Shivering, she had pulled on the gown from which she had scrubbed the most offending marks, then rubbed at the toes of her shoes.

Ma Lee had told her a great deal about the people she now

lived with. Molly was one of a band of wanderers with a flourishing trade in commercial poaching in the heaths and estates around London. All sale of game was forbidden but it was lucrative to sell the grouse and pheasants, rabbits and hares to establishments catering for the gentry and royalty. Nothing was ever said at the official banquets about the quality or source of the food presented.

But there was great rivalry between tinkers, particularly from Ireland, and the gipsies who were skilled, using nets and snares. Unfortunately two such parties raided a covert on the same night and fought out the matter so frenziedly with whatever weapons came to hand that many lay bleeding and dead from club wounds and the shot from short-barrelled guns. All Molly's family were wiped out and it was Jack who, riding back from his highwayman's patrol, found the girl shivering in the bushes and took her back to the citadel where she quickly came under Nick Caspar's protection.

'And he lets her go to other men?' Jade asked with distaste. She had come to realize that this sexual act must only be done with a man for whom one had at least liking and respect if there was not love.

'That's Nick's lay. He's a ponce. Sends out his girls an' gets most o' the pickin's. Rather have a magsman any day.'

'He has others besides Molly?'

'Cor, love yer! 'Course 'e has. Got a house in a far grander street than the Holy Land. All red an' gold papers, Molly says. They goes out for a short walk if there's no business that evening and it isn't long afore some swell stops 'em. Back they goes. Good money in it. Far better'n Rosie's. All quantity there but no quality.'

'Why does Jack stay here? Couldn't he afford a better place for Nan?'

'He's right in the centre o' things an' the Runners'll never break in. Watched all the way from St Paul's they are. 'Tis mighty safe.'

'I think he'll change his mind now Nan's growing up. And — you know he's ill, don't you?' She must remember the name She must remember the name of the Holy Land.

A shadow crossed Ma Lee's brow. 'Had that cough a good long time now. But he's the best pistolman in Lunnon. Even Nick knows that.'

'Why are you here?'

''Cos I got itchy fingers, that's why. Can't resist them fine ladies' dresses, and my Ben was a pickpocket. Run in the family, it did.' And Ma lumbered off, the floor creaking under her comforting weight. 'Got to go to the shop for a while.'

Jack had given Jade a comb and Paddy a cracked mirror he could not fence and she took both to the candle on the chair. The crack was unfortunate for one side of her face was a little higher than the other, not too noticeably, but it gave her an eerie look, like a girl not quite human. The bruises were gone from her eyes and there was only a faint trace down one cheek. Her brown hair tumbled from the centre parting to flow over her shoulders like dark rain. It occurred to her for the first time that she had been incredibly stupid. The green dress was not unattractive and there had been that hideous episode with Tom. She shivered and was about to drop the mirror when the doorway darkened and she saw beyond her own reflected face the hawklike features of Nick.

'Ma! Ma Lee!' she called, then her throat constricted.

'Gone out,' Nick said very softly, his hair red in the candle-glow. The mirror fell at her feet. She tried to think but her mind seemed stultified. Jack and Nan were out, she had guessed to Saul Isaac's house, but beyond that she was submerged in a pool of fear that seemed to have no bottom or end.

Nick closed the door with a finicky care and pushed the old chair under the handle.

'Don't say anything,' he whispered, and bending down he laid a knife at the far edge of the mattress. 'Don't make any noise at all.'

'Jack will kill you,' she said just as quietly with a curious cold resignation. Nick would not have attempted this if there had been any chance of being interrupted. For a moment she thought it might have been better to have been hanged, then she pushed the fancy from her strongly. At least she was alive. She would not always be here. Cowards were beneath contempt. But her heart beat irregularly and a sick dislike overtook her. It would be no triumph for him if he suspected she enjoyed any part of his seduction. You're a bitch, she told herself. A bitch. And he – what was he?

His fingers were at the buttons of her bodice, opening each one with scrupulous care, laying bare her breasts and rib-cage. He tutted at the sight of the long, fading line where Eliza's fingers had torn at the white flesh, then bent his head to draw his eyes down the narrow redness. A great shudder ran through her body. Green eyes locked with grey. 'Liked that, did you?'

She shook her head contemptuously.

'I should have said you did.'

'Of course there is all that experience. You should know,' she could not help retorting.

He smiled then lifted the shoulders of the gown and slipped them down as far as her elbows, constricting her movements. Her eyes widened and grew dark. He was pushing her sideways and downwards and she could do nothing pinioned as she was but slide to the mattress.

'Jack will kill you,' she said again, her voice sharp and high.

'What d'you think that chiv's for?' he asked softly but with an edge of anger. His lips nibbled at her breasts, not crudely like Tom, but with a gentle caressing that aroused the warmth inside her. The pleasurable tingle ran down to pulse between her legs. She stirred, moving her head from side to side, hating her own desire.

'See?' Nick whispered. 'It's not what you expected, is it? Fine ladies pay me a good deal for what you're having free.'

'Oh, please!' She strained away from him but there was nowhere to go. The mattress filled the small space and all she could see were his shoulders and the dark face edged with garnet. He smelt warm and animal and she was conscious of an overwhelming strength that would never allow her to rise.

'Real clean and pretty you look,' he said thickly. 'And those eyes!'

Her eyes were stabbing him through and through as she intended would happen to him in reality one day. But she could not keep her legs together for all the violence of her hatred of both himself and her. For all that she tried, he was parting her thighs and she was letting him do it.

'Haven't time to undress properly this time,' he told her, close to her ear, 'but that's something to look forward to next, eh?' He fumbled with his breeches.

Better than Rosie's. Better than Rosie's. Better — Ma Lee's words ran through her brain over and over again. Better than Rosie's.

She was struggling and his hands were on her upper arms, excruciatingly cruel. 'Don't be a fool. Do you want it to hurt? If you keep still at first, it won't. I promise you.'

Dizzily, she flinched from the hard rising of his body.

72

He put a hand over her mouth and pushed this new virile body towards hers with the other.

'Supposed to help me now,' he said softly. 'Come on.'

She refused to answer, close to tears but refusing to let them go. She tried to clamp her legs together again but he was between them.

'Christ Jesus!' Panic was uppermost, desire fled to leave only fear and detestation.

'Pray, do you?' he laughed mockingly. 'You do choose your times.'

Something pushed against the private place Mama could never bear to mention and all the soft tissues were tearing. A shriek reverberated against the palm of his hand.

He was inside her, thrusting through red tunnels of pain beyond which lay only the slightest vestige of the pleasure he had first summoned up to lull her into a sense of security. She moaned, half-fainting with each cruel penetration, her eyes shut so that she need not look at him. It seemed it would never end but at last the abominable ingress came to a sudden climactic end and he collapsed with a sigh.

She tried to push him away but he lay where he was for a long time while the red-hot chafing bit at her inside like acid. She moaned as he lifted himself away.

'Done you a real favour,' he murmured in a drugged enjoyment. 'Be as easy as shelling peas next time, now you've got rid of that troublesome little hindrance.'

'I hate you.' Her eyes burned intolerably but she wouldn't give him the satisfaction of seeing her tears.

'You'll tell me you love me one of these days.' He refastened his breeches and stood up to stare down at her. 'I can guarantee that.' His shoulders seemed to fill the room.

'Never!'

'We'll see.' Leaning across, he recovered the knife and pushed it inside his boot.

'I should cover yourself up.' Then he removed the chair from under the door knob without haste and went out.

She could hardly move. Ma Lee had been right. And yet, Paddy and Eliza had enjoyed their encounter. Once, Ma Lee said. It was only once that one went through this pain, but it could only be worth it if one suffered for the man one loved. Not for Nick.

Crying softly, she pulled down her skirts and restored her bodice to decency but she could not hide the blood that pooled the mattress and marked the green material.

Ma Lee had told Jack who was pale with a fury Jade had not expected.

'Rutting swine!' He almost hissed and took out the pistol to lay it upon the table, staring at it with red-rimmed eyes. He looked old and tired today.

Ma brought water and rags and Jade was able to make herself more comfortable. She also brought another gown from her seeming inexhaustible store and took the green one away to clean it.

Nan, though she did not know the reason for Jade's discomfort, was filled with a delightful sympathy. There were, Jade reflected, some compensations in her present way of life. People had been more distant in the past, except for Papa. Too late, she remembered the sea-horse. Now her luck was gone. Grow up, she told herself, there's no such thing. Life is what you make it. But it was the last link with home and the thought saddened her.

'Here,' Ma Lee whispered later, 'found this in your pocket. Don't suppose you want to lose it. 'Tis yours, ain't it?'

Jade nodded. 'My father gave it to me.'

'Funny little thing. What is it?'

'It's a charm. Thank you. Why are you so good to me?'

Ma shrugged and quivered all over, each fold of the yellow satin gown shimmering. ''Cos yer a game little cock-sparrer! Look. I'll give yer a drink after. Got camomile in it and other things. Good for stoppin' babies. Just in case you're worryin' like.'

Jade had never thought she might have a baby. It seemed terrible to bring a child into this environment, worse still a child of Nick Caspar's. Her face paled.

'Drink it all down,' Ma urged when she proffered the glass. 'Won't do you a scrap o' harm. I'll tell you what's in it so's if you do go somewhere's else, you'll never need fall if you don't want. The apothecary will make it up for you.'

Go somewhere else! Where? Jade drained the bitter brew. The prospect of Rosie's still hung over her head like the Sword of Damocles. But Jack wouldn't send her there, not after his furious outburst over Nick's behaviour.

She felt weak at the thought of coming face to face with Caspar next time. He had given her both pleasure and pain and once she had healed, the pain would never come again. She shivered and gave the glass back to Ma Lee, not wanting to think of Nick's hold over her when there was no longer anything to fear. He could overwhelm her like a storm and she knew it.

It was Eliza's day for coming. Jade half-dreaded, half-longed for her appearance.

'Goin' to give in me notice,' she said. 'There's no one's said anythin' amiss so they can't think I got anythin' to do with it. Have yer done the other reference?'

'Of course,' Jack told her, taking a paper from the drawer of the desk.

'Mama's in a worse tiz than ever,' Eliza said with dissecting cruelty. 'It's her little girl's birthday tomorrow and she can't have no party. Ain't it a cryin' shame!'

'They aren't really going away?' Jade asked. With Eliza leaving, there would be no more news of her parents. She could not bear the thought.

Eliza's gaze swept jealously over Jade's new, clean appearance, her shining hair.

'Yes, they're really goin'. To the Continong. Papa thinks the change will save Mama's reason. An' they say 'e's been told there ain't no hope for Miss Jardine an' they'd best to forget 'er altogether. Sad, ain't it?'

'Couldn't you let me go back? I wouldn't say a word! You know I'm fond of Nan and Ma Lee. I'd never want to hurt them. You know I don't know where I am so I couldn't find it anyway –'

'No,' Jack told Jade tiredly. 'You're a noticing sort of girl. The slightest clue and you'd have the law on us. Don't fancy having my neck stretched. It's my own fault for being weak in the first place. And now Nick's –'

'Nick's done what?' Eliza asked, her face turning an unbecoming red. 'Tumbled Miss Jardine? Well! Well! What's Molly goin' ter say? Eh?' From her injured expression and look of fury, she herself had coveted what Jade had thrust upon her unasked and unwanted.

'You'll tell Molly nothing if you've any sense,' Jack said firmly. 'But ravishing's a crime and that's another charge on top o' housebreaking and kidnap.'

'Ravishing!' Eliza smarted. 'A likely story. Anyway, she don't dare cheep to anyone. Thievin' an' fencin'. An' we'll all swear she wanted to; wanted to leave home for the thrill of it, wantin' to see how folks like us live, being a headstrong girl an' not wantin' to be married off to young Mandrake an' her mama sayin' she must.'

'Shouldn't you be going?' Jack suggested. 'You have what you came for.'

It was only after Eliza had left that Jade remembered she couldn't have gone home anyway. Back to Mama's deranged and disgusted eyes, her father's secret revulsion. She couldn't hide what had happened. Nick's lust for her had put her beyond the pale.

Jade woke out of a deep sleep to hear angry voices in Jack's room. Nan had not yet been disturbed so she got out carefully, shivering without the warmth of the blankets.

'What's all the fuss?' Nick said lazily. 'You never stuck up for the landed gentry before. Been robbing them for years. What's so different about Miss J? Got the makings of a real good whore, that little lady. Doesn't just lie pretending she hasn't noticed it. Shivers like a little thoroughbred colt. Make a fortune with her once she's trained.'

'Shut your mouth!'

'You know, Jack? You've got it hard over that child and you old enough to be her father.' Nick tutted in mock disapproval.

'You've got one last chance to leave her alone,' Jack told him.

'And if I don't?' There was no amusement left in Caspar.

'I kill you.'

'Don't be a fool!'

'I mean it, Nick.' There was a rattle that Jade knew was the pistol being put back on the desk top. The ensuing silence filled her with fear. Suppose Nick were to get the better of the Guv'nor? What would happen to Nan who was so pretty and so compliant? Unable to bear the suspense she pulled open the door so that she could just see through the gap.

The only light in the room was the flickering glow of one candle. The uneven radiance played over both harsh faces.

'Now, Jack –'

'I said I meant it.'

Nick's hand slid down his thigh towards his boot-top but the intervening bulk of the desk and the resultant shadow prevented Jack from seeing the stealthy movement.

Jade pulled the door wider. 'Jack!' she screamed. 'Look out! Please –'

But instead of looking at Nick, the Guv'nor turned towards her first, only for a second in which she saw that what Caspar had said was true, then his hand flashed towards the pistol. Raised it –

The knife flew towards him like a golden arrow and went into Jack's chest right up to the chased hilt. The pistol wavered; fell. Jack's body crumpled.

Nick's face turned towards her, smiling. His hair was dark fire. Trembling, she shut the door violently and pushed the chair under the knob as she had seen him do.

She heard him step across the room, stop and whisper close to the old panels, 'You've got to come out sooner or later. I'm willing to wait.'

She did not answer.

Nan stirred and said sleepily, 'What's – wrong?'

'Nothing, my pet. Nothing at all. I just had to get up for a moment.' Jade made herself return to the mattress and her place beside Jack's daughter. It would be cruel to tell her now. The night became a dark tunnel with only one end.

CHAPTER THREE

Jack knew that she could not stay shut up in the narrow closet for ever. There was Nan to think about. She needed food and drink. So Jade opened the door in the morning so that Ma or Drogo could bring in their breakfast and wondered how best to tell Nan that her father was dead. Surely it was kinder to say that Jack had been ill for some time and that his lungs had finally collapsed? Would she understand?

It was Ma Lee who came, rather less exuberant than usual, but with a look of anger that boded ill for Nick Caspar.

'Does she know?' Ma whispered.

'No,' Jade answered. 'I wondered if I should say his illness killed him.'

'Better than lettin' her know Nick knifed 'im.'

'Has no one – objected?'

'Everyone heard Jack threaten 'im and he had the pistol in his hand when Tom and Paddy O'Shea came in,' Ma divulged softly. 'Self-defence.' She shrugged. 'Nick's been wanting to be Guv'nor for a long time now an' Jack knew he was past it. Asked me to keep an eye on Nan and you only yesterday, after he found out about Nick and you, as if he sensed what was coming.'

'What – are – you whispering – ?' Nan asked, sitting up and rumpling her tight curls. She looked warm and sweet and very vulnerable. And innocent.

Jade's spirits plunged for a moment, remembering her own lack of innocence. But she could not have prevented it and what happened to Nan was far more important than the loss of her own chastity. Jack's daughter must be protected and she was perhaps the only person who could bring about that defence.

Her face burned as she envisaged Nick's price for allowing her to keep Nan with her. So long as he did not demand his pound of flesh today.

She went to Nan and put her arms around her. 'There's something you must know.' And she told the girl the story of Jack succumbing to his illness.

Nan turned on her a terror-stricken look. 'But – who will – look after me?'

'We'll do it,' Ma Lee said with false cheerfulness. 'We wouldn't see any harm comin' to you.'

'Oh, poor – Father.' Nan's huge blue eyes were awash with tears. 'Poor Father.' And she began to cry heartrendingly.

Jade held her for a long time until the girl's grief was partly assuaged, then she coaxed her to drink some milk and eat some crusty bread and later to lie down on the mattress until she felt a little better. Ma Lee went about her business.

'Very touching,' Nick said softly from the door. 'But leave her for the moment. I want to speak to you.'

Jade rose from her place at Nan's side and followed him into Jack's room. He sat down in the Guv'nor's chair, his knees spread wide, the light showing up the silken embroidery on his new waistcoat. His eyes watched her steadily but she gave no sign that this disturbed her. She waited contemptuously for him to speak.

'It was a fair fight.'

Her green eyes flashed but she knew better than to protest. There was Nan to think of.

'Never saw eyes like yours before,' Nick said and tipped the chair back to scrutinize her the better, starting at her small feet and travelling slowly up the length of her legs and thighs, over the shapely little breasts that strained against the new tight gown of faded yellow. Her throat grew constricted and dry but she did not move a muscle, giving him back stare for stare. He looked bigger than ever now that Jack did not stand between them.

'Come here,' Nick ordered and the chair legs crashed back to the floor.

She hesitated only for a moment. It would help neither herself nor Nan to rouse his anger. She entertained a vivid recollection of the strength of his bunched fists.

He pulled her to his knee, spanning her waist with his hands.

'I've got some plans for you.'

'I thought you might.' Her voice was perfectly even.

He laughed as though she had pleased him. 'Still hate me?' She did not answer.

'So, you do. But I mean to change that. I expect you know I have a house in a better part of London?' His hand lifted up the hem of the gown. Strong fingers stroked the firm skin around her instep and ankle, her rounded calf.

'I heard Molly say so.'

The fingers progressed a little higher, touched the satin smoothness of her flank. She could not repress a shudder that was only half repugnance. He's a murderer. He lives off women. He's cruel and vicious. The words spun wildly through her brain with the velocity of a runaway coach. Like the one that had disabled Nan. Forget all his vices, she told herself. He'll give Nan away to someone like Tom or the Maul unless I – unless –

For a moment the tips of his fingers caressed the warm little hollow of her crotch and she gasped and twisted in his hold. He laid his mouth against the point of her nipple and teased at it gently through the fine material. The sensation was quite delicious. She could almost forget the pain of yesterday, the terror of Jack's slaying. Almost –

'You'd like it better than here. A room of your own. Food brought in from the chop-house. Baths when you wanted them. A girl to look after you – '

'A girl? Would I have any choice?'

He lifted his head and his eyes were surprised and a little wary. 'Bargaining? I can have you without.'

'I might behave more to your liking if I could express my own – '

'Wishes?' The hand slid back down her leg and squeezed her foot.

'Not quite that.'

'You know perfectly well you mean just that.'

'I want Nan to look after me. That's what I'm after.'

He pushed her off his lap roughly and she staggered, her hip striking the edge of the desk. She bit her lip with the sudden hurt. 'Someone must,' she said in a practical tone as though nothing had happened. 'And if it's possible, I'd like Ma Lee as well. I won't always be able to keep an eye on Nan, not if I'm —'

'If you're what?'

'Looking after you. That's what you're saying is going to happen, aren't you?'

'It's hard to believe you're only fifteen.'

'Sixteen. It's my birthday. So Eliza reminded me.'

'Well!' He stared at her calculatingly. 'I'll have to give you a present then.'

She divined the present he had in mind. Perhaps she could endure it if he allowed her to have her way. 'The only thing I want is Nan. And Ma.'

'Sure there's nobody else while you're about it?' he asked sarcastically. 'The Prince Regent?'

She shook her head. Any faint hopes she might still have entertained of going home had vanished during the short interview. She had agreed to become Nick Caspar's whore and that was the end of being Jardine Benedict.

He looked around him with distaste, dragged at the skirt of the uninspiring dress.

'I've a mind to take you there this evening, only not in that. I'll have some clothes sent round and fetch you later in a carriage.'

'Only if you let me have —'

'Nan and Ma Lee,' he said resignedly.

'And a hot bath when I get there. Otherwise — I can guarantee nothing.'

'So that's the way of it.'

'What did you expect? It was only yesterday you forced me.'

He laughed unexpectedly but she was not deceived by his apparent good humour. She was sickened briefly that she had bargained with such a man. But Nan needed her. That's what she must always keep uppermost in her mind. You're a hypocrite, she derided herself. Oh, you want to help Nan. That's real enough, but there's a part of you wants him to teach you all he knows, only you must never let him see that too obviously.

Perhaps he understood her shame for he said sharply, 'I'll be back then. See you don't have a change of heart. And I suppose you'd better have that dim-wit ready too, not that I can see what use she'll be.'

'I can.'

He frowned impatiently and was gone.

Oh, God, she thought, what have I done?

But there was not too much time to worry about that. Ma had arrived with a jar of salve she said would help Jade's aches and pains if that rutting beast wanted his way with her again, and Jade, between using the stuff extravagantly and surprisingly unself-consciously, told Ma what was in store for her.

'You will come with me and Nan?'

'You'll be just as much a prisoner there –'

'For Nan's sake. Remember, Jack did beg you.'

'An' I promised,' Ma agreed slowly.

'At least there will be a proper room. Nan might as well have been a pet in a kennel! She will need you when I'm not there. And he promised baths, proper food.'

'It's just – I can't forget Nick an' what he done to you an' Jack.'

'We must both forget. What other solution is there?'

'Always said you was a game little wench. Know you'll 'ave Molly to contend with, don't you? But, of course, you must.'

'I intend to see that he keeps her in order,' Jade told Ma. 'There are ways.'

'You won't go thinkin' you'll be the only one for long?'

Jade shook her head. 'I won't do that. Could you get some hot water, enough to do Nan and me?'

'Anyone'd think you was both startin' some new, exciting life!'

Jade could not help laughing. 'I shouldn't imagine it'll be dull.'

Ma did as she was asked and the two girls were in the middle of washing their hair when the clothes arrived in a box. Jade's hair was streaming wet but she could not resist pulling out the garnet-red velvet gown and the mantelet trimmed with deep cream-coloured fur. Even the short sleeves were banded with it and there was a matching muff, a pair of shoes and stockings, garters of green, and a bonnet in the shape of a Greek helmet in the same red as the coat and dress.

She could not help wondering where the garments had originated. They were of very good quality and the faint scent that emanated from them was expensive. There were no under-garments, not even a petticoat.

There was another gown and pelisse she knew by their larger size Nick had thrown in for the 'dim-wit'. They were of dark blue trimmed with sable and would enhance Nan's gold and blue colouring. She was conscious of a faint alarm as she studied the clothes. It was almost as if he wished to see, or let someone else see, Nan at her best, and a vague, unformed fear took possession of her but only for a moment. Nick knew she would expect Nan to be treated no differently from herself, that was all. She had entered into a contract with him to do exactly as he wished so long as Nan was left alone.

Her wet hair dripped on to the velvet and on to the dusty floor. Ma thrust a towel towards her.

Once dressed in the strange-seeming finery the time seemed to drag. Nan became a little tearful over Jack but her tears only emphasized the glorious brilliance of her huge blue eyes, as the fur-trimmed blue accentuated the girl's beauty, and again Jade was disquieted on Nan's account.

'Real little beauty!' Ma pronounced, magnificent in red and a bonnet with an ostrich plume that nestled round the brim like a sleeping cat. She had all her things stuffed into a huge old carpet-bag Jade was sure Nick would frown on.

Jade became aware that she was quite taut with excitement. There was relief at leaving this dreadful citadel, of being away from the Maul who was so much more than a guardian. Maul was kept to terrorize and collect extortion money from clubs and hotels and gaming-houses. He had a penchant for young girls, Ma Lee had told Jade, and if Jade had not insisted upon taking Nan with her, it would have been just like Nick to have passed on Jack's daughter to the huge man as a chattel.

Drogo brought them some food, laughing and capering at their fine feathers, his beautiful Italian eyes sparkling. Jade had forgotten Drogo. The dwarf seemed more touching than ever today but Nick would never agree to letting her have the little man as well as the others.

No one mentioned Jack. It was as though he had never been.

They heard Nick long before they saw him. He super-imposed his personality by sheer force of weight. They had been sitting by the sulky fire which was usually tended by the old woman who changed the slop-buckets and for her services had a sleeping-place and a share of the food. Nan got up nervously, her eyes intensely blue in the candle-light, curls glittering. She looked taller, older, more womanly.

Nick was immediately aware of the change in Jack's 'dim-wit'. The cruel gaze appraised her then passed on to Jade. Ma and Caspar exchanged sour looks over the Greek helmet.

'Come on,' he said, and they went without another word.

Once inside the carriage, Jade crushed against Caspar, and Nan huddled against Ma's reassuring bulk, Jade had to pinch herself to decide whether or not she dreamed the journey. The warm clothes cushioned her from the cold that swirled around the windows so that the most she could see was a thin, white pall that turned the streets to shadowy tunnels lit for the most part by squares of windows or the lugubrious glow of infrequent gas lamps. People moved in the lanes and alleys, pushing close to the conveyance to beg without success, then shouting abuse after them.

Nick's strong thigh pressed needlessly close and Jade was conscious of the whiff of male body scent that came from his coat. She had a moment of panic in which she wanted to open the little door and hurl herself out into the cold mist to be lost in the maze of streets. But Nick would have divined her intention immediately. Even if she did get away he'd be so angry he'd retrace his steps and ensure Nan's fate was as terrible as he could make it.

They passed no officer of the law.

The house was arrived at in silence. It was tall and narrow and the once golden stone was soot-stained and a little dingy. There were bars at most of the windows. She'd been a fool, Jade thought, to have expected otherwise.

Nick jumped down from the conveyance, loomed huge against the icy vapour that set them all shivering, then plucked Jade from the temporary comfort of the interior. He swung her so easily, his fingers almost meeting around the small span of her waist, then, gripping her wrist, he took her up the steps and rapped four times on the middle panel of the door. A tiny, round window opened, then a bolt was drawn and a chain freed. A gust of warm air and patchouli billowed towards them.

Ma Lee hurried Nan after them.

A short, immensely broad-shouldered man in livery re-fastened the door. His nose had been broken and Jade imagined he had once been a wrestler, probably at a country fairground.

With the closing of the door, a red gloom surrounded them.

'It's upstairs,' Nick said briefly and impelled Jade up a narrow staircase embellished with a pair of shadowy cupids painted in gilt and a dim picture of a naked woman lying on a puce-coloured sofa.

They passed a door from behind which issued a muffled knocking sound and a man's husky laugh, then another and another shut on silence.

The room allotted to Jade was on the top floor. It was large and claustrophobic with its red and gold paper and heavy bed-hangings that smelt depressingly of stale cigar smoke, pomade and sweat. She moved instinctively to open the window which gave readily to show the bars outside. The crisp cold air blew round the place sending a gust of smoke up the chimney and made the candle gutter.

She rattled the window down again and saw Nick pushing a door that led off the main room. Looking round his shoulder she saw a small dressing-room that was papered in white and gold so that it gave an impression of space. A chest at the end had a good many drawers which ought to be useful to Ma Lee.

'Where's Ma?' she asked.

'She'll have to earn her keep downstairs. Don't want her underfoot up here all the time. You needn't look like that. She'll be here when she's needed.'

Nan, shivering by the bed, looked exhausted. She still obviously grieved for her father without the luxury of being able to talk about it.

'Poor Nan,' Jade said with another look at the narrow bed in the dressing-room. 'Come and lie down.' She helped the girl take off her cloak and saw her settled and warmly covered. Nan was asleep almost immediately.

'I thought she was to be useful to you,' Nick said sourly.

'It's only two days since you murdered her father.'

'You aren't supposed to say things like that.'

'I've always been truthful.' She began to unfasten the mantelet which slithered to the floor with a soft, luxurious sound. The bonnet came off next to reveal the brown silk banner of her hair. Nick lifted up the end of it and let it run through his fingers.

'You noticed how difficult it was to get in or out?'

'Yes.'

'Even when you do, and your job will be to attract some

84

gent with gold, you'll be followed.'

'I know that too.'

'Good, then we both know where we are.' The hand slid from her neck to the line of her back and fastened on her hip.

'You promised me a bath,' she said quickly. 'And supper.'

'Well, don't take all night.'

The bath was brought, a gaudy affair all painted clouds and cherubs trailing flowers, then filled with many cans of water. The copper jugs removed, Jade took off the dress and stepped into the water, revelling in the warmth and the almost forgotten pleasure, soaping herself all over, sighing with a bliss that was only slightly marred with apprehension of what came after the meal.

Ma Lee came up with a towel and the jar of cream from her portmanteau.

'Swine,' she muttered under her breath. 'Hates him, I do.'

'But he'll have to pay you more for working here. It was good of you to come.'

Ma looked suspiciously bright-eyed. 'No one never said such nice things to me.'

'Oh, go on! What about your – Ben, wasn't it?'

'Plain man, my Ben. No frills. Tell me if 'e ever hurts you, that Caspar.'

'Oh, Ma. We both know he will. I'd better make the most of the first few days.'

'Got to go now, love. He sent this up.' She displayed the house-robe she had left on the chair, an eau-de-nil garment, slithery and beribboned and decorated with cream lace. 'Hates to think of you havin' to wear it for 'im. Should have had that young lord you was to marry.'

'Shall I tell you what I might have wed? He had a high-nosed father with a strong look of Nick about him, and wandering hands. I was to live with both of them, I suspect. In fact, you'd never believe how like Sir Piers Nick Caspar is. Rupert would not have been faithful once he'd got the Jardine money, perhaps not until then, though he did want me. Very much, I suspect. But his father repelled me. I might have been no better off – worse really. So go and enjoy your supper, Ma, and look well after Nan.'

The woman kissed her. After she'd gone, Jade got out of the bath feeling perfectly whole and relaxed, then dried herself slowly. The satin robe slid over her skin with a sensuous pleasure.

Nick brought their supper himself, all set out on a tray, and Jade was so hungry she snatched the chops and gnawed at them like a puppy and mopped up the gravy with a hunk of new white bread, then relapsed with a burp of contentment. There was red wine in a glass, a refinement she had missed. And then she noticed how the shadows projected by the bars of the chairs were curiously like those of the gallows where the Mayberrys had been hanged together, how close the room had grown and how the odour of the bed-hangings had intensified. And Nick, observing her sudden silence, took the glass from her fingers and set it down among the chop-bones and crumbs. The fire spat as he turned the key in the lock.

I can't, she thought wildly, now that the moment had arrived. But he took off his coat and hung it on a chairback, then began to unbutton his shirt. There was nothing under the shirt but a massive chest with reddish hairs on it. His breeches followed, to display an undergarment he began, slowly, to pull down over his thighs. I shall never need to go to another art gallery, Jade thought, then was seized with a terrible desire to laugh until she was tired. But Nick would never understand. He'd think she mocked him and that was the last thing she felt like doing in the face of his overwhelming nakedness.

He approached her and pulled at the bow that held the satin robe around her. She snatched at it as it began to slide from her shoulders but was too late. It engulfed her feet like some pale sea-pool. He picked her up and carried her to the bed.

Dragging her against him, he wrapped his thighs around her, opening her mouth with his tongue, thrusting it inside in a way she could not pretend she liked. She closed her eyes against the sight of his face, dreading the inevitable uprising of his body. But when his mouth left hers and kissed her breasts she found herself responding to him in spite of herself and her intrinsic dislike.

Even the last hurdle, the entry of his body into her own, was not what she had expected. Whatever magic Ma Lee's preparation had wrought, she was glad of it for as Nick worked inside her, the pleasurable tingle with which she had grown familiar became, in turn, an aching need in which she strove as hard as he for consummation, then the penultimate agony that turned slowly to a wonder that anyone could endure such pleasure and live.

But even as she clung to him, drowning in her new-found delight, she knew that this was not the ultimate. Only with the man she loved would she find that.

Jade was awakened by a thunderous knocking on the door. For a moment she could not remember where she was, then she became conscious of Nick's arm round her waist and a stickiness between her thighs that reminded her of a night that had not been peaceful.

'Open this door, Nick Caspar!'

Nick stirred and moved heavily.

'I'll kill that bitch!' Molly's voice rose to a shriek. She continued to beat on the door and to shout obscenities while Jade got out of bed and wrapped herself in the eau-de-nil gown.

'It's Molly,' she said as Nick opened a reluctant eye.

'I know who it is,' Nick growled and dragged his body against the bed-head, scratching at the red hairs on his chest for all the world like a big ape. He caught at Jade's wrist and pulled her up beside him. 'Got a good mind to take that thing off again,' he whispered.

'She won't go away.'

'Shut your face!' Nick shouted, becoming angry. 'Go away, Molly Connor.'

'Anyway, Nan must be wide-awake now.'

'She'll have to learn her place or she goes.'

'I'll explain matters to Nan,' Jade said quickly, 'never fear.'

Nick, furious now that Molly continued to plague him, bounded from the bed and ran to the door. As it opened, Molly rushed in, panting, her cheeks burning with resentment and looking more beautiful than ever. The red-brown eyes narrowed as she saw Jade. Curses flowed from the pretty lips.

'Why did you bring her here?'

'My dear Molly, I don't need your permission to do anything.'

'Her whorish little ladyship won't look so pretty in another minute!' The knife appeared in Molly's hand and she lunged across the intervening space incredibly fast. Jade scrambled across the bed, having nothing with which to protect herself, but Molly seized the hem of the satin house-robe and drove the knife blade through it several times.

'I'll swing for you, Molly,' Nick grated, his face white, and approached her intimidatingly, thrusting his bulk between her and Jade. He clenched his big hands together and beat Molly about the face and breast until she was gasping and writhing with pain and the knife fell from her fingers.

Jade was almost sorry for the girl.

'Do this just once more,' Nick threatened, 'and you'll not be allowed back. I know you're popular with certain clients but you're not the only pebble on the beach. There's as good fish in the sea. Maybe better. I can do without you – or her if it comes to that. What I won't do without is money and what it can buy, and now there's no Jack to share it with I intend to enjoy that bit more. Jack and I were partners, now I'm sole owner. I'll give you one more chance, Molly. Behave and you can stay as long as you like. Lay one finger on this new girl and you go for good. Understand?'

The hot brown eyes rested on Jade with a terrible hatred. 'I – understand.'

'Get off to your room, then. Be along myself, presently. Just a little matter I have to deal with here before I go out. And don't get any ideas because I'm out, Molly. Toby will be keeping an eye to Miss Benedict and he'll have orders to treat you as rough as he pleases. Stronger than I am, is Toby. Still understand?'

'Yes.' Molly almost spat the word, then she sobbed uncontrollably.

'Off you go, then.'

The girl got up. Already her face was swollen and discoloured and her breasts must look the same. Jade realized she must expect similar treatment if she crossed the man who was, at present, so infatuated with her.

Molly had gone. Nick relocked the door and forced her back on to the bed. 'It's all in the line of duty,' he whispered. 'Just duty – never learn if I don't teach you, will you?'

But, as she lay beneath him, Jade could not help but remember Molly's swollen and tear-stained face. As Molly's heyday had passed, so inevitably must her own and then what would happen to Nan?

Then, the mounting pleasure of what he did to her became uppermost. He wasn't tired of her yet. She needn't worry for a few days yet. Weeks, perhaps. She must do as all members of the citadel did, live for today.

Eliza visited Nick a few days later. This time, Jade, although she recognized the girl's voice, could not bring herself to see her. Vera Benedict would never want anything to do with a daughter who had done the things she had since she came to this house. Any variation on the usual theme was known to Nick Caspar. He had painted her nipples with gold and rouge, had kissed every part of her body, and made her lie in so many positions she no longer knew which were acceptable.

Jade wanted to ask Eliza about Mama and Papa but they were fast losing reality. She was beyond their contempt and her own.

The house was claustrophobic but it was preferable to the Holy Land and Nan was settled now and happier than Jade had expected. Ma Lee was able to visit them frequently, never without her potions and pots of this and that, or bringing expensive, stolen garments for Jade's adornment at Nick's request.

Toby brought food from the chop-house and bottles of wine or champagne, and every afternoon or evening footsteps sounded on the stairs and doors closed on the floors below as the smell of cigar smoke floated to the top of the house. Men's voices and laughter were heard, and, when they left, Jade and Nan would run to the windows and watch them leave, seeing only the tops of their heads or their hats, the colours of their uniforms if they were officers. But sometimes the men looked older and Jade wondered that they wanted whores at that age. It seemed men were never past lust.

Then Nick would return, in his mole-grey coat, with his garnet-red hair, and press her down to the mattress or have her lie on him, but the ecstasy was over too soon and she knew that her hold over him was more precarious.

It seemed he knew it too for he spoke now of the day she would have to earn her keep and struck her when she said that she was not ready to go to any man.

Eliza returned and this time Jade listened on the stairs.

'The Benedicts go next week,' Eliza said. 'They day I leave. That reference of Jack's worked the trick with the Osbornes but I want a rest once Paddy and Tom do their bit. Sick o' housemaiding, I am.'

For the rest of the day Jade saw little but her parents' hopeless faces. But the bars on the windows and Toby's muscular body were ever-present to keep her where she was. She still had the sea-horse under the mattress and the sight and touch of it usually evoked her father's presence, but Eliza's visit had taken away that security.

It must have been close to Christmas when Nick told Jade they were to take a drive. She was delighted for the days passed slowly when he was not there and one could not bathe and eat all the time.

Leaving Nan in Ma's charge, for Nick refused to let the girl accompany them, Jade dressed in the garnet velvet that set off Caspar's unusual colouring, and followed him out to the carriage. It was the first time she had seen the house in daylight but it looked little different from any other in the long street. A few caped and shawled figures passed by, their breaths curling in the cold air. A cat ran across the cobbles and disappeared into a basement. And then, she stepped back as Molly came up to the door, her bruised face still vital and handsome in spite of Nick's brutality.

She did not even glance at Jade but the brown eyes entreated Nick's kindness. He ignored her as she had done with Jade and the girl heard her sob as she was hoisted into the interior of the discreet conveyance and the door closed behind them.

'Where are we going?'

'You'll see.'

Nick made no move to touch her and that in itself was strange. He still wanted her but she had come to need more than a pleasurable act. There had to be some special person associated with the business of giving oneself to a man and Nick fell far short of her total commitment. Somewhere, there was a man who might love her and whom she could love wholeheartedly and without feelings of shame.

She sat up suddenly at the sight of trees set down the pavements and a familiar frieze of chimney-pots. Nick pulled her to his side and set a powerful hand across her mouth. The house door was open and Papa was helping Mama down the steps. Vera's face was ashen and she walked like an old woman. Papa's shoulders were a little bowed but he had, as Eliza said, weathered the blows of fate much better. A cigar was held between his teeth and he puffed at it as he handed his wife into the coach that waited, a mound of luggage piled on top, and four blacks standing patiently, clouding the freezing air.

Jade struggled fiercely, screaming against Nick's grasp, biting at his palm, but he only laughed and held her the more strongly. She was forced to watch her parents being swallowed up into the maw of the vehicle, the coachman's whip flick over the black hides. The clop of hooves filled her ears, grew less and died almost to nothing.

She collapsed against Caspar, crying out incoherently, unable to accept what she had just seen but the house stood empty, the blinds drawn. And then, the tears past, she sat stone-like while Nick too smoked a cigar, then rapped on the ceiling for the coachman's benefit. She could not believe he would be so cruel.

He took her to bed on their return but she lay passive letting him do what he would and he grew angry at her lack of response and struck her several times. She rejoiced in the hurt for she had begun to fear she would never again feel any positive emotion. Bruised and tired, she heard Nick go down to Molly's room.

She crawled from the bed and went to see Nan. The idyll with Caspar was over but it had been foolish of her to let him see that.

The garnet velvet ensemble was gone when she awoke next morning. In its place was a much less pretty gown in grey and a cheap-looking mantelet. With her face pale and bruised, the dress made her feel and look drab and lifeless. What a contrast to her triumphal entry! Ma Lee looked concerned when she came upstairs to press her usual brew on Nick's newest mistress.

'I heard what he done,' she said. 'Takin' you to see your parents go away for good – Rotten pig.'

Jade had imagined herself past tears but she cried out and sank to her knees, overcome with a paroxysm of crying that ended as abruptly as it came. Then she got up. 'I'll not do that again. There. It's out of my system now.' She touched the gown ruefully. 'That can mean only one thing. He expects me to earn my living now though I suspect the tuition is cut short.' She made herself smile. Ma avoided her eyes.

'You know, don't you?' Jade said, unable to control a spasm of dread.

Ma Lee nodded. 'That Molly was talkin'. You and she and Barby are to go to Drury Lane tonight. Folks want entertainment after the theatre. Sam Goode will be watching from the chaise Nick hires to keep an eye on new girls 'e doesn't trust to come back. Fast little devil he is and can keep abreast of the traffic a treat. Not many young bucks could show him a clean pair o' heels. He'll watch to see where you go an' bring you back afterwards. You're supposed to lift anythin' you can in the way of valuables. Snuff-boxes or cuff-links, watches, things like that, or tie-pins.'

'That's right,' Nick said from the doorway. 'Now, get off about your business, you gossiping old bag of lard!'

Ma knew better than to stay. Nan retreated into the dressing-room and shut the door. Jade could well picture her distress.

'Molly's mouth was always bigger than her –' He used an expression Jade had only recently come to understand. 'Not much left for me to explain, is there?'

'Not much.'

'Take that damned thing off,' he whispered, suddenly vicious.

She obeyed, her fingers stiff and not managing the buttons very well. There were bruises on her body as well as her face. The smell of Molly was still on him and she could not help grimacing.

'Not good enough for you, eh?' Nick said softly. 'Get on the bed. Go on, do you understand? You need a lesson.'

Jade backed towards the edge of the mattress. He had not bothered to lock the door as he usually did. 'Hurry up, you bitch, and open your legs.'

She knew she could not refuse. He was undoing his breeches but never took his eyes off her. 'There'll be plenty of men who'll treat you like an animal,' Nick went on as quietly, then threw himself on to her with no preliminary, thrusting and slamming into her so that she fought against the savagery in horror. Even Tom had not been so brutal. Nick achieved a thundering climax but she felt nothing at all but despair.

After he had gone she tried to obtain hot water for a bath but he must have given orders she was to have nothing for she did not even have a meal.

By the time she was ordered to dress to go to the theatre, she was starving and weary, filled with anger because Nan suffered the same pangs. Ma Lee, who had brought the message that she was to ready herself, smuggled in a piece of sausage and bread which Jade gave to Jack's daughter. It had not been fair that Nan suffered for Jade's inadequacies.

'Whores always work best on an empty stomach,' Nick said coldly when she went, shivering, downstairs. 'Keep an eye on her now, Molly, but if there's as much as a scratch on her little white hide, I'll deal with yours. Remember? She's not going to appeal to anyone damaged.'

Barby, a voluptuous blonde girl in a strawberry-red gown and blue pelisse, arrived last. Her Junoesque appearance was reassuring. Jade felt she might be a bulwark against Molly should she prove spiteful, but Molly was back with Caspar and rejoiced that her enemy was laid low. That revenge was sweeter than that of inflicting physical cruelty for the present.

They had walked only the length of the street when Jade heard the clip-clop of the chaise behind them and had a glimpse of a little man with a face as brown and wrinkled as a walnut who leered and flourished his whip at her.

The evening took on the aspect of a nightmare. Barby and Molly walked on either side like jailers. Sam Goode looked spry in spite of his age. And her skin crawled at the thought of a stranger availing himself of her body.

Barby told Molly a risqué story and Molly responded with one from her own repertoire. Neither expected Jade to say anything. She walked in silence, listening to Barby's raucous laughter in a detached fashion, trying not to think beyond their arrival at Drury Lane.

She need not have worried about being conspicuous. The Lane was filled with prostitutes, some gay and colourful, others little more than children who lurked in the shadows, pathetic in their rags. Any man who walked alone was importuned, 'Can I go home with you, dear?' or some other such invitation. The words on children's lips had a special obscenity.

Once Jade had an overpowering urge to run as she had after the theft, but Molly, who must have been watching her closely, divined her intention and let her feel the prick of the knife between her shoulder-blades.

All this time carriages and chaises proceeded in either direction, occasionally opening the door to let in one of the ladies of the night.

'I'm one of them,' Jade thought emptily. 'I'm a whore.' The knowledge seemed insupportable. All the time she'd been in Nick's house she had managed to gloss over the fact because her circumstances had changed for the better. She could no longer excuse herself. Jade felt terribly alone.

'There's a swell cove,' Molly hissed, prodding Jade towards a crawling vehicle, but the man who peered over the half-door fancied Barby better. The woman laughed as she was all but dragged inside, screeching good-naturedly.

Carriages began to draw up outside the theatre. The performance was obviously due to end. Molly pushed Jade nearer the kerb where the link-boys' torches lit up the satiny brown of her hair. A sedan chair appeared, then another. Groups of people emerged from the lighted foyer, grand in their fine clothes, their fingers winking with rings.

One man emerged alone, his redingote trimmed with a black fur collar, his tall hat not quite concealing his face. Jade stared. It was – she'd swear it was the man at the Haymarket and on the balcony when the Mayberrys met their Maker. She could never mistake that impression of a moonlit landscape. He staggered a little as he reached the line of waiting conveyances. 'Maggs!' he called out. 'Where are you, fellow?'

Jade stepped forward, her heart beating violently. 'Let me,' she said, 'go home with you, please!' Even to her it seemed more of a command than an entreaty.

The carriage was coming forward and he was the worse for drink. For a moment she thought he was going to fling off her restraining hand but the light shone into her eyes and he thought better of it. Grasping her arm, he almost threw her into the musky interior and climbed in beside her.

'Home, Maggs.' His tone was as empty as her thoughts.

The wheels rattled over the sooty cobbles.

'Home, Maggs.' He leaned against the buttoned upholstery and watched her sleepily. If he dozed off they'd never let her into the house!

'I won't disappoint you,' she told him, regretting the darkness. He'd seemed attracted by her eyes but he'd possibly forget them before he got home. Then she remembered Sam Goode and the chaise.

'I don't – usually – pick up green-eyed drabs.' He'd not forgotten!

'No. I realized that. That was why I chose you. I don't usually importune men, either. This was the first time.'

'Why did you?' He was not so drowsy now.

'The – usual reasons.' Let him think her driven to desperate measures so that she could eat. Anyway, she *was* hungry. Nick had deliberately kept her without food all day.

Out of the window she spied the chaise and Molly sitting in the back. 'There was someone in there tried to pull me inside against my will,' she told him. 'He – seems bent on following. I hope he does not mean you any harm because of my preference.'

'You don't sound like a drab.' He pulled aside the velvet

curtain so that he could see the better. A link-boy darted alongside, the burning brand trailing smoke and flame. 'Be off with you!' the man shouted towards the chaise. 'I'll have the magistrates on you if you persist in persecuting this woman! Lose it, Maggs,' he ordered the unseen coachman. 'A guinea if you do.' And he tossed a coin to the link-boy who darted to retrieve it, leaving the roadway in comparative dimness.

More traffic appeared, all of which was more conducive to shaking off their unwelcome pursuit. The carriage swayed wildly and more than once Jade was thrown across the space between the seats to be caught against the broad, redingoted chest. She felt his hand slide across the thick silk of her hair, over the round of her shoulder. His skin smelt of good soap and his breath not unattractively of brandy and cigar smoke.

'I'm sorry,' she said breathlessly, 'that you've been put to this trouble on my account.'

'Oh, not entirely on yours, you may rest assured!' he answered carelessly. 'I have an aversion to physical violence, particularly over trollops.' An edge of cruelty had entered his voice and he sat up straighter as though the night air had revived him. 'So since I've no desire for a broken head, only that which five minutes with you will soon assuage, I prefer to lose the fellow.'

Any romantic illusions she might have entertained of his good looks being matched by him falling instantly in love with her and so solving all her problems, vanished like snow in June. With a few coldly well-chosen words she had been put into her place in his scheme of things. A quick tumble neither of them would enjoy, another guinea for the use of her body, and thrust out of the door like an unwanted cat to fend for herself.

'I'm glad you don't use paint,' he said after another rattling swerve that shook all the teeth in her head. 'And you seem reasonably clean.'

He'd very soon discover, of course, that she'd lain with another man earlier today and would throw her words back in her face! 'This was the first time.' She'd be shown the door faster than lightning took to strike.

'A seamstress, are you?'

Sewing girls earned notoriously little and were driven to sell themselves. 'Yes, I'm a seamstress,' she replied mechanically.

He made a disgusted sound that she felt, comfortingly, was

intended for the employers of such women, and not the women themselves. And then Jade remembered the woman on the balcony and wondered why he needed to resort to street-walkers. He could have had any woman he chose.

They sat in silence, while the carriage, driven more decorously now that Sam's chaise had been left behind in a tangle of late-evening traffic, came to rest in the mews behind a rampart of grand London houses not unlike the Benedict household. Her stomach muscles contracted as she remembered this morning and the empty house left by the departure of her parents. Soon strangers would move into it. Eliza said Papa had a prospective buyer. Her parents might already be at sea, bound for strange, new places, and she'd never see them again. The dormant pain came to life and she buried her face in her hands in impotent grief.

'I have no intention of hurting you.' The voice was sharp.

No. Only of using her for the requisite ten minutes or so, then casting her out of your life. But she had no right to expect anything else. He had an itch to slake and she had offered to do that for him. Fairy-tales were not built on such sordid foundations. Yet, ever since she had seen him in the box at the Haymarket, she had thought of him and his strange beauty, imagined him a kind of prince who might rescue her from danger and degradation.

'I confess – I am desperately hungry.'

'Well, I'd not deny you supper. It's customary to feed one's partner, I believe.'

'You've really never invited a whore in the past?'

'No. I doubt if I would tonight if you hadn't been so – persuasive.'

'You think I made you –'

'Oh, I'm not so vacillating that I need you to make up my mind for me!' Roughly he ejected her from the vehicle and jumped down beside her. 'There you are, Maggs. You did well.' The sovereign spun through the air to be caught with great dexterity. A shilling followed it.

Jade was propelled up the steps to the back door. A passage opened out, lit by a candle, the marble flags shining coldly. She shivered involuntarily.

'Come, wench. You don't imagine I'd bed you without giving you a bath first? God knows who you've been with. Up those stairs with you and if I find you still please me after supper, we'll sleep together.'

96

3

She was ushered into a bed-chamber more Stuart than Georgian, the furniture dark and heavy, the hangings of ivory and forest green. There was a gesso mirror surrounded by gilded fruit and leaves. A variety of objects lay on the dressing-table, silver-backed brushes and pins, an enamelled snuff-box, a flask with a silver top, all chased with the initials G.M. Gilbert, she wondered? George?

Jade heard him shouting for the bath and hot water, then he reappeared, the redingote removed to show her a handsome dark coat, breeches and a fine linen shirt and lace ruffles. 'Get you into that closet,' he ordered her. 'My housekeeper will think the bath's for me and I prefer she thinks so. I'm ashamed I've resorted to drabs after a clean record. But circumstances alter events, as you no doubt already know. I'll tell her I'm ravenous and she'll bring enough supper for a regiment. And I'll see she doesn't come back afterwards.' His tone was careless. The dressing-room was claustrophobic. Jade, pressed against the door, heard the advent of the bath and the inevitable copper cans, the murmured instructions to the unseen Mistress Pratt to bring a tray in half an hour.

Then the door opened and she was ordered out again and a guinea laid on the table. The man, changed now into a black and white robe, told her to undress and get into the bath which was the usual hip variety with a miscellany of Italianate paintings around it.

She was glad to shed the drab clothing and Nick had taught her not to be ashamed of her body. She stepped out of the grey gown and mantle, then removed her stockings and garters, the tawdry shoes with which she'd been supplied. For a moment, she stood like a carving in white jade, the firelight kind to her narrow body and small yet well-shaped breasts. She knew her hair was beautiful in its shining simplicity. Crossing her arms over the little white bosoms, she stepped into the bath as though she were indeed the novice she had made herself out to be, aware of his quick intake of breath at the sight of her nakedness.

All the time she soaped and cleaned herself, she was aware of his black gaze, the way his fingers drummed impatiently against the chair arms. When she stood up to dry her limbs, his eyes never left her. He tossed her another robe of ivory satin with a green girdle which she bound round her slim waist.

He sent her behind a screen when the supper tray arrived

and she swooped on it the moment they were alone, snatching at the drumsticks and the thin, cold beef, cramming it into her mouth so that he could not mistake her obvious need.

He poured wine and gave it to her in a goblet, all the time staring at her silken banner of brown hair, her elegant white body. She gave a great sigh when she could eat and drink no more, only warmed her slim fingers in the pink glow of the fire and curled up her toes in contentment.

'If you could purr,' he said, 'I believe you would.' It was his first sign of amusement.

'It's wonderful to eat when you were sure you'd have to starve.'

'I still think you too well spoken for a whore.'

'I cannot tell you why I am. Only – that the situation was forced upon me.'

'Do you expect me to believe that?' He leaned forward to touch the fall of hair, the hollow of her cheek. And somehow that contact led to other things and the robe was unfastened to fall away from the pale miracle of her body. Not once, Jade thought dizzily, had he made her think of any physical aspect of their incipient coupling. With Nick, each part he touched was marked with a label in unequivocal terms. With this man, whatever his fingers aroused became something else, a branch of stars whirling, a warm fire burning. Her breasts welcomed his kisses, her thighs and her body the caressing hands, the soft slide of his fingertips over the smooth skin. Her body opened out of its own volition, like the petals of a flower.

'Love me,' she whispered. 'I need someone to love me –'

He had not bothered to carry her to the bed. It was obvious he intended to take her here on the rug by the fire. She stroked his smooth chest and the well-muscled back, enjoying the soap-smell that was all over her as it was on him. The scent of the wine still hung about the room, mingled with the faint odour of tobacco. Her legs encircled his body. He thrust deep inside her. Stopped.

'You said you were not used to this life,' he said, and her senses screamed for him to go on with what he had started and might not finish.

'There was a man who took advantage of me. I could not prevent him.'

'I suppose,' he remarked, 'that one only gets what one pays for. I'd hoped it was not spoiled goods.'

'Then you hoped for too much! You'd best pay me and let me go.'

'I've made you angry.' He sounded pleased about the fact.

'I cannot afford to be angry.'

His mouth moved against her throat, her breast-bone, and she pulled at his thighs, urging him to possess her. And again he began those movements inside her body, rousing her to a pitch of pleasure that made her cry out so that he was forced to put a hand across her mouth. 'You'll make Mrs Pratt suspicious.'

The world was breaking up in a kaleidoscope of purest sensuousness, each coloured piece forming a pattern she thought she would never forget, and yet as soon as it ebbed away she could not remember a vestige of it. God has made it so, she thought, so that one must always strive to reproduce those sensations. No matter how often one does it with the right man there will never be satiation. And a warm golden snake seemed to coil in her loins, waiting to be reawakened when he wished it.

She held him to her until they both slept.

It was cold when she awoke. The fire had burned to ashes and a chill blue filled the window-panes. The cerulean tint lay on his skin as well as hers. They were liked drowned creatures at the bottom of a pool.

Soon, he would expect her to go. She burrowed against him, crying out her inability to leave him. He jerked out of sleep, pulling her towards him, then pushing her aside. Grabbing his robe, he put it on, then went to light a candle. Immediately, he became real, his face set in that same moodiness with which he had first treated her. His foot struck the tray with its remnants of the meal they had shared and he frowned, turning away from the sight of her slight body on the hearth-rug.

'Someone will come soon to see to the fire. You'd better get up.' His tone chilled her.

She rose slowly and thrust her arms into the sleeves of the ivory house-robe.

'You wish me to go?'

'What else did you expect?' he asked harshly. The effects of his brandy, the wine and his sexual encounter had obviously worn off, leaving him in the worst of tempers, yet, just after the consummation of their lying together he had held her close, murmuring something against her hair she had not properly heard. But the timbre of his voice had held something more than pleasure or surprise. He had not expected to enjoy her and was unable to hide the fact that he had.

'I — I don't know when I'll eat again. Couldn't I — ?'

'No, you couldn't.' He was brusque to the point of rudeness.

'Please? After breakfast?'

'Get dressed now,' he ordered curtly. 'I can't imagine how I could have been so crassly stupid as to tangle with a girl like you in the first place. The brandy, I suppose.'

Her stricken pallor must have awakened him to the extent of his cruelty. 'For God's sake, don't look like that! Are all your men glad to see you in the morning?'

'There have been no others but the one who forced me.'

The black eyes tried to outstare hers but did not succeed. 'It was you who invited yourself and I suppose I was maudlin —' He turned his back on her and went to the window to stare out on to the street. 'I had a reason.'

'I — I daren't go back,' she whispered. 'See? The bruises are not gone.'

His harsh intake of breath told her the marks remained.

'Let me stay a little longer? I'll not ask for any more.'

'Did I please you so much in my brutish cups?' he asked sarcastically. 'I confess I remember little of what transpired. Did I acquit myself creditably?'

Jade flushed and bit her lip. 'I should have called you — practised. Yes, you did please me, there's no point in lying because of your present insolence —'

He got hold of her suddenly and forced her towards the dressing-room, pushing her inside just as the door of the bed-chamber opened on a little knock. There was a thud of footsteps, the sound of a bucket being set down in the hearth. Shielding Jade with his body, the man said, 'Don't be too long, Betsy. I've — a fancy for breakfast. A great deal of breakfast.'

'Very well, Mr Masson.' The girl began an energetic raking between the bars.

Jade became intensely aware of Masson's body pressed against her own. She retreated towards the back of the small room, striking a chair in her agitation. Jet-black eyes were turned on her, a finger was pressed to the well-cut mouth.

The girl at the fireside seemed to have noticed nothing. She continued to work at the fire until a few flames were produced with the aid of the bellows.

'Here,' Masson said irritably, 'let me finish that.'

'Mrs Pratt would think little of it – '

'She will not know. Now, go away and tell her that I want my kidneys and bacon.'

Betsy put the empty tray outside, then came back for the coal scuttle.

'If you really do not remember what you did last night,' Jade said, 'I cannot take your money under false pretences. Give me another chance to earn it properly. Perhaps you feel that our grappling on the floor did not merit full payment?'

He turned on her savagely and grabbed her by her upper arms, but the action only made the unfastened robe fall to the floor. The dark gaze was drawn back to her body. She pushed her hands inside the breast of his robe and put her arms around him. 'I can't go,' she insisted softly. 'Not only because I have only brutality to return to. However unkind you are, he will be twenty times more so. He starved me all day yesterday so that I'd be compelled to seek out some man. That chaise – the driver was supposed to watch where I went and take me back. He'll know that I made you throw him off. I'm afraid – terribly afraid – '

Her voice had dropped to a whisper. She saw that Masson was responding to the stroking of her hands if not to the gist of her story.

'He? What's his name?' It was obvious that he was sceptical.

'I dare not say. He'd have me killed. Whores are expendable.'

'I can't make you out. You neither look nor sound like a light woman, yet you've had experience. I recall enough to know that.'

'Only with a beast I could not fight off. I swear it.' She sank to her knees and slid her arms around his legs. 'I swear it with my dying breath – '

'Oh, for heaven's sake get up!'

Jade, recognizing the signs of his returning irascibility, got up and seized the ivory satin, refastening the green girdle. She saw more than that. Her caressing hands had roused him. For all his pretence at severity and forgetfulness of what had transpired between them, he remembered enough to want her again.

The unmistakable sounds of breakfast approaching sent him

out of the closet and the door was pushed nearly shut.

'I feel lazy this morning,' Masson said. 'I'd prefer not to be disturbed until I ring.'

'Very well, sir.'

'Come and eat,' he called after a time. He had placed a small table in front of the now cheerful fire and pulled up another chair.

'Don't be too hopeful,' he said, seeing Jade's expression. 'I can really do little for you, except, perhaps, to find you some position. What are you fitted for? Oh, you're a seamstress.' Leaning forward, he picked up her hand and scrutinized it. 'How is it you are so unmarked? I should have thought you'd have borne the traces of needle-pricks. Are you left-handed?'

'I – I have not sewn for a while.' She did not look at him.

'I should have remembered. You've been training for a new profession. The oldest.'

She said nothing. What he said was true.

'What about family? Parents. Brothers or sisters?'

'I – have none.' Pain touched her and was reflected in her eyes and voice.

'I see,' he said more quietly. 'Life is not always what we want it to be. We cannot always find weapons against death and abandonment. Or cruelty.'

He had his own ways of being unkind, Jade could not help thinking, but perhaps he knew that for he turned his attention to the food set out on the tray.

'You said you had a reason for – '

'Accepting your invitation? Yes, I had, but that is my own business.' The firelight cast red sparks into his eyes so that he looked satanic. Jade remembered how he had appeared when she awoke, his admirable body overlaid with a patina of coldest blue. Like a marble statue in a moonlit garden. Only, he was very much flesh and blood and all his arrogance and disapproval of her way of life could not alter the fact.

She could tell him the truth. She could say, I am Jade Benedict, baptized Jardine. I was taken away by thieves and kept prisoner. Made to assist at a robbery of valuable goods. Compelled to help fence them to Saul Isaac who will swear that I did not complain that I was acting against my will. Forced by Nick Caspar after I had seen him kill Jack Flynn. Taken to another house where he taught me the rudiments of becoming a whore. Sent out, under guard, to sell my body –

Jade discovered that she could not eat a bite of the appetizing meal. She could never tell Masson her dreadful story. He might feel sorry for her if he believed her but she suspected he would not and neither would anyone else. Far better to remain an enigma. It was not his pity she wanted.

'You are not eating.'

'I cannot. I am afraid that you will put me out and that they will be waiting for me. Whatever else is a lie, that is the truth.'

'I have friends in high places. A cousin in Parliament. A word in the right quarter – If I thought the effort worth it!'

'He would still have me killed. You do not know the extent of his power.'

'The kidneys are excellent.' It seemed he had heard enough of her protestations. He held out a fork and she speared one but could not put it in her mouth.

'I fear you are telling the truth,' Masson said with an anger that heartened her for it was not directed against her. 'You ate so avidly last night that only terror would take away your appetite this morning.'

'Do you know why I spoke to you? Outside the theatre?'

'No.' The black eyes stared at her.

'Because I'd seen you before.'

'Seen me? Where?' He frowned. 'Though I imagined your face familiar.'

'At the Haymarket and outside Dances' prison. Newgate.'

'You went to see a hanging?' His mouth twisted with distaste.

'So did you! You stood on a balcony next to half a dozen drunken young lordlings. And there was a woman there who did not flinch or turn away. But you did.' Her voice softened. 'You detested it as much as I. But I could not go inside the house as you did. I could not move in case I fell and was trampled.'

'I do recall you stared up at me. I remember your eyes.'

'They were shut most of the time. I could not bear to see boys – ' She faltered and was silent. The fork clattered on to the dish of kidneys.

'My cousin wanted fuel for a campaign against hanging for children, and for offences that simply do not warrant such severity of punishment. I was to set down my own reactions – '

'And did you?'

'Aye. In a news sheet. Did you not see it?'

'I – I have not been in a position to obtain them.'

'No. They cost money, don't they? Damned if my appetite hasn't left me too.'

He threw down the linen napkin and they sat looking at one another. Jade became aware that the lower half of the satin robe had slipped away from her leg exposing her thigh, and that he was intensely aware of its firmness and whiteness. Its promise –

'Your housekeeper must know that you are not alone,' she said unsteadily.

'I realize she must. Two forks. Two cups. Orders not to be disturbed – '

'I chose you because I could not forget you – '

His dark brows drew together. 'None of that nonsense! I've been made painfully aware of the fickleness of women. That's the only reason I allowed you to importune me. I was sick to death of faithlessness and wanted revenge on her gender. Do you understand? It was merely a vendetta against your sex.'

'I understand perfectly. It makes no difference. I should still be glad you did not push me aside. Do you think it's an easy thing to stand in the winter dark and force yourself upon a stranger? Do you?' she cried out.

Her vehemence surprised him. Jade knew perfectly well where his disillusionment had originated. With the beautiful woman on the balcony. She had become involved with the older man, the one in the crimson redingote, and Masson suffered on that account. Sufficiently to take a whore to his bed, or his hearth-rug as the case may be –

'What will Mrs Pratt say?' she whispered.

'Damn Mrs Pratt. You'll share my bed with me, Miss – ?'

'Jade.'

'Jade?' He laughed harshly. 'The word has connotations, not of the most desirable.'

'I did not know. It was given me because my eyes were the colour of a certain stone. A green not of the usual – '

'Rest assured it means other, less agreeable things, but now is not the time to inform you. Later, my dear. You are not averse to earning another guinea or two?'

She was drowning in the dark, almost hostile gaze, the promise of his body, the desire he could not hide, even if it was mixed with the flavour of self-contempt.

'As many as you wish,' she replied and, for a moment, she

recalled the tiny carving in the pocket of the drab gown. Her luck was still with her. She had escaped Nick Caspar, the citadel in the Holy Land, the house with the red and gold paper, the cupids and the barred windows. Toby –

She was with a man who could transport her from ordinary physical relations into a region of necromancy and beauty though he obviously did not feel likewise.

Masson was picking her up in his arms, carrying her to the bed. She heard the swish of the curtains as he surrounded them in a privacy she longed for. Then his lips were on hers and she forgot everything but him.

CHAPTER FOUR

'What's your name?' Jade whispered.

'Does it matter?' His voice came out of the darkness, hard and unforgiving as it always was when he thought of the woman who had rejected him. 'This is likely to be such a transient relationship. Not the kind in which one exchanges confidences.' He meant it. Her spirits plunged to a dark abyss.

'She was a fool,' she said, 'to let you go.'

'What do you know about it?' He drew away from her, leaving a gap between them. She was cold without their previous contact, longing to come closer.

'I have only the evidence of my eyes. I saw how she looked at the man in the red coat when you were occupied elsewhere. Even then, I knew she would hurt you.'

'Be quiet, damn you!'

The soft violence struck her dumb but not for long. She had to engage his attention. She must!

'Is it – Gilbert? I saw your brushes – G.M.'

'No, it isn't.'

'I know it's Masson. Geoffrey – ?'

'If you must know, it's Gabriel.'

'It does suit you most beautifully,' she ventured.

'I didn't invite you to my bed to fill my ears with platitudes.'

He sounded no softer, yet more friendly. No, definitely not friendly, but inclined to respond to a touch, a caress. Jade leaned towards him and let her hair brush his unseen cheek. He liked her hair which smelt, at the moment, of chestnuts and herbs. Ma Lee had produced the concoction. She thought suddenly of Ma Lee and Nan Flynn and it was as though Nick's hand struck her, blow after blow.

But they wouldn't have given her up yet! Whores were invited to remain if they did their job well. No one would hurt Nan because she'd stayed away all night. She could have several nights so long as she found her way back with the money and some of Gabriel Masson's dressing-table trinkets. Ma Lee would not allow Nan to be harmed so long as Nick believed Jade would return. It was when he knew she would not that he'd turn his rage in Nan's direction.

Jade had a vivid recollection of how Nan looked in the blue, fur-trimmed clothes, her tight little curls glittering, her blue eyes huge and shining. Nick wouldn't forget how Jack's daughter could glow with a beauty that was without artifice.

Jade moved restlessly, was caught up unexpectedly and held close against Gabriel Masson's warm, sculpted body. She gave a glad little cry and let Nan slide from her thoughts. Gabriel was far from parting with her. He was surly and resentful when *she* came into his mind but he'd not think of her for ever. Already a night and most of a day had passed and Jade was still in his bed. And, if she'd not misread the signs, she'd still be here in twenty-four hours' time. Forty-eight. Mrs Pratt wouldn't like it but what her master did was really no concern of hers and Jade could not see him stand for nonsense from servants.

'You've not told me all you can,' Gabriel said. 'No name that could find your parents. No name to the man who initiated you into such a sordid way of life. Not even the name of the employer who paid you insufficient on which to live respectably. If there was such a person.'

'The world is full of seamstresses. All starving –'

'I know it well. My cousin is always full of such facts and figures. But your voice says you were never such poor employee –'

'What is your cousin called?' She wanted to distract him.

'Peter. But what is it to you? You're never likely to meet.'

'I will look out for news sheets when you have no longer any use for me. When I see his name it will remind me of a brief happiness.'

'Be quiet! Do you think I can't see through your tricks? Do what you've been trained to do, and do it quickly.'

'It should not be done quickly. That's like gobbling a meal

and having to suffer the stomach-ache afterwards.'

'Then show me how it should be done.'

'You want me, then? Really want me?'

'Damn you, I want you! I didn't mean to say it in case you've wrong ideas, but you've made me. I should sate myself and send you packing, only I'd regret it should there be a fraction of truth in your tale.'

'There's more than a fraction,' she insisted.

'I cannot rightly understand how you ever got into that satyr's clutches. Your seduct –'

'How could you when you are a man of good breeding and with such handsome possessions? You've never known hunger or want or cruelty.'

'You're wrong about the hunger. There's more than one kind, and at this moment I'm famished!'

'Then you've forgotten about her?'

It was the wrong thing to say. Some of the urgency left him and Jade wished she'd resisted the impulse to be indiscreet. As he would so rightly point out in another minute, that woman was none of Jade's business. He could not be expected to throw off love so recklessly.

'No,' he said, 'I've not forgotten her any more than you would if the same thing happened to you with a man you were set on. I loved Phoebe, or thought I did.'

'Then – why?' She was touched by his unexpected confidence which she saw he already regretted.

'She decided Jerome had more to offer –'

'The man in red?'

'Aye. He had more money, the key to any famous or noble home you can mention, and, obviously, a way with women. The Lewises have always admired style. I was too quiet for her, had farther to go, and she had not the time to wait. Nor would I wish her to –'

But he would! Although she could not now see his face, Jade knew that pain was there. He had wanted his Phoebe Lewis to walk with him instead of running after Jerome. His pride had been severely dented and it could be a long time before he recovered from the blow his love had dealt him.

'I still say she was a fool,' Jade asserted, her head against Gabriel's shoulder and her arm around his waist. 'To have you and let you go –'

'Don't talk so foolishly. What do you know about me? You are not paid to air your views. You know what you are paid for and why you importuned me on the street.'

'And you know why you did not refuse. You remembered me as I did you, so it was not so unsavoury as you make out. There was something more than –'

'Than what?'

'You know perfectly well! You insinuated my name had other connotations. What did you mean?'

'A jade can be a clapped-out horse or a woman in a similar state.'

Jade began to laugh. 'Well, I can assure you I'm not! And I don't intend to be. In fact, I feel very strong and extremely energetic and I shall stay so, I promise you.'

'You did not look so valiant last night.'

'No. I was wretchedly starved and afraid of – what I should find in you. All men are not so straightforward. You could have been perverted for all I knew. One of the hazards of a drab's life.'

'I should not have labelled you that. But Phoebe had made me cruel. Not that it excuses me. The more I listen to you, the more I regret some of the things I've said –'

'So long as you regret nothing you've done,' Jade told him, 'for I certainly do not. Indeed, I wish you'd give up talking and do some of them again.'

She laid her lips against his throat and ran her hand gently across the space between his shoulder-blades. He'd found that very erotic. And then, as before, his touch found places in herself that took her away from anything physical so that her senses soared above mere craving for bodily ease. She wanted to look into that bright kaleidoscope that showed her a hundred swift pictures of sensuous delights that would stamp themselves on her mind with shattering effect, before they dimmed and vanished, leaving always the promise of the next time. With him, there would always be a repetition.

He'd never let her go. Phoebe Lewis would become a shadow – not even that. She'd be lost in the quicksands of time. Gone for ever.

Jade shuddered uncontrollably and the world was a confusion of colour, of trembling, of a consciousness that Gabriel had turned back to flesh in the same moment as herself. She could go to sleep now. They both could.

She closed her eyes and was swallowed up in the waiting dark.

*

He went to see his housekeeper next morning. Mrs Pratt was obviously aware that her master was entertaining a trollop and, though she'd disapprove, she could not gainsay Gabriel the right to do as he pleased in his own house.

Jade did not look forward to her first encounter with the lady but if she had to fight a dragon in order to stay near Masson, she'd endure any coldness or criticism. In any case, Gabriel had enough arrogance for two.

The fact that she wore only the ivory satin when breakfast was brought was a mark against her, pointing out the inescapable fact that Jade shared Mr Gabriel's bed, but Jade could not bring herself to put on the dingy dress that had belonged to someone else and still smelt of another's flesh and sweat.

'You will, of course, treat this young lady with every courtesy,' Gabriel said from his side of the table by the fire. 'Should I not be here, she must have everything she wishes.'

Jade could not mistake the small spark of hostility in Mrs Pratt's grey eyes at her master's directions. 'Very well, sir.' She did not look at the girl again.

'I think she wants hot water – a bath – after we've eaten. I have to go out for an hour. You will have everything sent up straight away.'

'Of course, Mr Masson. How long does – the lady – expect to be here?'

'That need not concern you unduly for the present. But you will set aside a room where she may sit while this one is cleaned. I thought the small room across the hall. The one with the chaise-longue and the windows facing the street. One can see the plane trees and the passing traffic.'

'I'll have it made ready now, sir. Your bed-chamber's been neglected of late.' Mrs Pratt's lips curled as though she had entered a pigsty by mistake, though she took care that Gabriel did not see her expression.

'You seem not happy,' Masson commented after the housekeeper had gone.

'I hadn't imagined I could feel so – unclean.'

'Well, what did you expect?' he asked. 'I could hardly introduce you into my household as an old family friend; surely you know that. The servants are only too well aware of why you are here. It will surprise and probably shock them that I have at last introduced a mistress so surreptitiously –'

'Don't tell me you've never slept with a woman before!'

The words were out before Jade could stop them. 'I'd never believe that.'

'My dear girl,' Gabriel said drily. 'A man does not reach the age of thirty without some sort of experimenting. But there are numerous houses where one can gain experience. In your line of business. I should not have required to remind you of the fact that I need not bring anyone into my house. It's a compliment that I broke my rule for you.'

'Be damned to your compliments!' Jade almost shouted. 'You come dangerously near to patronage and I'd remind you that I'm of as good d –'

'As good descent as myself, I think you were about to say?' Gabriel put in silkily. 'I suspected so, all along, and now you've actually put it into words.'

For a moment, she hated the triumph in his eyes.

Once again, he had invited her to tell him about her past and still she could not, remembering all her encounters with Nick Caspar. The fact that she was powerless to escape them did not altogether outweigh the fact that she had responded towards him after the initial fear and abhorrence. Shame would prevent her from confession.

'So,' Gabriel commented, 'you still have much to hide. Well, I can bide my time as well as the next man. Now, if you'll excuse me, I must go. I've an appointment with my cousin, Peter.'

'Be sure to put the world to rights between you!' Jade could not resist saying.

He looked very handsome when he laughed but then his eyes turned bleak and she knew he was thinking of Phoebe Lewis who was to wed an old man who was unlikely to live for very much longer and then she would fall heir to all he possessed. She'd want Gabriel back afterwards. She couldn't help but expect Masson to be there when she was free. Money and position first, love afterwards. For a moment Jade hated her violently, then, remembering Gabriel's decision to let her stay, she ran to him and clasped him in her arms, her face only reaching as high as his broad, warm chest. 'Don't be too long. Please –'

'I do believe you mean that.' He looked surprised.

'I do.'

He bent his head to kiss her full on the lips. 'I'm sure you can hold your own with my staff while I'm absent.'

'I'm sure I shall.' He'd prefer her to show a brave front.

But she watched him go with misgivings and the room was empty without him. Panic visited her. She must not become too fond of him for there could be no future in that. A man like him could never marry a fly-by-night like herself, a woman who was previously owned by someone else, as well he knew. And he had his pride.

The painted bath and the copper cans were brought by two maids who stared at her boldly until she said, 'Do you take me for a peep-show? Go about your business! Your master would expect me to be treated with respect.'

'Sorry, ma'am, I'm sure,' the sly, sandy-haired one replied with a little bob that set the dark one off into giggles.

Jade could not keep up the feelings of resentment once they had gone. If Papa had suddenly produced a whore in *his* bed-chamber, the whole household would have been agog with excited conjecture and the woman would have assumed the interest of a Punch-and-Judy show or a mermaid at a fairground. Tomorrow they'd accept her as if she'd always been there. She thought, as she bathed and soaped her white body, of the gossip in the kitchen and, for a time, her heart misgave her. But it was inevitable, even justified. Someone must preserve decent standards, after all. And then, remembering each delicious moment spent in Gabriel Masson's arms, she could not help smiling. They'd all be so jealous! No one could work for such a man and not indulge in fancies about being in her place between the master's sheets.

Mrs Pratt came in to tell Jade that the small sitting-room was ready, her sour gaze flicking over the satin peignoir and the heavy mass of brown hair that Jade had attended to with Gabriel's silver-backed brush. She stared at Jade's little bare feet as she crossed the carpet and the girl recognized the envy in her eyes. It was as she had thought.

Jade thanked her for attending to her wants and waited to be shown to the room across the passageway. It was an attractive place, the walls covered in eau-de-nil silk with threads of silver tracing a pattern of branches bearing blossom. The chaise-longe was covered in green velvet and a leaping fire put rosy shadows on the fine, plaster ceiling. Some news sheets lay on a small table and there were books on a shelf in an alcove by the fire with a decanter of wine and glasses.

'It looks very nice, Mrs Pratt.'

The housekeeper had not been able to conceal her surprise at the quality of the newcomer's voice. 'The master left these for you to read. If you can –'

'Oh, I can read them perfectly well,' Jade replied, smiling. 'Can you?'

But the woman was not to be drawn and the atmosphere lightened after she had taken her leave, closing the door with a soft, disapproving click.

Jade poured herself a glass of wine, amusing herself by holding the liquid so that the glow of the fire shone through it. Then she went to the window to stare out into the street, surprised to notice that tiny flakes of snow had begun to fall, flakes that began to increase in size so that in a very short space of time the roadway was covered in a thick carpet that deadened the sound of the iron-bound wheels that normally rattled over the uneven surface. A few people, wrapped in cloaks and redingotes, passed by. Women thrust their hands into fur muffs and wore pattens to keep their shoes from the snow. A sedan chair glided by, its roof white.

She drank the wine, then took another glass, but its comfort could not prevent her thoughts reverting time and time again to Nan Flynn. She had been away for a day and two nights. Nick would be furiously angry that Molly and Sam had let her slip away, able to tell her story of abduction and rape to anyone who would listen. He would vent his frustration on Jack's daughter first. And for the first time, Jade realized that she could not remember how to get back to the house with the barred windows, and the intricacies of the Holy Land were beyond her. All she knew was that Nick's house was within walking distance of Drury Lane, but so were a thousand others. Even if she felt that Nan was in imminent danger of Nick's savage revenge she could not prevent it. A terrible picture of Nan's face, half-destroyed by blows from Caspar's fists, presented itself.

She paced the beautiful room, then seized upon the topmost news sheet. It was the one containing Gabriel's article about the multiple hanging at Newgate and of his opinion of a justice that hanged boys of thirteen and fifteen for theft. Are things more important than human life, he asked? The penal system needed a great deal of revision and soul-searching. He did not know how a judge or a magistrate could go home at the end of the day and look upon his own children, who, if they were hungry, might easily be persuaded to take a loaf from a baker's shop, or food from a street-stall, rather than starve to death.

There was another article in the next one, pointing out that not all people stole out of hunger. Were not Bluegate Fields and the Holy Land a living example of the fact that sufficient thieves existed out of cupidity and wickedness? This article was signed George Hoare and pointed out that he had been held up and robbed in his coach on Hampstead Heath.

Of course, both sides of an argument should always be presented out of fairness, but Gabriel's was an infinitely better piece of work. What a pity he still hankered after a woman who had enjoyed the spectacle!

She rushed to the door when she recognized Gabriel's tread on the stair, opening the door to greet him.

He had his arms full of boxes, his face flushed with snow and wind. Throwing aside the parcels, he lifted her up against him, his skin and his hair smelling deliciously of fresh air as well as expensive soap and pomade. Her face was quite wet from the melted snow on his fur collar. It began to trickle down between her breasts and she screamed with a mingling of laughter and relief that he had returned in such a good humour. He could have been cold and arrogant as he often was.

'You're drenching me!'

'Then I will have the pleasant task of drying you again,' and he set her down and took out a fine linen handkerchief, opening the ivory robe so that he could attend to the matter.

'This robe,' Jade said. 'Who does it belong to if, as you say, you've not had a mistress in the house before me?'

The look of pleasure died and he turned away from her. 'It was my sister's. She – died young and we were very close. I could not bring myself to part with some of her favourite possessions.'

'Yet you lend it to me? I could not imagine you letting any draggle-tail wear it!'

'I would not.'

'But why me?' Was she so special?

'My dear,' he answered, turning back again, 'I was much too fastidious to have you near me in that – rather pungent – grey affair, which I notice you too seem to dislike. So it was either nakedness or Anna's peignoir. Mrs Pratt would have given me notice had it not been the garment that met her eyes today –'

Jade was laughing now, her skin tingling very pleasantly from his ministrations with the 'kerchief. 'And what are these interesting-looking boxes?'

Her eagerness infected him for he began to tear the paper that enclosed them. 'It's almost Christmas. It's the day after tomorrow, so having given orders that your clothes be thrown away—'

'Oh, no!' She stared at him aghast.

'Oh, come!' His busy fingers were stilled. 'You can't regret them.'

'It's not that. I had something in the pocket of the gown. Something I valued.'

He got up, frowning. 'What was it?'

'A charm. A carving. Very small.'

'You'd better open these yourself. I'll look into the matter.'

'They won't be—burnt?'

Gabriel shrugged. 'I hope not.' His expression said it could matter little.

She turned her attentions to the parcels when he had gone but the expectancy was gone. Opening the first, she saw, under the snowy tissue, a glimmer of silvery green. It was a velvet gown, just the colour of her eyes. She tried to summon up a feeling of gratitude but could think only of her father's gift. 'Papa,' she thought, 'don't let it be lost! Or I have lost you, too.'

Leaving the dress in the box, she went to the door, straining her ears for the sound of his returning steps, then, when she heard them, she ran half-way down the stairs to meet him. 'You found it?'

'Don't hang about the stair like that,' he said sharply. 'You must learn to be discreet. What if one of the servants should see you so? Out of the bed-chamber—'

'But did you?'

'Yes.' He swept her up to the landing and back to the sitting-room. 'Any other woman would have had the floor littered with the contents of those boxes by now. Why does this charm have so much importance—?' He held out his hand and the sea-horse lay on the palm.

She took it from him and it was warm from the contact with his skin. She kissed it and closed it inside her own palm. 'It was given to me by someone I loved.'

'Indeed. Then it was fortunate you have it back.' His voice had changed, grown cold.

'Yes. Oh, yes, thank you.'

She knew he was disappointed that she had not been in such urgency to see what he'd brought her so she laid the carving on the table and got down on her knees to inspect the rest of his purchases. A velvet bonnet, a pelisse with a fur trim, elegant shoes and some boots for the snow, gloves, and an assortment of undergarments of the kind she wore before Paddy had abducted her.

'They must have cost you a pretty penny,' she said in a low voice. 'Far more than I could ever repay—'

'You make it sound like a business transaction!' he cried, exasperated. 'As I said, it's Christmas, a time for giving, and since I can no longer give to Phoebe—'

'You should have bought less-expensive things. I can never be to you what she was.'

'I saw them in a shop when I left Peter. The colour seemed right.'

'I'll wear them while I am here, then, just to please you—'

'Then go off naked when you leave, I suppose.'

A sense of the ridiculous overcame her and she began to laugh helplessly. 'I can just see Mrs Pratt's face as she sees me off the premises! Naked—'

Then he laughed too and took off his redingote. 'I shall expect thanks.'

'Thank you. Very much.'

'The thank you I envisaged took a more intimate form.'

'I should have thought you'd be tired of me by now.'

'He taught you your job very well. Nothing too gross but enough to stimulate the imagination. An artist, I should say, in his own way.'

'I wish you wouldn't—'

'Wouldn't what?' He took off the dark coat and loosened his cravat.

'Keep reminding me about him.'

'I can't help thinking about him.' He obviously resented the fact.

'You must have known, when you pulled me into your carriage, that there had been someone before you. Whores are never virgins.'

'I didn't realize, though, that you'd get such a hold over me.' He was down to shirt and breeches and locking the door.

'Have I?' Her green eyes shone.

'Over my body, that's all,' Gabriel said coolly, 'and I'm a fool to say even that. After Phoebe, I'll let no one come too close in other matters. This has nothing to do with love, I assure you.'

'I didn't expect it,' she replied slowly and watched him

finally undress. Beyond him, the snow swirled outside the window-pane, settling on roofs and chimney-pots, darkening the little room so that the pink glow of the fire was enhanced, making rose-coloured patches on the silk wall-covering.

'Good,' Gabriel murmured. 'May I suggest the chaise-longue?'

'I prefer the rug in front of the hearth.'

'Very well. It matters little to me where we lie together!'

She waited for him to shift the tissue-paper and the boxes but all the time the core of sadness that had come with his confident assertion that there was no scrap of love in his need for her grew into a hard lump that lodged in her throat. But why should he feel anything beyond a desire to gratify his senses? He had taken her in as one might a stray cat, partly out of curiosity, half in a hope to gain some pleasure from her presence. The fire crackled derisively.

She had known it would be a mistake to become too involved and now, insidiously, she was on the threshold of a passion that had more at its roots than that of an appreciation of his erotic skills and his body. She wanted what Phoebe Lewis had thrown away: the essential core of this beautiful, arrogant man who wrote fervent articles about justice and reform and meant them.

It was not until Gabriel kissed her throat and her breast that he became aware of the tears that had fallen so silently but she could not or would not tell him why she cried.

She was opening the door and Nan Flynn stood outside, her poor, pretty face discoloured with bruises, blood on her mouth. Her shoulders, under the snow-speckled shawl, were hunched as though the bones hurt. She gasped out incoherent words in her distress, but the only word that made any sense was Nick.

Jade held out her arms and cried out in an agony of distress. She pillowed the curly, golden head on her breast and somehow the fair, defenceless head became dark and masculine. Gabriel was saying, 'What in Heaven's name is the matter?'

For a moment she fought against him, pushing uselessly against the strong grip of his arms, then she became still and quiet, frozen with the horror of what she suspected was grim reality. While she lay here with Masson, who assumed, with every day, a greater importance in her life, Nan paid the penalty for her defection and she could no longer bear the thought.

'What is it?' Gabriel insisted, sensing her despair. 'I thought you were perfectly happy.'

'I am. But I remember someone who is not and I can never reach her – Not now.'

'You can't take all the sorrows of the world on your own shoulders.'

'I know. But she's ill-equipped to fight for herself as I can. She'll have missed me – She's grown attached to me. I have responsibilities.'

'Then, you want to go back?' His voice was hurtfully impersonal. 'If that's what you wish –'

She lay, exhausted with the strength of her own emotions. Although she had tried not to love him, she did. Everything about him was overlaid with magic, with a rightness that could never exist elsewhere. But he had been honest. Phoebe Lewis owned the part of him Jade craved the most. His heart and soul. She had his body but any experienced whore could have that for a price. Gabriel would never again part with the essential core of his being. Once rejected, he'd put that into an ice-pit and leave it there, imagining every woman would be, fundamentally, another Phoebe. Out for all she could squeeze from a man. Unfaithful –

'Of course I don't want to go back! Have you no imagination? I chose you from all the men in London because I saw you on a balcony one winter morning when the world had turned to a nightmare and you spelled out something else. I saw you suffer as I did when everyone around us saw only a spectacle, an amusement. I had never realized that death could become a mere phenomenon, a diversion. That is an abomination against God –'

'Don't flagellate yourself so. I see now why you cried yesterday, with such quiet bitterness. But who is this woman who so distresses you?'

'I – cannot say. I find I could not go back because I've forgotten the way and that makes it the more terrible. I cannot remember the road back from Drury Lane, and even then, I'd find only pain at the end of it. But it would be my pain. I'd not have to endure hers also – That's infinitely worse.'

'Please, try to forget. You've said you've forgotten the way to your past. It's out of your control, through no fault of yours. I decided to throw off the pursuit. I know you suggested it but I need not have taken any notice of that. My blame is as great, if not greater, than yours. You cannot condemn yourself. All along, I've told myself that you were

117

out for anything I cared to put your way but I see that I might have been wrong. You cared far more for the charm that was given to you by a past lover – than for the clothes I bought so casually.'

'Not a lover! My father –'

'Your – father?' He urged her to speak more fully of what distressed her.

But she could not tell him. She could only let him hold her until the present despair had been alleviated and he had caressed her into a better frame of mind. The bed-hangings enclosed them in a comforting anonymity.

'I think I should take you for a drive. You've been too much indoors –'

She sat up then, excited by the thought that he wished to take her out in public, then the thought of Nick and Molly, of Sam Goode, came back to haunt her.

'They – might see me. I'd not want them to pay you a visit. If they suspected I'd talked of what I know –'

'What a hag-ridden little creature you are! What could you know that would make you such a catalyst!' Now he was scornful.

'I know things that could lead to persons ending up on the gallows. Dying in the way that sickened us both. And I am not particularly brave. The sight of a Runner's truncheon might overcome any private resolution not to say a word –'

'I think you are brave. My servants, for instance – you held your own there.'

'Oh, that!' Jade dismissed them grandly in a way that made him laugh but all the time she retained that image of Nan, her fair skin discoloured and her young body racked with a pain she would not properly understand. Nick would inflict all of his rage and resentment on poor Nan. Ma Lee would be powerless to intervene once he had decided Jade had escaped him.

Gabriel did not insist on his right to possess her and this sensitivity did much for her morale. She curled up close to him, his gentle stroking the greatest comfort, the soap scent clean and fresh in her nostrils, dimming the recollection of the Holy Land, Maul and Tom. Someone came to light the fire. Gradually, it seemed impossible that she had ever lived through that shameful episode. She was intensely grateful to Masson for not treating her as merely a gratification of his bodily needs. Self-respect was returning slowly but surely and part of her could not bear to give it up. But there was Nan to consider –

'Don't think of it,' Gabriel said, rightly interpreting her shudder of distaste. 'They're bringing breakfast.' The fire was crackling invitingly beyond the curtains.

'I believe they are. It's a new day.'

A new, lovely day as far as Jade was concerned but it would not be so pleasant for some. If it were not so obvious that Gabriel Masson had unexpectedly become fonder of her than he suspected she could not have borne the thought of Nan Flynn's day.

The tray was set down; the sandy-haired maid announced, pertly, that breakfast had arrived and took her noisy departure.

'She's a little madam,' Jade said, seizing the robe that had once been Anna Masson's – Gabriel must have suffered on his sister's account but he had not allowed the tragedy to sour him. She must be as liberal-minded. Somehow, the meal became a delight. He in his black and white robe and the firelight reflected in his eyes, hers dwelling on the symmetry of his features, listening to the timbre of his voice. No trace of moodiness there this morning. Everything in her responded to the suggestion of an intimacy such as she had once envisaged in marriage. But she would not have found this in Rupert Mandrake. Her intellect told her he would have been missing at breakfast most mornings of the week and on those occasions Sir Piers would have been there, his profile like Nick Caspar's, his responses the same, cruel yet desirous – His nervous, fair wife would have no say in his actions.

Jade became aware that Gabriel watched her and his expression showed a certain contentment in her presence. She noticed the new interest with which he regarded her since she had cried out in her nightmare. It seemed that his emotions could transcend expediency. And as if putting the seal on so satisfactory a moment, he lifted up her hand and kissed it but made no move to take her to hearth-rug or bed. The fact that he did not intend to use her, even though he betrayed some feeling, was more to her than all their encounters and the sorcery he created. He did not know that he honoured her but she did not greatly care. He'd recognize the emotion for himself one of these days.

She smiled at him, her green slanting eyes warmed by the fire-glow and he pressed the hand and let it go.

'Get dressed, and we'll go out in the snow.'

Warm in the jade-green velvet and silver fur, her feet snug in the little high-heeled boots, she cried out for joy when she stepped out of the house. Children were throwing snowballs. Carriages were stopped outside gates. Lights streamed out of doorways where circles of greenery decorated the painted panels. Church bells rang for Christmas Eve. She loved him so much that she pulled him towards her in the buttoned interior of the conveyance and kissed his mouth and his cheek, his closed eyes. She wanted to say, 'I love you,' but she knew she must not. Not yet—

He pulled himself away as though he regretted his recent softness. 'What would you like to do?' His profile assumed its normal arrogance.

'We always went to church on Christmas Eve.'

'Which church?'

Her eyes clouded. 'A long way off. In the country—'

'We'll go to the country, then, and enter the first church we see. If that's what you want.'

'Oh, yes! Yes. That would be the nicest thing I could imagine.'

He looked at her strangely and she knew what puzzled him. Phoebe Lewis would have wanted some valuable trinket or an expensive dinner. She had only asked for a ride in the snow and the austere confines of a church. Let him decide which he preferred.

She held up her head in the green velvet bonnet and willed him to put his hand inside the fur muff imagining his fingers touching hers without urgency, while the snowflakes fell softly, but insistently, augmenting those that packed the confines of street and garden. But he had turned aloof, staring out of the opposite window.

The faint sound of bells made Gabriel rap on the roof and shout, 'Stop here, Maggs.'

Then he was handing her out of the carriage and they were helping one another through the thick whiteness out of which protruded the dark shapes of yew and laurel.

Breathlessly, they pushed at the thick door and found themselves in a small, white-washed building crammed with country folk at their devotions. She sank to her knees and prayed. For the souls of the Mayberrys, for Jack Flynn, for Mama. For poor Nan. For Gabriel Masson so that he might overcome the bitterness engendered by Miss Phoebe Lewis.

The sound of the bells and the carols were like a purification. It was only when they made their way out afterwards that she saw a familiar-seeming back preceding her to be lost in the ranks of farmers and their wives, the stalwart children. Molly Connor? Could it have been Molly? Jade's happiness crumbled like the snow with the sun on it. But for all that she hurried, she saw no one outside that resembled Nick's woman, though there were carts and traps and chaises enough beyond the churchyard gates.

It was imagination, she told herself, and turned back to Masson. Perhaps he had come to love her though did not realize it. The day must come when he would tell her so.

But the shadow of Molly was not so easily exorcized. Jade saw her in every dark corner on the homeward journey, inside every gate-post on the street where Gabriel lived. The sandy-haired maid who let them in with her sharp, knowing glance, shattered the obsession. She was real and the things she would say in the kitchen presently were equally irrefutable. This preoccupation with Molly had no foundation and she would not allow the thought of Nick's doxy to disturb her.

'Is there anything you would like?' Gabriel asked as they warmed their hands and feet at the fire. 'I'll send Joan or Lizzy out. There'll be little obtainable tomorrow.'

'Some shampoo for my hair, perhaps,' Jade said. 'I'd like to wash it tonight. Oh, and this other recipe.' And she wrote down the ingredients that made up Ma Lee's nostrum. It would be foolish to neglect Ma's sensible advice for a pipe-dream.

The two bottles were brought by the dark maid just as they finished tea, and the set of Gabriel's mouth indicated that he meant to take her to bed. It was going to be the most wonderful Christmas she had ever had.

Jade slid into bed like a seal in a warm ocean.

Christmas Day was intensely pleasurable. The smell of goose and rich pudding filled the house, filtering into all the bedrooms and attics. Gabriel, at her insistence – she felt a desperate need to know as much of him and his family as she could – showed Jade through all the rooms then took her into the one that had been Anna's. Opening drawers, he had taken out rings and brooches that were his sister's and a little painted miniature that showed Anna like himself, a creature of moonlight and darkness, wearing a garnet-coloured gown that sent Jade into a silence Gabriel could not comprehend.

When he pressed her for some indication of her reaction Jade said, 'She's very beautiful, as like you as a twin, or she was.'

Picking up a slender chain, he told Jade that she could have it for the carved sea-horse and teased the narrow gold through the little hole that marked the creature's eye so that it would hang properly on her slim neck.

'Don't you mind,' she asked, 'that this was hers, and you know what I am?'

'What are you?' The cool black eyes challenged her without warmth.

But she could not answer, nor tell him of the sudden pain that came upon her.

Then carol-singers came into the street and he opened the window so that she could throw out silver. The mufflered boys scrabbled in the snow and they ended up laughing while he seemed not to notice the pain that was mostly regret.

The dinner was glorious and she pressed her hands to her stomach, which seemed tight as a drum, and sat looking at pictures in the fire until Gabriel came to unbutton the green velvet gown and everything else until all she had on was the jade sea-horse on the chain. The dim sound of bells came on the dark, snowy air, and she gave herself up to him as though there were no tomorrow, no time but the present, shut in the curtained prison of Masson's bed.

'You've said nothing of yourself,' Jade reminded him afterwards, seduced by the feel of the sheets against her skin and the warmth of his nakedness.

'What is there to say?' He did not want her to pry.

'Have you no parents? Family?'

'I was born late when my parents had given up all expectations of children. Then Anna followed. It was a great strain on my mother who never really recovered from her ordeal. My father was proud as a peacock. But they were both old before I grew up, and died some years ago. Just before Anna did.' He sounded stiff and with more than a touch of spikiness.

'You sound reluctant to talk about them. Or yourself. Yet you badgered me --'

'They are not the things I would normally broadcast. They are of meaning only to myself.'

'So you have no relations?' she persisted, wanting to know as much as she could.

'Only one cousin, Peter, older than myself, but a friend as

much as a relative.'

'I'm glad you have someone.'

'Why should it matter to you?' His arrogance was again predominant. 'We are unlikely to have any lasting relationship. You have to admit that.'

She would not, of course.

'You'll have a country house. People like you always do.'

'There's a house at Englefield Green. It's little more than a cottage – on the way to Windsor.'

'I expect it's a mansion.'

'You might call it that. But I'd only show it to my wife.'

'Only you haven't one. Not now that Phoebe –'

'Damn you! Leave her out of your infernal prattling!'

She had gone too far in her efforts to gain some picture of his past. His face was filled with obstinacy.

'I'm sorry if I presumed.' She wasn't, naturally, but she wanted him in a better temper. But she had her own ways of breaking down autocracy and oppressive tyranny. He could be as stiff-necked as he liked but he could not hold out for long against her touch, her caresses. She was his mistress only but mistresses were often more important than wives. Wives were for child-bearing, for perpetuating the family line. Mistresses were for pleasure and diversion, and for the moment she most certainly pleased and diverted the arrogant Gabriel Masson.

It was colder next morning and the snow was harder and crisper. The leaves on the path were frozen into heart-wrenching patterns. Jade remembered the ride to the church with regret. She would like to have seen Gabriel's country house.

He was distant at breakfast and she knew that he was torn two ways about her, regretting the manner in which they had been brought together, yet needing and desiring her in a way that probably annoyed him. He did not take easily to relaxing his principles.

Masson broached the subject over an earlier breakfast than usual. 'You enjoyed yourself so much on Christmas Eve that I wondered if you'd care to repeat the experience?'

'You mean – go out?'

'Yes. The conditions are much better this morning.'

She had a fleeting memory of her conviction that Molly Connor had been in the church with all the country folk. Masson, seeing her hesitation, said, 'We needn't go anywhere.

It's immaterial to me.'

'I was being foolish. I caught a glimpse of a woman as we left the church. For a moment I thought it was – someone I knew.'

'And it's no use asking about it.'

She shook her head.

'I told you what you wanted to know,' he pointed out.

'A pen sketch only. Nothing of flesh and blood. I suppose – it's useless to expect you to fill in the gaps?'

'We could visit my ancestors.'

'I'd prefer someone still alive.'

'It's not possible to take you to Peter's. And there's no one else.'

'I can see we could hardly visit your friends.'

'You are intelligent enough to appreciate why.'

'Of course.'

Then, you refuse my offer to take you to my country house for an hour or two? I usually go there for a few days at Christmas, but this year there were – complications.'

'You mean a complication. Me.'

'Yes. Although it's none of Mrs Pratt's business what I do here, I can't feel quite the same about Mrs Beddoes.'

'I take it you like her. A great deal.'

'Yes, I do. She was my nurse.'

'And she'd never reconcile her image of an infant Gabriel with you in bed with a loose woman.'

'No.'

'But if I dress up in the nice, well-bred clothes you bought me and put on a demure expression, I might just conceivably pass as a human being?' Her eyes were suddenly bright with anger.

He did not ask her why she was so affronted. But she had a suspicion there was a hint of amusement behind the arrogant darkness of his gaze.

'Do you want to go or not?'

'You said only last night that you'd only show the house to your future wife.'

'Men say things they forget once a woman has pleased them.' He yawned.

'I should throw your offer in your face.'

'But you won't?'

'No.'

'You'd better eat your breakfast quickly, before I change my mind.'

'I've finished.'

'Then make yourself presentable.' He cast a glance at the fire as though he'd have preferred to remain beside it, and her heart quickened. He wanted her to see his country residence and his old nurse but had to cloak the business in seeming indifference. She'd be a fool to refuse.

Once ready, she kept a hand over her face as they moved from door to carriage.

'Cold?' he asked.

'No.' She would not say that she feared being seen and recognized.

Inside the conveyance, he looked at her with a detached approval that had nothing to do with the violence of last night's passion. He was two men just as she was two women. Perhaps that was the bond that drew them together.

It was sharp and tangy once they left the suburbs. The sky was blue and the sunlight emphasized the prisms of diamond fire in the frost and the water. Smoke rose from cottages with snow half-way to the window sills. Holly berries glowed scarlet. Blue shadows slanted over the whiteness and filled furrows and depressions. Crows splotched the purity of the fields in which Jade saw the imprints of fox and badger and a great billow of smoke and crimson light streamed out of a smithy. The sparks and the hammering were one with the thud of her pulse.

Masson poured her brandy to combat the chill. The sight of his fingers wrapped round the slim silver flatness of the flask gave her acutest pleasure. His half-seen strong, lean profile, the long line of his thigh and boot, the black hair that just touched his coat collar, there was nothing about him she found displeasing. If only they had been introduced before that traumatic evening that led to her downfall. He'd have seen her as she once was. Innocent. Pretty. The sort of girl of whom Mrs Beddoes would have approved.

The banging of the blacksmith's hammer against the anvil had grown faint and far away. Jade felt desolate. Masson was amusing himself because he was lonely. There was no one but his cousin who would doubtless marry and take himself away. Gabriel would have to marry in his turn, but it would not be a drab he'd picked up in Drury Lane. No man in his right mind would take such a risk. He'd grow tired of her eventually.

'May I have some more brandy?' The sound of her own voice startled her.

'Are you cold?' he asked again, pouring out a generous

measure. The sight of his pale face against the buttoned velvet upholstery tormented her.

'A little.' She was, but it was an inner cold that was much worse than that of chilled feet or hands. She had come to doubt her ability to influence fate and reality was a bitter thing.

A cloud of thin black trees floated by the carriage windows, each stick-like branch etched with white. This journey was not the happy one they had taken two days ago. Like a spoiled child she railed against the fact that she could not have what she wanted. It was not his fault. He had not encouraged her to expect more than she had.

If she was broody, Masson was equally quiet as though his thoughts, too, were of overwhelming importance or disappointment. There was just the crunch of hooves in the brittle snow, the carking of crows, the omnipotent rumbling of the iron-clad wheels, as though they carried her to destruction. Jade had a presentiment of a pain that would be too great to bear. Not even the glow resulting from the brandy could dispel that entirely.

It seemed an eternity before the cottages of Englefield Green showed their steep, sloping roofs and banners of smoke from twisted chimneys. Gardens had vanished into a uniform whiteness, dimpled with cavities of blue and lilac out of which protruded shrouded shrubs and fruit trees.

The carriage turned into a drive between gate-posts decorated with snow-covered deer. Jade supposed they must roam the wooded spaces around the village and Windsor. She liked the thought.

'You said it was a cottage,' she accused, seeing the house in a swirling distance.

'Artistic licence,' Masson said smoothly. 'We are all prone to exaggeration.'

That made her laugh for the first time and some of the Heaviness was lifted from her heart. Masson, too, lost his dark brooding and looked pleased to be so near his second home.

'What is it called?'

'Stagshaw.'

'I like that.'

'I used to spend a good deal of time here.'

'When they were all alive?'

'Yes. It made a difference when they were gone. I'd half

expect to see Mother sitting in the music room, playing the spinet, or my father in the stables. He loved to ride and hunt.'

'And – Anna?'

'She enjoyed both. Many's the wild ride we had with the branches scraping our faces. Or she would sit in the dusk, playing pieces by heart or memory, I never knew which.' He sounded devastatingly human for the first time. He missed his family and had been made fool of by a hard, predatory woman who used her beauty as a trap. Masson still bled from the wounds.

Perhaps the effects of the brandy worked on them both. They were both cheered, descending from the vehicle with faces that were anticipatory instead of dark with premonition.

The house was timbered after the Elizabethan style and the black and white, contrasting with rose-coloured brick, charmed her. It was not unduly large as it had seemed from the bend in the long drive, but warm and welcoming, a large stag's head protruding above the deep-set doorway.

'My grandfather, Peter, hunted that,' Gabriel said.

She stared at the magnificence of the antlers. 'Did he have to?'

'It had gone rogue. Caused countless damage.'

'That's different. I'd not kill so handsome a beast for any lesser reason.'

'They eat our trees.'

'I like trees too. What a dilemma!' She laughed now, carefree as a child.

'All of our emotions are divided. It's inevitable.'

'Yes. Inevitable.' She was suddenly at one with his mood and the day.

A little, stout woman ran out on to the wide step. Mrs Beddoes had once been fair and pretty. Her eyes were that milky blue of old people and Jade knew that Gabriel's nurse was probably almost blind. She would not, properly, see Jade's finery of green velvet, or her claim to beauty. Mrs Beddoes would rely on instinct only. Would she recognize Nick Caspar's hold over herself? The shabbiness of her recent life? If she did, then surely she was damned in Masson's eyes.

'Master Gabriel. We've missed you,' Mrs Beddoes said. 'But we thought it might be because you'd good reason. Is this the reason?'

The blind, baby-blue eyes were turned towards Jade. The old, still feminine hand was outstretched.

'This is – a friend of mine,' Masson told her.

The hand enclosed Jade's. 'A friend?'

'That's all,' he reiterated. 'She wished to see Stagshaw, so I brought her.'

The hand was long in relinquishing Jade's.

'And what's your friend's name?'

'Jane Benson,' the girl answered, heartsore.

'Aye. Miss Benson,' the old woman repeated. 'I think you'll be here again.'

'I don't think so.'

'Let the future look after its own,' Mrs Beddoes said, like an oracle. 'Now I suppose you'll be wanting a meal? Are you staying?'

'No,' Gabriel answered quickly, as though he could not bear to have Jade under this so special roof, 'it was a whim. A meal and a quick look around the rooms and we'll be off. I have to see Peter tomorrow. It's arranged.'

'Master Peter. You'll give him my regards.' The old pink mouth puckered into a smile.

'Naturally. Now what is there to eat?' Masson took Jade's arm.

'Plenty in half an hour,' the old lady replied. 'Fine it is to have you here.'

'Then we'll do our tour of the house while you make preparations. Come, my dear.' He crossed the flagstoned hall as if he had been a boy again.

Jade thought it the most attractive house she had ever been in. It was full of brick or stone fireplaces and inglenooks, attic ceilings and flowery bedrooms, oak beams and copper, patchwork bedspreads and baskets of logs. There were burnished warming pans and the kitchen, unexpectedly large, housed jelly-moulds, jam pans, a huge mechanical spit (she'd have hated it if they'd used a dog), glazed, brown crockery. There were bunches of herbs and dried hams hanging from hooks, cheeses set out on a black marble slab, rush mats and brass pokers. The four-poster beds were of carved oak and very inviting. Most were decorated with the massive initial 'M'. It seemed sad that Masson was the last of the direct line. He should have a son –

Everywhere there were paintings of past Massons, some dark, some red-haired. Red hair was always cropping up unexpectedly, Gabriel told her. Jade admired red hair.

The meal, when they were summoned to the dining-room,

3

where portraits of Masson's parents dominated either side of the huge fireplace, was positively gargantuan. Blue and white plates of broth, cold turkey and ham and boiled potatoes, sauces and piping hot vegetables. Dark fruit pudding ablaze with brandy. Nuts and pyramids of silver-wrapped mandarins. Cox's orange pippins. Sugared almonds. Dates. The servants came and went, busily.

Jade ate sparingly but enjoyed the wines which induced a delightful headiness that dispelled the last of her sombre misgivings. He would not have brought her here if he had not a greater regard for her than she suspected.

He leaned towards her and his black shadow spilled before him like a flood.

'We must go soon if we are to get back today.'

'Must we?' The words were out before she could bite them back.

'I fear so.'

'Would it be so dreadful if we stayed?'

'There's Peter. I told him I'd dine there tomorrow.'

'Oh, yes. You mustn't disappoint him.' She drank. Set down the glass. 'Does – does she like me, do you think? Mrs Beddoes?'

'Would she have done all this if she hadn't?'

'So it's thumbs-up as Nero might have prescribed.'

'Certainly it is not thumbs-down or thrown to the lions.' He kept his tone purposefully light. 'I should say she steers a middle course.'

'Just as well, since our liaison has no future,' Jade could not help saying, and all the satisfaction of the day seeped slowly away.

'How could it have?' Masson replied evenly, and his fingers drummed on the table-top. 'It was just that I could not let the season pass without pleasing Mrs Beddoes. She'd have been hurt.' He was very arrogant with the other servants.

And what about me, her heart clamoured unfairly? Why show me all this when it must be taken away again. He was cruel.

'Can't you stay, you and your young lady?' Mrs Beddoes came back to rub salt in the wound.

'No. Because of Peter. I told you earlier.'

'You should have invited him here.'

'Perhaps I should. Thank you, my dear.'

'No trouble,' the old woman said comfortably. 'It never is.'

She clasped Jade's hand very warmly as they were about to re-enter the carriage.

'She likes me,' Jade said, her heart lightening as she was handed inside. 'I'm sure she does.' And she waved her handkerchief in the growing obscurity. Mrs Beddoes would not miss the moving whiteness, however dim her sight.

'Well?' Masson enquired as they moved off, entering the claustrophobic embrace of the long drive. 'What did you think?'

'What else could I think but that it's perfect?'

The coach lamps swung, illuminating branches heavy with golden snow, vast, gnarled trunks with black hollows in them, the fugitive glitter of ice.

'It's the only word that describes it fully,' Masson agreed.

Jade, sure she would never see it again, settled in the corner as far away from him as possible, to lick her wounds.

Masson seemed not to notice.

They were at breakfast next day when Mrs Pratt knocked and entered.

'Yes?' Gabriel enquired.

'You did say that all the staff were to visit their families today?' the housekeeper asked carefully, not looking at Jade. 'You did mean – everyone?'

'I did. And you are all to take a hamper. You've all had to work harder since I did not, as usual, go to Stagshaw over the holiday.'

'But – if you are to take luncheon with Mr Peter –'

'Tell me plainly what is disturbing you,' Masson said a little grimly.

'There will be no one to – take care of Miss Benson.'

'What you mean is, that there will be no one to watch Miss Benson.'

Mrs Pratt flushed. 'If you are satisfied with the arrangements, sir –'

'I am.' Gabriel drew himself up with all of his dark harshness. 'In any case, both you and I are returning earlier than the rest. I cannot feel that any great fatality will ensue.'

'No, sir.' Mrs Pratt took disapproving leave.

'You trust me, then?' Jade was unexpectedly pleased.

'I do not say things I don't mean. You can amuse yourself?'

'Of course.'

Thinking of last night when they had returned from Stagshaw, her face was suddenly warm. He could not have pretended such splendid violence. It was like being seduced by a thunderstorm. Perhaps he interpreted her expression for he said, 'I will be back by three,' and took leave of her.

A little while later, Mrs Pratt took her departure after seeing off the other servants, all dressed in their best and carrying heavy baskets. Masson had been generous.

He had seemed unwilling to go at the last, Jade thought, and stretched out on the chaise-longue, her gaze on the green silk walls, to peel an orange. She revelled in its freshness and in the sharp, fresh scent it left behind.

She read the remainder of the news sheets and some sonnets from Shakespeare, then drank a glass of wine and ate three walnuts. But the time dragged without him. She was glad that he trusted her, but her mind hankered after the pleasantness of Stagshaw and the fancied approbation of Mrs Beddoes.

But it would be best to forget the visit and the sense of warmth and belonging that had come to her over the previous afternoon. Better to remind herself of the turbulence of last night's passion –

She went to the window and stared out almost unseeingly at the heavy, grey sky. Feathers of snow twisted out of the dimness, twirling and tumbling so slowly, yet so inevitably. She could not stop it. It would be like ordering back the tide.

There was a woman standing on the opposite side of the road. She had on a dark cloak that covered her head and she leaned, half-fainting, it seemed, against a gate-post. There was no one else in the snow, only the cloaked woman who seemed ill. Something in the sight evoked the memory of her dream. She must be mad, first thinking she saw Molly, and now Nan. But the drooping head lifted and the face inside the hood was Nan's.

Jade cried out and rushed for the stairs, almost falling down them in her agitation and haste. Wrenching open the door she half-expected to see the figure gone like a wraith, but it was still there, pricking at her conscience like a goad. She began to run through the sluggish snow, her new shoes wet through in a moment. 'Nan? Nan!'

The face was as it had been in the nightmare, swollen and patched with purple and blue. 'Oh God, I'll kill him,' Jade whispered and put her arm round Nan's waist. 'Come inside, my love, and we'll sit at the fire.'

Nan could hardly walk. Jade half-carried her up to the door

of Gabriel's house and into the hall that loomed large and chill. Nan found it frightening and clung to Jade almost as if she were still a child. All the way up the stairs Jade could only think how she would enjoy stabbing Nick with his own knife.

The girl rallied at the welcoming sight of the fire. Jade made her sit on the chaise-longue and loosen the cloak, chafing Nan's cold, wet hands until they felt warmer. But all the time her heart became heavier. They had found her. It had not been imagination that she had seen Molly. They had watched until they saw her leave the house with Gabriel. It was not far from the intersection where Maggs had lost Sam's chaise. They must also have seen Gabriel and the servants go out. 'I suppose Nick beat you,' she murmured at last.

Nan nodded and two huge tears burst from between her eyelids to fall on to the front of her gown. Jade was stricken with a terrible fear.

'What else did he do?'

The girl sat, heavy and unmoving, and Jade knew what Nick's revenge had been.

'Oh, Nan, I would have spared you that. Are you hungry? There's food downstairs.'

Again, the golden curls shook a negative. The tears continued to roll.

'You shall have wine, then, my darling.' Jade poured a good measure, her fingers trembling with a mixture of rage and pity. She held it to Nan's lips until the girl had swallowed most of it, then set down the glass.

'It's not the worst thing that can happen,' Jade said. 'At least we are both alive. See?' She touched the jade charm. 'I've still got my luck. Let me fetch you something to eat. Things will not always be so.'

Nan seemed calmer now as though the wine had made her completely relaxed, but Jade kept looking over her shoulder with a feeling of guilt. Gabriel had left her in a position of trust. He had probably done it to test her, not that it had been a very prolonged test. Mrs Pratt would be back in an hour or two, Gabriel sooner. But, as he explained, the servants usually had time off today. It was custom.

'Listen – Jade,' Nan whispered. 'They – mean – to kill – me – if you don't come back with me. We have to take – some – things from – this house –'

'No!'

'Yes. And – Sam is waiting in – a chaise to – take us to – Isaac.'

'I won't let you go back! Mr Masson will – ' But Gabriel would be placed in appalling danger if they stayed. She could not allow him to face that. In any case, Nick would see that he was informed that Jade was not only his whore but a thief and a fence. Jade did not want to see Gabriel's face when he read Nick's letter. She must take the threat towards Nan very seriously. When she thought of Stagshaw and last night – Her premonition had been right.

'We must,' Nan repeated. 'We must meet Molly – at – Isaac's house. And there isn't – much time. I should have come – sooner – but I could not – cross the road. My – bones hurt. Everything hurts.'

'Molly? Not Nick?' Jade stroked Nan's back comfortingly.

'No – Molly. She says – Nick told her – '

Molly would have enjoyed passing on Caspar's message. Jade was conscious of a bitter violence that shocked her. They had sent Mama out of her mind – her fastidious mind. They had removed her from a more than comfortable home, abused her. Forced her to see things that were too terrible to think about too much, destroyed her virginity. Killed her protector. Sent her out to sell herself, not that that had been the sordid business they'd originally envisaged! And now poor Nan –

There was nothing she could do, if she wanted Gabriel to be left out of the disgusting repercussions, but fall in with the wishes of Nick as reported by Molly Connor. The knowledge was like gall. She must forget Masson and yesterday. There was no point even trying to give him an explanation.

Nan had begun to look restive, to shift away from the haven of Jade's sympathy.

'Please – Jade. They'll hurt me – kill – ' Her eyes were alive with terror.

'Don't worry.' Jade knew that she could no longer make the girl suffer further. She refused to think of what would happen as a result of that recognition. Jack had died for her. There was no disputing the fact, and she must save Nan from future brutality. She wondered, fleetingly, what had happened to Jack's body. The river most likely, attached to lead weights. When it finally rose, if it ever did, no one would recognize him. Poor, unfortunate Jack. She must not think of Gabriel Masson. She must not – nor of Englefield Green or Mrs Beddoes.

'Take only small things,' Jade forced herself to say. 'The bedrooms are on the other side of the passage. 'Only little objects, please, Nan. I'll get my outdoor clothes. You're right. We mustn't stay any longer in case anyone comes back early.'

She heard the girl shamble rather than walk and pitied her recent ordeal. Nan had been so much of a child. Protected from anything that could harm or distress her. Resolutely, Jade pushed away the thought of Nick's cruelty. Going into Gabriel's bed-chamber, she took the pelisse and bonnet from the press, refusing to look at the bed, standing by the dressing-table to stare at the silver-backed brushes and trinkets. She would have to take something if she was to prevent Nan from being beaten again, or worse. The flask might be the best thing as Gabriel had another and he rarely bothered with the cravat pins. Jade slipped the articles into her reticule and forced herself to leave the room without another look. Then, she remembered she must give Nick the money she had earned and returned to the table where Gabriel's sovereigns lay undisturbed. She had never intended to touch the things. These too she swept into the green bag. Masson would understand that she could not go without the clothes he had bought. He may even remember how she had joked about her departure. But he would not laugh. She could not bring herself to think about his probable reaction.

'Nan!' she cried out to cover up the despair of her enforced flight from the refuge of Masson's house, his embraces, even his tart turn of phrase when he remembered Phoebe and must hurt another woman. 'Nan?'

The girl came slowly, but obediently.

'You said we must hurry,' Jade said, white-faced. 'Come, now.'

'Help – me? The stairs – '

'Of course,' Jade said gently, forgetting everything but Nan's hurts.

They emerged on to the street, Jade looking first one way, then the other, expecting to see Gabriel's tall, striding form, or Mrs Pratt's disapproving thinness. But there was only the trodden snow and the dim shapes of other houses. The sky had darkened again and the joyful sparkle of yesterday was drowned in the threat of bad weather.

It was difficult to guide Nan to the corner where she insisted Sam Goode was waiting. The chaise was in the side turning and Sam peered out, his walnut features frowning in case they did not arrive.

'Took your time, didn't you?' he commented, his toothless mouth twisted into disagreeable lines.

'We couldn't hurry,' Jade said harshly. 'Not after what Nick did to Nan. The poor girl can hardly move – '

'Oh, what a shame!' he derided. 'Now, pack yourselves inside or Isaac won't be there. Molly's waiting to fence the stuff.'

'To hell with Molly,' Jade retorted, and turned to stare her last on Gabriel Masson's house. There was someone now, outside the gate. Even at this distance it looked like Mrs Pratt. The tallish figure moved towards the door and Jade knew that very soon the whole neighbourhood would be alerted by the woman's cries for help. She must have returned earlier than she said she would. She would be aware almost immediately that Jade was not in the house, her curiosity being what it was, then she'd notice that there were articles missing. Nan would have been sure to leave drawers open. Jade bit her lip until it hurt. She tasted blood. Mrs Pratt had anticipated treachery and now she had it.

She helped Nan to mount the step, then got into the chaise herself. They were moving off and it was as though a hole opened out in front of her into which she would fall to degradation and hopelessness. Then her fingers moved automatically to her throat where the charm lay in its warm little hollow. So long as she retained this, somehow, everything would resolve itself, in time.

Nan clung to her and as Jade put an arm around the girl's waist she became aware of the sharp edges of Gabriel's treasures in the pockets of the cloak but she had not the heart to see what they were. She was imagining Masson's return, the avenging figure of the housekeeper, with her tale of Jade's theft and defection. He'd not believe it at first, then he'd look in the press and find her outdoor clothes gone, the flask and pins, the sovereigns and whatever Nan had filched. She should have vetted the articles before they left the house but she'd been too sick at heart. Gabriel – She wanted to scream.

The streets passed in icy blurs she would not recognize a second time but the foul smells told her they were coming close to Isaac's yard. An open door showed her a room with a rope across it, over which hung the stupefied bodies of sailors. They depended like dead things, the floor pooled with drink, vomit and urine. Some rat-like children huddled against a wall in the next yard, their skins white and green. The littlest cried hopelessly.

Jade roused suddenly and she scrabbled in her reticule for one of Gabriel's sovereigns then tossed it towards the miserable group. She would never forget the look on the eldest boy's face as the golden coin fell into the slush, just by his hand. He'd take it for a miracle. She smiled and hugged the knowledge to herself but the brief happiness faded as the chaise began to move more slowly then ground to a halt.

She could see Isaac's door at the end of the alley, the light showing in a narrow strip below it. 'Come, love,' she said to Nan. 'The sooner we go, the quicker it'll be over.'

'And don't take all day,' Sam shouted ill-naturedly. 'It's frozen I am, waiting your ladyship's pleasure!'

Jade could not have cared had he turned into an icicle. She and Nan had their own problems with the slithery snow but she had the impression of a door slightly ajar in the house next to Saul Isaac's. It seemed unimportant when she was bracing herself for the imminent meeting with Molly. She wondered what future Nick had in store for her and was visited by the ugly remembrance of Rosie's. He'd be sure to send her there this time, just in case she tried to run off again. No one escaped from Rosie's. The sweat broke out on her brow and in her palms. Rosie's –

Looking back, she saw the dark bulk of the chaise blocking the end of the lane. There was no way out there and none here. Lifting her hand she rapped on Saul Isaac's unprepossessing door.

'Who's there?'

'I have to meet Molly Connor here. She's expecting me. I was here the night the jade figurines were brought. You must remember me.'

The bolt was drawn with nerve-racking slowness. The Jew's tall, black-garbed shadow showed in the gap. 'Molly's not here, yet.'

'Then we must wait. I've brought things –'

'Please! Not outside!' Saul opened the door so that they might enter and tut-tutted at Nan's inability to make haste. 'Come in, foolish girl, while I shut the door from prying eyes.'

Jade could not decide whether or not to burst out laughing at his strange accent but the threat that hung over her stopped her incipient hysteria most effectively. One did not make fun of someone who had the misfortune to be different. In any case, the dark, hooded eyes were unfriendly.

No sooner were they both inside than Isaac turned to lock himself in, but before he could do so the door was thrust open again roughly and two Runners appeared in the gap.

Isaac gave a squeak of alarm and held his arms sideways as if to bar their way but they were rough and burly and he was swept out of their way like a straw in a torrent.

The door crashed to and one of the Redbreasts stood against it implacably.

'Told to expect two young ladies with something to sell,' the other man said, looking pleased. 'Taken me a long time to catch you unprepared, Ikey, but I knew I should one day.'

He elbowed the stricken trio into Isaac's study and fixed his eyes on Jade.

'It's you I was told to look out for, young miss. Given no name, I was, but a fair description o' both you and her. No mistake's been made, so save your breath for the magistrate. Now, what is your name?'

Jade did not answer. Her thoughts were too confused.

'Come on, now. Got to have something to put down in the record. You must know that.'

'It's – Jane Benson, and this is my sister, Nan.'

'Do all her talking for her, do you?'

'She was hurt as a child. Often she finds difficulty in speaking.'

'No problems with taking things, though, eh? Very well, Jane Benson, now let's see your bag.'

He took the reticule and emptied the contents on to the table. 'Hm. Five sovereigns – '

'I didn't steal those!' Jade said quickly. 'I – earned them.'

The Bow Street Runner laughed humourlessly. 'How?'

'How do you think!'

'Now, no pertness.' His face hardened. 'Warmed his bed, did you?'

'If you want to put it that way.'

'Not many ways you can put it, miss. Not without being offensive.'

'I suppose not. But I didn't steal them. And the hair shampoo and the other are mine.'

The big calloused hands picked up the flask. 'Suppose 'e gave you this?'

When she did not reply, he turned over the pins. 'Good stuff, they are. Gold and worth a little fortune.'

Turning his attention to Nan, he attempted to put a hand in one of the capacious pockets in her cloak but she shrank back with a gasp. 'Resisting arrest?' he roared. Nan turned as white as curds, slumped against Jade.

'She's not well,' Jade said sharply. 'I'll get it from her for you.' And she reassured Nan, detaching the garment gently so that the man could empty the contents of the pockets beside Jade's small haul.

Jade drew a breath of purest shock. Nan had robbed Gabriel of all Anna's mementoes, the rings, brooches, the chains, the beautiful miniature that was so much like Masson, everything, in fact, that reminded him of his sister.

'Oh, Nan! How could you!' she whispered in deepest distress. 'I said things of no great value.'

'Little things,' Nan insisted, 'you said – little things – and they are.'

'It's not your fault,' Jade agreed, seeing the hopelessness of their present position.

'Shut up, then, you pair o' light-fingered whores. Condemned out o' your own mouths, you two. The initials on the flask are G.M. and we were warned you'd take something on leaving the house of a Mr Gabriel Masson. Seems our informant was right.'

'Molly Connor, you mean,' Jade could not help saying. 'Why can't you be more specific? It was Molly who blew the gaff, as you would say –'

'And what would you have said?' the Runner enquired disagreeably.

'Betrayed us. Acted as Judas – the bitch!'

'There's no need for any high-falutin' melodramatics,' the Redbreast reproved but his expression showed that Jade was correct in her assumption. 'Now, if you two ladies –' here his tone was laced with sarcasm – 'will precede me to the door,' his big hands swept up all the valuables and glittering articles into a bag he produced from his pocket, 'we'll be on our way to Newgate.'

'Oh, God! Not there,' Jade whispered. 'Not there.'

'Yes, miss. There.' And the thick-set man took them both by the upper arm and propelled the two girls before him.

Behind them, Saul Isaac moved swiftly, and Jade, struggling against the ruthless arm-hold, saw him, over her shoulder, up against the mantel-shelf where the flintlock hung on its two nails. She was seized for a moment by a wild hope but the Runner, seeing her triumph, whirled round and saw the thin, dirty hands reaching for the weapon. 'For Christ's sake look after these two doxies!' he yelled to the man at the door, then launched himself across Isaac's desk, scattering papers and musty books and raising a cloud of dust that set them all sneezing and staggering. He grabbed Isaac's long arm.

It would have been funny if it were not so serious, Jade found herself thinking, then added up the case against them. It was frightening in its strength and Saul had made it worse by adding attempted murder to the rest. She had a horrid picture of the Mayberrys, their faces covered, their bodies swinging for the jollification of the city's tradesmen and townsfolk, for the watchers from the Holy Land and Bluegate Fields with a lesson to ram home for a rebel. It could never happen to Jardine Benedict – only it could! She dug her fingernails into her palms and realized that she might never be able to prove who she was, and without proof no one would believe a word she said. Her house was empty, her parents travelling on the Continent, the servants disbanded, only God knew where. There were only the Mandrakes – But, even if they acknowledged her, there was no salvation there. Rupert would not marry 'spoiled goods'. His lecherous rake of a father would possess her, then throw her aside when she disappointed him as she must after Gabriel Masson.

Gabriel. He would be doubly cruel having just suffered over Phoebe Lewis, half of him still hating all women. Eliza would disclaim all knowledge of her.

With a terrible inevitability, Jade saw Isaac brought low, a moaning sound escaping the grimed lips, the Runner force his arm behind the Jew's back so that the waxen face contorted with agony. His face was bleeding where the Runner had struck him with such enjoyment.

'I got the little bitches,' the other said, grinning, and spread his stalwart body against the door. 'We got them all, Jeremy Bowles, so we have! Just as she said, that Molly Connor!'

She had never envisaged anything so terrible. Sam Goode had gone, diplomatically, while she and Nan were arrested. A van had appeared, a dark, sinister thing, with two horses that hung their heads in the snow-filled atmosphere, as though ashamed of their calling.

They were dragged and pushed, with no regard for Nan's injuries, thrust into the dark maw of the vehicle with Nan screaming with fear and frustration and Jade steeped in a hell of her own making, envisaging Masson's present frame of mind. Later the Bow Street Runners would call at his house, detailing the sordid events that had led to the arrest. He must accept the fact that Jade had absconded when her accomplice called at the house that was empty of staff and master. The absence of her outdoor clothing would tell him as much, not to mention the theft of the articles that had belonged to his sister, Anna. He'd never forgive that. Even if he remembered all they had been to one another, that beautiful day in the snow and the country church, and after Stagshaw, he would never forgive the misappropriation of Anna's rings and brooches. The miniature that was all he had left of her looks. He would hate her. Jade shrunk from the conviction.

They were taken to Bow Street, though Newgate would be their inevitable journey's end. Down a flagged passage to a door that intimidated. The key grating in the lock. There was the smell of humanity at its worst, of urine and other disgusting things that could not be prevented in a place like this, buckets in the corner and dark shapes with shadowy faces that waited like vultures for the moment they lapsed into somnolence or sleep.

Jade and Nan were thrust inside and the key turned with a malevolent click.

'God help us,' Jade murmured and looked around for a space where she and Nan could rest for the ensuing hours. There was nowhere but against the wall, cheek by jowl with the previous occupants, all of whom would be harlots and pickpockets or worse.

Huddled against a malodorous corner, the intimidating shapes only a finger's breadth away, Jade forced herself to stay awake, taking off the charm that encircled her throat and putting it in the pocket she had stitched in her petticoat in case of future dangers. Close to the embroidered hem, it was unlikely to be found.

A woman had come out of the gloom but Jade screamed at her and the noise brought an acid-voiced gaoler who threatened to slit the gizzard of the next whore who disturbed his peace.

Next morning, most of the occupants of the room were bundled into the van and taken away in its intimidating darkness, shoved close to one another so that one escaped no finer point of torment. The old lags, hardened and experienced, made conditions a continuous hell and Jade was hard-pressed to keep them off herself and Nan who could not understand this odorous proximity. Her cell in the citadel had not fitted her for their present predicament.

Hungry and apprehensive, they were disgorged into the inner courtyard of Dance's prison, the smells and the sounds beating against gorge and eardrum, infecting both with fear and loathing.

'Jade,' Nan whispered, green-faced, 'where are we – and – what will they do?'

'I'll take care of you.'

'I'm – so – frightened. Why – didn't – Molly come?'

Because she told Jeremy Bowles. Because she was jealous of Nick's penchant for me. 'I don't know, sweetheart. Please, don't think of it. It will be all right –'

'It – will not.'

'Stay close to me. We mustn't be separated.'

They were herded like sheep inside the cold tomb of the building, the echoes of their footsteps flung back from wall and barred doors. Hands plucked at them through those bars. Voices pleaded and cursed. Nan covered her ears in dread.

They were thrust and jostled, struck and bullied, impelled into a huge cage of a place where the straw stank and hammocks were slung in a Stygian gloom. Then the keys turned inexorably and they were surrounded by women in rags of clothing, their hair matted and their faces filthy. Teeth were bared in vulpine pleasure.

'Cor! Look at the pretty little wenches! That velvet! The cloak's too good for 'er. Shall we 'ave it? 'Urry, Lucy, afore those – turnkeys come back. Won't be easy to decide 'oo it all belongs to after, will it?'

The noisome bodies pressed close. Nan, shrieking, was divested of cloak and gown, only her strength preventing the removal of her undergarments.

Jade, her arms held by two skinny but strong women in little but the remnants of former clothing, had her pelisse taken off, then the gown that Masson had chosen because of its colour. The buttons were jerked off to disappear into the dirty straw.

''Urry, Lucy, do!'

The gown was stripped from her body. A hand was laid on the bodice of her shift, but Jade, tried beyond endurance, sank her teeth into the engrimed hand. Blood dripped from the bony fingers to stain the white lawn.

A turnkey with a lantern appeared, alerted by the screeching and crying, and dragged off the woman who had tried to tear off Jade's underclothes. The sight of Nan, her golden hair revealed, as well as her well-developed breasts and inviting hips, Jade's narrow elegance, made him purse his lips in appreciation. He beat off the shadowy figures and cleared a space for the two newcomers.

'Let me find one o' you dollymops near them when I come back and I'll have your guts for garters. Gutter filth! Not fit for human society.'

'Didn't think so last night, did yer!' someone shouted from the back of the room.

'God blast you for a poxed whore,' the turnkey said so savagely that no one spoke. 'Be back in ten minutes an' if I find anyone near these prisoners, I'll see they get a flogging. Personally –'

The threat seemed genuine for no one harassed herself and Nan once the man had gone. Someone tittered as though they knew a joke that Jade did not and she could not help feeling uneasy. A thick silence fell.

Without their warm gowns, the December cold struck at them, setting both girls to shivering. Jade insisted that Nan cuddled close to her so that their bodies would generate some heat but it was still cheerless. Nan coughed and could not stop.

'Won't be cold for long,' the unseen woman said in a thin reedy voice that was bounced off the damp walls. Someone else sniggered and Jade's sense of unease was accentuated. Those women seemed to be waiting for something to happen. A low chorus of laughter died away into a pit of disquiet.

The key turned again. No one moved. Jade strained her eyes into the darkness. There were four figures advancing into the room. Two of them were coming towards the corner where she and Jack's daughter huddled close for warmth.

There was a threshing and rustling from close by and a woman's voice, thick with anger and contempt, said, 'Get off me or I'll scratch your rotten eyes out.' But her bravery was in vain it seemed for the noises went on into a beastly rhythm that Jade understood too well. The woman was crying now, but very softly in case she was punished as well as violated.

The turnkey who had protected them was looming over Jade and the girl she held against herself. 'You won't need her,' he whispered, 'but my friend will. You'll not need fear those others if we're your protectors.'

'Protectors!' Jade could not keep the bitterness from her tone.

'It'll pay you – and 'er – to keep a civil tongue in your head.' His tone was sour.

'Will it make any difference?' she enquired coldly.

'Not really. Except that I can see that your life is heaven or hell.'

'And Nan's?' Stagshaw and Masson receded into infinity.

'Can't rightly prevent anyone fancying 'er, can I? Not in this place. I'd have me work cut out lookin' after you. Be reasonable.'

He set down the dimmed lantern a little distance away but the glimpse of their white undergarments and smooth, clean skin worked on him for he was down on his knees in a moment, pushing Jade back on to the straw, the smell of which sickened her as much as the urgent body that now sprawled over her own. Out of the corner of her eye she could see the shadowy figures beyond the lamplight, coming closer, the glow reflected in their eyeballs like that of the rats she had seen in the pit with the dogs. The women would enjoy her discomfiture, the bitches!

Gabriel, she thought, panic-stricken. Save me. Please don't let this man do what he wants. But Masson would be sitting in the room with the green silk walls, brooding about herself and Phoebe. Hating all women – Drinking –

Though she kicked and struggled, the white drawers were removed and the shift raised so that her breasts and loins were exposed.

'God, but you're a tasty little bit,' he breathed, his mouth smelling of onions and beer, his body of unwashed flesh. Her stomach revolted as he pressed the wet lips over her own. She could hear Nan's stifled tears and cries, then realized that the fourth man must be with her. Rage was added to her revulsion.

'No!' Nan was saying in her slow way but there was the sound of a heavy slap and a silence then a grunting activity that made Jade want to vomit. Her body was being thrust apart. Gabriel. Help me. Forgive me –

The man was inside her, his breathing fast, the onion smell fanning her cheek. Every part of her resisted him. She had felt something for Nick Caspar, some degraded fascination, but this was bestial. After Gabriel it was an obscenity. She discovered she was whispering vile things she had heard at the citadel that, instead of deterring the man, only made him more excited.

'Thought you was a lady,' he whispered back, enjoying himself the better. 'Seems I was wrong. You're bad as the rest.'

And then it was over and he lay over her winded and gasping, seeking her mouth, but she turned her face into the straw that was preferable to his kisses.

They were getting up, fastening their clothes, going away, taking the light with them.

Jade covered herself. Nan lay where the man had left her.

'Are you all right? Nan?'

'Will – they – always do that?'

Jade could think of nothing to say at first, then she whispered, 'Someone new will come, then it'll be their turn.' But Nan was so pretty. They would not tire of her easily. The night stretched ahead, an eternity.

CHAPTER FIVE

She could not remember how long they had been there. A more kindly gaoler had gone round the cell seeking their cloak and pelisse though the gowns were not returned. Nan seemed ill and to have no strength. She had lost weight, too, not that that was difficult in this awful place. Just to survive took every ounce of willpower Jade could summon up. Some days she despaired.

They obtained food, insufficient and miserable though it was, because Jade paid for it in the dark with the unwilling gift of herself. Nan was so flushed and feverish that she obtained a respite for the girl by saying she had the gaol fever which might even be true, though Jade doubted it could have come upon her so quickly. Nan's brutal possession by two men in quick succession had been the root of her illness. She had lost heart and was vulnerable to the germs in the place.

Those episodes in the night, when not only the gaolers but male prisoners who could afford the bribes were let into the women's quarters, scarred Jade almost beyond endurance. She knew herself to be unfit for decent society, for any sort of life afterwards. Dirty, her hair matted and smelling of the straw she lay upon, her only motive was that of protecting Nan Flynn, pressing water to the girl's cracked lips, using some of her own meagre supply to bathe the hot forehead. Speaking to her gently, keeping her as comfortable as was possible.

The dreadful miasma of the atmosphere was worse, in many ways, than the cruel boldness of many of the women. Never did they draw one breath that was not tainted with the smell of ordure and urine, of the vomit that resulted from the drunken habits of those women who had, or were brought, money. It was not sufficient to buy them freedom but it bought oblivion. There was a tap in the yard from which ale was dispensed for those fortunate to be able to afford it.

Jade came to know them all. The old, pitiful women, homeless and abandoned, who had committed small thefts to keep breath and life in their wizened bodies. It seemed iniquitous that they, forced to steal food because of starvation, should have to suffer. Peter Masson would be appalled if he could catch a glimpse of this living hell.

Thoughts of Gabriel's Parliamentarian cousin led Jade's mind inevitably to Masson himself and she shrank inside the pelisse as though he saw her present debasement. He'd remember only the fact that she had spun him a tale about never being able to go back to her dubious past, then running off in expensive clothes with the articles he treasured most. He'd not have cared about the flask and the cravat pins. He knew she could not go out of the house, once her old garments were destroyed, without wearing the green velvet. But the things that belonged to Anna –

Following so closely on his disillusionment with Phoebe Lewis, her apparent defection must have hurt him unbearably. Perhaps she could, after all, tell her tale in the court at Bow Street? Could she stand up and say who she was? How she had been abducted and corrupted, made to lie and steal, importune, sell herself to any gaoler who would feed herself and Nan? The Mandrakes would not thank her for dragging them into such sordid circles. They might not even recognize her as she was. Her parents certainly mightn't, but in any case they were not to be found. But Gabriel's disgust would be such that she wouldn't want to live once he had repudiated her. She had never felt so low, so disinclined to return to the world she once knew. If it was possible to return! There was certain proof that she had been implicated in crime and Molly would have given details to her Bow Street Runner, Jeremy Bowles. The address of the house of the collector, Isaac, of course, and his attempt to kill the Runners would be on the official record. She would not speak for fear of what she might do to those she loved. She could not. It was too late.

It was when Nan had seemed a trifle better, though white and wasted, that a pock-marked man came to inspect the prison. He was dark and foreign-looking with the resolute expression of a fanatic, and his face, as he surveyed the big, noisome room with its over-abundance of prisoners, blanched with a mixture of distress and disbelief.

Jade learned that evening, when as always she was visited under cover of the darkness, that the man was a Friend, a sort of Quaker, called Stephen Grellet, a Frenchman living in America, with evangelical leanings and drawn to problems in England.

She was so interested that the business of being forcibly served lost much of its usual abhorrence. Grellet was travelling in the ministry, had visited munition makers to tell them that what they did was dreadful, had been several times arrested and in fear of being put to death. But, influenced by John Wesley, he had gone on trying to put right the wrongs of greed and privilege, and had even called a meeting in St Martin's Lane so that thieves, prostitutes and pickpockets could speak of the reasons for their fall from virtue. Huge numbers of criminals had, unexpectedly, come, and the Chief Police Magistrate, seeing that this could help the cause of crime prevention, had offered rather satirically to show Mr Grellet all the scum of the capital city.

Stephen Grellet had said he'd be satisfied with a permit to visit London's prisons. Although the gaolers had warned him about the women's section, he had insisted on his right to see every part of Newgate. His dark eyes, seeing the sick and the old, with insufficient clothing, sprawled on straw that was an abomination of filth and disease, the infants who'd had the misfortune to be delivered in the place, must surely be touched, Jade reflected, thankful that her possessor had finished with her and was on the point of taking himself off without a word of thanks. No one had ever thought fit to thank her. She was becoming hardened to the fact.

The only likeable gaoler was the older man who reminded her of poor Jack Flynn who had loved her in his own way, and died for her. He seemed in a position of authority. She would not have minded lying with him quite so much. But he had noticed her and it was not impossible that she could beg him to have the others leave herself and Nan alone.

Her opportunity came when it was his turn to inspect the inmates for disease and its effects on the rest. His face was like Jack's, an intermingling of distaste and a recognition of more decent values. He lingered with herself and poor Nan who was no longer golden and beautiful but a pathetic wreck of her former self.

'She needs nourishing food,' Jade said, 'but I have no money to send out for it.'

Her eyes conveyed the message that there were other ways to recompense him. He wavered and was lost in the backwash of a glance that was green as Mediterranean waters. The pelisse was still pretty even if she had lost most of her freshness and youth. Her innocence. She smiled wryly.

'We are forever pestered by those who would take advantage of us,' she whispered, knowing that he would remember the glimpse of white undergarments under the opened pelisse. Off-white, she amended, and longed for a bath as she had never wanted anything else. Except Gabriel Masson. She still loved him and always would but there was no future in hoping he'd relent. She had spoiled him for feminine society. Her throat was gripped by a pain she had imagined half-mastered.

The gaoler recognized the torment, was sorry and desirous in turn. She was the most gallant and bowel-racking little bit to come out of this arena. He'd be a fool not to see the invitation she'd held out. His brother-in-law was a butcher. He could get calves' foot jelly and broth and the like with no great effort. He could say it was for the Governor. 'See what I can do,' he said gruffly. 'Me name's Dick.'

Jade read his mind and was overcome with a relief that made her weak as a baby. She despised herself but it was not entirely her fault that she had been made cognisant of the value of what lay between her legs. Men had done that for her.

As he went about his business, she met the satirical gaze of the gipsy-like harridan who plagued most of the more sensitive women incarcerated with her.

'Must be nice to be so popular,' the woman sneered.

'It is.'

'Wouldn't be if someone took a chiv down your face.'

'Perhaps not,' Jade agreed, but the questionable triumph of her new hold over Dick and its possible rewards was pushed back in a tide of apprehension. The nights were long in Newgate and a spoiled face would mean that she had no way of gaining what Nan so badly needed.

All day, she watched her tormentor, Bella Scrivener, and her little clique of friends, none quite as dangerous as herself, but still unpleasant and not to be ignored.

At dusk, just when her nerves had reached screaming point, the door was opened to admit the usual, furtive, night-prowlers. There seemed more than usual.

''Aven't 'ad a tumble for ages,' an old, saucy voice remarked, 'an' I must say I'm ready for it. Come on, one of you.'

Someone laughed, more out of hysteria than amusement. It was easy to be brave when one was no longer singled out. Nan, thankfully, was fast asleep.

Jade waited, her palms and her body wet with perspiration, dreading the advent of her usual persecutor, or, worse still, one of the male prisoners. She forced herself not to tremble. They liked it if one showed fear and repugnance. It fed their ego, added a fillip to the slaking of needs already aggravated by prison regulations. She always tried to divorce herself from the entire proceeding which had grown meaningless with any-one but Masson. Don't think of him – or Mrs Beddoes's disgust.

She thought instead of the Frenchman who had come to better the lot of men and women in prison, of politicians who would try their best to abolish hanging for anything but anarchy and murder. But her mind would not focus on any-thing but the identity of the man who could come for her.

It was Dick who bent over her and laid a parcel in the straw, who lay down beside her, trembling a little, as she had wanted to do earlier. She was touched.

'What did you bring?' she whispered.

He told her and she became limp with gratitude. She'd had a terrible fear that Nan would die and leave her alone but his gifts could restore her friend.

'Thank you,' she said, and shut her ears to what went on elsewhere. 'You aren't used to going to other women, are you? I daresay you've a good wife.' A wife who would be middle-aged and who would not turn to her husband as she once did.

'Aye. I have.'

She touched his face gently. 'Let me thank you another way. I couldn't do without you. You know that. He – didn't come tonight. That man I hate –'

'I told him and the rest you aren't to be bothered again or I'd have them up before the Governor. I said I was to look after you in future. They didn't like it.'

He touched her tentatively as if he thought she might break. Break! After what she'd been through since the night of the party when the Mandrakes came. To her horror she found that she was crying. She had an image of snow – and stags.

'What is it? Is it that you don't want me –'

She shook her head. 'It's that woman. Bella Scrivener. She threatened me today and I fear she means to mark me at least.'

He stiffened. 'She's bad.'

'I need something to protect myself. A knife.'

'Don't know if I can –'

'Then, next time you come, my face will be cut open, or my breast –'

His hand, that had begun to explore inside her shift, was suddenly stilled. 'Can't have that, then, can we?' he whispered thickly. 'I do want you. Never wanted anyone so much in all me days.' He was overcoming his initial scruples and his breath quickened as his hand slid down over her navel and below. She helped him remove any obstacles. 'Jack,' she said as he prepared to take her, 'you won't forget the knife? Bella looked at me so fiercely and I have Nan to look after.'

'Dick,' he muttered. 'Me name's Dick. Forget about Bella for the now.'

But she preferred to think of him as Jack. Jack who had loved her though he fought against the emotion. Who had not sent her to Rosie's.

He was very gentle with her, pathetically grateful for her favours. It had not really seemed like selling herself. But she cried silently after he went, only rousing when she heard a cautious footstep in the straw, pushing herself backwards against the wall, her stomach muscles tight as a spring.

But it was Dick returning, kneeling, pushing the haft of the knife into her hand. 'Mind you, if you're found with it, I'll have to deny any knowledge. You know that. It's nothing to do with me.'

'Thank you.' She could breathe more easily now.

'You know,' he whispered as he prepared to go, 'a man could die in you. Die he could and be glad to.'

She watched him lose himself in the dimness. The room was as quiet as such a hell-hole could be. But she could relax now that she had protection of both kinds. Reaching down, she touched the charm through the soiled material of her petticoat. Her luck still held. Grabbing the pelisse around her, she waited for morning.

Jade thought that Bella Scrivener had seen the knife pass

from Dick to herself for she had made no trouble apart from the occasional sneering observation. It did not do to be too well-spoken.

Nan had been disbelieving when she was shown the luxuries that were to make her well, though Jade insisted she tried not to attract attention when she ate of the forbidden fruit. They huddled together, their backs to the room while Jade watched for trouble and saw that every spoonful was finished. Nan was still pale and listless so the excuse that she had the dreaded fever was accepted. Jade sat over her like a vixen over a cub, sheltering her from abuse and discord.

Dick came, of course, for his nightly rewards. He was mad for her, Jade realized, but she could not mind him as she had done his predecessors. He was a decent man who had improved their lot out of all recognition.

The dreadful sameness and demoralization of the passing days was alleviated by another visitor, more than one, in fact, but one woman was more memorable than the rest for all that she was quietly dressed and wore a high, white cap that was so spotless that it had the effect of making Jade feel a slut. The once beautiful pelisse was marked and spoiled, her face was white and her eyes dark-ringed, her hair so wild that it would take a hundred brushings to disentangle it.

The visitor, who was called Mrs Fry by the Assistant-Governor, had apparently been in communication with the Frenchman, Stephen Grellet, judging by the snatches of conversation the prisoners overheard. Her calm face betrayed a deep disquiet and sorrow, the more she saw of the wretchedness of the conditions and heard of the truly bestial behaviour of women like Scrivener and her cronies.

The ladies had brought a bundle of flannel garments for the children and they busied themselves helping to clean up the infants and some of the sick, including Nan who still lay, white and disinclined, by the wall.

Some of the ladies held their noses, which actions provoked a torrent of scurrilous abuse from the hardened prisoners, but Mrs Fry had a habit of staring quite quietly which discomposed all but the worst and her keen eyes missed nothing. Her expression was very gentle as she gave the warmly dressed infants back to their mothers and she smiled encouragingly at Nan and said that she hoped she soon would be better. It was strange, but, although the other visitors had quickly had enough, Mrs Fry seemed reluctant to go.

Bella Scrivener said terrible things about gentlewomen who went slumming after they'd gone but the babies were quieter that night, wrapped in the warm flannel, and even Nan recovered some of her old prettiness.

Gaolers came for Jade and Nan Flynn two days later, and several more women.

'Where are we going?' Jade looked around desperately for Nan who could not keep up with the rest.

'Bow Street, dearie, but you'll be back, never fear.'

She struggled to return to Nan but was struck hard and told to keep in line. The sinister van waited in the prison yard which was flooded with slushy water so that their feet were soaking before they began their journey. Shivering, the two girls crouched on the packed benches that ran down each side of the conveyance. Both cloak and pelisse were crumpled since they had been slept in for the best part of a month. Their nails were none too clean but their hair looked better since Dick had brought Jade a comb. Nothing, however, could eradicate the pallor induced by confinement.

'Why – are we going out?' Nan asked.

'They must be hearing our case.'

Nan fell silent again. They wouldn't be too hard on Nan, Jade decided. She wasn't truly responsible. Jade would tell her story, about the runaway coaches. Then she saw that she could not for that would be to connect the girl with the Holy Land and Jack who had been a highwayman and thief. Molly, for reasons of her own, had not given their names to Jeremy Bowles. Of course, to say that she knew Jade was Jardine Benedict was to connect herself with abduction and robbery. Jade, wondering why Bowles had not also apprehended Molly, understood now that Bowles had a foot in both camps. There were thief-takers who had dealings with criminals. Jonathan Wilde had been a glaring example. Nothing had changed since his day.

The Runners had insisted that Jade gave a name to enter on their records before they delivered her to Bow Street on the occasion and she had said the first thing that came into her head. Jane Benson. It sounded near enough her own.

It would be as Jane Benson she would be tried and transported. She would be transported, wouldn't she? Remembering Gabriel, it could not matter what happened.

They were unloaded, like a herd of cattle, at the magistrates' court, dragged out so that their cloaks were half-pulled off to reveal their scanty underclothes. But Jade was hardened now to the sight of desire in men's eyes. She and Nan were not yet scarecrows enough to arouse no interest.

Again, they were crowded on to benches in an ante-room, while every now and again a woman was called and left the place either quiet and pale, or noisy and belligerent. But that was only a mask to conceal fear.

'Jane Benson. Nan Benson.'

Jade, lost in her own dark thoughts, did not move. Then she became aware of a dark-jowled man with a ferocious expression, bawling in a tremendous voice, 'JANE BENSON!'

She stumbled to her feet, took Nan's hand. There was a great icy vacuum where her stomach should be and her hands were frozen.

'Asleep, were yer? Get a move on, yer light-fingered doxies! Come on.'

Unbelievably, she was staring at a large clock on the wall. Five past eleven. She thought she would see the time for ever. Five past eleven. There was the dock, the witness box, a kind of platform railed off at the other end of the crowded room. It was a nightmare from which she must surely awake.

Everyone stood up, chairs scraped and squeaked, murmurs died into silence.

Jeremy Bowles was giving his version of the affair. 'Acting on information received —' Then, after the long recital and informing the court that Jane Benson spoke for both sisters, he stepped down.

Another Runner stood up and he, horribly and unexpectedly, was recounting the story of the theft from the collector's house. 'There were men with the accused but as they were masked it will not be possible to trace them.' Molly had been determined that Jade was to be securely pinned down!

The collector appeared next and when asked if he recognized the girl who had robbed him, looked straight at Jade and pointed an accusing finger. 'I'd know her anywhere. The light was on her face. That's the girl.'

'I understand some of your lost property was found at the house of the man, Isaac.'

'Some. I identified a few articles. The rest must have been sold.'

'Quite. Quite.'

A pause while the man sat down, then a voice shouted,

'Mr Gabriel Masson.'

Jade thought she would faint. She swayed, her eyes closed with shock and shame. Gabriel was there when she opened them again. There was no trace of feeling in his face and his eyes were dead. She had done this to him. It was like—murder.

He began to give his own version of the affair. 'I had been to the theatre. I admit that I had been drinking heavily and when I was importuned outside the building I did not refuse the girl though normally I would have done. I committed the unpardonable folly of taking her into my own home after the girl in question spun me a story of being afraid of some man who had interfered with her against her will. To bolster up her tale she pretended a chaise was following her. I had my coachman shake it off.

'I'll not deny that I let the girl stay some days since she had played on my sympathy very cunningly. Like a fool, I believed everything she said.

'On Boxing Day, it is my custom to allow the staff to visit their homes. Mrs Pratt, my housekeeper, as good as told me I was mad to let the girl stay in the house alone for a short period while I had luncheon with my cousin, Mr Peter Masson. In my arrogance and certainty of her honesty, I allowed the girl to remain in the house by herself. I see now how crassly stupid I was.

'Mrs Pratt decided to return much earlier than planned, being, justly in this case, of a more suspicious nature than myself. Reaching the door of the house, she saw two women getting into a chaise at the corner of the road, one of whom she recognized by the clothing she wore, provided by me since her own were already disposed of as being unfit, as the whore who had engaged my attention at Drury Lane— Who stole jewellery belonging to my sister—jewellery she knew belonged to a dead woman.'

The recital went on tonelessly but Jade heard no more. 'The whore who engaged my attention.' Inexorably, the cruel words were burned into her brain. She would see them always. Always— She covered her face with her hands.

Gabriel had stepped down when Jade again became aware of her surroundings. Mrs Pratt was in the witness box, pointing out herself and Nan. 'It was them who robbed the master and got into the chaise. I swear it.'

A darkness came over Jade's mind. She was dimly conscious

of Gabriel staring at her from the side of this dreadful room, and his face was no longer dead but hatefully alive with disgust and repudiation. Her thoughts became entangled with the snow, the sound of church bells, Mrs Beddoes, Mrs Fry and Stephen Grellet. Bella Scrivener. Jack Flynn. Nights in Newgate that were too shocking to remember without wanting to spew. Her eyes entreated him but he turned away. She knew that she had lost him irrevocably. Dimly she recalled that it had been her intention to reveal her identity. They'd have heard of her in Bow Street. But the face of Sir Piers Mandrake seemed to fill the entire courtroom, blotting out everyone but Nan who shivered at her side. Jade no longer had the strength to fight. She was aware of her lips forming answers to questions she could no longer remember, even fancied she saw Molly, smiling at the back of the court.

'Jane Benson and Nan Benson –' a loud voice proclaimed, but she heard no more. Sickness and self-disgust overcame her and she slumped forward across the rail. Something momentous had been said but it was lost for the present.

She came to her senses in the side room. Someone was holding a cup of water to her lips. Nan's eyes, shining with tears, were close to her face. The girl looked waxen-pale and very afraid. Transportation, Jade thought, was enough to strike terror to any woman's heart and soul. They talked of it constantly, Bella and those others. Had they been given seven years or fourteen? It would be fourteen.

'Molly,' she whispered. 'She was there – Why did she hate me so?'

'She – was – jealous. Don't – swoon again – will you? That man – Masson – he looked as if – he detested us. It was – Molly's fault. I'm afraid when you – aren't there.'

Jade pulled herself together. 'I won't be so foolish again, I promise.'

There was no more time to think for the van had come back for them and they were forced outside into the wet, then its unprepossessing confines, pressed against women who cursed and wept now that they had been sentenced but never looked once at Nan and Jade.

Newgate loomed up, outwardly beautiful, inwardly warped and ugly. Jade noticed they were not jostled this time like the others and when they came to the usual door where the remainder of the women were halted, she and Nan were ordered to go on. There was a great upheaval behind them as those who had not gone to Bow Street rushed towards the bars to welcome those returning.

'Jane Benson!' a voice screeched, a voice Jade recognized as Bella's. 'Not too much of the lady to have your pretty little neck stretched, are you! Going to top you, I hear, you and that milksop. Needn't have fed her up on all those nourishing slops, need you! All wasted now.'

Jade struggled for a moment against the gaoler's arm. 'No! Oh, no,' she whispered, but it was not herself she saw hanging from the gallows. It was the Mayberry child and Nan Flynn. She could not bear Nan to die for so little. 'I'm not Jane Benson,' she insisted, 'I'll tell you who I am –'

'The Queen, maybe,' the man suggested cynically. Women said anything when they went in fear of their lives. 'The Hempress Josephine?'

'I was taken away by thieves –' Her voice had grown hoarse.

'Now, miss. This isn't goin' to 'elp. You know it ain't true.'

They had come to a row of five low doors. The second gaoler was unlocking one, then with a swift, brutal push, had precipitated Nan inside the darkness beyond it. She had no time to utter a word before she disappeared.

'We must be together,' Jade said, her mouth dreadfully dry. 'She's only a child –'

The door in front of her opened with a creak and she had no opportunity to say any more. She was conscious of a violent impetus, then the clang of the door closing again. Screaming, she threw herself against it but the key had already turned and she was in darkness.

Her eyes had grown accustomed to the dark and she made out a low, vaulted ceiling that, in itself, was oppressive. A little greyish light filtered through a double-barred window no bigger than a handkerchief. Her fingers, exploring in mindless panic, touched walls that were lined with strips of wood and studded with huge nails. A narrow barrack bedstead smelt of other bodies, of urine. Fear released everything one normally controlled.

Jade leaned against the wall that separated her from Nan, thinking she heard a low moaning but it was only the winter wind against the glass. The door, she had noticed, horror-stricken, as she was forced into solitary confinement, had been four inches thick. Little sound could penetrate such a fastness.

Shuddering, she slumped to the edge of the soldiers' cot,

seeing only Masson as he had appeared at Bow Street, immaculately dressed in the dark, elegant clothing that echoed his unusual colouring. Moonlight was no colder than his face and his eyes. He moved and spoke but there was no life in him. She and Phoebe, between them, had turned him into an automaton. They had destroyed him.

The living-dead face was etched on to the retinas of her own eyes, the mouth edged with bitterness. 'The whore who engaged my attention.' The words rang in her brain with ever-increasing power to wound. She was filled, suddenly, with a terror that he might find out about the men in the women's quarters. But he would no longer care what she did.

Had it been Molly, smiling at the back of the court? Had Nick Caspar been there? She would have noticed Nick for he'd have been head and shoulders above everyone else. It seemed strange that Nick was not there to see her brought down. For the first time, Jade saw that Nick might not have had a hand in her betrayal. He'd punished Nan because of Jade's defection, there was no refuting that, but it was Molly who had seen her leave Masson's house that day, who had gone to Jeremy Bowles, over whom she probably had some hold, perhaps of the body, or of some discreditable secret she had wormed out of one of her special customers. Molly would have her own ways of obtaining useful information, and men were weak in certain circumstances.

'I'll never trust another Runner as long as I live,' Jade told herself, then pressed her hands to her mouth in case she screamed. How long would she wait for the day when she was given her last breakfast from the coffee-shop across the way? Would Gabriel watch her from the balcony as she was hooded and got ready for the rope? How different his next article would be! It would be more like George Hoare's who had viewed hanging from the point of view of the man who was menaced with pistols and robbed of his valuables, left humiliated on a moor.

It seemed an eternity since she had eaten. It was almost obscene to be hungry. What use to feed a body that would soon become a corpse? She buried her face in the noisome palliasse, uncaring of her revulsion.

She was shocked out of her trauma by the stealthy turn of the key in the lock. Jade had forgotten that women prisoners, even the condemned it seemed, were the perquisities of the gaol staff. But she still had the knife concealed in the pocket where her father's charm was kept. It had been a good idea to sew it so near the hem.

There was no need to reach down for it. Dick's voice came to her out of the gloom, chastened, distressed. 'It's me.'

She could not bring herself to move. The relief, after the fear, was too great.

'There's a gentleman wishes to see you. It's about your case.'

That made her laugh discordantly. 'A gentleman! Here?'

'A Mr Gabriel Masson. But you don't have to see him, love. Only if you want.'

She sat up, trembling. 'Gabriel? Gabriel here?' Her voice had changed.

'Downstairs. Waiting. But I'll tell him to go if you say the word–'

'No. No. I'll see him.' He had remembered the night after Stagshaw. He must have–

'I'm right sorry things turned out as they have,' Dick said slowly and heavily as if she were already dead. But she wasn't! And Gabriel had experienced some change of heart. He and his cousin Peter were against hanging. Even her apparent duplicity hadn't put him off her entirely. Jade felt transformed, rejuvenated.

'It's not your fault,' she said automatically, wanting Dick gone, in a fever to get out the comb and try to subdue her hair. 'I hadn't realized they knew about the collector. Isaac might have told them. He'd want to paint me at the blackest. Probably said I slept with him so that I'd influence him to buy the stuff!' He wouldn't dare mention Flynn and Nick Caspar for fear of what would happen to him inside prison. There were worse deaths than hanging.

'You never thought–I took advantage?'

'No, Dick,' she answered gently. 'I never thought that. You were kind where everyone else was cruel. I think Nan would have died if it hadn't been for you. How is she? Tell her I'm here, on the other side of the wall. Thinking of her.'

'I will. And you're sure you want to see this man?'

'Quite sure. How–how long can we have together?'

'Half an hour or so.'

'Thank you, Dick.'

The darkness did not seem too inimical. She occupied the time by tugging uselessly at her hair. The pain in her scalp banished the remainder of her self-pity. That could help no one. Setting aside the comb, she went to the window. By standing on tip-toe she could catch a brief glimpse of the sky that was swollen and heavy with snow. No moon or stars would break through that thick blanket. She would remind Gabriel of the church in the snow. Their growing happiness. That she was compelled to do what she had out of pity for Nan.

There was a scrabble of sound and the door yawed open. Dick stood in the gap with a lighted candle. 'Here you are, sir. The prisoner, Jane Benson.'

'Do your prisoners always sit in the dark?' Gabriel asked harshly.

'If they've no money to buy candles.'

'Take that. See that this woman has light whenever she wishes.' But there was no kindness in Masson's voice. He did what he thought was right, not because he was touched by her plight. 'Some heat too and wine. I'd not put a dog in this cell.'

The words of explanation and extenuation died on her lips. Dick had gone out, closing the thick door, and Gabriel stood watching her in silence. How beautiful he looked in the candle-light, like some dark angel of vengeance. But his features were stiff and unyielding as his set body, the implacable stance of his legs and thighs, the feet planted apart as though he barred her way. He had blotted out Stagshaw —

Her voice came from a great distance, thick and distorted with pain. 'It – was not as you think – '

'How was it, then?' Distaste twisted his lips.

'I was made to do it.'

'As you were made to rob that other man? Come, Jade. You must do better than that. Why not tell the truth? You saw that I was well-dressed, had a carriage of my own, that I smelt strongly of the brandy I had drunk, uselessly, to put Phoebe from my mind. And in your cheap, opportunist, guttersnipe way, you set out to entrap me with a body doubtless used by any man with the misfortune to come your way. It's a wonder I don't have the pox – '

She took a step, raised her hand and struck him violently so that his head snapped back and he reeled against the door.

'By God, you'll pay for that. I came to tell you what I thought of you for what I can only call your betrayal but you should not have raised your hand against me.' He stood upright now and there was a trickle of blood at the corner of his mouth. His eyes were terrible in their bleakness. 'What a fool I have been. A double fool. Women are all the same –'

'Are they? What about Anna? Your sister.'

He was silent for a moment. 'Cheap words,' he said chillingly, 'after you took what I prized most. God damn you for speaking her name in this place.'

'It was not I who took them. Nan did that, though she's not responsible for her actions.'

'No more lies, please,' he said wearily and wiped the cut with his 'kerchief.

'Had I known what Nan had, I'd have left them behind. Truly.'

'Oh, no, you would not!' he replied, seizing her wrist in a brutal hold. 'You came with the express purpose of robbing me when you'd had a surfeit of being bedded by me. It's an old trick with whores. Peter knows it all. Get a foot over the door, a meal inside you and then the body of your host. Pretend you like it, wheedle some new clothes and finery out of him – Take, take, take.'

'I did not!' She screamed and lashed out at him. 'It was you who took away the clothes I had!' She could not after all tell him she was Jade Benedict. He'd never listen and there was now no one to whom she could confess her past and be believed. She was Jane Benson, tried and convicted, here till she died one morning at eight o'clock.

'You'd have got them just the same. Every artifice practised by doxies was known to you. Well, you can earn another guinea with which to bribe your gaoler before I go. I'll not be back again.' The strong arms that had once held her so differently were thrusting her back on the dirty palliasse. She kicked and pleaded, cursed and reviled him, but he seemed impervious to either words or actions. He went on with the business of taking off the pelisse and the shift, her nethergarment, with an almost scrupulous care. His face might have been carved from marble.

However loudly she cried out there would be no one to hear. Squirming back against the wall she was aware that he unfastened only his breeches. With a harlot one needed no finesse. There would be no magic this time.

Catching hold of her by her waist, Gabriel stretched her out beneath him, then his hands were on her wrists so that she could not again scratch at his face and neck.

'Gabriel – no –'

But he was stronger and he was determined to commit this

last humiliation on her. He thrust into her angrily, each hard stroke a punishment that became, insidiously, no real castigation. The restricted bed creaked. Her world had narrowed down to that creaking bed, the brown vaulted roof above her, Gabriel's face, sweat-filmed and shut-eyed, rising and falling with every cruel ingress, his whispering curses. 'Whore! Prostitute, harlot, doxy. Filth, tart. Drab. Scum. Seducer. Tell me now that you've only been with one man apart from myself. Tell me and I'll stop.'

Her silence enraged him to further obduracy and she could no longer hold back the moan of protest. Her just-audible pleading had no effect. For him she had lost all identity, all claim to being human.

He had finished with her at last. Straddling her exhausted body, he stared down at her with a furious gaze. 'I'm glad I need never see you again.'

'No more pleased than I am,' she said with a soft violence. 'I wish I could say that you'll live to regret it, only you're so full of gall and your own misery that it's not likely.'

'There's the payment for –'

'Slaking your itch? It'll cost you more than a guinea this time! Beast!' She was shaking, sobbing.

'It's all you're worth.' Contemptuously, he got off the bed and covered himself. Putting a hand in his pocket, he dropped the gold piece on to the filthy mattress.

'I really do hate you.' She got up on to her knees and drew the pelisse round her.

'How can that concern me now?'

'You *are* wrong –' she insisted, shutting out the memory of snow.

'I heard all the evidence. There was no mistake.'

'Fabricated –'

'Even yet, when you are to – ?'

'Die. Go on, say it! So much for your precious humanity, Mr Gabriel Masson.'

He was very white now that his rage was burnt out.

'Will you watch me too? Will you? And that poor girl in the next cell who is slow and not too intelligent through no fault of her own because two gentlemen like yourself ran her down in the street for a prank? Some jape that was! To spoil the quality of a child's life.'

His eyes narrowed and she knew that she had made him doubt himself. 'We'll make interesting copy for you, no doubt, as we kick our lives away, the sight enjoyed by rich as well as poor. I'm glad I'm going to die for you've sickened me of fine well-born men who pretend philanthropy and practise rape.'

'You admit that accommodating men is your trade —'

'But even a harlot can pick and choose. Even a drab can decide upon whom to bestow her privileges. Go now,' she said wearily, 'I'm tired and you've hurt me. I'd prefer to be alone. I will tell Dick you are not to be admitted again.'

'Dick. So you know his name.' His eyes accused hers.

'What else is there to do here?' she said bitterly. 'At least he was kind.'

He turned away just as the door opened, whispering something she could not hear, pushing his way past Dick who looked after him amazed.

'All right, are you?'

Jade could have cried with the violence of her emotions, for the gentleness in his tone. 'Perfectly. I think I'll go to sleep now.'

He lingered. 'Good night, Dick,' she said more sharply.

'Good night.'

The door closed on them both. A dreadful silence fell upon the place. Dry-eyed, she relived the past, unhappy episode. The flickering of the candle reminded her that it would only last so long. She blew out the flame and lay down, covering her sore, sticky body as best she could. It was odd, but she almost preferred the main women's quarters to this in spite of Bella and those others.

There was no escape from Gabriel and what he had said and done. Again and again, he forced himself upon her, took her and threw the guinea on the bed.

'Gabriel,' she whispered, 'oh, Gabriel.' The tears she had held back came now, hot and agonized. She thought she would choke on her grief. 'It won't do,' she muttered to herself. 'It won't help.' But it blurred her mind and drugged her body so that she did, eventually, fall asleep.

Jade had lost all count of time. Mostly she sat in a brown shade, at other times in pitch-blackness. The candles were precious and she only resorted to those when her nerves screamed out against isolation. While they burned she paced the nine foot by six foot cell, her shadow a grotesque companion. Sometimes she talked to her shadow as though it had a separate existence. Gabriel's eyes haunted the corners of the room. She could not forget his bitter mouth, his cruel hands. He made no further attempt to see her.

She spent Gabriel's money on a fire and wine for them both. Wine warmed away the devil of despair and helped her to sleep. She would hold up the glass to the fire or the candle flame and imagine herself back on the chaise-longue in Masson's green-silk room, red wine to drink, an orange to peel and scent the chamber with bitter-sweetness. The news sheets, the softly falling snow, then Gabriel's return, his fingers unfastening the buttons and hooks on the jade velvet gown. The thought of Stagshaw was too painful.

Then his subsequent savagery would impose its shadow over the memory of happier days and she would bite her lip until it bled. Feverishly, she would think of other things, tracing an imaginary journey taken by her parents in France and Italy, but that train of thought always ended in a sharp vision of Mama in a pink dress, a pretty doll who got smaller and smaller and vanished into nothingness. She saw Drogo, grinning, his dark foreign eyes glittering, his stunted body capering in childish amusement. Ma Lee, all shuddering bosom and too-bright red hair, holding her, angry with Nick. Nick himself dressed in mole-grey, his garnet-coloured hair fascinating her while Molly watched in impotent fury.

But it had not been impotent at the last, that anger. Molly had succeeded admirably.

It had been a shock when, one late afternoon about a week after Gabriel's visit, the door had opened to show her Nick's huge shape. Jade's eyes had widened with disbelief. Curiously, she was not afraid of him. The threat of death reduced every other emotion.

The gaoler with him was not Dick who would have come first to ask her if her visitor was welcome. Caspar had obviously greased this man's palm well to take him up unannounced.

'So this is where you and the dim-wit are.' Nick stared uneasily at the low roof.

'Don't tell me you are surprised!' Jade mocked.

'I didn't know. I swear it. Molly got drunk and blabbed to a customer. A customer I know well. So here I am.'

'Why?' Jade asked, her gaze hard as she remembered Nan. 'There's nothing here for you. All I regret is that you revenged yourself on someone else. Always were a bully, weren't you?'

His hand flashed towards her face, slamming her down against the head of the barrack bed. Dizzily, she saw him go to the window, stare out at the unprepossessing view. Reaching down, she uncovered the pocket and took out the knife, slipping it inside her sleeve. She could only die once and she could think of few people she hated as much.

'Stupid of you to get rid of Sam that evening. Hasn't done you any good, has it?' He shrugged and came back, confident that she was cowed. 'A good lay, was he? That man?'

He struck her again when she stared back with contempt. 'I asked you a question.'

'Very well. Yes, he was.'

'Tell him any little indiscretions in moments of weakness?' He took hold of her finger, pretending to examine the dirt-engrimed nail. 'I take it there were several?'

She shook her head. Nick bent the finger right back until the perspiration broke out on her face and palms. 'No! I didn't.'

'Tell anyone. The Redbreasts? Magistrates?'

'I said nothing. Surely Molly told you that? She was there, at Bow Street.'

'You might have said things out of court.'

'Well, I didn't. I was too ashamed of any connection with you to hurt anyone from the past with such divulgences. It could only have smeared them with the same filth –'

'Didn't always think I was,' he whispered, and squeezed her breast until she gasped with agony.

'Always, I did!' she cried out. 'Always.'

'You shouldn't really have said that. Any little confidences passed your pretty little lips here? Lots of company at night, I heard.'

'For the last time, I said nothing at all.' Her face was white with a sick pain.

'See that you don't then. I can easily send someone even up here with a big enough bribe. Molly'd enjoy coming up with her chiv, especially after the beating she had for putting you away. She could make your last days hell.'

'It's too late for revenge,' Jade said slowly. 'I won't say that I never had the urge to speak. I did – twice. But the silly thing was that no one believed me.' She began to laugh, harsh rasping laughter that bruised her throat.

'No mention of my name?' He had his hand around her other breast and this time she screamed.

'I think I believe you. Some nasty moments I had after I found out about Molly and Bowles. He's due to have an accident.' Nick sat up and began to unbutton his coat. 'You know, of course, that I was in love with you? Only you spoiled it by letting me see I was nobody. Not good enough. It's never good for a man's morale to look down your nose at him. I've a mind to tumble you. Just once more. Might never see you again and you get under a man's skin.'

'No,' she said, and let the knife slide down into her hand. 'I've got my own protection and I'll never let you touch me again. And don't think I'll be afraid to kill you, because what have I got to lose? I haven't given you away, or any of the others, and at this late stage I don't much care what happens to any of you. So knock on the door to let that gaoler know our conversation's at an end and never let me see you again.'

They stared at one another over the gleam of the blade and her hand was perfectly steady. He tried to outstare her but failed.

'You little bitch,' he whispered, almost admiringly. 'Wish it was you and not Molly who was besotted. I still don't think we've seen the last of one another.' Then he rose and went to the door. Banged on it three times, waited while the door swung open. Not until she glimpsed the gaoler did she let the knife slip down behind the bed.

'Pity,' Nick said from the aperture. 'Sleep well.'

He was gone and she shook with reaction. Her breast hurt dreadfully and her head ached. The backs of her eyes were hot and sore as if sand had blown into them. But she did not cry. She couldn't cry for Nick Caspar. But neither did she sleep. He had successfully taken away her sense of security, the hardly won resolution that could help her to face what must be endured.

Her eye-sockets were black with weariness next morning. Dick came, his feet dragging, his face pale. He did not look at her. Then she knew with a sudden cold fear that the execution date was fixed. It was when people averted their eyes from you that you knew that hope was gone.

For some reason, the instant she assimilated the knowledge, she thought of Mrs Fry, remembering the calm, resolute face, the way she forged a passage through the filth and squalor of the women's cell, her smile for Nan Flynn.

Did Nan understand? It seemed important that they be together.

Dick set down a bottle, the last he would ever bring. ''Tis Geneva,' he told her. 'Dulls the mind better than wine. Gave some to her as well.' He jerked a finger in the direction of the wall separating her cell from Nan's.

'The Governor will be coming to tell you himself, so you'd better put that under the bed. Overheard them talking, I did. Knew I couldn't hide it from you.'

'When?'

'Day after tomorrow.'

'Oh, God –'

'Don't take on. Have some of this. 'Twill be better.' Uncorking the bottle, he poured out a generous measure, then turned to see to the fire, being extra liberal with the fuel. He could afford to be now. Then he lit a candle and took a peep out of the pocket-handkerchief window. 'Going to snow, I think.'

'Will it snow the day after tomorrow?'

'Don't, Miss Jane!' He stumbled away from her and she was locked in with her own thoughts, but the gin had restored her to a false calm. Nick had said it wouldn't be the last time they met. Perhaps there was some string he could pull. He had his own sort of power.

The Governor, purposefully matter-of-fact, his eyes anywhere but on her face, came with a woman assistant, to tell Jade what she already knew. The prison chaplain followed but Jade was more concerned for Nan's welfare than her own spiritual well-being. She listened with only half an ear to the prayers.

'Is there no confession you wish to make, my child?'

'None.'

'It's better to unburden oneself.'

'I have nothing to say.' Gabriel had taken away her will to fight just as she had murdered his trust, his self-respect. They had destroyed one another.

'Very well. If you change your mind, send for me.'

'Tell Nan I am thinking of her constantly.'

'Honour among thieves, eh?' The chaplain allowed himself a small joke.

'That lady, Mrs Fry. She's not expected at Newgate today or tomorrow?'

'And what would you want with Mrs Fry?'

'She would listen –'

'I would listen.'

'But she's a woman. One could tell her things –'

'It may be a long time before Mrs Fry comes back.' Too late for you, he was thinking, no doubt. Too late.

The pain in her breast and her weariness sent her to lie on the grimy mattress, the pelisse hugged closely around her. The interplay of light and shadow on the ceiling soothed her and she slept for a long time to dream, surprisingly, of pleasant things. Days at Ayas Bywaters, the excitement of the prospect of moving to London. The white gown with the jade-green embroidery round the skirt. Plumes in her hair and little green shoes. Gabriel's silk sitting-room, he sitting in his black and white robe, feeding her with kidneys and beef, then carrying her to the bed, drawing the hangings so that they were in a tent of sorts, like an Emperor at war.

But the day in the snow was the best, she in the new, pretty boots and green velvet, the church and the bells cutting the clean air. Gabriel making love to her. The kaleidoscope shattering into beautiful fragments –

When she was awake, she asked Dick to fetch her chestnut shampoo and some of Ma Lee's nostrum. She preferred not to go to the gallows with a seed of any man's child in her. Dick probably thought her mad to wash her hair in order to go to her death, but it was no one's business but her own.

Later still he saw that she had hot water and a towel and watched her against the firelight as she teased and coaxed and parted the silky brown mop to a semblance of beauty. Noticing the bruises on her body when she took off the pelisse in case it became wet, he was angry.

'I suppose it was your fine Mr Masson!'

'I had another visitor while you were not here. There was something he wished to know and he found it difficult to decide whether or not I spoke the truth.'

Dick's face darkened. 'The swine.'

'It looks worse now than it is. How is she? Nan?'

'Not in such good spirits as you. She's fretted constantly. But I always tell her I've seen you –'

'Couldn't you let me go in there? For five minutes?'

'I couldn't, lass. And think how she'd go on when you left. 'Twould be cruel.'

'Yes. I see.' She could not dream of upsetting the girl even if it were possible.

Dick had not asked for her body since she came into the condemned cell. Perhaps it was too macabre, or too distasteful, to make love to a woman as good as dead. Not that Masson or Caspar had entertained such scruples!

For a time, bitterness took over. It was quiet, the blanket of snow muffling all sound, then the chaplain came again to pray for her. She repeated the familiar words mechanically. God seemed very far away.

And then there was a period of silence, of the fire crackling and sparking, while however close she crept towards it, her body remained made of ice. A time of confused thoughts, of grappling with the questions of why her life had been directed along this deadly channel with only darkness at its end. She could not see the purpose of it all. And the Geneva had either lost its strength or she had grown accustomed to it. She could forget nothing.

Ashen-faced and still, she realized, with the first glimpse of slate-blue through the double bars, that this was the morning. She was stunned and disbelieving but the sounds of hammering were proof enough.

A new sound penetrated the fastness of her cell. At first it seemed like the far-off rumble of the sea on a rocky shore and then she knew that it was the steady growth of the Newgate crowd. Cold and snow wouldn't prevent Londoners wanting to see a double hanging. The chestnut vendor would have lit his brazier and the luckiest spectators would be huddled round it. Bang, bang went the hammers.

The door swung open to reveal a new gaoler with a tray of breakfast. So she would say no goodbye to Dick. 'Eat that up sharp as you like,' the man ordered brusquely. 'The time's getting on.'

After he had gone, she ignored the rapidly cooling food but sipped the coffee which was thick and bitter and put some life into her. She must not crumble. In front of all those people she must be brave. They liked the condemned to make a good end. The thought made her want to laugh.

But she could not help starting up, retreating to the back of the cell, when the door groaned open for the last time. The Governor stood there and his features betrayed displeasure. 'Jane Benson – ' His voice droned on and she found herself clutching at the sides of the barrack bed, dropping to the floor, her knees pricked with the straw. He could not have said what she thought she had heard. It was some sort of trick.

'And so, instead, your sentence has been commuted to seven

years' penal servitude which you will serve in the colony of New South Wales.'

He had gone and she was still there, without any feeling in her body, her mind blank. Then, very slowly, she took out the sea-horse and stared at it.

'You did it,' she whispered. 'You did.' Then a violence of reaction overtook her and she leaned over to vomit her insides into the dirty rushes.

It was not until she was thrust into the communal cell where Nan already waited, wild-eyed and emaciated, that Jade knew it was true. They were to live and go to Australia. To Botany Bay.

'So you didn't get your neck stretched,' Bella Scrivener mocked. 'Can't think 'ow you got away with it. Open up for the Governor, did you?'

Jade smiled suddenly. 'That's my secret,' she answered and took Nan into her arms. Perhaps those articles in the news sheets had contributed to the last-minute reprieve. Or more probably Nick had some hold over an official with a dark secret that could ruin him. What did it matter? They were alive and the future waited. A challenge.

She had always liked a challenge.

PART TWO

AUSTRALIA

CHAPTER SIX

Ma Lee visited the two girls before they were due to sail in the *Caroline*. She brought each of them a gown, Jade's green and Nan's blue.

'Couldn't let you go in your drawers, now, could I?' she said when Jade thanked her.

'Thank you, anyway.'

'Had a bad time, 'ave you, love?' Ma saw through the façade of cheerfulness. 'Could have been worse, though. Not much worse than hangin' an' you could have got fourteen years. Usually do when you're reprieved. Looks as if someone pulled a string or two.'

'Nick did say something—'

'Don't mention that swine.' Ma cast a disillusioned look around the vile cage in which they spent their days. 'Still, if 'e snatched you off from under the hangman's nose you gotter give 'im credit.'

'How are they all?' Jade asked, pulling the gown over her head. If she didn't wear it, it would disappear during the night. It was fresher than most of Ma's dresses, she noticed with gratitude. Nan's made her look so beautiful and her eyes so extraordinarily blue that she'd have to watch her even more carefully than usual. Dick would help. They'd never have managed without him.

'Oh, just as usual,' Ma answered. 'Molly's back wi' Nick, now that she's over the beatings he handed out. He'll never forget, though, that it was she got you sent away. Have to sing small, she will. Serve 'er right.'

'Ma!'

'Hope he brains her one day. She's trouble.'

'Perhaps, with us gone, she'll change. Jealousy is very destructive.' Jade smoothed down the green folds and thought of Gabriel. He had punished her then left her to her own devices. But she couldn't have expected him to overlook her apparent duplicity. Phoebe's husband wouldn't make old bones. She'd see to that. Gabriel might succumb on the rebound. In either case Jade would never see him again. No one came back from Botany Bay unless they were free colonists with money of their own for the passage.

'Feelin' down, are you?' Ma dug into a capacious pocket. 'There you are, lovey. Bit o' mother's ruin. Tide you over tomorrow night.'

Jade frowned. 'Tomorrow?'

'Allus shocking the night afore sailin'. Didn't no one tell you?'

'No.'

'Should stay awake if I were you. Not that you'll 'ave much choice.'

'Thanks for the warning. You've been a good friend, Ma. If I should get back, how can I get in touch?'

Ma grinned wryly. 'Get back? How? Sprout wings, will you?'

'If I should –'

'Got a cousin in Lavender Street. Number twenty. Name o' Lil Stalker.'

'Good. I'll remember that.'

'Regular little beauty she's turned out,' Ma whispered, jerking her head in Nan's direction. 'Wouldn't have believed it once. Don't look like a –'

'Dim-wit?' Jade supplied sharply. 'She isn't! You've all been wrong.'

'Didn't mean no harm,' Ma said quickly. 'Really, I didn't.'

'I know. It's just that I hate that tag. She deserves better and I'll see she gets it one of these days.'

'Allus said you were the gamest little wench I ever knowed.'

'Nonsense!' But Jade was warmed and encouraged by the woman's approbation. If she ever saw England again, she'd go to Lavender Street in search of Ma's cousin Lil.

'Given up all hopes of *them*, have you?'

'My parents? Oh, yes.'

'You might trace them –'

'Mama wouldn't want to be found.'

'You knows best, dear.' Ma rose purposefully and fastened her cape over the splendid bosom. The suggestion of tears fought with the unreal red of her hair. 'Wish I hadn't to go –'

'I'll send you a letter via – Lil's, wasn't it?'

'Stalker,' Ma agreed gruffly. 'Won't say I'd be able to read it but I'll find someone. Nick's usually got a clerk or two in tow.'

'Don't let him see it.'

''Course I won't. 'Bye, Nan, my chick. And you –' Ma looked long and sadly at Jade's barely composed face, then went off, pushing her way through the little groups of women whose only thought now was of the *Caroline* and the journey to the other side of the world.

After they had lost all sight of her, Jade poured out Geneva and they both drank then gave some to the pathetic old women who never received visitors or comforts and had no way of buying their freedom. No Masson or Stagshaw in their past.

Bella Scrivener came to taunt Jade about the forthcoming voyage. 'Won't be no merciful Guv'nor nor no Dick where you're goin', Miss Highfalutin'.'

'There won't be any you, either!' Jade retorted.

That made the other women laugh. They enjoyed seeing someone like Bella being had the better of, and applauded Jade's turn of wit where others would have used their feet and fists, or foul language. But sleep was long in coming.

The gaolers were in a state of nerves next day. They fully expected trouble and that was what they got. The less stable of the transportees spent their last coins on drink, then proceeded to tear up their mattresses or palliasses. One who had procured a strike-light set fire to hers, and the women's quarters were lit up with a glow of red, which, with the watching circle of wasted and depraved faces bathed in its rosy light, was like a foretaste of Hell.

The turnkeys had to turn out in force, being scratched and spat upon, and chained the worst offenders to the wall. But they could not stop them shouting and venting abuse and no one had a wink of sleep. Dick was not there so, again, Jade was not able to say goodbye, but, once taken out in the morning and put, shivering, into the open wagon with the chained viragos, she saw him standing outside the prison gate, his coat collar turned up around his pale face.

Their eyes met over the side of the brutal conveyance and both knew it was for the last time. He was very like Jack. Even Nan thought so. It was almost as though Jack had not died, but lived on to be kind to some other friendless girl who found herself inside Newgate.

Jade lifted her hand and let it fall. Dick turned away and moved off slowly until he was swallowed up in the crowds who had come to jeer and fling mud. The wagons began to rumble over the cobbles, and, at every stage of the journey, there was someone to catcall and throw refuse or stones. The chained women, quiet and wild-looking, could not escape the hail of missiles and Jade was sorry for them. Their reaction of last night was understandable when one considered what they had to put up with in prison, the fact that they were leaving behind homes and relatives with no hope of return.

But her thoughts returned inevitably to Gabriel. Gabriel tender, Gabriel amused, Gabriel preparing to take her to bed. Then a Gabriel so horribly changed who treated her worse than the lowest drab and left her with no trace of self-respect.

Jade was still bound up in thoughts of him when the wagons rattled over the uneven quayside and the masts of the *Caroline* rose from the dark Thames water. Somehow, the shrouds and rigging seemed like the strands of a great web. Somewhere aboard would be the spider at the centre.

A broad, red-faced man was in charge of seeing the women aboard. His thick lips spewed out their names as if they had been toads. 'Benson.'

Failing to recognize the alias, Jade did not reply.

'BENSON! Jane and Nan. BENSON!'

She pushed Nan forward, wondering ruefully how many other women were there under an assumed name. The wide, highly-coloured face surveyed them from toe to crown. 'Deaf, are you?'

'No! Tired,' Jade snapped, wishing she'd held her tongue. But it was no fault of hers or Nan's that they were in this position, and a bullying overseer was hard to take. He smiled and the quality of that smile put her on her guard.

'Benson,' he said softly. 'Remember that, I will. Go on up the gangplank. You'll be met at the top. Benson. Are you Jane?'

'Yes.'

'Very well, Jane Benson. I'll find out later how you've settled in. Go on, girl! We haven't all day!'

'Johnson!' Jade heard him shout as she and Nan, carrying their small possessions, weaved their way over the treads of the plank and were met by a dark, hirsute man who took them round the waist and propelled them towards a hatch down which they were obviously intended to descend. He seemed in no hurry, however, to relinquish them. The broad, strong fingers dug themselves into the firm young flesh, sliding downwards over their flanks and thighs as though he examined a couple of mares.

Jade, waiting while Nan climbed over the side of the hatch and on to the open stair below, itched to strike away the black-haired hand, but dared not risk incurring his anger. It was out of the frying-pan and into the fire. The ship must prove to be as, if not more, disagreeable than either the citadel or Newgate. But there were ways of circumventing the lesser evils. The fountainhead was the best place to aim for and the captain could hardly be worse than his minions.

All the while she made her way carefully into the disconcerting darkness below, she wove a picture of the captain who would be handsome and gentlemanly and well-disposed towards petite, pale-skinned women with green eyes and silky brown hair and a good deal of experience in pleasing the opposite sex. But the vision was superimposed by the remembrance of Gabriel Masson. She was never going to forget him. His black and white colouring haunted her as she descended to utter darkness.

She never saw the man who directed her along a narrow space between what felt like shelves and turned out to be bunks. By this time, her eyes had grown accustomed to the light that filtered from the deck and her heart misgave her. There was no room to swing a cat and the absence of air would produce abominable conditions. Claustrophobia attacked her.

Women were crying in the shadows, and behind them Jade made out the bars of the cells that lay beyond the bulkheads.

'Nan? Nan!' Her voice rose.

'Quiet!' a man growled.

'I'm looking for my sister. She needs taking care of.'

'I'll take care of her.' He laughed crudely.

'Please. She came down just before me. She'll be frightened.'

Nan's face appeared in the gloom and Jade seized her before she vanished again.

'Come, love. We'll take these two bunks in the corner near the hatch. There may be more air that way. At least we'll get it first.'

'Wanting it first?' the sailor mocked. 'Always willing to oblige.'

Jade ignored him. He would be far too busy once the

chained prisoners were released. By tomorrow he'd have forgotten them.

'Benjy!' one of the unseen women was moaning. 'Benjy –'

'Shut your face!' the sailor ordered roughly. 'Bad enough having to see you troublesome whores settled without having to listen to that row.'

Feet came down the ladder and another shape appeared at the light aperture. The noise of approaching prisoners was now considerable. 'Johnson. Bates. Murphy. Wright. Fauld –' The list seemed interminable and the space was rapidly filled.

Jade's spirits flagged but her curiosity was aroused by the sound of what must surely be hooves on deck above their heads. They were not heavy enough for cattle. Probably sheep or goats, she reflected. There was the distinct noise of fowl. She had a strong desire to laugh. No one could have anticipated sharing the journey with large numbers of livestock. The deck rang with the clatter and somehow the homely bustle was reassuring.

They were given bread and soup without flavour. There was no telling what had been the base of the watery liquid. The bread was coarse but Jade enjoyed it. They would be forced to eat ship's biscuit before long and she'd heard enough tales of weevils to put her off for a lifetime.

Later in the day, just when the women's nerves were screaming for release from the dark and the suggestion of entombment, they were taken up on deck, ten at a time, for a walk round the ship, or those parts of which the captain approved. Sailors and soldiers watched their every move, some stern, some with the obvious intention of getting to know the female prisoners better. The cold river breeze ruffled their hair and twisted the folds of their skirts, brought colour to their cheeks.

Jade found it wonderful, savouring every moment, sniffing the river air as though it had been nectar instead of smelling of pollution; dreading the return to the unsavoury darkness that hid so much heartache.

She looked up suddenly, aware of being observed, and saw a young officer watching her. He was quite young, only in the early twenties she judged, and he looked clean and pleasant. She warmed to the trace of compassion in his regard. It was as though he knew that she was innocent of any wrongdoing, on this dreadful ship through no fault of her own. She smiled, aware that he reacted to the salutation, that he feasted his eyes on her face, the green gown, the faded pelisse with its fur trim, the flying banner of her hair.

A sharp voice barked an order and the lieutenant hurried away, leaving behind a sensation of comfort and hope. They must cling to any kindness, she and Nan. It took months to reach Australia. Three-quarters of a year perhaps of confinement and frustration.

Jade drew a deep breath, clutched the pelisse around her to combat the chill of the wind and saw a man approach. This must be the captain. The respect shown to him by the other men made that obvious. He was tall and comparatively slender, giving the impression of an almost Spanish elegance. The brooding eyes were black and so was the hair that was visible under his hat. His skin was sallow but his features were good, his expression contained and dignified.

She recognized the moment he saw her. The deep eyelids were raised and the full benefit of that dark stare was on her, travelling downwards without haste, returning as slowly to rest on her face. Jade raised her head proudly just as the wind snatched at her hair, dragging it back to show the beauty of her bone structure and ivory pale skin. Green eyes locked with black. No promise here of warmth or hope, Jade thought, still aware of the man's good looks and air of distinction. Even his long hands were refined, the fingers graceful. It was as though he could make no movement that was not in good taste. And yet, she shivered as she looked at him.

The black eyes went from her to Nan and stayed there. Again, the scrutiny from head to toe, a lingering when the inspection reverted to the shining blue of her eyes, the innocence of her demeanour, the glinting gold of the boyish curls.

He turned his head to say something in a low voice to the man at his side. The man replied as quietly. A gull flew over the ship and Jade's attention was taken away briefly by the sparkling whiteness of the bird against the dim shrouds. Her eyes took in the solidity of the upper-deck, the long lines of the masts, then returned to the spot where the captain had been. But it was empty. Already he was several yards away, apparently unimpressed by the faces he now barely looked at. His boots made sharp clacks on the unwashed boards. He was gone.

It seemed worse than ever below after the tantalizing taste of freedom. The woman who had cried earlier still said,

'Benjy, Benjy—' as if she were deprived of an arm or a leg. But Jade's mind was filled with another name. Gabriel. How could you be so cruel? Gabriel— But if he had been unkind it was because he imagined her false and predatory, wanting only Anna's trinkets. Any man would be bitter and unforgiving having been given such fuel for disillusionment. She saw his face in the dimness above the narrow bunk, cruel and condemnatory. Her body remembered what he had done. She would not shrink from the memory. What was over was finished with. What she must do was to reshape her life as best she could. All her old enemies were gone as if they had never been. Eliza, Molly, Nick Caspar, Gabriel—he too was an enemy.

Her fingers searched for the secret pocket, encountering the knife, then the charm. I still have you, she thought. You are still there. She still had her luck and her protection.

They sailed with the tide. It was not always so. Sometimes the ships waited for weeks and the women would go mad with grief and despair, knowing themselves still in England, their loved ones only a few streets away in many cases, yet as far removed as the stars. Children grizzled and fretted, disturbed by the change.

Nan cried as they left the Thames estuary and bowled out into the open sea and Jade comforted her as best she could retaining a mental picture of Mama and Papa under a cypress tree in Italy, the sky a hot blue and the landscape shimmering.

It was later in the day when the heat of the bulkheads was uncomfortably close and the smell of unwashed humanity almost unbearable, that a clatter of footsteps on the ladder, a whiff of sea air, and the flickering of a lantern roused everyone from a drugged somnolence. A child stirred, moaned in a half-sleep.

'Benson! Benson! Your presence is required.' The voice was satiric.

'Where?' Jade asked, swinging herself down from the bunk.
'You'll see.'

She recalled the broad-faced man, the soldier with the hairy hands, and was apprehensive. All the way up the ladder she worried about the summons but there was no way of evading what must come. She told herself that it didn't matter what happened to her body, only to her spirit, and the thought cheered her.

The breeze caught at her throat, charged with the bitterness of salt, but it was clean and refreshing after the bulkheads. Her legs adapted themselves to the motion of the ship and she smiled as she saw the sheep penned to one side of the deck and the crates of hens. Two cows stared at her out of dimness with thick-lashed eyes.

She followed the man, her steps lagging as they approached a door. A knock. A contained voice bidding them enter, then she was inside a well-appointed cabin with mahogany panelling and fittings, glints of brass and beams, a lamp that cast a yellow radiance over a table set for supper. Across a crispness of white linen cloth and silver cutlery, she saw the captain's dark brows draw together in a barely perceptible frown.

His dark eyes went from her to the man who had summoned her. 'I said Benson.'

'She said that was her name, sir.'

'Is it?' The quiet voice was cool but the reserved gaze descended from her face, taking in the quality and the good cut of Ma Lee's green gown.

'I am Jane Benson.'

'It was the other –'

'My sister is not quite –'

'Not quite what?'

'Responsible, sir.' Jade, recognizing the intelligence that confronted her, realized that the captain, while desiring Nan's body, might be swayed by the fact that he could expect little in the way of the mental stimulation he must surely require.

'And why is she – not responsible?'

Jade told the story of the two carriages and of the effect on Nan Flynn. 'She's little more than a child. I am forced to become her protector. A difficult task when she is so pretty.'

'She is beautiful.' The quiet voice fell silent as the dark gaze renewed its assault on Jade's figure. The effect of the lamplight on her eyes seemed to please him.

'You may go,' the captain said softly to his messenger, 'but see that the oil of tar is used below to sweeten the air. I could not help but notice the stench.'

'Yes, sir.' The dark mahogany door closed and she was alone with the master of the *Caroline*.

'Your wits seem sharp enough considering how young you appear.' He approved of what he saw, that was obvious, even if she were not so conventionally handsome as her supposed sister.

'Will you take supper with me?' he asked. But it was, of

course, an order.

Her blood beat a warning tattoo. He still had that quality that made her turn just a little cold. It was foolish, of course. The captain was a gentleman. Everything about him proclaimed the fact, his spotless linen, his polished boots, the impeccable cut of his clothing, the slim hands with their well-tended nails. His fastidiousness was in their favour because she could not imagine him putting up with smells and uncleanliness for long.

Her eyes took in the exquisite neatness of the captain's table, the places set for two. It would be wonderful to eat in civilized surroundings for a change. She had not enjoyed such style since her sojourn in Masson's house.

'I would be delighted to sup with you.' It was the conventional reply.

'Very well. Sit down.' He made no move to pull out her chair but captains did not fuss around felons. Gabriel had spoiled her once he had accepted the fact that she was not what he first thought. He must be regretting that weakness.

Composedly, she took her seat, her hands clasped in her lap, all the time aware of his silent assessment.

'What on earth are you doing among that rabble?'

'I was convicted of theft and –'

'And?'

'Importuning. It seems to be almost a worse offence than murder.' She smiled ruefully. He must know that already. She wondered why he asked.

His face showed no expression but he studied the hands she had raised in a defensive gesture. 'Is it true?'

'I'm afraid it is.'

'You say nothing of extenuating circumstances? Most would protest their innocence.'

She shrugged. 'No one, so far, has cared to listen.'

'But there were compelling reasons?'

'Quite compelling,' she agreed quietly. 'But I am to pay for my sins.' She shrugged and smiled again, then meeting his eyes she felt the colour rise to the neck and face and her throat constrict. Another door led to a cabin off this one and there the captain would sleep. But not alone. That was perfectly obvious.

He rose and went to the door. 'Bell? Bell!'

The man who had fetched Jade came soft-footed. 'We will take supper,' the captain informed him.

Bell poured out sherry into crystal glasses that caught prisms of light from the lamp, then left the cabin. Jade sipped at the golden liquid. It was smooth and not too sweet, reacting on her starved senses quite pleasurably. She saw the tall, restrained figure in a new light. He might prove difficult, reserved men usually were, but at least he would not be crude. Things might have been so much worse. She noted the sheen on the panelling with a gratitude that surprised her. She'd not properly understood the importance of beautiful surroundings. The Caroline might be packed with convicts – the men would be in the opposite bulkheads – her decks half taken over with livestock, but this cabin was gracious and well-appointed and there was a delicious smell of food that brought the saliva to her mouth.

'Tell me about the reasons for your transportation.'

She shook her head almost violently. 'I'd rather not. I'm not good at making excuses and, anyway, what's done is done.'

'You may encounter grave difficulties.'

'Undoubtedly, I shall. But whining will not solve problems.'

She fancied that she saw approval where there had been no apparent emotion.

He leaned across the spotless linen and poured more sherry.

'Thank you,' she said, with a hint of laughter. 'I've had nothing but Geneva since my fall from grace. I confess I enjoy the suggestion of luxury.'

'You'd be a fool not to,' he agreed. 'Not that I'd ever accuse you of stupidity. How old are you?'

'Sixteen.'

'So young?' His lips twisted briefly into the semblance of a smile. 'And your sister?'

She almost said the wrong thing. He'd smell a rat if she said Nan was the same age. No one would ever believe they were twins. 'A year older.' That was possible.

'A pity her mind's affected.'

It was better that he believed Nan worse than she actually was. 'It is a pity,' she agreed.

'But you are sharp enough for both of you,' he observed.

She said nothing. What was there to say? Picking up the glass, she drank the contents with a dreamy content. Time spent with the captain was time snatched from the hell of below deck. His speculative stare made her flush. Another horse on the merry-go-round, she reflected, and knew that he read her thoughts. Her heart beat faster.

The soup had wine in it and other good things but she knew better than to utter judgement on that served to the prisoners. That could come later when she knew him better. He was not in the least like any other man she had known.

After the soup came delicious cutlets and vegetables and these she ate greedily. It was weeks since she had eaten anything so mouth-watering. Cheese and fruit were placed before them and more wine brought. Her senses swam a little, and the captain's face assumed, more than ever, the good looks of a Spanish grandee. She was impressed.

'Captain Joel, sir,' Bell murmured and opened a box of cigars, cut the end off one and punctured it with a little sharp, silver object, then took his departure.

Captain Joel leaned back in his chair and surveyed Jade through a haze of fragrant smoke. The outlines of the fruit in the wooden bowl shivered. The polished mahogany retreated into a warm, gleaming redness. Everything was red. Walls, ceiling, the carved chairs, the waxed floorboards, the table without its white cloth. The captain's lips were red as he chewed upon the cigar, frowned at it and stubbed it out on a silver tray. She was surprised she hadn't noticed the redness of his lips until now but perhaps the wine had coloured them.

Captain Joel rose to his feet with no suggestion of haste and walked to the second door. Opening it, he stood against it and beckoned Jade to follow. She hesitated. 'Come,' he said brusquely. 'Surely maidenly doubts are out of place, considering what you have been?' The dark gaze impaled her. It was as though he had switched off politeness and breeding and become obscurely unpleasant. Suddenly, she found him totally frightening. She knew that it was stupid and irrational, but somehow that waiting figure was far more intimidating than Nick at his worst.

'You're a whore,' the captain said softly, but brutally. 'A self-confessed whore at that, yet you keep me waiting. You said you were convicted for importuning –'

'I was made to. That's not quite the same thing.'

'I invited your confidences, remember? You withheld them.'

'I'm sorry. You did, but I did not find the telling easy.'

'I've never liked sluts. Not even doxies who look like ladies, or speak like them. There's something in the thought of what they do that makes me want to punish them.' Each word fell like acid on to some delicate fabric, spoiling and mutilating.

She felt behind her for the door latch but he was too quick for her. Her hand was torn free, the raised sneck scoring a piece of skin out of her thumb. She let out a gasp of pain and found his face very close to hers, the sallow skin damped with perspiration.

'Why?' she whispered, 'when you dislike women so –'

'You did not look like a harlot. And neither did she. That pretty sister –'

'She isn't!'

'Ah, you love her, don't you.' The cruel hand dragged at her wrist.

'Yes. You're hurting me.'

'As I'd hurt anything that was so unclean. You've not the face of a draggle-tail, but you have the body. You're corruption, Miss Jane. Filth, Putrescence. Excreta. It's an abomination to show such a lovely face to the world when all the time what's down below is a cess-pool.' He thrust her inside the adjoining cabin and put his back to the door.

His face terrified her. No suggestion now of that cold elegance, the remoteness.

'Take off your gown, Miss Benson.'

She stared around her. More polished panelling and a wider bunk than the prisoners were allowed. The edge of it was carved with the shapes of flowers and birds and the linen was very white. Some books stood on a shelf and a robe hung on a hook behind the door. There was no speck of dust or dirt anywhere. Even the floorboards were waxed so that their reflections seemed to plunge towards the depths of the ship. The lantern on the wall creaked as it moved with the motion of the vessel.

'I said, take off your gown. Unless you wish me to tear it from those pretty shoulders. But I have nothing to offer you in its place.'

The floor tilted a little and Jade staggered towards the edge of the bunk. Her fingers moved mechanically over the little rounds of silver until the gown began to fall away from her breast, revealing the none too immaculate shift. She saw his lips twist with distaste.

'Have you ever tried to keep yourself clean in a place like Newgate?' she cried out. 'At least I managed to have water brought to me as often as I could –'

'How?' he asked chillingly. 'By –?' Here he used an expression that sounded even worse, coming as it did from a mouth that was well shaped and conveyed something very different, apart from the redness she so disliked.

'Nothing I will say will make any difference, will it?' The gown dropped to the mellowed floorboards.

'And the rest.'

Silently, she obeyed.

He watched her in the way of a cat with a mouse. It was cold without her clothes and she shivered. The movement disturbed her hair which fell over one shoulder, like brown rain, as far as her navel. She saw something else that had so far escaped her notice. From under the impeccable pillow, a few thongs of leather protruded, little ribbons of hide with knots at the ends. A sort of scourge.

Captain Joel moved forward. The slender fingers extracted the small whip, ran themselves over the narrow thongs lovingly and raised it. She screamed as the six little strands struck her shoulder, turned her back to protect herself, and felt the strips come down on her shoulders and spine. The knots flicked wickedly over her white skin. She could feel the trickles of blood, twisted her body round to escape the biting lash and felt his hand strike her face so that she fell upon the bunk.

She was gazing into the cruel features, her mouth contorted in protest.

'Turn over,' he whispered and dropped the scourge to the floor.

'Why?'

'Do as I say!' he ground out and put his hands around her narrow waist.

'I don't want you like all those other, drunken lechers. Not that way.'

Her senses whirled. She found herself staring at the faultless pillow, not quite believing what he meant to do. And then his body was over hers, taut as whipcord and as uncaring. She had never known such pain, and when he left her she wondered if she would ever move again.

It was nearly morning before she slept.

He did not send for her for ten days. They were days in which she lay in the hold, her body flinching from any contact. Children cried and women fought among themselves but she hardly noticed. Nan cared for her diligently as Jade had done for her in the past and the doctor produced a salve.

The food grew worse and not even the frequent explosions of gunpowder and the lighting of fires between decks could clear the miasma of impure air. When Jade was once again able to get out of her bunk – Bell had carried her there after the episode with Captain Joel – she found that some of the women had fallen ill and seemed quite feverish. The poor woman in the opposite bunk, Amy Grey, was pregnant and incapable of caring for her small son, little Daniel. Her mind wandered back constantly to the village where she spent her girlhood. The soft voice, speaking of thatched rooms, of love potions, of thick woods where wild creatures lived cheek by jowl with owls and pigeons, blackbirds and wrens, evoked a way of life that Jade recognized from her own youth. The small boy, still unbreeched and beautiful in an Italian or Greek way, all firm, round cheeks and brown, heavily-lashed eyes, entranced her with his suggestion of old legends. He was a baby Adonis, a Paris, a Narcissus. He pleased her entirely with his sweet nature and his comeliness. He filled the voids in her life as she held him in her arms to comfort him in the unavoidable absence of his mother. Amy was in another region, another time. Daniel responded to Jade, smiled for her, hugged and kissed her so charmingly and wholeheartedly that more wounds than those of her scourged body were healed. He was the child she would have wished for had her life been different.

She began to think that Captain Joel was done with her. Because of him the other men had, so far, made no demands upon her as they did on the rest. Pale and tired from nursing Amy, she was taken up the deck for exercise, the sea-winds stronger and colder than ever, the sheep bleating and the hens clamouring. A woman, dead of the fever, lay wrapped in sailcloth, ready for burial. All the women needed medicaments and better food or few of the transportees would reach Port Jackson. The doctor's face showed worry.

The sharp clack of bootheels on planking alerted her. Instinctively, she reached out to take Nan's hand. The flat, dark gaze stopped on them both. Thin, cruel lips quirked in a grimace she detested because she suspected what lay at the root of it. After Joel had moved on, her heart beat irregularly.

But all her misgivings could not remove him. Jade recognized the fact. If he summoned her, she must obey that command. She could not forget how he had looked at Nan. He had preferred the girl's innocence, her curly head that was reminiscent of a boy's.

Nan was asleep when the ladder quivered and the man entered the women's quarters. 'Benson,' he said. 'Nan Benson!'

Jade was, immediately, wide awake, her spine trickled over with ice. She let herself down and was ashamed to find herself trembling. Joel still hankered after Nan or he had summoned her knowing that Jade would take her place.

She followed the messenger and was shown into the same beautiful cabin. He was not there and she let her hand slide over the reddish wood, the feel of it like satin against her fingertips. Spray blew over the portholes and she was reminded of fireworks. The white foam separated, slid down the glass. Another shower followed. The woodwork creaked and the lamps flickered. She became increasingly conscious of the force of the gale. The perils of nature did not compare with the fear she had for the captain. Not that she would show it. Half of the satisfaction he gained was from the panic he inspired.

She was studying a painting when he came and heard nothing until he said, 'It was Nan Benson I asked for.' But his tone betrayed the fact that it was Jade he expected.

'She was asleep.'

'And you wanted to come?'

She flung back her head. 'Why not?'

He laughed very softly. 'Will you sup with me, Miss Jane?'

'Of course. I wondered when you'd repeat the invitation.'

'I've never met anyone quite like you.' His fingers drummed against the panelling.

She shrugged, smiling, wary as a deer.

'And what have you done since I saw you?'

'I was in bed for a week. Now I'm nursing those who have fever. There's an epidemic, Captain. The women are ill. They need medical supplies. Better food.'

'Indeed?' The dark brows arched and cruelty flickered behind his eyes.

'I have said what I felt was required. You did ask.'

'I asked you once why you importuned men.'

'Because I was abducted from my home and forced to submit to a man I could not escape.'

'You expect me to believe that?'

'That is entirely your affair. You must believe what you will.' She braced herself against the hostile stare. His fingers ceased their tattoo against the glowing wood. 'Did you expect virtue on a transport ship? Or did you welcome the voyage and the contact with women like me? The opportunities for chastisement?'

'How perspicacious of you.'

'Believe me. Some more of those women will die.'

'Do you expect me to cry over fallen women?'

'Amy Grey is a poor soul who stole bread to feed her child. She's never looked at another man.'

'I think supper will not be long.'

'Damn supper! I'll choke on your food knowing that they will lie hungry –'

He laughed involuntarily. 'How positive you are!'

'As if you didn't welcome that. Is this your first voyage to Australia?'

'The second. I admit I prefer a show of spirit.'

'You'd not get that from my poor Nan, for all her marvellous looks.'

'I need a mind that's razor-sharp. I admit I did ask for her but it was you I wanted. Needed – I knew you'd come.'

Bell had knocked and was in the room. They both stared at him as if he had appeared from another planet. The crisp, white tablecloth mocked them. The crystal glasses gave off their rainbow glints. Jade weakened.

Bell smiled and poured the sherry with infinite care. 'A rough night, Captain?'

'Aye, it's rough. I'll expect to be told if it gets worse.'

'Of course.'

'Leave us for the moment, then. Quarter of an hour till the first course.'

It was quiet after he'd gone. Joel came eventually and put a hand under her chin, tilting her face upwards. It was the strangest kiss, the kind one gave one's mother, not in the least like Caspar's, or Gabriel's.

The thought of Gabriel, as always, saddened yet exhilarated her. She saw him on the balcony of Phoebe Lewis's house, then in his own, the black and white robe pulled about him, accentuating the splendour of his body.

Captain Joel's hands strayed about her, arousing nothing but an impotent dislike. She could never forget the last time. It was a boy he wanted, not a girl with a narrow, white body, her breasts small as lemons. The captain liked his own kind better. It was as if he flouted his true inclinations.

It was a relief when the soup, rich with wine and vegetables, arrived. Even as she enjoyed the savoury mess, Jade deplored the watery substance the women, and probably the men, enjoyed. She must make that point while Captain Joel understood her views on the subject.

The meat course was delicious beyond words. Her companions had not had meat since the *Caroline* put to sea. They never would have it. Why pretend?

She spoke of the deprivations, hoping that he would take notice, knowing that it was unlikely. Mrs Fry would have seen that these voyages were different but she still struggled with Newgate, coming when she could, attending to her home and children between visits, a woman divided in loyalties.

Jade remembered Daniel with gratitude. Nan would be with him now, but tomorrow he would be hers. She drank copiously, hoping that the wine would make what followed the more bearable.

It did not. The captain was sadistic and nothing would ever alter the fact. Still, it was ten days since the last time. But she felt her stomach muscles contract when he stood up at the end of the delicious meal and walked quite steadily towards the cabin where his bunk was situated.

'Come,' he said; 'come.'

And she went.

Amy Grey was desperately ill. Though Jade had mentioned the insufficiency of the food and the need for medicine, nothing seemed to have changed. Some of the women had spots and suppurating sores, but Jade, perhaps because of the dinners with Captain Joel, remained reasonably healthy. And so did Nan since Jade pocketed some of the delicious meat and fruits. There was nearly always an opportunity for pilfering.

The captain pretended not to notice, but Jade suspected he must. He was no kinder, which made his initial courtliness all the stranger. Their meetings began as any supper party might, with Bell in attendance, his deft hands pouring out and serving. Then the captain spoke on various subjects, most of them interesting, protracting the meal so that it could last for as long as two hours, and then, perhaps due as much to the effect of the wines he drank as to his feelings about prostitutes, a devil seemed to possess him.

Always he held the threat of his penchant for Nan over her head so that Jade dared not refuse his summons. Each time she hoped that the evening would end on a different note but it never did.

Sometimes, during the much-looked-forward-to exercise period, she would see the young lieutenant, and though, at first, when she'd become Joel's mistress, he had flushed and looked the other way, gradually the sympathy he'd shown the day she arrived returned. Perhaps Bell, who was Joel's personal servant, had mentioned the captain's peccadilloes in the officers' cabin.

She was glad that Lieutenant Carey had ceased to resent what she was unable to avoid. It had hurt her when he withdrew his tenuous friendship. More than once recently he had accompanied her down the ladder to the dark prison below the deck, expressing concern over the plight of the prisoners, contriving occasionally to touch his hand on her shoulder as though it had been an accident.

It was galling to see the free settlers on deck, the women prim and virtuous and tight-lipped when the transportees came on deck, moving themselves and their children to a safe distance as though they'd be contaminated. Poor Amy and some of the others would have been equally respectable had they experienced the same security.

But, remembering the Holy Land, Jade could see the other side of the affair. Anyone must have reservations about women like Eliza and Bella Scrivener, the amoral Molly.

It was strange to think that, but for the American War of Independence, she might be on her way to Virginia. America, at least, was settled long ago, but New Holland, or Australia as it was now called since the Dutch links were superseded, was still comparatively raw. The latest Governor, so Jade heard, was a great improvement on Captain Bligh who had got himself deposed for his unbearable strictness. Lachlan Macquarie, so the ship's gossip went, had started off well-born but poor, an Ensign in some Highland Regiment. Supposedly kind and charming – she could have wished Captain Joel was of that disposition! – he had achieved promotion very rapidly after service in New York, Charleston, India, Ceylon, Egypt, England, a second spell in India, then was appointed Governor of New South Wales.

His private life had been less happy, the lady settlers had said, imagining their convict co-passengers to be deaf or stupid. Macquarie had been married, romantically, to a pretty West Indian heiress who died, tragically, of consumption. But he'd later married a distant kinswoman, Elizabeth Campbell of Airds, in Scotland, and had arrived at Sydney in fine style with his own regiment and a good deal of pomp. He was reputed to be in favour with Lord Castlereagh, and had been presented in Court, moving in the best British society.

He'd been disgusted, apparently, by the ramshackle appearance of Sydney and was already having many buildings removed which had spoiled the wide symmetry originally envisaged in the plans for the new town's streets. Hospitals and churches were built, and the new barracks held eight hundred men. A road had been built across the Blue Mountains, an impossible triumph.

The women went to Parramatta but it seemed that nothing improved that dreadful place of waiting.

'What can one expect from such dregs of society?' the smuggest of the free ladies said from her chair in the sun, then cried out as Jade tripped over a rope and stumbled heavily on to her foot.

'I do believe the strumpet did it on purpose!' she complained indignantly, her small, virtuous eyes quite pig-like though she never suspected. Lieutenant Carey took hold of Jade's arm and told the woman the matter would be investigated, then drew the girl aside. They stood at the rail, he unsuccessfully trying to project the sort of ferocity the free ladies would expect.

The sea was a deep, turbulent green, marbled with white where the *Caroline* forced her way through the waves. There was no land in sight, no bird to be seen. The sails flapped and strained against their ropes. A thin shower of spray wet her face deliciously. The young officer, she was well aware, admired her.

Carey's eyes followed the brown hair as it whipped back against a projection.

'Did you stand on her foot purposefully?'

'Yes. What are you going to do about it?' she demanded hardily.

He grinned ruefully. 'You know perfectly well I'll do nothing. She deserved it, the complacent, carping bitch.'

She smiled and her eyes were the colour of the sea. A little pulse beat at the base of her throat. Then she moved and grimaced with the renewal of pain across her shoulders.

'Has he beaten you again?' His voice was suddenly hoarse with a rage he was unable to suppress. He surveyed the circle of wearily marching women with unseeing eyes.

'You did know, then. I wasn't sure.'

'Not at first and I do apologize for my disapproval. It was—

jealousy, I suppose. But no one could envy you such a privilege. Why do you always agree—'

'Because he would take my sister instead and I could not bear the thought.'

'She looks worried,' Carey said, his eyes seeking out Nan. Her short curls were bright as the sunlight but her eyes were enormous with apprehension and doubly beautiful. 'I'd better send you back.'

'Thank you for understanding.'

'I'd take the stripes on my own back if I could.'

'Oh, you mustn't become too involved! I am, after all, a condemned woman, and you deserve better.'

'I can never believe you did anything—' His voice had dropped.

'Oh, but I did,' she whispered. 'I really did.'

'Is there something wrong?' Captain Joel said suddenly. Neither had heard him approach nor knew how long he had stood there.

'She—attacked me,' the pig-eyed lady said in a high-pitched voice.

'Indeed?' The captain's eyes narrowed.

The lady told her exaggerated tale and Lieutenant Carey could hardly contain himself.

'I beg pardon,' he interposed, 'but I think the lady is mistaken. I am certain now that I've heard the prisoner's version that she did not see the rope and fell over it.'

'Perhaps I should interview the girl in my cabin. I'll soon get the truth from her.'

Carey turned white. 'Very well, sir.'

'See that the rest are taken down. At once. Then bring Benson to me.'

The captain turned away. Even Carey's lips were pale. 'If he hurts you—!'

'That's my business. I stepped out of line. In more ways than one!' She could not hold back the burst of laughter that was half hysteria.

The free ladies moved away, staring over their shoulders at the brazen huzzy who found rebellion amusing. Whispering and bridling, they went off to the comfort of their cabins.

Jade stood by the rail while Carey ordered the female convicts below, then rejoined her.

'I wish you did not need to suffer on that woman's account.'

'Perhaps he will do what you have done. Turn a blind eye.'

'He's a devil.'

'Does he listen to you or to any of the officers?'

Carey shook his head. Jade had forgotten how good-looking he was in such an endearing way. For the first time she regretted having lost her virginity. She could not pretend she hadn't found sexual experience exciting and rewarding, but there was an innocence about Lieutenant Carey that made her just a little sad. She wished that she had given her own purity to Gabriel Masson. Endlessly in her dreams she went to Gabriel with the one thing she could never give him in reality but he no longer wanted her. Always, he closed the door on her and left her standing in the street. Molly and Caspar waited in the chaise, two shadows in the dark.

They had reached Captain Joel's door. Carey knocked.

'Come in.'

'The prisoner, Jane Benson, sir.'

'Come in, both of you.'

The captain had his back to both of them. He seemed intent on something he could see through the porthole, though all three knew very well there was nothing but sky and water.

He swung round disconcertingly just as Jade and Carey looked at one another enquiringly, obviously disliking the suggestion of complicity.

'Lieutenant Carey, I believe I heard you say the following words to the prisoner. "I'd take the stripes on my own back if I could." To what stripes did you refer?'

Carey's face burned. He could not think of anything to say.

'He was being gallant,' Jade said. 'I complained that my back hurt and told him how it had come to be so painful. It was entirely my fault. What else could he say? I'd embarrassed him.'

'That's not true! I knew already –'

'Oh?' The captain's voice was silky. 'How? How did you know?'

'Whispers. Rumours –'

'Oh, come! You can do better than that, Carey.'

'Cabin walls are not so strong that things cannot be heard.'

'Two noble young people, both trying to take the blame,' Captain Joel said mockingly. 'Which do I believe?'

'I was the only one who could have told him,' Jane said tiredly. 'Those panelled walls are perfectly soundproof.'

'Only a beast would treat a woman in that fashion!' Carey burst out incautiously. 'I can't imagine what perverted pleasure you get out of it.'

Joel stood perfectly still. Everything about Joel could have been dead except for his eyes. Jade could not bear to look at them. But she understood. Joel had seen them talk together and had been jealous. So jealous that he had encouraged the lieutenant to the folly of speaking out of turn.

'You may go for the present,' the captain said at last. 'But I expect to see you here tomorrow at nine o'clock. I will deal with Benson as I think fit.'

'You'll not beat her again! I won't let you.' Carey, driven beyond endurance, lunged across the room and struck the captain a blow that made him reel back and strike his head on the edge of the porthole.

The first officer, who had been passing, stopped, hearing the sounds of the scuffle and the raised voices. He pushed open the door.

Collin had been aware of Jade from the beginning of the voyage. It was plain that had not Captain Joel expressed interest, Collin would have claimed her as his. His eyes flickered from her to the captain, then to Carey, then back to Jade. She could have sworn that the tableau amused him. She was conscious of a futile anger.

Collin did what was expedient.

'Carey! What do you think you're doing! For God's sake, man –'

Joel stood up, holding his jaw. Blood trickled from his temple. The sallow skin was dreadfully pale. 'Clap him in irons,' he said softly. 'Tomorrow, he'll wish he'd been more discreet. He'll stay chained until we reach Australia.'

'You can't,' Jade said. 'It was all my fault.'

'Oh, but I can.'

A second officer, summoned by a secretly smiling Collin, appeared. Carey, dumb and uncomprehending in his state of shock at the severity of his sentence, was led away without a struggle.

'How cruel you are. He had done nothing to harm you, except to repeat what someone else had told him. You made him do it.'

Joel hit her across the face. 'You shouldn't have looked at him as you did. As though you invited him to your bed.'

She shook her head. The burning pain in her cheek was accentuated. 'I didn't. Truly –'

'You don't know the meaning of truth. No woman does

You can go back to your sty and tomorrow Carey will begin his punishment. Now, get out for I'm sick of the sight of you. Bell? Bell! Take her below.'

'Captain Joel —'

But it was useless. Joel went into his sleeping-cabin and Bell, not too gently, returned her to the bulkheads. Her head swam unpleasantly from the captain's blow and the stench of the airless place. How would Carey endure all those months of silence?

Nan was nursing Daniel while Amy muttered, tossing and turning, her mattress wet with sweat. Jade wet a cloth and put it over the young woman's forehead. As she smoothed down the crumpled gown, she felt the unborn child move. But Daniel's mother was not fit to give birth. She ought to receive medicines, be put into a clean, airy room. If only Carey had not lost his temper, she might have pleaded with Joel. Made him listen —

Two women fought together in the darkest corner over a trifle that could not possibly matter, frightening the children, but the noise, for once, seemed preferable to silence.

Carey was forgotten. Amy had passed one more stage towards death. Her sunken eyes were wild with delirium and she could not stop talking, oh so quickly, of the past, as if she had only a short time to remember.

Jade saw Amy's father, gaitered and bewhiskered, her mother contained and secretive. 'But did you love me, Mother? Did you?' Amy was never to be sure.

She spoke of her husband so touchingly that Jade was torn with memories of Gabriel who had treated her, fleetingly, almost as a wife, pleasing her without any demands, though he had wanted her badly enough.

Amy, strangely, said nothing of Daniel who was with Nan when he could not be with Jade for whom he had the greater preference. But Nan was very good with the child and extremely patient as though she recalled the frustrations of her own life after the carriage struck her. Daniel kept her occupied when Jade was absent. They were good for one another.

Jade sat up with Amy that night, using precious water to damp the cloths for her head, or her cracked lips, listening to the story of Amy's past. It was astonishing how vital such a quiet, unassuming woman could be when she revealed her secret hopes and fears, her joys and grief, probably for the first time.

'Davey,' she said very strongly, just before dawn. 'Davey? Davey, love.' Her hand became limp and slid away from Jade's grasp. Her head turned on the mattress and did not move again.

Captain Joel would have to take notice of conditions below now, whether or not he wanted to. He was paid half of his convict dues on arrival at Port Jackson, and already several women had died. He'd not want to forfeit the second stage of payment altogether.

She tried not to think of Carey. The rats below —

Jade summoned the doctor as soon as she was able.

'She's dead, of course, the infant too.'

'I knew. And so will others be before long. We must have more help in the way of medical supplies, better quality food. They eat vastly differently above deck, as I've reason to know,' Jade said bitterly.

The doctor looked at her keenly. He must recognize her in the lamplight. Everyone had seen her on deck, knew how she had visited Captain Joel, and now displayed her deep feelings over the barbarity below.

'I'll speak to the captain.' The tanned face was pleasant and reasonable.

'Tell him I put you up to it. My name is – Benson.' For a second she had almost said Jade Benedict, not that it would have meant anything, except having to make unwelcome explanations. 'He had that young officer imprisoned indefinitely, you know, out of jealousy. He provoked him into that blow, which, you must admit, left little visible trace, for I looked.'

'No one may assault the captain,' the doctor pointed out drily.

'I suppose not. But only a few days in irons would have sufficed.'

'My dear girl, it's obvious you know nothing of regulations – '

'Regulations! You seem, Doctor – ?'

'Marsh.'

'Marsh. You seem to feel much as I do, even if you prefer not to say too much to a convict.'

'A strange convict! Though there are male prisoners of better quality who forged and embezzled. I've spoken to several and sad misfits they are in that den of thieves across the way. I confess I pitied them.'

'I did not forge or embezzle.'

'I'm not your judge, young woman. I was surprised to find someone like you in such desperate straits, that was all.' He looked kind and a little sad as though her situation troubled him. 'Surprised and sorry.'

'Perhaps you should not allow Captain Joel to perceive such sympathy,' she answered. 'He's done enough to show me, at least, that it's not healthy. I'm glad that I have friends where I'd not suspected it, though. Couldn't you steal the keys to the dispensary, or must you ask him for everything?'

'Like everyone else, I must apply to Joel.'

'Perhaps if you stressed the danger of – plague?'

'My dear, we are far from those conditions!'

'How will he know?'

He smiled suddenly and looked much younger. 'You're a persuasive lass, I'll say that for you. Now,' he turned back to Amy, 'what's to become of the little boy? It was a boy she had?'

'I want to care for him,' Jade said quickly, before he had some other idea. 'And my sister has been happier since she's helped me with Daniel. Sometimes, as you must know, I am called elsewhere.'

Dr Marsh frowned. 'I have never been ship's surgeon before, and, believe me, I think I never will again. A country practice will suit me better than this hell-hole. You know how to care for the child?' His tone suggested that the little boy was unlikely to reach Australia alive, but Jade was determined he would.

'We've managed perfectly well for several days but all the children would do better with more time on deck.'

'You all would.'

'Please, Doctor Marsh,' Jade was impelled to ask, 'do all you can for Lieutenant Carey. He must be suffering dreadfully. I feel so – responsible.'

'I intend to, if I am allowed –'

'I hope you will be.'

'I'd best see what else is wrong down here. Present a stronger case. But ever since we set sail, it's been discouraging to be so fobbed off. I'd willingly break open the medicine cabinet except that I'm too much of a coward to pay the penalty. Does that lower me in your estimation?'

'No. Not now that I have seen –' Her eyes were flooded briefly with hot tears but she dashed them away fiercely.

Another woman nearby rambled in fever and the doctor

went to attend her. Amy, wrapped in her blanket, was taken away and the bunk washed with carbolic, then the gangway subjected to the ministrations of a white-washing with quick-lime. More tar-oil was burned on Dr Marsh's instructions.

Jade sat with Nan and the sleepy Daniel who curled against her breast like a puppy. She stroked his curly head, let her fingers trace the warm outline of his bunched fists, the little rounds of his knuckles. A slight comfort returned. Perhaps Joel only spoke of Carey being submitted to further punishment to keep her amenable to his sporadic need for sadism.

All day she expected the captain to send for her but he did not. Another of his unpleasant revenges, she thought, to have her avid to say something, then to deny her the opportunity.

She fed the baby soup that seemed better than usual. Either she or the doctor must have touched some weakness, or perhaps Joel had done a few calculations about the number of transportees he might have left to hand over. At half-rate the voyage would be a disaster. A reasonably healthy woman, she was told, would fetch around nine pounds and a man between ten and fifteen, more if he had some proper trade like joinering or building or with a working knowledge of farming.

The free settlers would be getting restive, too, about the increasing mortality rate, imagining the fever spreading to themselves. Someone he could ill afford to displease might complain about the treatment meted out to Lieutenant Carey. She did not even know the boy's Christian name. He looked so young –

Jade slept fitfully, Daniel beside her, the green pelisse covering them both. Gabriel would no longer recognize it. I love you, she thought, in spite of what you did. I do love you – Gabriel.

She took the baby with her for exercise next day. It hurt to see the wonder in his brown eyes when he saw the sky filled with scudding clouds, the soaring masts and the great billowing sails. He found the water even more remarkable, holding out his hands towards it and chattering excitedly. Even the free ladies were captivated by him though they looked no more kindly on Jade who they obviously blamed for Carey's punishment.

Joel came as he always did when the female prisoners were on deck. Jade realized that this was intentional, that it was his way of feeding on his perversion. He stood like a bird of prey, hating all of them.

The more obvious whores eyed any male on duty, sending signals behind the captain's back. Jade had to admit that she felt some of Joel's revulsion but she was a little afraid when he stopped in front of her, staring palely at the child in her arms.

'Go on, the rest of you! Now, what's this?' The small wound on his temple showed red in the wind that crept inside all their clothes, shaking the boat's timbers, and filling the vessel with creaks and groans.

'His mother died yesterday. Someone must care for him.'

'Is there no mother with other children? Someone more fitted – '

'I want to look after Daniel myself. I've been doing it for nearly ten days now. He seems to take to me.'

'I think you are too young.' The proud, narrow face was determined.

'I'm not too young for other things!' she whispered violently, knowing what he meant to do. 'Why is this so difficult?'

'I will make other arrangements,' he said inexorably.

'But he won't interfere in anything!' she rushed on, desperately. 'Nan is very good with him. Between us we can do everything that's necessary.'

The black eyes were suddenly alive with purpose. 'Please do not argue. You've become arrogant, Miss Benson. The time has come to change that.'

'I beg you,' she insisted softly. 'Don't do anything too precipitate. Please?'

He walked on, his elegant hands clasped behind his back, his pale profile remote. It was another way of frightening her. Of course it was!

But a sickness settled over her spirits. She joined the perambulation but the deck had begun to tilt and sway and it was difficult to keep her feet.

Collin came to order the prisoners below. Jade felt his assessing eyes upon her. The settlers' wives had returned to their cabins. The green waves were frighteningly high and a great many sailors were up in the shrouds or lashing objects to the deck and rails. It would be an uncomfortable evening and a worse night. She was dizzy just looking at the clouds.

Conditions in the bulkheads were unpleasant and even the worst offenders had stopped squabbling and gave up their energies to cursing the elements instead of the magistrates who condemned them and the captain who did nothing to make their lot any easier.

The day passed uneasily, the food slopped on bunk and floor, the children requiring pacification, women thrown, occasionally, to the dirty boards as the *Caroline* ploughed her storm-ridden way across the sea. Almost everyone was sick, including Nan, and little Daniel was the only bright spark as he refused to bow to the effects of wind and weather, remaining excited by the sounds of the storm and the pitch and roll of the vessel.

Jade could hardly believe it when Bell unlocked the door and called out, 'Benson!' She put Daniel into Nan's arms, the girl having recovered, and went towards him, pulling the pelisse around her to combat the fury of the wind that blew through the tainted confines of the hold. The sounds of frightened sheep and goats were cast below. Overhead, there were thumps and crashes galore as objects were riven from moorings. She clung to the ladder, her fingers almost torn away from the greasy props, gasping as the full force of the gale struck her.

Shuddering and wet from the heavy spray, she reached Captain Joel's cabin, hurried by Bell through the half-open door. Everything in the beautiful place rattled. The door closed behind her but Joel was nowhere to be seen.

Chilled, Jade went to the swinging lantern that had replaced the usual lamp. The rocketing glow spilled over dark beams and hurried across the smooth, dark red walls of polished wood. The silver shifted, clinking like bells. A glass was overturned, rolling against the raised edge of the table. Mechanically, she stood it up but it overturned almost immediately so she left it where it was.

The captain came out of the bed-cabin and motioned her to sit at the table. He was wearing a clean shirt and had obviously just finished shaving. It seemed incredible that he had only cut himself once, the result a small nick on his throat.

She could not keep her eyes from the red blemish. Equally incredible was the fact that he intended to dine as though nothing were amiss. All the urgent matters she was longing to introduce must wait until they had partaken of the farcical meal. She knew the rules well enough by this time.

Silently, she sat down, her eyes downcast, aware of him and

of each careful movement. She itched for him to spring to his feet, to throw something in a fit of passion, but the only excitation of feeling he ever showed was when she was in the next cabin and he had drunk sufficient to arouse both hatred and desire.

The soup was spilt before it reached the table, Bell retreating impassively before the naked hostility in Joel's regard. The captain fastidiously placed a napkin over the dark spots on the cloth. Jade could not touch hers, only turning it over with the spoon so that the captain began to drum his fingertips on the moving table top. The decanter, with its broad, heavy base, did not shift at all. She was glad of the wine.

The food was not to the captain's liking and he pointed this out chillingly.

'It's the weather, sir,' Bell said stolidly. 'Makes things difficult.'

Both drank more than they ate. Joel finally lit his cigar but the smoke turned Jade's stomach. She was glad when he stubbed the cigar out on the silver salver.

'Daniel,' she said. 'You will allow me to have the child? It means a great deal to me. I would do anything to keep him.' She should not have admitted that!

He watched her broodingly, his fingertips touching under his chin. 'As you would have done anything to prevent Lieutenant Carey's punishment?'

'Yes. Not because I had any designs on him. I felt – feel only friendship. How is he?'

Joel shrugged. 'I have not seen him.'

'You didn't mean that he must stay there until we reach Australia? He'll go mad.'

'I must treat a rebellious officer as I would a mutinous convict. It is a serious matter for an officer to strike his captain.'

'Then – the lieutenant – ?'

'I'm afraid so. Now you will make some wild outburst about hating me. No? Oh, of course, you wouldn't want me to refuse your request for that felon's child. A thief's brat, but you would saddle yourself with him as you have that mindless girl.'

Jade bit back the words that clamoured to be spoken. Nan was safe so long as Joel believed her incapable of thought.

'May I ask how she can be competent to look after the boy if she is as soft-brained as you'd have me believe?' How gentle his voice was and how merciless. Their eyes locked. In spite of herself, Jade flushed.

'She – she has a natural aptitude. He'd be quite safe. I've left him with her many times and she has an instinct to do what's best for him.'

'Either the girl is perfectly sensible, in which case I could not reasonably object to your joint charge of the Grey child, or she is feeble-minded and I must put him in another's care. Take your choice, my dear.'

The cabin tilted, sending the lantern light across the long, cruel face. Shadows followed it, blotting out all but the black gaze.

'No answer, Miss Benson? I confess it's the first time you've had nothing to say.' The golden glow rushed back, showing her his thin smile.

A terrible anger possessed her. He had made it impossible for her to keep them both. She wanted to rush at him, hurt him, hear him plead for mercy. She caught sight of the silver knives but they'd be too blunt. But there was always the knife Dick gave her in Newgate. She could pretend to fiddle with the hem of her petticoat, extract the knife and frighten him into making some promise that would satisfy her.

It was hopeless. As soon as her back was turned she'd be put into one of the isolation cells in the bulkhead and Nan would be the recipient of the captain's attentions. And Daniel? He'd rather throw the child overboard than see that he was cared for. Few of the women would welcome the responsibility. They all had problems enough.

There was a knock at the door.

'Who is it?'

'Collin, sir. You should come up. The wind's worsening and some of the sails dragging. I'm worried for the mizzen mast.' The man's eyes were on Jade.

'I'd better come. Give me five minutes.'

She heard Collin clatter away. The empty dishes shifted and a glass fell to the floor. Her green eyes were dark and hard as stones. He could not fail to see her detestation.

'A pity I must go.'

'Is it?' As soon as she had spoken, in a deliberately insulting fashion, she knew it was a mistake. His face warned her what she must expect. Fear made her move. She was half-way to the door when she heard the scrape of his chair, the crash as it overturned.

Outside, in the passage leading to the deck, the wind seized her like an enemy, buffeting and snarling, punching her in the back. There had been no time to put on her pelisse and the cold cut through to her bones.

She could not decide which way to go to escape his anger. Voices to the left deterred her. None too fast, she half-ran, half-beat her way towards the open air, the captain staggering after her.

She slipped on the deck, over which the sea had poured, leaving it shining wetly. Jade found herself flung hard against the sheep-pen, just making out the sodden lumps of greyness that huddled miserably in the confined space. Some tarpaulin had been lashed over the seaboard side of the pen, sheltering the beasts to some extent, but they bleated desolately at every change in the ship's progress.

Clinging to one of the rails, she felt under the gown for the pocket where her knife was, touching the jade charm briefly. Turning her head she had a swift glimpse of the sea, white and boiling, not far below.

She must have let out a cry for she made out the wavering darkness of Joel's silhouette coming towards her. Somewhere close by she heard Collin's voice. 'The rope, you fool. See to that rope!'

Lights swung, casting thin waves of illumination that showed her drenched shrouds, distant figures that clutched at anything that provided a hold, snatches of pale faces and soaked hair, straggling ropes and torn sail.

The captain lurched, grabbed at her tangled hair, dragged her to her feet. He struck out at her brutally so that, for a moment, she hung across the edge of the ship's side, pain gathering across her back where her body hit the wood and brass. The spray leapt up like a living thing, pouring over her head and shoulders, streaming through her gown. She shuddered violently and was flung forward again with the roll of the vessel.

Her outstretched hand struck the captain of its own accord and she was aware of his body falling towards her, now queerly joined to hers as if they were one person. She fought against the dead weight, pushing at him frantically, surprised that he suddenly fell away as though released from some bond.

The swinging lamplight bathed him transiently and showed her the sheep cowering in the pen from which sea water was swilled to flood the deck anew.

There was a dark patch on the captain's shirt-front, a widening redness from which protruded the haft of her knife. She had not consciously struck him. He had been thrust on to it, she told herself, over and over again, before her thoughts were drowned in the shriek of the gale and the creaking and flapping of wood and sail.

Again, Jade was impelled forward to clutch out at the sheep-pen. The loud bleating was accentuated. A man came out of nowhere and for a long, dreadful moment she thought it was Collin. But it was Dr Marsh. She wanted to cry with relief as he stared down at the obviously dead man.

'It was an accident. He struck me. I ran. I took this up to protect myself, and the ship rolled and cast him towards me and on to the blade.'

Marsh bent down and picked up the body after throwing the knife on to the deck. Lifting Joel, he heaved him over the side. 'As you say, the captain was washed overboard. Take that knife and clean it. Something tells me you may have further use for it. Now, for God's sake, go back to his cabin and say you were told to wait for him. Tidy your hair and put on something dry. I'll come down when I can, supposedly to look for him.'

He was gone before she could say a word.

In the sanctuary of the captain's cabin, she tried to push away the thought of the events of the past hour, busying herself with the tasks set her by the doctor. She wiped the knife and concealed it, then cleaned the bloodstain from the wet gown and hung it over a chair near the stove that Joel always had lit in his cabin. As the steam rose from the wet material, she dried her soaked hair and attended to it with the silver-backed brush on the top of the set of drawers by the porthole. The contact with the brush revolted her but it must be endured. At any time, someone could return and realize perfectly well that she had been on deck.

A good deal of muffled shouting penetrated the confines of the cabin but no words emerged from the confusion of sound. She shivered inside the green pelisse, unable to forget the moment when the captain's body had turned still and heavy against her. But she was not a murderess. She had intended only to protect herself. Not that she wasn't glad he was dead! Holding out her fingers to the heat of the stove, she discovered that her hands were shaking.

The gown dried quickly and she put it on in a fever of haste, having discovered that there was blood on her shift. There was no time to wash it out now, for fear of discovery. Even if she had to cut herself later to account for it, it would be worth the resulting pain.

How unexpected the doctor's actions had been! She had not imagined him so decisive. For the hundredth time she wondered why he had concealed her complicity in Joel's death. Because he was good and kind? Yet, he'd admitted to a tendency to cowardice, to seeking the way that was easiest. Or was it because he wanted something from her? She'd seen enough of men to have become cynical.

The door opened suddenly and Collin was in the gap. Her stomach muscles tightened. She had never really liked the first officer with his florid good looks and assessing eyes, and, with Joel gone, he would be in charge of the *Caroline*.

She must keep her head. Jade yawned convincingly and stretched. A glance at the clock and she pretended surprise. 'Is it that time already? Captain Joel said he'd be back soon.'

A glass clinked against a fork but the vessel seemed not to pitch so much.

Collin said nothing but his eyes spoke volumes.

'Is the storm abating?' she asked quite steadily, aware of his gaze travelling over the gown, lingering on her shining hair.

'Aye. It is. When did you last see the captain?'

'Oh – soon after you told him his presence was required.' She shrugged.

It occurred to her that she might have expected Collin to return much earlier. As if he read her thoughts, Collin said, 'It seems Doctor Marsh was right. I was on my way a second time and met him in a state of agitation. He'd seen the captain by the sheep-pen. The lantern light had swung over him and he was in no doubt that it was Joel. He lost sight of him for a minute as the lantern swung in the opposite direction, and when it returned, the light showed him a figure sprawled over the ship's side, then it vanished. He says he came to the cabin to find out if Joel was here.'

'Yes, he did, and I said the captain had been gone only five minutes. It never struck me that there was cause for concern. There was so much coming and going and the storm was so fierce I never thought of so terrible an accident –'

'Doctor Marsh voiced no fears?'

'I do remember I thought him anxious but I put it down to the weather conditions.'

'I fear Joel's overboard, then.'

'Oh, God. I never thought.' Reaction came and Jade could feel the colour recede from her face. She was sick and dizzy, stumbling towards the chair. Collin caught her just in time. Jade was aware of being lifted up against him, of the smell of sweat and sea water, the feel of warm flesh.

'I – I should go back,' she whispered. 'Back to – my sister.'

'I can spare no one to escort you at present,' Collin said softly. 'There's too much to do. You'd better have the captain's bed. After all, you've shared it for long enough, haven't you! Why change matters now?'

He kicked open the cabin door and put her down on the bunk. Her senses swam. Dimly, she heard Collin go away. She remembered nothing more.

She awoke to strong sunlight streaming in through the porthole and a sensation of foreboding that sent her spirits plummeting. At first she could not imagine where she was, then the whiteness of the pillow reminded her of the captain's fastidiousness and his cruelty. His death.

The *Caroline* still bucked like a nervous colt but there was none of the terror of last night and the sky was blue beyond the round of glass. Dr Marsh was in the cabin, hurrying forward as she struggled to sit. Still she could not believe that the kind, undistinguished face could hide such resolution.

'You saved my life,' she told him, then realized that the sheet had fallen away from her and that the shift had been removed. Quickly, she covered her nakedness. The blood was all she could think of, the blood on the white bodice. Collin must have seen it.

'What's wrong?' Marsh asked solicitously.

'My shift – '

'I took it. Collin told me he could not rouse you and feared you were ill of the fever that attacked Mrs Grey and the others. I took off your gown to examine you the better and saw – well, you know what I discovered. I washed the garment myself and will fetch it soon.'

'You don't think – ?'

'Collin has said nothing. I think our secret is safe.'

'And Nan and little Daniel? Lieutenant Carey?'

'I explained to your sister and I think she understands. The baby is well.'

'And Carey?'

'Desperately depressed,' Marsh told her.

'I feel well enough to go back. I must.'

'Captain Collin insists that you remain. You have had a

great shock.' The doctor's voice was carefully unemotional. He looked anywhere but at Jade.

'You are good,' she said. 'Always, when I think all men are cruel and predatory, I find one who reminds me that it's not so.'

'You exaggerate.'

'No. It will be easier now for you to obtain what you need from the dispensary. I think Collin will be glad for you to treat us all well so that he'll get the benefit of all those second-stage payments.'

'I expect so. Now cover yourself up and go back to sleep.'

'I still – worry. Mainly for you.'

'Don't. The story's accepted. If there was any blood on the deck, the sea washed it away. And sheep are not good witnesses.'

She could not hold back a smile.

'Were the animals all safe?'

'A few fatalities, alas, but we must look on the bright side. There will be meat in plenty for a week or two. Enough to bolster up the prisoners' soup and make nourishing stew. Things will be better now, you'll see.'

But she could not rest after he had gone. Over and over, she relived the captain's death, thinking of what might have happened to her had it been Collin or one of the other officers who came as she stared, horror-stricken, at Joel's body.

Slowly, she understood that the danger was past. She'd be haunted, many a time, but no one was going to denounce her, or Dr Marsh.

She was sitting up in the shift which was clean, dry and returned by the doctor, together with a bitter-tasting potion that eased her mind miraculously, when Collin came in, flinging off his coat and boots as though he were there to stay. His eyes were experienced. He looked pleased with himself.

It would have been better if she hadn't been in bed, but what difference did it make? She'd have been back there in no time at all. Collin was Master now and only what was good enough for Joel would be good enough for him.

'You look better,' Collin said, unbuttoning his shirt and putting off the tied wig. His hair was short and wiry but his head was well shaped. In spite of the dissolute expression and pouched eyes, she could not say that his looks repelled her. It was his calm assumption that she was a chattel to be purloined, used when he wished, without a by-your-leave.

'I am better.' She'd not demean herself by pretending continued illness. That would only put off, temporarily, the inevitable.

'Well enough, I hope, to accommodate me?'

'If that is what you wish.'

'It is.'

'The king is dead. Long live the king,' she murmured.

'You're a surprising wench. Such delicate irony –'

'And from a convict, too,' she mocked. 'We were not all born in the stews.'

'Do not be presumptuous.'

'I'm sorry,' she said though it was a lie. She had remembered Nan and the baby, young Carey. What happened to them could depend on her and she couldn't fail them.

'Get out of bed,' he said a little hoarsely and let his shirt fall to the floor. Jade recalled the fact that Captain Joel had put on an immaculate shirt and shaved himself before dying so unexpectedly. But she fancied it would be the way he'd want to go out of one life and into another. The only flaw had been the nick on his throat –

Her bare feet touched the polished boards. Collin's eyes drank in the shape of her body under the revealing undergarments, the tress of hair that hung over one breast.

'Come here.'

She went to him, suffering his hot touch on her skin as he drew off the clothes, one by one, until they lay at her feet.

'I always wanted you.'

'Did you?' She tried to look pleased, as though the remark surprised her.

He pulled her towards him, his mouth on her lips, her throat, the points of her breasts. His fingertips roused little frissons of pleasure against her back and hips. Jade made herself remain perfectly still.

'You're a cold creature,' Collin said, disappointed. 'A wonder Joel was so faithful.'

'I could lie and suffer you,' Jade said quietly. 'But that would give satisfaction to neither of us.'

'What, then? I sense a bargain.'

'I promise to be all you could want –'

'If?' His hands had strayed below and she knew she could not keep up the pretence of remaining unmoved for much longer.

'Don't give my sister Nan to one of your officers. I beg you.'

'It may not be easy –'

'You are captain now, and she's only a child in mind.'

'Pretty, though –'

'But not a *woman*! Would you force a little girl?'

'No –'

'That's what it would be.'

'Very well.'

'And I want the dead woman's baby. Amy Grey's child. He has no one but Nan and me.'

'If that's what you want. Why should I object? What's an extra child?'

'And Lieutenant Carey?'

'What of him?' The probing fingers were stilled.

'It was because Joel was jealous of him that he was in trouble. The captain fancied I looked on him with more than friendship. But I had only spoken to him twice. It was all so innocent. The captain was a very sadistic man, not like you. The wave that claimed him was perhaps the best thing that happened on the *Caroline*. You must know he was not normal. Don't punish Carey any more. I know that he was provoked beyond endurance. You, I know, will be fairer.' God help her for a sanctimonious hypocrite!

'I can't promise –'

'Oh, but you can! You must.' She put her arms around him and thought desperately of Gabriel Masson, but none of that disembodied magic was evoked. Nothing could be the same as those days in his house.

'Let me think. While we are abed together.'

She would make him agree. Nick had taught her too well how to enslave a man. Before she was a week older, she would have better food for the prisoners, a crèche on deck for the children, Carey in the charge of Dr Marsh, the key to the dispensary. There was nothing that could not be improved. It was only until Australia was reached, after all.

Jade was dimly aware of being carried to the bed. Collin, for all his pretentious arrogance, was preferable to what she had so far endured aboard the transport ship. Anything was better than Captain Joel.

She allowed her body to relax. Collin was an adequate lover. It was not too difficult to simulate passion. But he was not Masson. However hard she pretended, that shatter of rainbow fire eluded her. There was comfort of a sort, a kind of fulfilment, only it was a cheap, tawdry thing compared with Gabriel's love. A love she had deliberately thrown away.

CHAPTER SEVEN

Collin became increasingly amenable to the changes Jade had envisaged. Her first request, that Nan be found some work above deck involving children, had, after initial problems, been granted. No one could take exception to the girl who was clean, quiet and attractive to the sons and daughters of the settlers as well as to those of the convicts. Nan was accepted.

The new captain had, by dint of reorganization, cleared a small cabin of lumber and installed the Benson sisters and Amy Grey's boy. Needless to say, the free ladies were not so kind about Jade, considering it quite disgraceful that she had gone straight from Captain Joel's bed to that of his successor. Captain Joel had been such a gentleman, so distinguished and reserved. There had been that unpleasantness about Lieutenant Carey but that minx had been at the bottom of it with her deceptively innocent looks and beguiling smile. The smile was more in evidence now that Collin was so indulgent. A pity he had not a wife aboard to keep him in order. It was no great punishment for a convicted woman to wine and dine with the ship's captain every evening and to escape the hold that should have been her lot. Botany Bay would rectify that.

It was since her reign that the women prisoners had spent far more time on deck and she herself could be seen with the children, telling them stories and playing games with them while her poor, inarticulate sister saw that none fell overboard. But their own children enjoyed the extravagant tales, too, and would hover around the area set aside for the pursuit, wide-eyed and enthralled. No one could deny that the *Caroline* was a happier ship under the change of command.

For all that she had only the green gown and pelisse, Jane Benson was a remarkably personable girl. But it was rather shocking, the ladies whispered among themselves, that because she allowed Collin the freedom of her body, she was almost as free as themselves. Nevertheless, all that would change once the voyage was over. Miss Benson would become a transportee again and sold to some farmer who needed a strong woman who would work eighteen hours out of the twenty-four. That would keep her in her place! Why, she had even stood up for some whores who had used foul language and were put in irons and gagged. She was reputed to have asked Captain Collin what *he* would have said if he'd been shut up in that cesspit below. Mrs Elizabeth Fry would have had plenty to say if she were aboard, she'd told him.

Everyone knew of the Quaker lady who found English prisons so abhorrent, but the free ladies disapproved of anyone who neglected her own children in order to improve the lot of bawds and thieves and who allowed her relatives to take charge of the older ones as Mrs Fry did.

Jade, overhearing some of these acid conversations, longed to cry out, 'Elizabeth Fry is worth a thousand of you! Her children are with uncles and aunts because her husband's business failed and they have not the money to give their large brood the good life they wished. The relatives have taken them out of love and necessity. Mrs Fry is a saint who will be remembered long after your bigoted tongues are silenced.'

But she said nothing. It was not her place and she'd not embarrass Collin who responded very adequately to her own reform measures. They had achieved a comfortable relationship, could talk to one another without reserve. He had not made her forget Masson but she knew now that no man would ever do that. That knowledge was the only thing that depressed her. Masson was so far out of reach.

Dr Marsh had wrought wonders. The transportees had fought off the spread of fever now that he was allowed to treat them properly. Great endeavours had reduced the numbers of rats, cockroaches and bugs, but nothing would do away with the acrid smell of stale bilge water and the stink of unwashed humanity. Even those prisoners who could have washing facilities did not always make use of them.

There was no doubt now that Jade was queen of the vessel. Collin, though an excellent sailor and not soft with his officers, denied her nothing. The cabin was attractively furnished and Nan and the child had appetizing meals served there.

Whatever she suggested, Collin acceded to. Indeed, she often thought she overstepped the boundary of caution in her quest for change aboard the *Caroline*.

Wrapped in her pelisse, she would walk in whichever part of the ship pleased her, knowing that Collin would never gainsay her. Her new-found arrogance made her bitter enemies among the women settlers to whose most spiteful remarks she was by now quite impervious.

It pleased her to note the frowns and pursed lips, the whisking away of the rather dull skirts. Why was it necessary to dress up supposed goodness in drabness?

It occurred to Jade during these provocative peregrinations that she was flying in the face of providence, but it was so amusing. She could not help herself and Collin was putty in her hands. She had never known such a sense of power, though, she had to admit, it did sometimes pall.

A year ago she had been so young and untouched. She had known nothing of physical relations. Now she knew almost too much, was a little afraid of having changed so radically. Was she corrupt? She fancied she was and yet she had never wanted anything for herself except the freedom to breathe God's air wherever it suited her most. If she were truly degenerate she'd ask for money or trinkets. She'd be another Phoebe Lewis. That was the one thought that kept her within the bounds of convention.

The arrival at Tenerife was thrilling. The sight of land, and such beautiful land, was the greatest pleasure. It was hot and the mountains shimmered bluely. The dominating peak, Collin told Jade, was Pico de Tiede. She had never seen anything like it. There were no peaks around Ayas Bywaters or London. The steep blueness enthralled her and the waterside was so colourful with a brilliance of flowers, small boats and a coming and going of donkeys and carts. Spanish-sounding music floated across the water and the moon was huge and golden.

Collin was busy and Jade did not see much of him during the day but a good deal of new food came aboard, fowl and pumpkins, mulberries and figs, onions and other vegetables, as well as fresh water and fish.

Dinners became delicious banquets and Collin brought back rolls of material so that Jade and Nan and the baby could have new clothes. The only time Jade was disappointed was when Collin was invited to meet the Governor of the Canary Islands along with some of his officers. They had, he said next day, had sherbets made of ice brought down from caves in the mountains she so admired. He described the splendour of the occasion and she wished she could have been there but there was no way in which a convict could be admitted even if she were not condemned to remain aboard. Collin could not risk his captaincy by removing her from the vessel, much though he had wanted to.

When the *Caroline* sailed, Jade stared at the island and the tantalizing point of Pico de Tiede until her eyes were tired. She did not think she would ever see it again.

The only flaw in her present way of life, apart from the necessity of pleasing Collin, was the behaviour of Carey. She had been overjoyed when she saw him for the first time, though shocked by the change in his appearance. He looked older and very white and drawn. His back seemed bowed as though he expected that, at any time, more punishment would come down on his shoulders. Carey's manner was altogether stiff and unforthcoming, and it was not until she saw the look he gave Collin that she realized he had been told of her relationship with the new captain. He had forgiven her the sordid liaison with Joel but it seemed that the more normal but equally unavoidable one with Collin affronted him.

Jade tried to see the matter from his viewpoint. He had suffered on her behalf but it was because of Collin's weakness for her that Carey was to have no further imprisonment with the dark and the rats.

She was so upset by Lieutenant Carey's hostility that she was forced to protest. 'What say do I have over my own affairs? You know the procedure. The captain takes first choice of mistress, then all the rest of you according to your rank. If I had complained – and I could not – my sister would be forced to suffer. I might have been refused care of the baby. And you –'

He stared at her coldly. 'And me?'

For the first time she wondered if he had not blinded himself to the extent of his punishment. He had been ill and Joel might not have had time to remind him. She could not allow Carey to hate her needlessly.

'You were to be kept confined below until we docked. For months. In the dark.'

'Oh, Christ!' he whispered. 'Christ. Christ –'

'Didn't Collin tell you? And your imprisonment could have extended beyond the voyage.'

He shook his head violently and his face was grey.

'I asked Collin to rescind the order. I felt so strongly about the matter.'

His eyes flared open, no longer young and pleasant. 'In bed, I presume?'

'It doesn't matter where. You are not to be shut up again.'

Carey's mouth twisted. 'Sometimes I wish I had died.'

'Don't say that! I have just as much reason but I would never take such a viewpoint. I've been subjected to things you can't imagine. Now that sounds self-pitying and I'm ashamed of it, but, because of what I'm doing now, several persons lead happier lives, including yourself. You'll forget in time —'

'I loved you.'

'You'll love someone else.'

'Doctor Marsh thinks highly of you. Does he know — ?'

'About Collin? Oh, yes. I asked him to take good care of you, but he'd have done it anyway. The doctor knows a great deal about me. Fortunately, he does not censure me.'

'I'm tired,' Carey said in a low voice. 'Excuse me.'

After he had gone Jade could not rid herself of the hard lump of misery in her throat. Not even the soft folds of the new, pretty gown and Daniel's delightful chuckling could compensate for the lieutenant's unhappiness. She wondered if she should have remained silent about her part in frustrating Joel's cruel intentions. Resolutely, she put the thought from her mind and took Daniel to see the animals in their pens. Nan always enjoyed watching the sheep and the goats, the squawking hens. She often enticed the ship's cats into the cabin to stroke and pet them. Jade had never decided whether Nan's rape by Nick and the Newgate turnkey had been forgotten. The girl must think of it sometimes, but she had not allowed the bestiality to colour her life. She remained sweet, gentle, endlessly caring. What if they were separated as soon as the arrival at Port Jackson? Surely they allowed family units to remain together? Jade vowed she would see that they did, even if she had to say Daniel was her own son. Who would know or care?

Jade tried to speak to Collin about what would happen when they reached Australia but he would not be drawn, only plied her with wine, took off her new gown and underwear and carried her to bed. He had grown as skilful as Nick Caspar but though she enjoyed the bedding with an appreciative and lusty man who could contrive to hold her at just the right pitch of excitement until they both reaped the reward of their intercourse, he was not Gabriel. Often, after Collin had fallen asleep, usually sprawled across her, for the bunk, though wide, did not allow them to lie side by side, she would summon up Masson's face out of the dark. It was astonishing how clearly she saw him. She had forgotten not one feature or any line of his body. If she had the materials, she knew she could paint his likeness. She had been a more than adequate painter at Ayas Bywaters.

They reached Rio and the long, looming mass of the great continent behind the high, rounded peaks made her strangely insecure. It was another step on her journey to servitude. She was not naïve enough to imagine that her unknown future was to be a bed of roses. There would be thorns in plenty, work and heartache. Her bones hurt with foreknowledge.

Again there was the loading of fresh merchandise, medicines for the depleted dispensary, much-needed water. More material from Collin for clothing and sidelong looks from the respectable women who appeared to envy her in spite of the irregularity of her position. Perhaps the security of husband and children were not always enough to make for real happiness.

The few times she set eyes on Carey, he was studiously unaware, looking in another direction or going to another part of the ship. She tried to make allowances for him, the fact that he'd been disgraced and degraded, abominably treated. But the obvious ostracism hurt her far more than she would show. He was right of course to ignore a girl he had loved and who had slept with both masters of this vessel. Romantic love did not marry easily with physical relations. Carey would have been happy seated at candlelight dinners, a rose in a glass, the candles burning between them. Jade in an off-the-shoulder gown and her hair dressed in ringlets. He might have held her hand, brushed her lips with his, but his body was unawakened – he'd have had a mistress otherwise – and he'd never understand that it was not so terrible to exchange chastity for things like happiness for people one loved. She had not left him out of her bargain with Collin. But all her reasoning did not alter the fact that she ached for his patent misery and wished that matters had been different, that he might have respected her.

Sometimes Collin had a few of his officers in his cabin for a card game and rum-drinking and Jade would be expected to take especial pains with her appearance, to help serve the refreshments, encourage the captain when he showed signs of losing. Carey never came and she wondered if he were ever invited.

The next real excitement was some very bad weather when a man fell from the topsail yard and drowned and another was swept from the deck. Her eyes had met Dr Marsh's at the news and the hint of complicity reminded her that where Carey had rejected even her friendship, the doctor welcomed it.

The first sight of South Africa made her heart beat faster. Table Bay was incredible and Table Mountain a golden-curtained mirage. There was a great busyness on board, cannon shifted to make room for prospective purchases, and some of the women transferred to accommodate sheep to add to those on the deck, which had been depleted in the storms in which Joel had vanished. Boars and sows were added to the menagerie, horses and two bulls which must give the crew a severe headache for they were anything but gentle.

More attractive supplies were the trees that would be planted on arrival to enhance the streets of Sydney, the baskets of quinces, oranges, lemons, pears, apples and bananas, figs and all kinds of grains. There were oaks and sweet-smelling myrtle. The colours of the fruits dazzled her and she could not wait to feed an apple and a banana to Daniel who had never tasted such delights.

As they drew away from Africa Jade realized that the next step would be the last. No more *Caroline*, no more Collin. He was not to remain like some of the others who were promised land for their services on the transport. As if he meant to have as much of her as he could, he would appear unexpectedly during the day and shut himself and her in his cabin where he would undress her rapidly in case he were disturbed and could not spend the usual time to rouse her. But his energetic plungings rarely failed to satisfy her. She had been made to give and receive pleasure from men's bodies. Was it so shameful? It seemed worse to back-bite and criticize, Jade thought, as she rose after he had gone. Making other people unhappy was a worse sin. Flushed and languorous she would face the battery of condemning eyes, tell her interminable stories, all about lost princesses, but with happy endings she could not envisage for herself.

Of Australia, she made herself think as little as possible.

They saw Tasmania first. Jade was gripped with a spasm of fear that she thrust away before Nan or Daniel sensed it. Ten more days and they would be set ashore in a hostile country. She fingered the little green charm around her neck. It'll be all right, she told herself. I *will* make it all right. I will –

'Damned if I won't be sorry to part with you,' Collin said

gruffly at dinner.

She stared at the silky red wood of the walls and ceiling as though to imprint them on her mind's eye. The ship's decanter glittered and the crystal broke up into rainbow fragments that reminded her of times with Masson. So long as she had been on the *Caroline* there was always the thought that the vessel might turn and go back. But no such miracle would take place. Masson was gone most irrevocably. The dormant pain became alive.

'You look sorry, too,' Collin persisted, perplexed by her silence. She had seemed happy after Joel disappeared but he had no illusions about her loving him. The minx had wheedled a great many privileges out of him, but not one on her own account. He had, of course, given her presents but she had never asked for those. She really was the oddest and most fascinating creature. He toyed, briefly, with the notion of applying for land in New South Wales though this had not been his original intention. He had a wife and children in Greenwich and a home in the Surrey countryside he'd not relinquish easily. It was only because Grace was pregnant that he'd not had her on board. He expected a letter at Port Jackson, telling him if the child was a boy or a girl.

That charm Jane had taken to wearing around her neck now that she was no longer confined below was quite valuable. He reached across the table and touched the carved stone. 'You never told me how you came by this,' he said, noting how, in the candle-light, her eyes were the same, subtle green. 'And how you kept it in Newgate, I'll never understand.'

'If I want something badly enough, I fight to keep it.' Her mouth was defiant, and, he'd swear, a little afraid.

'It worries you, doesn't it? Port Jackson. Parramatta. The place is much better run than when it all began in 1787. You would have been right to feel apprehensive. Teething troubles are always overcome.'

'It's been so long since we left London – '

'A question of avoiding the frequent becalming on the African side. To get the benefit of the winds it's always been the Canaries and Rio de Janeiro, then the run for the Cape.'

'It seems a lifetime.'

'But it's not all been so bad, has it?' he teased, his fingers stroking the warm firm skin below the trinket on her neck. 'Have I ill-treated you?'

'No,' she admitted, though he noticed that she did not

214

respond to the touch.

'Tell me what you fear,' he suggested, wanting to woo her into a better frame of mind before bed.

'Separation from Nan and the boy. I've tried to say this many times of late but you always fob me off. It matters to me.'

'I'll have little say once you put foot ashore. I must hand over the official records and whichever officer meets the vessel takes charge.'

'If you set down in black and white that Daniel was my child. That Amy Grey's died with her, no one would argue or care very much. Would they? They'd not separate us then.'

'Why you should want to hang a mill-stone round your neck –'

Her eyes flared, magnificently angry. 'Would you, if you had a child, call it that?'

Collin shrugged. He was not excessively paternal but, so far, his offspring were girls. He'd welcome the news that this latest arrival was a boy. 'I would not. I meant only that you'll have problems enough without the responsibility.'

'I'm not afraid of responsibility.'

'But I should warn you that it does not follow that sisters would automatically,' Collin pointed out, admiring her spirit, 'be taken into the same household.'

'I will worry about that when the time comes. And you will indicate that Daniel is my baby? It would make things much simpler.'

'You're a young witch,' Collin said huskily and ruffled his crisp hair, a sign Jade recognized as that of capitulation. 'More wine, my dear?'

She allowed him to fill her glass. He'd be amorous now and she *was* grateful. It was the prospect of Daniel being taken from her that had made her nervous and irritable. For the first time she admitted to herself why Daniel was so important. He was like Gabriel except that he was not so pale-skinned. Anyone who resembled Masson would always have a claim on her that would not easily be broken.

There was no longer any excuse to remain at the table. Collin took her in his arms. He was a little tipsy but not so drunk that he could not cope with the buttons on her gown or pull the shift over her head. He burrowed his head in her breast and ran his hands down her back, pinching her buttocks and pushing them close to his own body, then slid his knee between her thighs. For a moment, she thought he meant to tumble her to the polished floorboards but he was too fond of his comfort. He swept her into his arms and his mouth closed over her breast, slid down to her navel and the round of her stomach.

He was not Gabriel but he was better than loneliness and the spectre of a land that was reputed more hard and cruel than most. Better the devil you know, went the old saying.

She stretched out on the bunk and opened herself to receive him.

Australia seemed to go on for ever, a long, low fuzz of silvery green with crescents of pale sand, without any of the beauty of Tenerife or of Rio with its sugar-loaf peaks and wealth of foliage and parrot-coloured flowers, the sea that was blue and green combined.

But there was the hint of mountains in the distance and they made her pulse quicken. She loved mountains. They were pure and self-contained, lifting themselves from the squalor beneath. One day she meant to climb a peak and sit on top of it, quite alone. Perhaps she'd believe in God again up there with the clouds and the birds and the song of the wind.

The settlers were restless now, the women casting doubtful glances at the long, wooded stretches they imagined full of savages, the men hopeful and tense in turn. There was much packing and less time for disapproving looks and spiteful asides that were intended to be heard. The captain's whore would soon find out what a pioneering life was about, though if she employed her usual tactics of lying down for any man soft enough to grant all her hare-brained schemes, doubtless she'd survive.

Lieutenant Carey, aware of the imminence of their separation, allowed Jade the benefit of a frosty smile. His was the wrong kind of love, she told herself, then reflected that any woman Gabriel turned to would meet with her own dislike. He, she could easily hate for going to someone else. But it was wrong to imagine one could ever bind another human being, wrong to want their total subjugation. People were meant to be free, and one must understand that.

Dr Marsh, who had provided Jade with essential nostrums from the medicine cupboard, continued to like and admire her. She would be sorry to see him go but he was returning to England in search of a country practice. Nothing, he said, would induce him to serve on another transport ship, then he had bent his head over her hand and kissed the back of it so tenderly that the hot tears pricked at her eyes like thorns.

The great heads of Sydney harbour engulfed the *Caroline*, showing Jade an immense stillness of silver water smudged with the dark silhouettes of islands. This was as beautiful in its own calm, reflectful way as the more obvious beauties of their previous ports of call. The shore line was thickly wooded, the colour of the foliage still that same grey-green, yet seeming to belong to the land that lay behind it, so mysteriously contained, but throwing up a wall of blue she knew now to be the range that cut off the flatter coastal lands from the little-explored interior. Strips of blonde sand spread in fans across tiny bays.

A glimpse of the distant quayside sent her heart to her throat. She stretched out her hand to grasp Nan's wrist and held Daniel close. The almost completely land-locked harbour still charmed her. The cliffs of the heads made her mind reel with their splendour. The bays and coves were made for lying in the sun, for small boys to explore. But she was not free to determine what she would do. Somewhere on that fair-seeming settlement was the building where she must spend her days. Seven years was an eternity.

Collin was suddenly at her side, his arm going round her waist in a clumsy affection. She could not look at him.

'It won't be so bad, my sweet, and anyway –'

'I wouldn't be here at all if I hadn't misbehaved? That's true.'

He was obviously relieved she did not intend to rail against her fate.

'Thank you for that matter of which we spoke.' People crowded to the rails and she would not wish to compromise him by mentioning Daniel.

'It was little enough, remembering what you have done for me,' he replied in a low voice. 'A pity it's ended.'

Jade discovered that the intolerant gaze of the most unpleasant of the free settlers was upon her. Freda Symons had always hated and envied her. She knew she could not bear to work for someone so virulent, a woman who could make her life intolerable.

The male prisoners were assembled ready for departure and a detachment of soldiers on the quayside obviously waited for them. Sick at heart, Jade made herself look at the buildings that showed between the lightly-leaved trees. Such odd leaves, they were, long and narrow with pale undersides. The men began to move down the gangplank dejectedly, a wild-looking lot who had obviously not troubled to wash and shave themselves overmuch. Those who might have been more particular had not dared to assert their right for fear of reprisal. She remembered Dr Marsh's remarks about the clerks and forgers and how he'd pitied them.

Lieutenant Carey watched her jealously and she wished Collin had not kept his arm around her so openly. The doctor smiled from his place near the sheep-pens. For a moment Jade was back in the storm with Joel dead at her feet and the lantern swinging. Her lips formed the words, 'Thank you.'

'Come on, you bitches!' the second officer shouted when the men had reached the quayside. 'Haven't got all day! All of you in line.'

'Goodbye,' Jade said quite steadily and walked away to join the line of waiting women, the bundle containing her small possessions in one hand, the other arm occupied by little Daniel who squirmed and exclaimed over the wonderful things he could see and pressed damp little kisses close by her ear.

She did not hear Collin's farewell, being fully occupied in negotiating the gangplank, Nan close behind, but, looking back from the quay, she saw them all, Collin, Carey and Dr Marsh, the men who had contributed to her knowledge of life during the long months. There was no way of holding on to those relationships and she did not think she wanted to, apart from Marsh. She would miss him most.

'Come along, now!' a harsh voice roared, precipitating her into the present. She found herself face to face with a red-faced man in uniform. He was sweating profusely and batted off the flies that hung round the waterfront with a hand like a side of ham. He was big and crude and Jade was aware instantly of his speculative glance. Her face showed no emotion but her heart thumped uncomfortably.

'What's your name?'

'Jane Benson.'

The man consulted a paper. 'And son, Daniel?'

'That's right. And this is my sister, Nan. We are to remain together. There must be some house or farm that needs two women.'

The bloodshot eyes continued to look at Jade, then passed

on to Nan. Her hair clung to her head in damp clusters of curls and her skin was a better colour than most of the women's since she had spent half the voyage with access to the deck.

'Look a lot better than the rest of that miserable lot.'

Jade said nothing. She had the terrible feeling that this man would claim them both. 'We are to go to Parramatta,' she said at last.

'I'll decide where you have to go,' the officer replied. 'Stand in here beside me. Who's next?'

All the time he checked the other prisoners, sending them on to another man for disposal, Jade was in an agony of certainty that she was intended for the soldier beside her. He was like one of the boars they had taken on at Cape Town.

For the first time she noticed the line of carts and carriages that waited beyond the quay, the groups of men who scrutinized the women one by one as they reached the barrier. Every now and again a woman was taken out of the line as if being hired long before reaching the women's quarters at Parramatta where much of the exchange was effected.

The last of the female transportees passed out of the officer's jurisdiction, he turned back to the Bensons. 'You'll have to do,' he said. 'No one can say you aren't the best of the bunch. Pity about the child, though.'

'What do you mean?' Jade was cold.

'Didn't want anyone lumbered with a family, but there wasn't anyone else who'd have done for Mr Heriot. Particular gentleman is Logan.'

'Mr Heriot?'

'Owns a big property and needs a housekeeper.' The officer smiled cynically. 'Friend of the captain's, were you? Saw him up there with you. Looked as if he didn't want you to go. And you're better rigged out than the rest, you and your sister. Easy, really.'

'How do we get to Mr Heriot?'

'His man's come to fetch you. Here! Johnson! Get Johnnie Dart down here, will you? He'll know what's to be done with these doxies, begging your pardon, lady. And no trying to scarper, either. You wouldn't like the bush very much. Soon kill off the little feller, there. And Mr Heriot doesn't like to waste his money.'

'What do you mean?'

'Come now, you can't be that innocent. Special treatment

costs a fair amount and since Mr Heriot wanted the best, he paid for it. Be glad I took the trouble.'

'I'm very grateful, of course,' Jade said, hoping that the irony was not too obvious. 'Have you performed this service very often for Mr Logan Heriot?'

'Once or twice.' The officer grinned. 'But I didn't get anyone like you before. Couldn't say which of you he'll favour. The last had red hair and the one before that black.'

'Catholic tastes, obviously.'

He smiled again. 'Pity I promised him. Something tells me you'd not pall on a man. Still, if Logan's pleased, I'll get some rum, or brandy and cigars. There's always a compensation for a good deed. Oh, there you are, Dart. I've done my best for your master. Take them away.'

'He expects one woman.'

'Captain Collin attached a note saying the girls prefer to remain together – a family unit. He says that, separated, you'll get nothing out of either. Together – ' He shrugged. 'Logan'll have to suffer them all. There was no one else he'd have looked at. Now, go on, man. I've to see the rest of those harlots bedded.' And the captain strode away, humming to himself.

If Logan Heriot sounded like a bombastic, arrogant lecher, his messenger was not. Dart was a slimly-built but strong-looking man of about twenty-six, dark and grey-eyed, his face burned brown. In fact, every exposed part of his skin was baked by the sun. It was fascinating to see the little pale lines that radiated from the corner of his eyes when his face smoothed itself out.

He looked from one to the other, then back at Nan.

'Which of you – ?'

'Me,' Jade said firmly. 'I'm sure some post can be found for my sister. And she is good with the baby. If it's a big house – '

'It is. A very large house.' Dart continued to look at Nan as though the sight pleased him. But it was not in an un-pleasant way, Jade reflected. He was gentle.

'Then, there may be a garden. A corner of a garden – for the child?'

'That will be up to Mr Logan, of course.'

'Of course. Now, the baby's tired. Do we start the journey now or do we stop in Sydney?'

Dart seemed to take her decisiveness for granted. Of course, with a master like Heriot he'd be used to being ordered about.

She thought she disliked her prospective employer already. She'd never cared for bullies, men who bought things that were better earned.

In a daze, they followed Johnnie Dart along the quayside, gaining glimpses of brick houses and white-washed walls beyond the trees whose polished leaves caught the light. The sails of a windmill turned.

They were no longer homeless. Gradually, Jade's pulse returned to a steady beat. It would be all right. It had to be. Daniel was almost asleep. She turned back for a moment but the figures at the ship's side had gone and she could recognize nobody. She hurried after Dart, the past gone and the future reaching out towards her with strong, imperative fingers.

She could never remember how many days they journeyed to Elsrickle. The place was named after a Border hamlet, Johnnie told them. Heriot was proud of his obscure birthplace in spite of the fact that most of his life before coming to Australia was spent in Edinburgh where his father made a good deal of money which was passed on to his son.

There was plenty of time to learn a great deal about the man who had bought her. He'd been attracted by the Windsor district on the upper Hawkesbury where the soil was fertile, but a drawback remained in the heavy flooding that occurred, often without warning, carrying away crops and cattle, occasionally humans.

'People in the lower houses have been forced to cling to their chimneys during the floods,' Johnnie said. 'Creates havoc afterwards, cleaning up, but most think it's worth it, even if it's not too comfortable on the roof.'

'But Elsrickle isn't like that?'

'Heriot's had his land for a while and took care that it was higher up. A cautious man.'

'Yet he orders housekeepers he has never seen? A dangerous lottery.'

'Doesn't like to be away from the place.'

'And housekeepers are expendable, aren't they!'

'Could 'a' been much worse if you'd all gone to the women's prison,' Johnnie observed and stole a side-long look at Nan. It seemed he liked to reassure himself that she was all right.

'Yes, of course,' Jade agreed, repressing her irritation with Heriot's high-handedness. 'I suppose we have been very lucky.'

She must not jeopardize a good position by indiscreet criticism that might be repeated. Johnnie's loyalties were most certainly with his master.

'How did you come to be in Australia?' she asked.

Johnnie's expression did not change. 'Same way as you. Worked out my seven years and got my ticket-of-leave. But I'd grown used to it here and even if I'd had the fare, what is there in London but opportunities to get into worse trouble? Nothing's changed for the better, so I hear.'

'No,' Jade agreed, remembering the Holy Land. 'It has not changed.'

'Your sister,' he asked quietly so that Nan could not overhear. 'What did she do?'

'Nothing, except be born into the wrong family. She's never done anything wicked, but bad things happened to her over which she had no control. I'm glad they have not spoiled her. I hope they never will. But I won't let them!'

He did not ask about herself. A nice, discreet and caring man, Johnnie Dart. Already Jade liked and respected him enormously. For the first time in weeks she thought of Stagshaw.

They had travelled to Parramatta by boat. The vessel was crowded with people, trees, baggage, and even a few goats and hens that served to amuse Daniel. Nan could not keep away from them. Seldom reacting favourably to men or women, all her feeling seemed devoted to animals and children. A pity she'd not lived in the country and wed a farmer, Jade reflected. A farmer would not demand too much conversation.

In Parramatta, they saw chain-gangs, long strings of men shackled to one another, all in grey which reflected their hopelessness. They showed burnt faces, skinny, brown arms, and sparks of lechery when they saw the two girls, their soft, pretty dresses outlined in sunlight. They must be starved of women.

Their overseer had not missed the sly, lustful glances and roared at them, bringing down the lash on more than one pair of shoulders. Jade was sorry for them. They were forced to dig roads, the dust flying continually into their lungs, the flies around their heads. She hated flies. But she was also aware of the dangerous hostility engendered in these grey 'caterpillars', the hard eyes that followed the progress of the overseers with the ever-ready whips.

Collin had told her that, in the beginning, the convicts had refused to do many of the pioneering tasks allotted to them, hiding or breaking their tools or running away into the hostile bush which claimed many of them. Stricter supervision had become necessary. Some had been flogged an inordinate number of times, many dying under the scourge, more brutalized irredeemably. He had mentioned a figure of three thousand lashes for one man, administered in the barbaric fashion of allowing the man's back to heal and then enforcing the second-stage punishment. It occurred to her that there must inevitably be repercussions from the repression that was the antithesis of the original method of treatment which had been almost too haphazard.

After Parramatta had come the buckboard over a track that was so primitive as yet that they were bounced about like peas in a pod. Daniel, amazingly, enjoyed the jerky motion almost as much as the incredible wild life. Johnnie told them the names of the flowers, trees and the strange creatures that abounded. The kangaroos delighted the little boy most and the parrots that weighed down the branches like garlands. But it was the ghost gum that both attracted and repelled Jade with its suggestion of polished bones and shrouds, its colours of moonlight. There were the scents of eucalyptus, trees that shed their bark and kept their leaves. Gum that seeped from knots and cracks in the wood.

Black shadows moved silently in the shade of the eucalyptus, some of them barred heart-jerkingly with white, giving the illusion of drifting skeletons. There would be soft miasmas of mist and the smell of smoke, glimpses of bark huts that were not hammered together but formed of leaning slabs. They saw red gums that Johnnie told them were so hard that they could never be cut by ordinary methods.

The painted shadows were the aborigines, the original occupants of the country, who had strange customs of their own that went back farther than anyone could tell for certainty.

The journey was broken at settlers' homes and these were primitive affairs of timber frames panelled with sheets of soft wood from the cabbage-tree. The gaps were filled with clay and twigs and painted with white-wash. Roofed with reeds and long grasses, the floors hard-packed mud in some cases, they were odd yet curiously comfortable abodes.

Both girls and Daniel would share inadequate beds and were

not addressed unless it was unavoidable, though few ignored the child who seemed to grow more beautiful every day, and more lovable. He was not like Amy. His father must have been very handsome, Jade thought, filled with pride that he was now hers.

The mountains moved closer, the ghost gums more frequent. The heavily-wooded slopes levelled out into flatter ground, but Jade turned always towards the mountains with their high, sunlit bastions, the suggestion of canyons that separated one range from another.

She spoke to Johnnie of the great ranges. 'Will they ever be climbed?'

'They are climbed. Already there is a road built –'

'A road! Across those!'

'The Governor and his lady have travelled it and seen what lies beyond. They call it Westmoreland. But behind that lies far more. It's endless, this Australia.'

Daniel could not help laughing at the peculiar hiccuping amusement that rang from the woods. 'Kookaburras,' Johnnie said patiently and that was even funnier. Jade had not laughed so much for months. Kookaburras!

The first they saw of Windsor was a very beautiful new church on the hill and some white houses surrounded by fields and fences. It was an almost English scene except that the trees were covered with those old, horizontal leaves that shivered in a warm breeze and gleamed like silver. Jade made Johnnie stop so that they could wash the dust from their faces and hands and brush their hair. First impressions were the most enduring.

It was some distance from the low houses that the patches of land grew larger and the houses more imposing. They drove past more sheep than she could remember seeing in her entire life. Some horsemen in the distance waved to Johnnie, recognizing the buckboard, no doubt, but no one came near.

Johnnie took the vehicle through wide gates, closing them carefully behind him, then they were bowling up the long drive, the horses obviously pleased to be home. A big house took shape with a long colonnaded porch, the white pillars etched against a black shade in which glass still contrived to glitter. The main block of the house was oblong, the white front broken by long, shuttered windows that gave the building a look of secrecy.

Jade could not conceal her surprise. It was so grand. Surely there would be room for Daniel and Nan? One little room stolen from the rest—

The trees that surrounded it had been there for a long time. They were the perfect backcloth to the edifice. At the foot of the gently sloping ground the river sparkled and eddied, fringed with scrub and shrubs, more trees.

The horsemen had apparently alerted the household for the buckboard had no sooner come to a standstill than the door opened and a man came out on to the pillared porch.

Jade sat perfectly still, the baby clutched against her. It was not possible, she told herself. Not possible. She stared white-faced.

'What's this, Johnnie?' the man asked impatiently and stepped into the sunlight.

The picture Jade had imagined in that first disbelieving look was shattered in the sharp light. The black hair and eyes were Masson's but she was now aware of the differences between them. This man's skin was darker and he was probably younger than Gabriel. He was in his shirt-sleeves, something Masson would not have permitted, however great the hurry, and Logan Heriot was, it appeared, anxious to see what he had paid good money for in Port Jackson, yet displeased by the complications arising from the presence of two extra persons.

'I said one woman,' Heriot went on brusquely as Johnnie sought for words. 'Did you fetch another for yourself? I've suggested it often enough.'

Johnnie flushed.

'He did not!' Jade said explosively, then fell quiet as the black eyes switched to herself. 'Our papers said we were not to be separated. Your great friend, the docks captain, has the document saying we three were to remain together. They are all the family I have. In any case, in a place this size there must be work for both of us.'

'I said I wanted no convicts' brats. What's Jeffers thinking about?' Heriot demanded of Dart and pushed the damp hair from his forehead.

Johnnie shrugged. 'He said no one else would have suited and that he could not guarantee the arrival of another ship for some time. Months, perhaps.'

'H'm. Perhaps I could not have waited that long.' The dark gaze wandered from one girl to another. 'What has she to say for herself?'

'Very little,' Jade said quickly, then went on to the reasons for Nan's disability.

'There are worse fates,' Heriot remarked, 'than a quiet woman around the place.' His tone suggested that Jade could do well to follow Nan's example, yet she did not believe he'd welcome a great show of meekness.

'Well, you'd better come in,' Heriot said carelessly. 'What's your name and hers?'

Jade told him as they went inside the hall. The floor was of cedar polished to gleaming smoothness and waxed. The smell of the wax haunted the place. A cage containing a magnificent parrot stood near the door and Daniel reached out to touch the bars.

'Don't let him do that,' Heriot said sharply.

'He won't contaminate the wretched thing!' Jade cried before she could prevent herself.

'I hadn't thought he would. Rajah bites.'

'Oh.' Jade removed the child quickly. 'I'm sorry.'

'Perhaps, Johnnie, you could take Miss Benson's sister and the boy to the kitchen for some refreshment. Mrs Doyle will see to them.'

'There you are, Nan,' Jade said, handing over the baby. 'You are to have tea. See that Daniel behaves himself. We don't want to start on the wrong footing.'

'This way,' Heriot indicated, opening a door and waiting for her to pass him. She entered the room almost unwillingly, but, once inside, she could not restrain the feeling of pleasure that took possession of her. Another cedar floor in which the few pieces of furniture were duplicated as in a red lake, a fine fireplace with a mirror above it reflecting the flames that danced on the five-branched candelabra. Two enormous paintings of people in eighteenth-century dress. The long windows were shaded by shutters but cracks of sunlight scored white lines down the muslin drapes and lay like daggers on the floor.

'You're quiet enough now,' Heriot observed. 'Not that it isn't an improvement.'

'I was waiting for you to tell me my duties.'

'Duties? Didn't Jeffers tell you?'

'Not in so many words, but I understood well enough. You have no wife and your home is isolated. You want a woman.'

The bald recital in Jade's quiet voice seemed to disconcert him. He laughed abruptly. 'Can't quite make you out but it's early days yet. At least you've got the right idea. No false modesty later, eh? Can you keep house?'

'I can do anything you wish so long as you are kind to Nan and the baby.'

'Isn't it normally the master who makes the provisions?'

'It's the only thing I'll ever ask of you.'

She was aware that he was studying her in a different way and there was nothing juvenile in that regard.

'You weathered the journey better than I'd have thought. All of you.'

'Yes. We were lucky.'

'Lucky?' He raised one eyebrow a little cynically.

'I think that's the right word.'

'You'd be a tigress if anyone touched your family, wouldn't you?'

'You know that already.'

She could see him reflected in the dark red boards. The shadowy Heriot was all Gabriel and her heart leapt briefly. They were not in the least alike! Gabriel had been tormented – almost violent. Heriot, apart from that second in which she had shaken his composure, was utterly self-possessed. She tried to visualize the day's end but could not. Men were all different yet essentially the same. Apart from Masson. 'Who is Mrs Doyle?' she asked.

'She cooks for the household. I've a brace of maids, too.'

One of whom would have been his bedmate no doubt in the absence of his housekeeper! Something in the set of his mouth told her that Heriot was a lusty man and never intended for celibacy.

'I think we'd all be the better for a bath,' she told him. 'And we have clean clothes with us.'

Heriot summoned one of the maids and asked the girl to have water heated and to send food to the dining-room. Lizzie was also to see that a room was made ready for Nan and Daniel. 'I've several unused,' he pointed out. 'And Miss Benson will occupy the one usually reserved for my housekeeper.'

A curious expression flitted across Lizzie's broad, sun-tanned face.

'And get on with it, wench!' Heriot growled, intercepting the knowing glance. 'We have more visitors than expected, unfortunately, and there's more to settle before – evening.'

He had been going to say bed. The reason for her presence was obviously in everyone's mind. Perhaps he had not bothered with the maids and was hungry for satisfaction.

227

After the tiring journey she was not sure if she could cope with a strenuous night. Lizzie looked too mannish for his taste.

The dining-room was beautiful and bare as the previous one had been. The same waxed cedar floor with a rug or two flung down, only the essential furniture. Another portrait of a woman who resembled Heriot and who looked the image of Anna Masson.

'My mother,' Heriot said, noting the direction of her gaze.

'Is she – in Scotland?'

'Dead,' Heriot said, 'not that it's any of your business, really.'

'There were no other children?'

'No. I was an only child,' he admitted grudgingly.

'Like me,' Jade said unthinkingly and could have cut out her tongue.

'Oh?' He was on to the mistake immediately, taking up a stance in front of the empty fireplace as he had no doubt done before the leaping flames in some shiversome house in Edinburgh. 'Then what's all this about a family to be kept together?'

'Nan is an adopted sister.'

'And – the child?'

'Mine,' she said steadily.

'My dear, you don't look old enough. The brat's two if he's a day and you are how old? Add a year or near enough from conception –'

'Nineteen.'

Heriot shrugged. 'If you say so. I'll admit you have the effrontery for someone of more mature years, but come, let me see what I have –'

'Bought?'

'Aye, if you insist on the word!' His accent, which she presumed to be the Scots tongue he'd held on to as he had his memories of Elsrickle, she found both pleasing and mildly irritating, but she supposed she'd become used to it.

'Supper – ?'

'Damn supper! They'll knock first. They always do –'

'When you are entertaining a new housekeeper?'

'Quiet, lass.' He was unbuttoning the sprigged bodice, pulling aside the shift so that he could better see her breasts. His fingertips teased at the nipples and his eyes were on hers so that he could watch her reaction. A hand clutched one buttock very firmly. 'Just how I like a woman,' he remarked. 'Nothing too overblown. I've no fancy ways so don't expect it. As you'll note, everything about me is straightforward – '

Quite suddenly, Jade burst into peals of laughter. 'I hope it will be – later,' she managed to say once she had partially controlled herself.

Heriot was by now laughing as heartily as herself. 'Damn! There they are with the confounded chops. Always act in a hurry when I've got – distractions.' He buttoned the bodice regretfully.

The meal was plain and good. Every now and again, the candle-light on him, Heriot was shatteringly like Masson. They said little.

Afterwards, Jade was reunited with her 'family'. It was the first time she had bathed Daniel properly. It had been just a matter of a good wash-down on the *Caroline*. He was in a great good humour, still trying to say Kookaburra, much to his own and Nan's amusement, chattering about the gaily-tinted bird in the hall, then falling asleep in the disconcerting way of small children, when it was least expected.

A little cot had been made up in Nan's room and barricaded around with chairs, the backs forming a chain of safety bars. Mrs Doyle, voluble and very Irish, peeped in to see Daniel in his temporary crib. 'Shouldn't be surprised if Mr Heriot doesn't get one o' them convicts to make a proper one. He's the sweetest wee feller, to be sure.'

Though Mrs Doyle was a former transportee, her offence had been small and she had long since imagined her own fall from grace quite forgotten. She enjoyed working at Elsrickle and gave Heriot as good as she got. Heriot often had to employ parties of transported men, some of whom were frightening characters and not easily controlled in such an isolated spot. For them, Mrs Doyle had nothing but contempt, but the two girls so newly arrived were very young and her tough old heart had gone out to them in a way she had not been able to do with the two previous women who had been older and who had queened it over the rest of Heriot's staff, exploiting their position. Light-fingered, they'd been too; though Mr Heriot had been generous about that and not reported them as he should.

Jade had not enjoyed anything so much as her bath, for a long time. She had hung up the clean gown in the steamy atmosphere to remove the creases, and, as she stepped over to the long mirror, she approved the fine green material so prettily striped with woven silks. It clung to her body, revealing every curve, and the neckline was scooped provocatively low. The jade carving lay in the hollow of her breast-bone. The material had been Collin's last present.

Brushing furiously at the waist-long hair, she thought she had not felt so hopeful since before the ill-fated night of her introduction to London society. How unpleasant the Mandrakes had been. She could have been so miserable if she'd been married, in spite of all Mama's money and Papa's fondness. Poor Mama. Was she better now? Where in the great continent of Europe were they at this moment?

And where was Masson? Her arm fell away and the brush clattered to the top of the chest. Slowly, she pushed the long, soft strands away from her shoulders and went for a last look at Daniel. She wished he had been Gabriel's child but Ma Lee's nostrums had been efficacious and must continue to be so long as life was so uncertain. She did not want any man to feel obliged to marry her once it was possible, and that could not be so until her seven-year term had expired. There were nearly six still to be served unless there was some miracle and she were pardoned. But those so far freed had all been men of culture and who'd been able to contribute to the good of the new country.

She had no talent which would earn her freedom. Or perhaps she had, she reflected wryly. Logan Heriot might have influence. He must know the present Governor, Lachlan Macquarie. They were both Scots after all.

Heriot was waiting when she left the little boy. Judging by the look in his eye she was not going to be allowed to keep the dress on for long. He bent his head and inhaled the scent of her hair, then slid his arms around her so that her back was to his chest, cupping his hands over her breasts. 'I'd have killed Jeffers if he'd sent you to anyone else.'

'You'd never have known.'

'There's nothing else you have to do?' he asked, but it was more an order than a question.

She shook her head.

His hands slid over the firm round of her stomach and pushed apart her thighs, stroking the insides. She gave a little gasp of pleasure and was aware of his own, unmistakable response. Heriot picked her up quite easily and kicked at his bed-chamber door. It was very masterfully done.

The room was large and as plainly furnished as the rest.

She could see them both in the shining floor, his tallness accentuated, herself a mystery of trailing dress, floating hair and shadowy eye-sockets. The bed was covered with white and enclosed in flimsy draperies to keep off the flies. She became aware of the distant sounds of sheep, of the strange birds in the trees behind the house.

'Tomorrow,' she said, 'I'll have to start earning my keep.'

'Why wait till then? You can start now.' He laughed easily.

She wondered at her brief anger. Masson had laid out his guineas on the bed-table though his technique had been more gentlemanly. He and Heriot were poles apart.

'Why the look of baffled fury? It was a whore I asked for, not a wife.'

He was right, she supposed, but women did have a habit of dressing up the moment. She had a panicky conviction she did not care to be made love to so lightly. Even Nick had the excuse of an overwhelming passion.

'And that child,' Heriot went on, setting her down none too gently on the bed. 'I don't want to hear him. One cheep and he goes.'

'Is that all, sir?' She had imagined him as soft as Collin and that had been her greatest mistake. Even Masson had come round to a sort of gentleness.

He laughed at the indignation in her green eyes. The dress slid away under his suddenly impatient fingers. He whistled.

Jade's face burned. 'Is it so different from what you usually buy?'

'I hadn't expected –'

'It was too hot to wear anything but the gown.'

'I can't say I object.'

She could tell by the narrowed eyes and indrawn breath that he desired her quite violently. But it was a crude, un-formed desire. Heriot was used to prostitutes and imagined her as typical as they. If they were to achieve any kind of bearable relationship she must remove from him the idea that she was the same.

'So long as,' he said, 'you remember who's master here.'

'I don't care to be reminded that you – bought me.'

He laughed openly. 'But I have! You'd fare far worse if I sent you back to Jeffers marked "unsuitable"! You do know that, don't you?'

She turned her face away, not answering, and he became angry. 'You needn't put on such airs. After all, what are you?

A transportee and a harlot. All the women Jeffers sends me are. Why must you have different treatment?'

'You make it sound a very cold transaction.'

'There'll be nothing cold about it,' Heriot told her unrepentantly. 'I didn't send for you to admire you from afar. And it's quite a few weeks since I had a woman. I'm only flesh and blood. Aren't I good enough for you? If not you can take your brat and your feeble-minded sister and get back to Parramatta. So look at me, damn you!'

She sprang at him so suddenly that he was unprepared. Her nails raked at his cheek and his eyes widened with fury. 'You bitch!'

'Don't call Nan that! Everyone does it!'

He grabbed at her wrists, panting. 'All this because of her?'

'Not all. Some.'

'And the rest?' Some of his anger was abating as he looked down at her. She was so small and remarkably plucky. Then he became aware of the scratches on his face.

'Well, what's it to be?'

When she did not answer he took off his clothes and thrust himself upon her.

It could have been different, she knew that. But his initial approach had made her aware of exactly what he thought of her. He was insensitive but there was something in his forceful love-making that roused her at the last. She tightened her legs about him and clasped her arms around his back, feeling his head relaxed upon her breast. Unsatisfied, she lay awake, wondering if he were asleep.

His voice came out of the dark. 'Try harder next time. Eh?'

She turned her back on him while he chuckled and smacked her on the bottom. She thought she hated him.

After the first morning, Heriot was always gone by the time she awoke. He worked as hard as any of his sheepmen. They had a long bunkhouse some distance away. It was only Johnnie Dart who ever came to the house.

Heriot was fairly undemanding with his household staff. Mrs Doyle was a good plain cook and he appreciated simple food. Lizzie and Dora took care of the hard work, the scrubbing and polishing, and washing of linen and curtains.

The sparsely furnished rooms were no great trouble to keep

tidy and clean and much of the house was not used unless Heriot entertained, in which case he had his guests to stay since the distances were sometimes considerable between neighbours and friends.

Beyond Elsrickle was one small farm owned by George and Bess Davies, who employed a small party of convicts to help work their modest piece of land. Heriot told Jade that the Davieses had lately been joined by relatives from England who had acquired the acres beyond theirs. Both settlements were on flatter ground which was more easily cleared and sown but nearer the Hawkesworth than Heriot would want to be.

Jade saw the convicts for the newest settlement pass by some days after she had arrived. She had taken Daniel down the drive to see the kangaroos and parakeets and the long, hopeless train of grey-clad men had raised the dust so that all she saw were shadows. The chains clanked depressingly. A whip cracked.

Daniel had drawn back as though he sensed their hostility and despair.

She told Heriot that evening at supper. Nan had not wanted to join them. She was happy enough with Mrs Doyle or looking after the baby or the chickens.

'Macquarie wants few more convicts and many more settlers. But who will make the roads then or clear the land?' Heriot frowned as he pushed aside his plate. It was darkening and a few stars showed in the purple sky. The ghost gums reared in a white rampart beyond the windows.

Lizzie brought in a rhubarb-and-pumpkin pie and a dish of fresh fruit. Heriot loved baked fruit pies, a throwback to his Scots upbringing, but Jade always chose the fruits or a piece of cheese.

She took a peach from the dish and bit into the plushy skin so that the juice ran down her chin. Jade dabbed at it unsuccessfully.

Heriot gave her an assessing look. 'Not so much the lady now, eh?'

'I never said I was. I just happen to like good manners.'

'And mine don't come up to expectations.' The good humour left his face.

'No,' she answered calmly, enjoying the spark of exasperation in his eyes. The light of the candles was not on him and his shadowed features were again like Masson's. Her heart gave a great bump against her rib-cage. Even though she had not seen Gabriel for so long and their parting had been so bitter, she had not forgotten one moment of their affair.

'I can't imagine why such a paragon found herself in Newgate. Or slept with enough men to pick up some very fancy little tricks when you forget yourself. As you did last night.'

She threw down the peach so that it squelched against the plate. 'I seem to recall your orders were to try harder. Wasn't that the gentlemanly way you expressed yourself? That first night?'

'Now I suppose you'll tell me some heart-rending tale of how you were seduced and thrown out of your father's house. How you *had* to live off your body.'

Jade felt her face grow pale. 'I had no intention of doing so. But if you despise me so much I think perhaps it would be better for us all to go to the centre at Parramatta. If you can spare someone to take us there.'

'Well, I can't,' he raged, pushing back his chair. 'All I did was to grease Jeffers's palm to send me a doxy and what I get is a creature of moods and fancies who lies like a corpse one night, then acts like a courtesan another. At least my previous women were predictable. Can't you get it into your head that I work hard, it's lonely out here without a woman and I want someone I can sleep with – be comfortable with? You seemed, at first, to understand that.'

'Why didn't you stick to the others, then?' she asked, infuriating him further. 'They seem to have suited you. Perhaps you took more trouble with them – '

'You can forget it if what you want is to be wooed like some simpering miss! I told you earlier I'm a straightforward man. We even laughed about it and I hoped we'd be friends. What was it put you off? When it came to the point.'

'The way you spoke about Daniel and Nan. Then you made it so plain that each time you took me to bed you expected value for paying Jeffers. Did I ask you to do that?'

'Did I ask you to bring your family with you? It's my bread they eat and my roof that shelters them.'

'Yes.' Her voice was toneless. 'Perhaps I had lost sight of that obligation.'

He banged noisily at a fly that had penetrated the fastness of the dining-room. 'Must I like them into the bargain?'

'No more than I am compelled to like you.'

Now his face was white. He flicked the fly to the floor and stood on it. His aversion to having them indoors was shared by Jade.

'You did mean it,' he asked, 'that the child was yours? I've never been sure.'

She hesitated. Perhaps he would not dislike Daniel so much if he knew the truth. But then there would be no legal hold over the child.

'Does it really matter?' she said with deliberate lightness.

'I never know when you are telling the truth.'

'I was made to lie in the past but I didn't enjoy it.'

'Ah, that mysterious past of yours about which you say nothing.' His face darkened. Ignoring the tempting pudding, he poured a measure of brandy. Heriot had no liking for the rum that was Australia's universal drink.

She sat silent, the half-eaten peach in front of her.

'I don't know what to make of you,' he said, jamming the glass down on to the polished table, the sound as harsh as his expression. From the nearest trees the kookaburras mocked them but Jade was far from laughing now at the ridiculous sounds.

'You must decide what you believe. But we've stolen nothing from you, not like your other women.'

'Only my peace of mind. I can't think why I put up with you –'

'I'm sorry.' She rose from the table. 'I'd best leave you.'

'Go to that brat! And you addle-pated sister.'

She found herself picking up the knife beside her plate. Heriot touched the old scratches on his cheek. 'You see?' The brandy was working on him. 'You'd kill for them. Why can't you feel so positive about anyone else?'

'You can't have it both ways,' she told him. 'You don't want entanglements and I can't give myself unless I feel some kind of affection – So you have an impasse there, Logan Heriot.'

'Damn all women! I've a good mind to call your bluff. Send you away –'

He went out of the room, slamming the door behind him.

Jade put down the knife, suddenly afraid. Just because Heriot was a harder nut to crack than Collin had been, she mustn't blind herself to his good points. However reluctantly, he was making himself responsible for her two dependants. He did not and never had pretended that she was to be anything but his mistress. And she had heard much of Parramatta. Enough to know that she could not subject Nan and a baby to such crudities. It was reckoned almost worse than Newgate. Besides, she was indeed what Heriot imagined her to be. It was madness to give herself such delusions of grandeur. Jardine Benedict had been a very different proposition from Jane Benson. She only rebelled against Heriot because he had, so far, shown no tenderness. A woman needed that. However cruel or arrogant a man was, a spark of gentleness nullified the rest. She should, perhaps, teach Heriot how to be kind.

She went to Daniel who was peacefully asleep, his cheeks warm with the heat – the sound of voices issued from the kitchen, Mrs Doyle laughing, Johnnie Dart's kind soft tones and Nan's hesitant replies. Johnnie was surely falling in love with Nan. How did she feel about him? And what must inevitably happen to any relationship between them if Heriot decided to send them all packing?

In the moonlit silence of her own room, Jade saw the moths press close to the window. The birds were quiet so it must be later than she imagined. The Indian cane matting was rough but cool under her bare feet. Wide awake, she lit a candle and compelled herself to read for a time, but uncertainty and a niggling unhappiness prevented her usual enjoyment in the pastime.

She replaced the book on the chest of drawers which, on a closer scrutiny, appeared to be of cedarwood polished to simulate mahogany. The chair, also locally made, had a rush seat. In time, she supposed, this early Australian furniture would have a place in history much as the English oak and American cherrywood, Italian walnut.

How she had loved Papa's Chinese lacquer cabinets. Determinedly she exorcized the memory of Papa and Mama. Just because she was stupidly out of her depth, she must not become maudlin. She despised such weakness. In casting off her old identity, she must also stop looking back to the past. It was by her own wish that she was cut off and that Australia was her home. This was her country now and it was up to her to make as best a future as she could, and not only for herself.

Restless, she got out of bed and walked the floor, the thin white garment clinging to every damp curve, her hair too heavy to bear comfortably.

The door crashed open just as she was reaching for pins to swathe her hair on top of her head. Her heart jerked. Gabriel had looked just like this the night he visited her in Newgate. Pain rushed upon her like a black tide. She would never be free of him.

'What do you want?' she asked quietly.

Heriot gave a queer, unhappy laugh. 'You're my mistress. If you don't know – !'

'I didn't mean at this moment. That's plain enough though I wish you were not so drunk –'

He slapped her so hard that her ears rang. 'Don't get too fancy with me, woman!' His Scottish accent had never been so defined. 'I'll come to you as I please, drunk or sober, and you'll not deny me.'

She put her hand to her cheek. 'I admit I worried in case you sent us away –'

'Haven't made up my mind, but my body needs easing. It's a virginal couch this and I've a mind to take you on it.' He clamped his hands around her arms and forced her to the edge of the bed. His eyes were narrowed and he breathed quickly as though he had been running.

'Logan. Not this way –'

'Why not? If other men can have you and make children on you, haven't I as much right?' With one strong tug he tore the gown from neck to hem. 'Haven't I paid for the privilege? And dearly.'

One arm pinned her to the white cover. His other hand was busy with his breeches' fastenings. Brutally, he pushed her thighs apart and lowered himself on to her. The smell of brandy told her he had been drinking ever since he left her and she turned her face away from his attempted kiss.

She fought him strongly but it made no difference. Ruthlessly, he slaked his passion in her, and, unexpectedly, she found herself responding as she never had before. It seemed she preferred him the worse for drink, the master he had originally envisaged. He excited her this way.

He was lifting her from the edge of the bed, her body lapped in ever-growing circles of content. Settling her against the pillow. The bed creaked as he climbed in beside her and measured his length against her. His head pressed against her breast.

'You'd be – too much of a lady – to enjoy –' His voice trailed away.

'On the contrary, I rather liked it,' she said.

But he was already asleep.

CHAPTER EIGHT

At first Heriot remembered little next morning but Jade recalled how he had looked asleep with the moonlight blanching his skin and darkening his eye-sockets and his thick hair. Sleeping, he was the image of Masson. It was all too easy to imagine herself back with him. The illusion was perfect even if it hurt.

Awake, Logan was himself, annoyed that he had gone seeking the disturbing girl who had replaced his former mistresses, realizing she could take it as a kind of capitulation.

The sight of Jade, her hair tumbled and every inch of her body visible through the white veiling, was enough to make any full-blooded man stay here all day. The ornate, cedarwood bedhead framed her as though she were a painting. She sat up against it, the sleeves of filmy white not really concealing her slender arms, the nipples showing through the flimsy covering over her breasts. The breasts he had kissed only last night, inspiring a flood of passion he now remembered all too well in spite of the fumes of brandy that had sent him here. He had never sought out one of his previous whores. They had always come to him, predatory and predictable. He had made out that they had been preferable to Jade with their honest lust and practised tricks but the pleasure of the previous evening had surpassed any other he had experienced.

He couldn't stay, of course. He had the reputation for being a conscientious master, expected to appear as usual. Half of him was eager to begin the day's work. The other half wanted to push her back, to unfasten that tantalizing garment, to cover her body with his. It was impossible to believe that only a short time ago he had not known she existed.

Thrusting his hand inside the white material, so deliciously virginal, he encountered something that was not at all chaste. Jade's breasts were firm and warm, entrancing to kiss. Her belly was flat and satiny, oddly cool. Not that it would always have been so flat. That child she worshipped had been enclosed inside it once.

His desire abated. Daniel must be her own son. She could not love him so violently if he were another woman's. If Jade had to make a choice, it would be in favour of that dark little gigolo of a brat. He knew it in every bone.

Why did it matter? She was like the rest, a ship in the night.

Jeffers would have the record of her past. Perhaps he should see him, ask to look at the official documents that contained their names. Once he knew all about her it would be difficult for her to assume an importance she would most certainly not warrant. He was being a fool. Another week or two and he'd go, assure himself of what he already knew to be true. That she was not worth the heart-searching.

He wondered, his fingers still against her skin, who had fathered her child. None of the women Heriot had slept with had borne children. He thought that might be the real root of his dislike of Daniel. Somewhere in the past had been a potent, virile male who had impregnated this girl who found him so wanting.

With a shock, Heriot realized that he was not as detached as he would have wished. The little minx had wrapped herself around him and the warning signals told him to tread carefully. She was a talented harlot and unworthy of a vestige of heartache. Resolutely, he rose from her side and flung on his clothes. He would work later than usual today and that would put her in her place. Perhaps he would not come back tonight.

Jade saw him later, when she went out into the paddock, riding his horse as though he were glued to its back, with no look of Masson at all, his shirt-sleeves rolled up to his biceps. He was dedicated and competent, a Scotsman who had probably had little except his own determination and the frugal reward of his father's lifetime savings. But she would not let herself become deluded into thinking that Heriot was ever to become as amenable as Collin. He had taught her a salutary lesson in humility and one she would not easily forget.

He did not come to her that night and she was surprised by her sense of disquiet. Surely he did not really intend to throw them all off as she had suggested? She sat up, ostensibly reading but listening to every creak of the house. Perhaps he had been distracted by one of the girls in the bunkhouse? He must have sought his pleasure there in the past, though perhaps not. It would not be good sense for the master to take the women brought there by his own sheepmen for their exclusive use and pleasure.

He could not imagine he would be punishing her by his absence? If only she did feel so strongly about him. It was

239

having to pretend to him that went against the grain. No, her apprehensions were all on behalf of Nan Flynn and the small boy Heriot thought her own. She had managed her life so far and could go on doing so. It was Masson who had spoiled her for other men. Damn, damn him! The blurred letters danced unintelligibly on the page before her.

She was relieved when Heriot appeared at breakfast though naturally she would not allow him to see that. One never laid all one's cards on the table.

Oddly enough, that was what Heriot said he had been doing. He'd been gambling until quite late and had fallen asleep where he sat. It was a long time since he'd played cards and he insinuated they could take quite a hold on him.

'How nice for you,' Jade said insincerely, and smiled.

He did not look as if he had been up half the night. The whites of his eyes were quite clear and the lids were not puffy. He'd committed the indiscretion of taking one of the bunkhouse doxies. And he, knowing the trend of her thoughts, would be watching for her reaction. Perhaps he amused himself with aborigine women. Gins.

'Can I expect peace tonight?' she asked calmly.

'Peace?' His brows came down in a frown.

'Surely you understand? Will I be free from my evening duties? I happen to be in the middle of an exciting story and I wondered only if I'd have the chance to find out how it ends.'

'You may have the chance to find out how a good beating feels,' he growled, outraged that she should find his lack of attentions merely peaceful.

She could not really understand why she required to goad him, or why his discomfiture should give her such pleasure. Surely she ought to welcome his absences? Jade had never had to combat pique before.

They parted still on cool terms, Heriot unforgiving because she had shown so clearly that she preferred his absence, Jade knowing that such tactics might only estrange him altogether and result in the loss of a good place.

When Daniel lay down for his afternoon sleep, she walked across the paddock and skirted the nearest of the sheep pastures. Some of the women peered from the back windows of the bunkhouse but they'd see little but a cool, pale dress and a shady hat, one of several imported from Manila.

A black cockatoo flew out of a bone-coloured tree, the only

colour a few red feathers by its tail. Its song was melancholy.

In another tree, a crow carked ceaselessly, drowning the noise of the sheep. Jade, drawn by the noise, went towards it, aware, out of the corner of her eye, of a few distant figures busy in the largest of the pastures.

Nearing the tree she saw the crow, struggling and ruffle-feathered, its leg seeming tangled in something not at first discernible. Sorry for the creature, she ran towards it, and, seeing her so close, the bird flapped the harder, screaming. Some distance away, another tree was full of crows though not one came near because of the racket set up by the trapped bird.

Steeling herself against its struggles, she traced the tangled cord to a particular branch and discovered to her horror that it had been secured there deliberately. Anger flooded through her. She began to pick at the knots urgently. The task was made more difficult because, in the creature's efforts to escape, the knots had been dragged tighter.

She turned her attention to the bird's leg but this was even more difficult to free as it flew wildly against her face, scoring her cheek with its claws. Determined not to be defeated, she scanned the ground for anything that was sharp and found a flint close by the fence. Returning, she sawed away at the cord until the final reluctant strands gave way and the crow, limping and fluttering, took itself off in the direction of the others.

The cessation of noise made her aware of other sounds that grew nearer. Heriot was riding back, the sweat gleaming on bare forearms and face. His expression boded no good. 'What are you doing, you stupid bitch!'

She recoiled for a moment from his fierce anger, then said very clearly, 'Someone purposely tethered that bird. It was no accident.'

He flung himself to the ground and glowered over her like a thundercloud.

'Someone purposely tethered it!' he mimicked hatefully. 'It was no accident!'

She could not help herself. Jade delivered a stinging slap on the damp, mocking face. The next moment she was seized and turned over. His hand came heavily on to her almost unprotected seat. It had been too hot to wear more than the gown. Jade screamed and kicked strongly. One of the sheepmen laughed.

241

Heriot, having missed his pleasures last night, was quickly aware of her near-nakedness. Giving her a last blow for good measure, he righted her only to find a small tempest assailing him. His jaw ached from one particular slap that found its target. He held her away from him, wrists imprisoned.

Her breast was heaving and her eyes flashed hatred. 'Don't you mind that one of your men is a sadist?' There was the noise of distant cheering.

'I asked him to tie the damned crow there.'

'You beast!' She kicked at his nearest shin.

'Have you ever seen a lamb without eyes? Just bleeding cavities?'

She grimaced. 'No. But what has that – ?'

'To do with my order? A great deal.' Her bosom was not rising and falling so fast now and he regretted it. Jade roused was a good deal more bedworthy than Jade restrained. 'See all those crows over there? Now that you've set this one free, the one who kept them at a safe distance, they'll be over the flock in no time, pecking away. Blinding. Now do you see?'

Jade forgot the crushing pain in her wrists, the hot soreness of her backside. There was a new picture of suffering before her and it was worse than one captive predator.

Heriot, aware of her recognition of that bungling, said more evenly, 'We'll have to waste time shooting at them now and I can ill spare the shot. And the unnecessary delay.'

She stared at the ground. 'I'm sorry. But I wasn't to know.'

'In future, remember that whatever you see, there's usually a reason.'

'Yes. Will that be all?' She used the tone she knew would infuriate him most.

'No! It isn't all. I won't be playing cards tonight and I'll expect you where you damned well ought to be. In my bed as soon as supper's over. Understand?'

'How can I resist such a charming invitation?'

'And I'll get some sort of response from you even if I have to resort to a taste of what you've just had. Is that plain?'

Their eyes locked stormily.

'Perfectly clear.'

'Then get back to the house before you do any more damage. It's not safe, for one thing. There are snakes and I'd prefer it if you stayed in the paddock; that's what it's for. And if there's a thunderstorm and any fire breaks out you're more likely to be trapped outside here.'

She turned away from him, her head in the air, but he was beside her in three long strides, his arms locking her hands to her sides. His mouth came down brutally hard, making her struggle for breath. It was as though he had branded her with a heated iron.

More ragged cheers came from his men. She could not decide which she detested most. Their good-natured jeering or Heriot's determination to subdue her.

Yet, hurrying back across the grass after he released her, she was forced to see her own folly and his rightful annoyance at her interference. Her buttocks still throbbed hotly from the beating she had so unexpectedly received. But he had not had all his own way. His face would bear a few bruises too.

Unexpectedly, she was smiling. Despising herself, she made herself frown.

Bathed and rested, the scratches on her cheek hidden under a dusting of powder, she appeared as usual at the evening meal. All afternoon, she had heard the shot-guns blasting away and then the noise stopped and she realized that they had trapped another bird to act as scarecrow. She wondered how they had done it, and Mrs Doyle told her they'd probably hung some bits of meat on a branch to attract numbers of the creatures, then selected one.

There was so much to learn. If Heriot had not turned so hateful she might have asked him some of the things she wanted to know. She had to nerve herself to greet him. He had attended to his toilette under the pump for his skin and his crisp hair were still damp. But he had put on a clean white shirt, she presumed for her benefit. It was a start.

Instead of keeping up her policy of aloofness – it seemed far better that they made up their differences – Jade engaged him in conversation over the meal, just as if nothing had happened.

Heriot, surprised and probably flattered, told her of discoveries he had made. The scribbly gum that appeared carved like an Egyptian column, the grey galah birds that showed pink undersides when in flight, how camels would be a far more sensible animal to traverse Australia's deserts than the horse, and how whaling would be the next valuable export after wool. How ant hills rose as high as a house.

'Come and look,' he said, going to the window. 'There's a moon.' And he showed her the ghost gums that stood out now like apparitions, gleaming like satin, their leaves shrouds of greyness. The mountains, so blue by day, were now ramparts of bronze and purple.

She thought she knew now why she resisted him. He was superficially like Masson, yet he was not the man she loved. She had been more generous to a turnkey than to this sheepman who allowed her family to remain at a fine place like Elsrickle as though his was the obligation. He had taught her as many lessons as she had thought to teach him. Did she really want him as a kind of human lap-dog?

Jade knew that she did not. 'I'm sorry about the crow,' she said, then added, 'I still don't like anything that's fettered,' in case he thought she was weakening.

'And I don't care to see an animal cruelly blinded,' he retorted. 'Think how you would feel if it happened to yourself.'

She did think. But Heriot had never been imprisoned without real cause as she had been. He knew nothing of those hateful nights, her body violated without the slightest compunction by the very men who were supposed to guard her. She could never forget the desperation and humiliation. It would always colour her reaction towards the captive. Only he did not know and she intended he never should, no more than he knew that he was a perpetual reminder of what she had lost and had no hope of regaining.

She could not say that she wanted to bed with him. Always there would be a part of her that had nothing to do with the stroking and caressing, the mouth on her breast, the hand between her thighs. But Heriot had grown a little more discerning, just as she had become more accommodating, less hostile towards the realization that this was to be her life so long as he wanted her. And tranquillity for the child. Daniel was the true focal point of her life and he was happy here.

Heriot had made love to her more than adequately. She decided she must be grateful, then was surprised that her feeling was now a little more than gratitude.

Heriot was by now fully aware of his mistake. Never before had he thought of a woman as more than a gratification of the senses. In Edinburgh he had met innocent misses but they had less appeal than the whores with whom he secretly consorted. They excited him with their flamboyance but he knew that somewhere there must be a woman with whom he wanted to conceive his children. He wanted an heir now that he had built up an estate like Elsrickle. And Jane Benson had become so satisfactory and so desirable that he had the uncharacteristic wish to please her, even, one day, to marry her. He did not flinch away from the unexpected thought and was amazed at the change in himself.

He had bought her a gift that might bring them together and then he had recalled his intention of visiting Jeffers before making an utter fool of himself over a confessed felon. He'd always been level-headed.

Heriot told Jade over breakfast that he had the necessity to go to Port Jackson and that he had bought her something as an early or late birthday present.

'Is there anything you'd like me to bring back?' he asked. 'From Sydney?'

'You said – something about a gift –'

'Apart from that.'

'Some paints and brushes. Turpentine. I would like to execute some miniatures.'

'So you're an artist?'

She shook her head. He had the exquisite pleasure of watching her rise from the bedclothes and swing her legs over the edge of the bed. Her feet and ankles were so white and well shaped. 'I always had a feeling for colour and was encouraged to paint. My father –'

'Yes? Your father –'

'Always said I might be good if I took it up properly.'

'That is not the occupation of an under-privileged girl.'

'I have never said I was.'

'Where is your father now?'

She shrugged. 'We were separated, unavoidably. I have lost trace of him.'

'I wish I knew more about you!'

'Perhaps you'd not like what you hear,' she replied.

Oh God, if she were not so distractingly beautiful. Why had he let himself fall even half in love with a convict!

Heriot stumped off in search of breakfast, scowling at Lizzie without being conscious of the fact. Lizzie smiled grimly. The master seemed to have bitten off more than he could chew this time. Like a little race-horse kicking up her heels that Miss Jane was. Real thoroughbred face and figure she had and that ornament she wore on that thin gold chain looked expensive in a funny kind of way.

Lizzie manfully thrust down envy. A lot better than those two previous hussies, this one was, and thought a lot of that Nan and the baby. You couldn't really say she was a good person, not sleeping in the master's bed so openly, but you could depend on her, and she never queened it over herself and Dora. And she had to face it. They'd all go running if Mr Heriot asked any of *them* to be his mistress. He was a fine-looking man when he wasn't frowning. Lizzie Smith wasn't blind or stupid. Heriot did not hear her sigh.

Jade arrived as soon as Lizzie had gone. She wore a gown sprigged with small flowers and looked so innocent and charming that he could hardly believe he'd forgotten himself so thoroughly last night. Pictures of Jade lying naked in the dimness infiltrated his mind. She could be so wanton, so distractingly voluptuous – His mother would turn over in her grave! A thief from Newgate! And he loved her.

'You'll find your present in the stable,' he said gruffly.

'How shall I know where to look?'

'You'll see it without any trouble.'

Even the act of popping a fragment of food into her mouth made him aware of her in a sexual sense. A nice thing if Lizzie came back and found them at it under the table. What a bit of gossip for the kitchen and the bunkhouse! He watched Jade hungrily, then took his unquiet body off before he forgot himself. Batting angrily at the regiment of flies, he went for his horse, stopping to stroke the little brown mare with the white mane and tail that was his gift to Jade. She'd be able to ride. All girls with her background could. Jade had class.

It was not until Daniel was fed and washed that Jade went to see her present. She was astounded by his generosity. Livestock was expensive in so new a country. Logan had told her a story about the cattle belonging to the first settlers wandering off into the bush and being found years later, their numbers increased. There had been lean times after the beasts vanished. And here he was giving her a mount that must have cost him a pretty penny.

The mare was saddled. Jade had not ridden since she lived in the country but one never forgot how. She swung herself up on to the neat brown back and dug in her knees. It was not very feminine to sit astride but no one was likely to see her if she rode away from the sheep enclosures.

Kicking gently, she set the mare trotting but the sensation of riding again was so pleasurable that she was soon galloping along the dirt road, oblivious to everything but the thrill of movement and the current of air against her face. She should perhaps have tied back her hair which swirled first this way and then that, but she had no ribbon and, anyway, she did not want to check this miraculous freedom.

The long, colonnaded shape of Elsrickle had passed from sight some time ago and she was riding between fairly thick woods through which she caught glimpses of bright water. The sight of the water tantalized her, reminding her of the dust that coated her skin and parched her throat.

'Stop!' she cried out. 'Stop. Stop. There's a good girl.' Sliding down, she looped the bridle over a branch and made her way through the undergrowth towards the river's edge.

One minute she was alone in the resinous gloom, the next she was held by the ankle and dragged down to the narrow strip of bank. As she fell, she saw the newly-cut edges of fallen trees, spaces in a clearing and a low cabin-like building some distance away, then they were blotted out by a man's silhouette.

Breathless from the heavy fall, she tried to free herself from the iron grip but the man was too strong. He had raised his head and she saw his face, long and pale, engrimed with dust. Pale blue eyes narrowed, piercing her with their intensity. His shaven head and the grey garments told her all she needed to know. A hard, dirty hand came over her mouth as she opened her lips to scream. A chain jingled as he moved. He was tethered like a goat and smelt like one.

'There's no one will see us down here,' he said softly, 'and it's no use thinking I'll be punished for having my pleasure of you. Passed Mr Heriot's the other morning we did and saw you. The Davieses said you're a transport like ourselves. 'Tisn't a crime for one convict to lie with another. Expect it, the authorities do. Couldn't believe my eyes when I saw you through the bushes.'

Green eyes blazed hatred and he laughed. 'Oh! Got to fight for you, have I? Come on. Open up before I hurt you. As you may imagine my time's not my own.' He had planted a leg on either side of her and the pressure of his arm across her lower face stifled her. She was conscious of a swift panic. He was stronger than anyone she had ever known. Stronger than Caspar.

The other calloused hand was up inside her skirts, tearing at the top of her undergarment. She tried to draw up her knees but his thighs weighed her down. Wriggling her right hand free she raked her nails across his cheek. He closed his eyes tight and growled like an animal. 'Do that again and I'll kill you,' he grated. 'The river's there in front of us and I'll drop you in when I've finished with you.'

She knew he meant every word.

Every scrap of colour left her face. But she bit against his palm, and he seemed to like that. His soft laughter frightened her more than his anger. Turning her face away from his seeking mouth she saw an axe lying a few feet away. How far? The length of her arm? More, she imagined, squirming below the tough, aroused body. She stretched her free arm towards it and her fingertips stroked the edge of the shining blade.

But his head was turning too and he saw what she intended. 'You little bitch,' he said softly, and dragged her away so that the weapon was decisively out of reach. 'First you'd have the eyes out of my head and now you'd split it open. Heard tales about you, me and my mates. Some of them were on the *Caroline*. Weren't exactly famous for keeping your legs together, so why so coy? Who's to know? And don't scream. A couple of turns of my wrists and that little neck would snap like a flower stalk. The current's strong here and you'd go a long way before you were washed up. If you were ever found! The abos like human flesh, I've heard, or they do up in New Guinea. Not good enough for you, eh? You've got a choice. Either let me have what I want and no tales told or I have you anyway and get rid of you afterwards.'

Her clothes were tearing now and the hard thighs were pushed over her own, pinning her painfully against the earth. His lips ground against her mouth so that she tasted blood. But she refused to lie still. What he said was true. No one would know but herself but she would never feel clean again. The long chain clinked as he shifted his position.

The pale blue eyes burned coldly, narrowed to shining slits. She could see her face reflected in pupils that were cruel as winter. With an effort, she tore her mouth free of his and screamed. He brought his full weight down on her legs so that her face twisted with pain.

'I warned you –'

But he never finished the sentence. A boot came out of nowhere and kicked him in the side. He gave a startled gasp and whispered an obscenity. The boot struck again and he rolled away from her. With a bound, he was up on his feet, the axe in his hand. He could not run away, not with the chain round his ankle.

Heriot stared down at her, ashen-faced. 'Are you all right?'

Jade grimaced as she tried to move. 'I think so –'

'What he means,' the convict said, 'is did I tumble you. Tell him I didn't. That it was only horse-play. Only a kiss –' His skin sweated.

She wanted to tell the truth but could not. The threats stayed with her. She swallowed, her throat drier than before.

Heriot gave a shout of rage and sprang towards the man. The axe was swung high. The chain made a rattlesnake sound. She was chilled.

'Logan! Come away. He'll kill you. He said –' She stopped abruptly.

'Oh, so it was just a kiss,' Heriot said harshly. 'A bit of fun, was it?'

The axe quivered threateningly. Jade scrambled awkwardly to her feet, stumbling with the pain in her thighs. The man had all but knelt on them.

'I'll have your hide,' Heriot promised grimly. 'It's Denver, isn't it? I've heard about you from George. And you can put that down. Davies and some of his men are coming. They tether you away from the rest of the scum because you always make trouble. Well, you'll not get away with this.'

The strong, sinewy arm slackened. The axe tumbled to the ground. Heriot went forward and struck Denver with all the strength of his bunched fist.

The man's pale eyes flared open and he made a grab at Heriot. In a moment they were both struggling in the dust, panting and grunting, the links of the chain clattering. Denver was strong as a wild-cat but Heriot was surprisingly resilient. Fists flew and the ever-present dust rose in a cloud that dimmed both flailing figures so that Jade's heart was in her mouth, wondering which was victor, fearing for Heriot.

She pulled her gown to some semblance of decency, wincing as she did so. The sound of hooves penetrated the gasping, scuffling uproar and she turned, thankfully, seeing a broad, grey-bearded man dismount, his grey eyes alive with anger.

'It's my man, Denver, I suppose?'

She nodded, speechless for once, but he recognized the anxiety in her expression.

'DENVER!'

Several sunburnt, husky riders appeared, crowding around Davies. There was a sudden silence. Slowly the dust began to disperse. Heriot came out of the thinning cloud, his cheek cut and the collar of his coat hanging free.

'He attacked this woman. Then, when I remonstrated with him, he threatened me with the axe. The man's a beast – '

The small grey eyes surveyed Jade. 'What was she doing here in the first place?'

'I was riding along the track. I was thirsty and came towards the water to drink. He – grabbed my foot as I passed the bushes.'

'I gave her the mare that's tied to a tree back yonder. I wasn't sure how well she rode. So I watched and saw her come this way. After a few minutes I decided to follow. I saw the mare, heard Jane scream, and found Denver assaulting her,' Heriot said angrily.

'Assaulting?'

'They were on the ground. As you can see, she struggled. Her clothes are torn. He meant to ravish her. That's obvious.' Heriot glared in the direction of the now-visible convict who stood perfectly still in the shimmer of dust. There was something so inimical in Denver's icy gaze, such pent-up violence about the strong, rangy figure in the grey clothes, that shaven skull, that Jade shivered.

'You're a pig, Denver,' George Davies said. 'Did he – harm you, ma'am?'

She shook her head. 'Bruises only.'

'Your mouth's bleeding,' Heriot pointed out, and produced a handkerchief. 'You'd best clean it with that.'

'Bring her to Bess,' Davies interrupted. 'She'll have some remedy. A tot of rum, too, I expect, and a needle and thread. As for you, Denver, you'll be thrashed. Again. I never knew anyone invite so much trouble.'

The wintry gaze turned to blue fire. 'For tumbling a whore! It was she wanted it! And I can hardly run off – '

Jade was conscious, briefly, of the concerted stares of all the men Davies had brought with him. Their conflicting expressions shamed her. They half-believed that man. Heriot could not control himself. He swung a vicious blow to Denver's head that rocked him, then sent him crashing to the ground. Black eyes clashed with those of palest ice. Suddenly Heriot was Gabriel in that Newgate cell.

'Two hundred lashes,' Denver said.

'No –' she protested swiftly. 'That seems –'

'Far too little,' Heriot interposed as Denver was hauled to his feet. 'I'd like the punishing of him. I'd let my arm fall off before I stopped.'

'Logan –' But it was useless. Nothing she said would make any difference to Denver's fate. If she had gone a different way – if she had not stopped to drink –

She was like Phoebe Lewis, bad luck for the men with whom she became involved.

Heriot's arm came around her. She was dimly aware of Denver being hustled away, still arguing his innocence. 'Asked me, she did! Only pretended to object when Mr Heriot came along. Why would I be such a fool, and in sight of the house? Had anything in breeches on the *Caroline*! The doctor gave her anything she asked for. The captain – Some lieutenant – She begged me –'

Heriot's arm grew stiff and unyielding. Like a fetter. Like the iron and chain round Denver's leg. She heard Davies's men go. A kind of silence –

'I can't go to that house –' she whispered, 'not after what he said.'

'You can and will,' Heriot told Jade in a voice she hardly recognized. 'If you don't, the scandal will be heard as far as Port Jackson.'

'You can't believe him.'

'How do I know you didn't see him from the track? That you didn't come down purposely? You said yourself the greatest thrill you had with me was when I all but raped you.' His face was Gabriel's, tormented, accusing.

'Logan. I swear –'

'I've caught you out in lies before, remember? That "sister" of yours?'

'White lies, meant to hurt no one.'

Brutally he turned her to face him. She cried out at the resulting pain, then held up her skirts to show him the marks on her body, then her swollen and bleeding mouth, the dark patches on her arms. 'In spite of the fact that he said he'd break my neck and throw me in the river, I fought him. There were all kinds of rumours aboard and Denver distorted them all. The doctor was a saint who did what he could in that hell below deck. He was like a father. The lieutenant was a kind of brother –'

'And the captain?'

'I could not refuse. He had the same power as yourself.'

Heriot was trembling. 'I want to believe you.'

'You must. I want to stay here! I want to be with you. For all kinds of reasons.'

He stared at her, white-faced.

'I feel better now. You are quite right, we have no choice but to go to the house. I can't say I'll relish it but I'll put a brave face on it for your sake. I don't want you hurt or diminished.'

'Jane –' He caught her to him and she flinched. 'He *has* hurt you. There's no pretence. Can you sit the mare?'

'If you'll set me on the saddle.' She laughed ruefully. 'To think that an hour ago I was enjoying myself so harmlessly!'

Heriot said nothing and Jade could not tell if he really believed her. But he was careful with her when they reached the mare, riding his own horse slowly until they reached the open door of the Davieses' house where a stoutish woman with large breasts and wide hips awaited them. Her look for Heriot was reasonably friendly but for Jade there was no welcome, only a chilling politeness. 'Sorry you've had this trouble, miss, I'm sure. Let me see the damage. Come into the bedroom and I'll take that gown to repair. Heriot, help yourself to the rum. You know where it's kept.' Not that he would enjoy it.

The bedroom was plain and a little dull, the cane-bottomed chairs uncomfortable. Jade longed to be back at Elsrickle. She took off the gown slowly, every part of her body aching, aware of Bess Davies's scrutiny. 'Don't bother about my underthings, but I can't go back with the skirt so damaged.'

'I'll fetch you some water and iodine,' Bess replied stolidly. The floor creaked as she walked.

Jade sat in one of the stiff little chairs when she had gone. She felt sick and degraded, sorry for Heriot's shame. An unobtrusive mistress was one thing, a woman who courted trouble so blatantly was another. The memory of Denver's filthy lies was like being immersed in scummy water. Mud always stuck.

Her reflections were broken by the sound of voices from the back of the house. Then there was a silence eventually broken by a sound like a pistol-shot. A pause, then another. Someone screamed after the tenth crack. Her body was swept with waves of coldness. She wanted to cover her ears but what would that accomplish? It was the first time a man had been flogged on her account. But shutting out the noises would not prevent it.

She still sat, like a statue, when Bess Davies returned with the dress, her eyes the only part of her with any colour. The broad plain face showed no expression as the gown was handed over and the water and iodine placed on the table by the window. 'Come back when you've finished,' Bess told her coolly.

The iodine stung her mouth but Jade did not notice. She had lost count of Denver's lashes by this time and the cries had turned to moans than dwindled to nothing.

She forced herself to join Heriot and the Davieses in the low, shuttered room that still contrived to be overpoweringly hot in spite of the shade. A glass of rum was pushed into her hand She coughed as she drank it, hating the taste, but felt better when she had got it down. All the time she thanked Bess for her trouble she felt Davies watching her. Heriot exchanged neighbourly chit-chat without much enthusiasm. While she had been in the bedroom Bess had repaired Heriot's coat collar. The cut on his cheek was daubed with iodine and looked red and angry. He hunched his shoulders as though his ribs hurt.

At last Heriot rose to his feet and said they must go.

'We'll be seeing you again, though?' Bess looked only at him.

'Aye. I'm off to Sydney, but later, perhaps. Did you want anything while I'm there?'

Jade stared out of the window while George debated. The sun was blindingly white beyond the eucalyptus trees and the kookaburras laughed madly. She could not help seeing Denver's cruel eyes. He would be past seeing her now but he'd remember her and Heriot when he recovered. He'd be a bad enemy.

It was not until they were well away from the place that Jade turned to Heriot. 'I wish you weren't going away.'

'It won't be for long,' Heriot said, then wondered for the hundredth time why he insisted on leaving her.

She missed Logan but there was more time to spend with Daniel. The child flourished in spite of the heat. He wore only a little pair of breeches and a hat to keep off the sun. Everything interested him, in particular the tame kangaroo that lived in the paddock behind the house. He called it Jump and they were often to be seen playing together. Fortunately Jump was good-natured.

Nan loved the kitchen and the fowl-yard, the goat and the horses. She was learning to cook under Mrs Doyle's tuition, and Johnnie Dart often came to supper, praising her efforts. Flushed from the heat of the oven, the blue gown making her eyes the bluer, her golden hair damp, Nan herself looked good enough to eat.

Jade called the mare Polly. Daniel was extra fond of the old nursery rhyme, 'Polly put the kettle on', and the thought of a little horse performing such a homely chore always made him laugh. Many things made the small boy chuckle. His was a serene nature. Sometimes Jade could hardly contain the upsurge of happiness she felt on behalf of both her protégées. It seemed not to matter very much what became of herself so long as they flourished. It was a pity Logan did not take to the child, but he might change. She could not help wondering what business was so urgent that he had to go to Sydney.

Heriot had some Dutch furniture as well as the cedarwood beds and chests. She enjoyed polishing these, her fingers tracing the plain, satisfying lines of presses and tallboys. There was one cabinet with marquetry inlay and a domed pediment on which Delft vases stood in white and blue symmetry that pleased her more than most. She brightened the brass-edged keyholes to burnished splendour, wondering who had brought the piece to New South Wales and what Heriot stored in it. Men kept such sentimental things. Masson had preserved his sister Anna's treasures. Heriot had been devoted to his mother. The Mandrakes probably kept the house full of decadent French secretaires and verre églomise or Venetian rococo. She was overpoweringly glad she had not been married off to Rupert. Perhaps Tom and Paddy had done her a favour when they took her away so summarily.

She stood, the bowl of beeswax in her hand, and remembered Nick, so clever and cruel. She might have become reconciled to Nick if he had not taken her to watch her parents leave the house. Any fascination she had felt died in that moment. He could not have shown her his character more plainly. But the recollection of his passion, his dark red hair and grey eyes and coat, still had the power to thrill her body if not her mind. There had been a bond between them, tenuous and unhealthy perhaps, but a kind of thraldom she now regretted. She had betrayed herself in that fleeting need of him. If it were not for that, she could consider herself reasonably virtuous, for what had happened since was beyond her control, apart from falling in love with Gabriel. Heriot sleeping had a magic that did not exist when he was awake, a spell that took her back to the sojourn in Masson's house, a time that could never be repeated, something she would always yearn for, quite uselessly, of course.

Having exorcized her demons with hard work, she fetched Polly and set Daniel on her back, exulting in the child's pleasure. Nan had not wished to join them, being much too absorbed in Mrs Doyle's culinary masterpiece for tonight. A galah and two lovebirds occupied a large cage on the back porch and the colourful interplay of flight excited Daniel. She could forget Denver and his useless hatred. Davies would watch him even more closely after this.

But an unaccustomed noise put her on her guard immediately. The sound of steps on the path was unexpected. None of the sheepmen ever came to the paddock and Johnnie only came after the day's work was ended.

She snatched Daniel from Polly's back and turned to face the interloper. He was not so frightening, she decided almost immediately. He was tall and fair and his expression touchingly diffident. Yet there was something in the line of his chin that promised a kind of firmness. He smiled, and she could not hold out against him.

'I'm Henry Lambert,' he said, and his voice was educated. 'I planned to see Logan but Mrs Doyle says he's away.'

'He is.'

She had no idea how lovely she looked, her hair loose, the sunlight outlining her pale dress, the child clasped to her breast. Her answering smile would have disarmed a mysogynist.

'I haven't seen him for some time. I've been away –'

'And you find that Logan has had a change of staff.'

'A pleasing change.'

'Thank you. Some refreshment, Mr – ?'

'Lambert.'

'Of course. I was a little startled to see anyone, that's all. Logan has few visitors as a rule.' She looped Polly's bridle over a rail and put Daniel on to the grass. Immediately, he began to toddle away. She ran after him and scooped him up. Both were laughing.

Henry Lambert stared at them as though he had seen a vision.

They went into the house and Lizzie brought wine and

biscuits and took the baby for his afternoon nap. Jade, now that matters were on a more decorous footing, wondered how much Henry surmised. He must know that all Heriot's house-keepers warmed his bed. The veneer of politeness never faltered, but it was not the cold correctness of Bess Davies. She thought Henry quite charming and discreet.

When he spoke to her of his connections with the East India Company she was interested, begging him to tell her more. A long pageant of important names passed between them. Lord Wellesley and Warren Hastings, the Earl of Moira, Lord Teignmouth, Lord Minto, Ranjit Singh, Tipu of Mysore, Cornwallis – the huge country of India came alive under Lambert's expert knowledge. She saw the great elephant herds, the temples and rivers, the silks and spices, the jewels and the beautiful women. She saw too the flies and disease, the beggars at every gate. She did not want him to go, revelling in the sophistication of his talk, the spell of his voice.

'I have heard,' she said, 'that the Company was built on slavery.'

'Everything is built on slavery,' Henry told her. 'All the great empires were dependent on cheap labour and the whip. The ancient Egyptians could never have had their necropoli without a regiment of poor workers who dared not stop laying bricks. Australia is being built on the forced labour of convicts. I know Macquarie regrets it and is pushing now for more free settlers with means, but they will still need muscle to clear the land. Felons –'

Like Denver, Jade thought, and was silent. Such hatred – she was cold.

'Perhaps,' Henry said, divining her change of mood, 'I should go –'

'Oh, no! I have not been so diverted for long enough. Are you still with the Company?'

'I still have ships trading in India and the Spice Islands but I have also interests in New South Wales and Queensland.'

'What sort of interests?' Jade curled up in the big comfort-able chair and took up her wine glass. A strand of brown hair curled over her shoulder and down to her breast. Her eyes were very green.

'I have recently dealt in opals.'

'Oh, I love those stones. They are so alive compared with diamonds and sharp, shining things. I've always preferred opals, amber – jade. Their smoothness.'

256

28

'I notice that the trinket you wear is a particularly fine specimen. Very small but intricate. Quite valuable.'

Jade put her hand over it. 'It is a good piece. It's a wonder,' she admitted frankly, 'that it wasn't stolen, but I suppose Providence looked after me. It was given me by my father, oh, a long time ago.'

Unlike Heriot, he did not ask her about the past.

'You found your opals in Australia?' she went on.

'A good way from here. I needed a change and the *Isabelle* had put in at Port Jackson so I sailed on her, up the coast, away beyond Port Macquarie, where the country belongs to those black shadows in the bush.'

'Were you afraid?' She had found the aborigines sinister.

'I was cautious. Cowardly, I fear.' He laughed gently.

'I don't believe it. But, the opals! I was told they were to be found in Mexico and in parts of Europe. No one mentioned New Holland.'

'No one knew. No one really knows now apart from a man I befriended. Of course, it can't remain a secret and I couldn't wish to keep it so. But what I've found has brought me a far greater fortune than all my trading. I'm satisfied.'

'How did you meet?'

'Well, I decided I couldn't skulk on board for ever. For one thing there's something so compelling about a land mass one has never explored. And I had company. We took horses and provisions and rode inland, keeping a sharp lookout and making diagrams to help us find the way back. We found a river with small islands in it and fig-trees growing on the banks. There were parrots and cockatoos, black ones, and many birds I could not name, only draw pictures of them –'

'You paint?'

'Yes, not well but enough for the results to be recognizable.'

'Go on!'

'The banks were thick with emu and kangaroo, some wallabies. We made a fire of dead wood. There was plenty of that. While we were eating and drinking we noticed that the animals were behaving oddly, seeming afraid of something. The gilans were chattering their heads off and Richard, my partner at that time, noticed a black cloud along the horizon. The guide turned white; he knew what it was. The natives call it the willy-willy. If you're caught in its vortex, you're dead. As you can see I missed that! But it was bad enough. The birds became utterly quiet and that in itself was sinister.

The kangas got into the water. That blackness turned into a funnel-shape. Pure sand, spinning and whirling just above the ground, rushing up to the darkness above it. The sound of it was like a thousand dervishes. Oh, I was rather shaking in my boots – '

'And then what?'

'We threw ourselves down underneath anything that was handy. And then we were in the centre of a swishing shriek (or a shrieking swish!), and a sensation of being in a vacuum. I remember hot sand dropping on to my face and hands. It was very dark and bits of tree hit us. We could hear trees being torn up by the roots. It was like a devil bent on – taking us away, I suppose.' Henry shrugged, but she could tell that it had been no light experience.

'You were fortunate to escape.'

'Luckier than the poor travellers we stumbled upon next day. Two were lying dead and the third, who was some distance away, was near to death. He was aboriginal, guiding the others. The sand clung to the grease he'd smeared over himself and a boomerang was still clutched in his hand.

'We cleaned out the abo's eyes and nostrils and gave him brandy, but it was useless trying to carry on any sort of conversation.' Henry swiped out at a fly with much the same disgusted expression as Heriot's. 'Sign language was better. We never found out who the dead men were as they carried no papers. They had some crude equipment such as miners might carry. Their horses had vanished. Pick-axes protruded from the sand layer.

'After a restless night for everyone, we got up to see that the ground was patched with boulders. Richard and I knew that they hadn't been there the previous night. There was a big one under the blue-gums and Richard gave it a bang with one of the pick-axes. Astonishingly, it split open and a kind of rainbow fell out of it. We picked up the shiny, coloured powder and it fell away through our fingers in particles of blue and green, orange and violet.

'I struck another and the same thing happened, except that a piece was left clinging to the coating of ironstone. Just a toothlike chip but enough to tell me it was an opal in its natural state.

'The aborigine had recovered by this time and he saw our attacks on the boulders. He shook his head as if to tell us we were wasting our efforts and kept pointing into the distant scrub. We had nothing to lose, so we went with him. We couldn't take the boulders with us and we could only destroy the opal at their hearts.

'I should say we went about forty miles or thereabouts. The soil was white and dusty and there was a good-sized hill facing us. Every now and again a turkey showed itself and we killed one for supper. The air was still filled with sand from the cyclone but it was thin and no real problem. The wild duck and pigeons had begun to settle almost normally.

'The darkness lifted after that and the sun showed red as fire through what was left of the sand. There were some bark huts, as though recently men had camped here, and white mounds of excavation beside a windlass. Two shafts that led underground.

'Well, we went down the shafts and found worked-out tunnels – dug through softish clay and struck something hard and glassy. The clay crumbled and there was a kind of opalescence shot through with glints of fiery colour. Underneath this we were able to break the roof of opal and the candles and lamps showed us sheerest magic. We dug a treasure from our small part of New Holland's unexpected bounties – '

'Australia's,' Jade corrected, enervated by the story, thrilled by the under-played marvel of discovery.

'I tried to trace the two men who died,' Henry told her, 'but there was no record of either them or their dealings with any buyer. It was, and still is, a mystery. We sank other shafts, of course, and found more. There must be tons of it elsewhere, but I never believe in taking what will never be of use to me. Richard and I became rich and so did the men we had with us. We swore we'd leave the rest for someone else. I bought a new ship with my part of the money and kept some of the best of the opal once it was cut and polished – '

'I should love to see it.' The moment Jade had spoken, she realized it was a mistake. Henry Lambert was a friend of Heriot's. She was a convict, serving a seven-year term for theft and importuning. It was presumptuous to expect to be treated as an equal.

'Of course you must,' Henry insisted warmly. 'I'll arrange it with Logan.' Then, seeing her expression, said, 'What's wrong?'

'You could hardly say anything else when I practically begged for an invitation. But it isn't practicable, is it? Everyone round here knows who I am. A transportee acting as

Logan's housekeeper.'

'People have been transported for very little,' Henry observed quietly. 'I heard a quite dreadful story once of a boy of thirteen who poached because his family was starving. He was flogged to excess and ended up in an asylum. I've seen prisoners crawling like dying dogs and it really seemed that they were not criminals at all in the truest sense. I'm not easily swayed and I'd swear you were good. I will say that if I ever hear anyone speak ill of you. It's very true that it's impossible to cast the first stone with any degree of right. We all have our miserable little skeletons in the cupboard and I'm no exception. I still want you to come and see my collection and would be honoured by your presence.'

She could not speak. She was so used to censure and the casting up of her unsavoury past that she had forgotten how it felt to be treated as an equal. For a moment her eyes glittered with unshed tears and Henry Lambert's face was a blur of brown and gold and shivering grey. Nick had grey eyes but they were not like this man's. Henry had something of the quality of Dr Marsh. A generosity that demanded no return.

'Logan may not feel as you do.'

'I'm sure he will.'

'Is it far? Your house?'

'The other side of Windsor.'

'Oh. It's only an hour or two's journey.'

'That's all.' Henry finished his wine. 'I must go now.' He sounded quite regretful.

'I've enjoyed talking to you. And thank you.'

'What for?' He looked surprised.

'Your faith.'

'Oh, that!' He got up and she saw that he was taller than she'd first imagined. He looked like a kindly Viking – if there were such a thing. Those Papa had mentioned had been beasts like Denver. But kindness could be superficial.

'I hope we may see you often,' she said, and meant it.

'Oh, I'm sure you will, now that I've discovered the reason for Logan's defections. He used to visit me much more, not that I blame him. He's been lucky.' The pleasant, good-humoured mouth twisted.

Jade wondered how it would look if she ever confided in him. It would be a pity to shatter his illusions. He envisaged her as a victim, but she had never really thought of herself as that. She had always seemed more or less in control of her destiny.

They shook hands and she watched him ride away. She had not felt so stimulated since the awful business of Denver and meeting the Davieses.

One moment she was asleep. The next, Heriot was in her bed, his body warm and urgent, his kisses on her throat, her eyelids. She opened her arms and took his head to her breast. Drowsily, she welcomed his caresses until her own passion was awakened.

'Heriot! I missed you. I'd not realized how much until you were here.'

'It's been an eternity. Hell –'

She laughed softly. 'Surely an exaggeration?' She raised her shoulders so that he could take off the bed-gown. His lips travelled the length of her body. The bed-coverings slid to the floor. Blue lines of moonlight penetrated the shutters and striped him like a zebra. Gabriel, she thought. You are Gabriel.

He entered her body, arousing acutest desire. Gabriel, she thought, drowning in circles of longing. She was like a pool in which a fish had jumped, sending out ever-increasing ripples. She moaned and clung to him but he was not Masson. Never could be. She was shaken and grateful, aware of a sensuous gratification, but there were no shimmering patterns of rainbow fire.

Rainbows. Henry Lambert had likened the opal dust to their iridescent beauty. Strange and ever-changing. Like life. Like love. True love.

Remorseful, she continued to hold Heriot when he was still, glad that he was there. Loneliness was the enemy. She must be glad for what she had. The moon and stars were not for everyone. Kaleidoscopes were mirages. They spelled out what was unreal. A child's dream.

'What have you done in my absence?'

'Taught Daniel how to ride Polly.'

'Polly?'

'That's what I called the mare.'

'And?'

'Tried to learn how to cook. Mrs Doyle is teaching Nan. She is marvellous but I cook very badly. You'd have stomach pains regularly if I made your meals.'

'There's no need for you to cook. You know that.'

'I polished all the furniture. I enjoyed that. It's the smooth, satiny feel of it I love. Like cool skin. Quite sensuous.'

'What else?'

'I entertained a friend of yours.'

'Oh?'

'Henry Lambert.'

'I meant to call on Henry but I found I wanted to see you more.'

'I liked him.'

'He's all right. Can be obstinate though you may not think it. He was probably on his best behaviour.'

'Yes, I could imagine he's far stronger than he allows anyone to see. That's why you like him. You don't get all your own way. You thrive on friction.'

'You've obviously given him a great deal of thought.'

'He wants us to visit him. Told me about his opals.'

'He asked you?'

'Yes –'

'I shouldn't have thought – Do you want to go?'

'Very much.'

Logan rolled over on to his back and stared at the shadowy ceiling. 'It could be difficult. You know that.'

'When I said the same thing he seemed unconcerned. Did you get all your business done?'

Heriot had not seemed to move away and yet she was immediately conscious of a sense of withdrawal. Whatever that business had been, he had not been pleased with the outcome. Intuition told her it concerned herself, but he had still wanted her the minute he got home. Jeffers. He'd asked to see the papers and would believe Collin's falsification. But nothing, it appeared, would destroy the feeling he had for her.

'I could not get the painting materials. It might be a long time before you have those.'

'It doesn't matter.' It did, though. She had been so set on capturing Masson's likeness that this news was a blow. Then she took in the import of what Heriot had just said. He spoke as though she would always be there. His affection for her was much greater than any disillusionment.

'How good you are to me. My time here was to be a punishment –'

'Don't speak of it.'

'Very well. But I can still thank you.' She rubbed her cheek against his shoulder. 'I've much to thank you for.'

'Go to sleep now,' he answered gruffly. 'I'm tired and so must you be.'

But she was not. Long after Heriot was asleep she lay in the warm darkness, glad that he did not intend to change anything. He had been the first lover to give her any kind of security. She would have to be careful not to give him too much cause to resent Daniel.

Her loving, beautiful Daniel.

Now that Jade had Polly, she accompanied Heriot on some of his rides about the sheep station. She could not help but be aware of the curiosity of the men. They had women of their own for she glimpsed them sometimes on the fringe of the trees that surrounded the bunkhouse, and heard their laughter.

There were dogs too, to help herd the sheep, so Elsrickle was a busy place. Heriot showed Jade a burnt clearing. This, he explained, had been the result of a bush fire they were fortunate in containing. Some of his livestock had been lost.

'Didn't they run away?' She saw no sign of fencing.

'My dear woman, sheep only stand still and allow it to happen. It's a peculiarity they have. Even if they were cold, they'd let themselves freeze.'

'Poor creatures. If only they'd had the sense to run!'

'Aye.'

Jade stared about her at the charred remains of what was left of the trees; the dark ash of what had once been living things. 'Thank God it did not spread any farther.'

'We fought like demons and, luckily, the wind changed at the vital time. I have Johnnie Dart to thank as much as any-one. Without his organization, the story could have had a vastly different ending.'

'He's a good man.'

She was glad when they left the desolation and rode towards a copse of wilga trees. The thick leaves were the colour of pale limes and round as pennies. Jade thought them quite beautiful and the shade delicious. Few trees in this new and exciting country gave any shelter. The sun was held off while they enjoyed its verdant canopy. The light that filtered through gave off a soft, green translucence. Everything about Jade was bathed in the greenness, her skin, her light-coloured gown, the sheen on her hair. She had an eerie fascination.

'How beautiful you are,' Heriot told her huskily. 'I've no fancy words but you know that I love you?'

'Do you?'

'And that I want to marry you – though at one time it was the last thing I intended.'

'Only you can't. There must be special dispensations to wed someone like me – '

'Someone like you! Anyone would think you were a leper!'

'I am to people like Bess Davies and that cousin of hers, Freda Symons.' She had discovered that the new settlers were her old enemies from the *Caroline*. Jade winced as she imagined the conversations that must have taken place between them.

'We can make do without their company.'

She shook her head.

'Here, you rely on your neighbours.'

'Any woman can make a mistake. She should not be expected to pay for it for the rest of her life.'

'But we must always be rated lower in the scale than the virtuous free settlers.' She could not keep the irony from her tone. 'The Davieses will not have forgotten the business of Denver. The thought of that man disturbs me.'

'Chained dogs only snap their teeth. They catch nothing.'

'He must hate both of us.'

'Forget him.'

She put back her head and looked at him. 'You have not mentioned Henry Lambert again. Perhaps he has had second thoughts about that visit.'

Heriot shook his head. 'Not Henry.'

He was right, for a note arrived next morning asking them both to come for supper the following evening and to stay overnight.

Jade was unexpectedly excited. She had been nowhere since she came to Elsrickle, apart from the traumatic ride to the Davieses' place. After her chores were completed and she had played with Daniel to the mutual delight of both, she indulged in an orgy of bathing and hair-washing and going through the limited but satisfactory wardrobe she now possessed. She chose the delicate green gown that was always her favourite. Collin had bought the material at Tenerife and Freda Symons had been vituperative about that in her hearing. But the unpleasantness could not dim her pleasure in the garment. Jade had liked all of her green outfits. She still had the pelisse. Sponged and restored, it would warm her in Australia's winter.

Heriot could not keep his eyes from her when she was ready, the snowy petticoats showing as he swung her up into the seat of the small carriage which had been cleaned and polished and made comfortable with cushions. She was aware of his pride in her as they drove along the river road, the fine houses lost in their enormous acres, the eucalyptus leaves gleaming in the light.

Windsor looked peaceful and attractive, the church perfection on its high perch. People looked at them with the curiosity to which she was now accustomed. It seemed that she was to be more than a nine days' wonder. Men hailed Heriot and he shouted back in good humour, looking so pleased with himself that Jade was touched. Could she stay with Logan Heriot for the rest of her days? She thought she might.

After Windsor, the carriage turned up a long, tree-lined road, well fenced and showing glimpses of parkland and massed shrubs. There were yellow flowers and the brooding paleness of the ghost gums, the brilliant darting of parrots and cockatoos.

The house itself was a haunted echo of beauty, rising high above Lambert's domain. Horses grazed in large numbers and geraniums of all colours flaunted their velvety blooms between the white pillars of the colonnade. Vines hung from the porch.

'It's a beautiful place,' Jade said. 'But it has not the same welcoming look as home.'

'Home?' Heriot's black eyes kindled. 'That's how you think of Elsrickle?'

'I suppose I do. And to think that I dreaded seeing the station at the beginning. I was so afraid Captain Jeffers meant to keep me and Nan for himself. He singled us out from the rest. Previously it had always meant – '

Heriot's smile vanished. 'What did it mean?'

'Oh, use your imagination!' She was annoyed with herself for arousing his dormant jealousy. 'As your mother would have said, "you ask the road you know".'

He turned to look out at the pelargoniums.

'I've looked forward to this for two days. Don't spoil it.' She reached out and linked her fingers through his. 'Please?'

Henry Lambert came out on to the sunstriped steps, smiling. He could not have failed to see Jade's impulsive gesture. Coming to the carriage he opened the door himself and held out his arm so that she could alight. Her eyes sparkled with a pleasure she could not hide. Not since she had lived at home had she felt so surrounded by those who vied for her favours. Lambert, as much as Heriot, liked her more than ordinarily. She felt fifteen again and looking forward to the party that had ended so abysmally. But she could not wish, uselessly, that nothing had happened. Events shaped people and one must not allow them to warp one. She had descended to rock bottom and now floated upwards on a reasonably stable cloud.

The room they were taken to was grander than anything in Elsrickle. The floors were polished cedar but this chamber was twice as long and had a Spanish influence. White walls and dark furniture and not much of that. Touches of red to go with the shining floor. White sheepskin rugs here and there. Long red curtains and filmy lace separating them. Pots of geraniums on white window sills.

Henry and Logan were talking but Jade was walking around the great room, one minute bathed in the white light from a window so that her gown was outlined in narrow fire, then plunged into shade so that she resembled some wood or water sprite.

Cool, mint-adorned drinks arrived and they relaxed, Jade listening to the badinage that passed between the two friends, at home in a harmony she had thought gone for ever. Blue-gate Fields and the Holy Land were a long-past nightmare, never to be repeated. The ghost of the period with Masson obtruded briefly, all holly-adorned, snow-crowned, tantalizingly redolent of roasted chestnuts and the feel of ice under the feet. But what place did winter have in Australia's heat? Heriot shifted his position and his shadowed face was Gabriel's. Her heart leapt.

The opal collection was housed in another long, low, shuttered room with cabinets of glass, a room that reminded her of the jade and soapstone collector. The shelves were covered with velvet against which the gems gleamed under the candle-light, one minute green shot through with a mottling of rainbow colours, the next glistening darkly, their edges a fiery orange, their surfaces smooth as Greek marble and showing only a kind of grey-blue lustre. She could not wait for the candle flame to be blown their way so that the miraculous interchange of green and orange began all over again, seducing her senses so that she wanted them as she had seldom wanted anything else.

'I thought opals were whitish with pink and little specks of yellow,' she said.

'There is a variety of such milky gems but they cannot possibly compare with the greens,' Henry told her. 'Or the orange pin fire.'

'Aren't you sorry you can never wear them yourself?'

'Often! But I do have some very handsome cravat pins. Indeed, I am wearing the best in your honour.'

'I hadn't noticed. I was looking at you, rather than at what surrounded you.'

Henry was pleased. 'You are very lucky this time, Logan. I must admit I envy you.'

'You'll never get her away from me. Only over my dead body.' Heriot was only half-joking.

A little frisson touched her spine. 'Don't talk like that!'

'Superstitious?' Heriot asked, satisfied that she feared for his safety.

She turned away from the opal cabinets, catching the last spots of fire in their translucent hearts. Though most of the stones were unset, some were made up into jewellery.

'What did you admire the most?' Lambert asked.

'Oh, the brooch in the form of a peacock's tail and the set of ear-rings beside it. And there was a lovely ring, a sort of cloudy lavender and lime with little diamonds round it. I liked too the long, oval-shaped one with a claw setting. It showed the most beautiful flashes of green and a lick of purple. Why did you have them set? Have you a fiancée?'

'Not yet.'

She sipped the last of the mint-flavoured drink. 'I can't think why.'

'A new country suffers in that way. The women are in a great minority and the worthy ones are almost invariably plain as pikestaffs,' Heriot said.

'And into which category would you put me?' Jade asked wickedly.

Heriot laughed.

'You are in a class entirely of your own,' was Lambert's reply. 'The rules will never apply to you.'

'You've no other guests?' Heriot demanded.

Lambert shook his head. 'There's no one else I really wanted.'

Did he mean it, or had he foreseen what would have happened? Everyone within a wide radius would now be aware that Logan Heriot had a mistress who had been notorious aboard the *Caroline*, a transport vessel, and who had thrown herself at a convict called Denver, causing him to be flogged to insensibility. She also had a son to another man and a sister not quite normal. Lambert had been discerning. She was glad she was beyond the pale, for cruelty and censure were qualities she recognized all too clearly and wanted to avoid as long as she lived. That could be construed as cowardice but dining with Logan and Henry seemed far more agreeable and she had never wanted to become a social climber like poor Mama.

Mama had grown dim and unrecognizable, a tiny figure in sugar pink who dwindled into nothingness. But Papa was still clear. A little weak perhaps, but full of love and caring. She hoped she might see Papa again but it would not be until he was old. If ever –

A tall, thin woman came to tell Lambert that the meal was ready.

Magic took over from regret. It was all candle-light and flowers and dishes that were rare and delicious food, some of which Jade did not recognize.

Henry had a spinet which he played very well. He played 'Greensleeves' with just the right touch of nostalgia and a glance at her gown to show that she was involved in his choice. She felt that she had never been so content. Nan was developing into a happy woman. Daniel was a joy. Henry was a true friend and Heriot loved her to distraction. What more could she want? And why did she have the sudden certainty that it could never last?

The notes of music dropped into a well of perception.

CHAPTER NINE

They saw a good deal of Henry after that night. Jade continued to regard him as a cherished friend. Logan was surprisingly indulgent about their liking for one another considering that he never lost his suspicion of Daniel. Women never really cast off their children though they did change in their feelings about their men. Sons clung to their mothers. Logan should know. He had worshipped his and resented his father's place in her life.

Their days revolved round sheep and horses, the crops on the land nearer the river. Self-sufficiency was vital when one lived so far from Sydney and everything must otherwise be imported or transported.

Occasionally, Heriot was forced to accept invitations from friends or acquaintances he did not wish to estrange, and, at these houses, he noted there was almost always some single woman of good character who was sat next to him. Jane Benson, of course, was not invited but not one of those so-called good women could rouse in him an iota of what he found in her. The match-making was abortive.

There was only that one facet of their relationship that disappointed him. Jane had not become pregnant by him and there was that boy who proclaimed that she was in every way suited for perfect childbirth. Hardly out of the schoolroom, she had fallen for another man's child. A potent, virile male, while he –

Daniel had become a symbol of what was lacking in himself.

Jane had few wants. A pair of shoes, some toiletries, shampoos and suchlike and the occasional expedition to town. The apothecary's was one of the few regular calls. But Heriot liked to please her with unexpected purchases, bolts of material, a carpet for her room, bulbs and seeds for the garden she had begun, though it had to be well fenced off from the sheep and kangaroos.

On her birthday he gave her pearls and Henry one of the rings she had admired, the larger opal with the small diamonds. He would never forget her expression when the boxes were opened, the incredulity that swiftly became a kind of pain. How brilliant her eyes had become. Her voice had become small and high-pitched, then changed as Nan brought Daniel in, dressed in his best clothes and carrying a posy of flowers picked from the little garden. All the love he wanted from her was there in the look she gave the small boy and the hug she gave to the girl who was not really her own sister.

He had become so hungry for Jane's love that he could not contemplate the remainder of his life should she turn against him. He had her affection and loyalty but it wasn't enough.

Possession of her was a joy and a torment. But she was still with him and obviously wished to remain. One day he would make her feel as he did. Somehow he must.

It was late February when the rains came. The sky had been

heavy and grape-coloured, the air intensely enervating. Daniel had been fretful and Mrs Doyle full of Irish dolour. 'To be sure, Miss Jane, and it's going to be real bad.' She watched a streak of jagged lightning strike one of the ghost gums with an unholy pleasure. 'There, what was I after tellin' you! Real bad, it is.'

Nan sat with the child while Heriot and Jade went round the house, closing all the windows and listening to the artillery of rain against the roof. The woods smoked and the sound of the sheep almost drowned in roll after roll of thunder. The blue-white flashes were the worst for they lit up the rooms in some vast electrical madness, showing Jade cowering maids and even Heriot's face set in a kind of apprehension that worried her. The thunder of the rain became an integral part of their lives, never ceasing or even slackening in its ferocity.

'The livestock,' she murmured, as they stood side by side at the french windows.

'Will survive. Or most of them will. There's not much we can do. It's nature. At least we're better off than the Davieses and Symonses. I admit I fear for them.'

'Shouldn't we see if they are all right?'

'You'd show concern for people who ostracize you?'

'Isn't there something in the Bible about turning the other cheek?'

'I never cease to marvel at you.' Heriot grabbed at her and pressed his body close to hers. He could feel her heartbeat, quickened with either fear or anticipation. 'If I were struck by lightning at this moment, I'd be content.'

'Heriot!' Her voice was crisp. She felt suddenly that she was so lucky now that she must help others. 'We don't matter! Elsrickle is safe. Those neighbours of yours are on low ground and you told me that once the Hawkesbury rose nearly forty feet. We should be doing something constructive. I admit we can't leave at this moment. But the minute it slackens –'

'God knows when that will be. If we left now we'd be pounded into the ground.'

'There's that track above Elsrickle.'

'Aye, there is.'

'When it stops, shall we – ?'

'I'll get no peace if I don't! But you cannot leave the house. I won't allow it.'

'If you go alone, I will not have peace of mind. Let me come with you.' Her hand stroked his forearm. 'Please.'

'You can't know what the conditions will be like.'

'I can. I know that my garden will be swept away. But I can make another.'

Now, Heriot thought, she spoke of the future as though it were everything.

'I'll not let you go into danger.'

'We can take food and dry clothes at least. Anything less would be inhuman.'

'They don't deserve your consideration.'

'Will Henry be safe?'

'Eminently.'

'Good. I'd not like the though of him being in danger.'

'No,' Logan said. 'You think a lot of Henry, don't you?'

'As a friend,' she replied quickly. 'Nothing else.'

'Nothing?'

'Only as a good, kind, dear friend,' she reiterated firmly. A great flash of light showed her Heriot's face, whitened by the storm into a facsimile of Gabriel's. 'You are my lover, not Henry.'

Not her love, Heriot noted. Her lover. There was a difference. It was ironic that this was what he wanted once.

There was a terrible excitement about standing at the window, the stream of water gushing past the all too fragile barrier of glass, seeing the world lit up as the vicious light speared the sky and anything else that came in its way. The fields below, the great stretch of water had become one enormous lake that spewed out floating objects, trees, sheep, pieces of bark, garden furniture, each thing swirling as though in the centre of some vortex, spinning, disappearing downstream while something else took its place.

When the deluge showed signs of abating, Jade ran to the store cupboards, turning out blankets and sheets, spare shirts and garments, a side of bacon and one of salt beef, butter, a sack of flour.

Johnnie Dart ran from the bunkhouse and Heriot asked him to saddle the horses to the buckboard and help stow away the goods under tarpaulin. It would be a rough ride and the food and clothing must be kept dry.

The voice of the river had grown loud and aggressive. The violent channel down which the debris was tossed like so many children's toys, was even more turbulent as if the river had grown some cruel new gullet that worked ravenously, eating everything that came its way to ensure its own limited existence.

Johnnie rode ahead to tell the Davieses help was on its way. The buckboard slithered and jerked on its perilous journey. In spite of its elevation the high road was nothing more than mud and Heriot frequently had to lay down branches so that the wheels could gain some purchase. The road was made originally because during the last bad floods no one had been able to get beyond Elsrickle. The chain gang had made it in just over three weeks but it had been improved since. After this it must certainly be repaired.

It was not such a great distance but it took them a long time. It was moonless and the rain still fell though much less strongly. Jade was soaked after the first ten minutes but there was an exhilaration in the need for continual striving against the wet and the mud. Her shoulders ached and her body was chilled for it was much cooler since the worst of the eruption. Heriot was a vague glistening shape, working and encouraging the horses to greater efforts. The poor beasts were lathered with sweat by this time, plunging and slipping.

A feeble glimmer came out of the sodden dimness. The flicker of lamplight. Johnnie shouted, 'Leave the stores up there. Come down on foot, the path's washed away.'

Jade stepped down into an ankle-deep morass. She clutched at Heriot's arm.

'Don't let go,' he warned. She heard his boots squelch in the quagmire. Together they ploughed through the thick slough towards the anaemic light. Johnnie appeared, holding up a lantern. The yellow glow showed the dark line to which the floodwaters had risen, then ebbed away. Jade felt a swift flash of sympathy.

They pushed open the swollen door but there was no sign of either of the Davieses. Only the lamp burning in a spoiled, empty house.

'They'll be at the Symonses',' Heriot said, half to himself. 'They're on lower ground.'

'I always thought Bess bigoted,' Jade told him, 'but she's brave. No one could say otherwise. How far is it to the Symons?'

'Two miles. And we couldn't take the buckboard. There's no track.'

'Then we'll take the horses, and the lantern, of course.'

'You'd be prepared – ?'

'Oh, Logan! You know you want to go. We have to, otherwise we're no true neighbours and in Australia we have to be.'

'You should stay here. Johnnie and I will go.'

'And what would I accomplish? I'll be far more use helping you. I'm not made for skulking in corners while you get on with everything that matters.'

'There's no one in the bunkhouse,' Johnnie said unemotionally. 'They let the convicts go before they left the house.'

'What else could they do? Leave them to drown? But they'll be hiding somewhere.'

'They can't get to Elsrickle, can they?'

'Be sensible,' Heriot said. 'Remember the struggle we've just had? No, they'll be hidden close by. Another reason for leaving with us. I certainly couldn't leave you knowing they were loose. I haven't forgotten Denver.'

'No more than he's forgotten you,' Jade could not help saying.

'I have not the time to worry about one renegade. Johnnie and I will fetch the horses and we'll pick our way along the bank.'

'Can we take any of the things I brought?'

Heriot shook his head decisively. 'We'll have our work cut out to get ourselves there. Two miles does not sound much on horseback, but there's never been a viable road beyond the Davieses' place and the Symonses have not had the time to do more than mark the track. Come on, Johnnie.'

They were no sooner gone for the horses when Jade was assailed with memories of Denver, his greyness, that shaven head, the arrow-painted garments, those ice-blue eyes that turned grey with hatred of anything right or decent. The thought of him lay like a shadow on her heart. Every slightest noise, the slap of the rain, the creaking of soaked timber and slopping floorboards seemed the sound of his coming. Despising herself, she ran, in a sweat of fear, to bolt the bloated door, then set herself to mopping up some of the mess of water against Bess's return.

Somewhere in the dark, Denver lurked with his freed and complaisant cronies. Desperate men always listened to the anarchist. Jade forced herself to think of something else. Determinedly, she made herself wash away the black tide-mark from the kitchen wall. The bedrooms defeated her with their spongy mattresses and sodden pillows. They'd have to bake in the sun before they could be used again. A thunderous knocking sent her pulse beating fast.

'Who is it?'

'Damn you, Jane! It's Johnnie and me. Who else would it be?'

Thankfully, she pulled the bolts and Heriot saw her, milky pale, a dark line around her forearms where she had dipped into muddy waters.

'I – remembered the convicts were free.'

'Of course. You did right. But we'd best go.'

'Yes.' She seemed frantic to leave and he could not blame her. He noticed also the changed appearance of the kitchen. This attempt at improvement touched him as much as her efforts to better their relationship. He knew, too, that she did not love him. One could achieve quite a rapport without actually being in love. It had ceased to matter. The fact that she had any sort of feeling for him was enough. For the present. He wanted the future to be different, though, even if it meant making friends with that child. Nan was easy to like and, anyway, she would soon be Johnnie's business. He wasn't blind.

The door creaked suddenly and Jade saw a shadow in the dimness. Two – three shadows. As she had lived Denver's appearance in her mind, now the reality came over her a hundred times worse than in imagination.

Heriot spun round sharply, his eyes assessing the possibilities of the wrecked kitchen. It was impossible to retrieve the shotgun that was strapped to the horse under a cover of tarpaulin. He hoped they had not found it first. But there had not been time. The horses were beside the trees, tethered against their departure.

Jade remembered the knife she had used minutes ago to scrape off some of the thickest mud. As the first of the men took a step over the threshold, she retreated towards the table.

The man was tough-looking, his nose battered like a boxer's. Her first feeling was one of relief. Had Denver been with them he would have come in first and far less tentatively. Heriot stiffened. Johnnie drew a deep breath.

'Come in, boys,' the man said. 'It's Mr Heriot and his whore, and John Dart.'

The shadows became a small knot of jostling men, their clothing soaked, their wrists still red and sore from the chains. Jade could not take her eyes off the tell-tale marks.

'Where is it, then?' the pugilistic man demanded, keeping out of range of Heriot's bunched fists.

'Where's what?' Heriot asked. He was longing to rush at the man, Jade saw, but he would be remembering her presence. Her dependence. She saw the knife at that moment, half-hidden under a pile of rags. She moved slowly in front of it and shifted one arm behind her back.

'The things you brought for George Davies. We're hungry, ain't we, lads?'

'Aye. Hungry.' A sharp, pallid face was turned towards the girl. The rat-like smile brought a touch of coldness to her spine. It was too reminiscent of Newgate. And there were twice as many of them.

Her fingers touched the wooden handle of the knife, drew it towards the table's edge with infinite patience.

'We left everything up by the track when there was no one in the house.'

'Garn! We don't believe that. Mebbe you should have left her there too.' The rat-faced man moved a step closer and bared the sharp teeth in a grin. 'Wouldn't miss a few slices of the loaf, would you, Mr Heriot? Would you like to see how we does it? Might give you a few useful hints. I know we none of us ain't had a woman for a time. A sizeable time, but it's something you never forgets how to get on with, is it?'

'Where's the food?' the battered man asked again. 'Me belly's as flat as a board.'

'I told you,' Heriot said harshly, and his face was grey under the sunburn, 'the food and dry clothes are up at the end of the track. You're welcome to them. Go on, go and take them. The Davieses aren't here. They were intended for their use.'

Two of the men made to go out of the room but the rat-faced man called them back. 'We can get that wi'out his permission. But you're not going to let that tasty little piece stay here, are you? Keep us all warm, she could. Sleeps with anything, Denver said, or have you forgot? Nearly had her, he did. Said how nice it was until Mr Heriot arrived to spoil things. Put him in a real good temper if we was to let him finish what he began. Eh?'

Someone laughed and somehow the original intention to fill their stomachs had turned to something much more ugly.

The convicts were growing bolder. One of them picked up a jar of rum from the corner and held it to his mouth, tipping back his head to gulp at the fiery contents. They were forgetting the punishment for disobedience. There were six of them to the three from Elsrickle and one of them was a woman.

'Don't look so pretty, do she,' one commented, reaching for the stone jar, 'not with her hair in rats' tails and dirty —'

'She don't have to look nice. All that matters is that we can dip our wicks. Anyway, I don't see much wrong. Pretty little pair of oranges she has, don't you think? Just fancy one in each hand.'

Someone sniggered. Heriot's face was ashen and his eyes were so furious that so far no one had dared to go near him. The jar was passed to the rat-faced man who drank deeply, then doubled over in a fit of coughing.

'Gore! Give us that,' the man next to him warned. 'You'll spill the lot.'

'Who's going to be first? With her ladyship? Must say this do give you the right feelin's. Makes me remember poking at my old woman and I ain't thought about that for long enough. Whips do have that effect on you.'

She had hold of the knife properly now. The crude vulgarities seemed worse with Johnnie Dart there to hear them. She minded his presence there more than Heriot's.

Emboldened by the effects of the rum, the unwelcome visitors drew a little closer.

'Don't you dare touch her!' Heriot barked sharply, his hands closing over a sodden chairback.

'And what'll you do, eh, if we did?' Rat-face jeered, a dribble of rum still running down over his pointed chin. 'We've as much right to her as you. She's a convict. Convicts should be for other convicts, not for men wi' money to burn. A fine feller you are when you're in bed with her, but we should have what *we're* entitled to and a convict woman's one of them. So hand her over peaceable like and we'll go like lambs. Or rams! Funny that, isn't it! Then why aren't you laughing like the rest of us, Mr Po-faced Heriot, eh?'

'Got you over a barrel, we have.' The flat-nosed man, made brave with rum and anticipation, lunged suddenly at Heriot. But Heriot was quicker. He swung the chair over his head and brought it down with a crack that seemed to reverberate against the stained walls. The man crumpled without a sound.

Rat-face had taken advantage of the incident. He flung himself at Jade, hands outstretched, and thrust himself against her. For a long moment she was aware of stinking clothes from which the damp exuded like a poison, of rank breath and a slobbering mouth that fastened, leech-like, on her throat.

Sobbing, she swung her arm round and struck at the upper part of that arm that held her fast against the edge of the table. Heriot was roaring like a Highland bull, the chair flailing towards yet another rum-emboldened figure.

And Johnnie was circling round the table, a spade in his hands, his blue eyes uncharacteristically hard.

Rat-face screamed. Blood spouted over her clothes and on to the wet floor. She pulled out the knife and thrust towards his chest, but he was already backing away. 'Fer gawd's sake, what's all the fuss about? You ain't no bleeding virgin to take on so. My arm. Look what you've done to my arm!'

'Damn your arm.'

They were all retreating now and the man with the battered face was pulling himself to his feet. Johnnie was making menacing motions with the edge of the spade. Part of the chair had broken off and lay on the floor.

Jade could see nothing but the blood on her clothing. She wanted to take it off but she had nothing here to take its place. This was like the aftermath of Captain Joel's death. She might have killed that rat-faced man and this time it would have been murder. She could not regret her actions.

The pugilistic man took hold of one of his comrades. They were no longer really aware of what they had done. Drink had too great a hold on them. Dimly, they realized that they were outmanoeuvred and outwitted.

'Damn you, you bitch,' Rat-face whispered. 'I hope Denver does get you one of these days. He'll be sorry he missed you.' Blood still trickled over the hand that was clamped over his wound. I'll tell him you did this.'

'Do,' she replied.

There was a sudden wild dash as Heriot and Johnnie crashed forward. They stuck in the doorway, squealing and cursing as blows fell about them, for all the world like a herd of pigs. And then they were gone, squelching through the mud, reviling the three left inside the house, voices and sucking footsteps growing fainter.

277

'Have they gone towards the horses?'

'No,' Johnnie answered. 'The other way.'

'Thank God. We mustn't stay another moment. They may meet the rest and come back. And Denver won't be so easily set back.'

Jade forgot about the blood. The rain or the flood would wash it away. She must stop thinking about what might have happened. It hadn't.

They left the house precipitately, the door left open on the night and weather. The darkness, as they pushed and struggled their way towards the line of the trees, took on a new and frightening dimension. Jade pictured Denver and his party of comrades standing perfectly still in that hostile obscurity, waiting to reach out for them as they drew close enough.

A branch touched her shoulder and she gasped.

'Hurry!' Heriot ordered tersely. 'Hurry.'

They reached the horses and Heriot checked that the shotgun had not been disturbed. Mounting with almost indecent haste, they turned in the direction of the Symonses' homestead.

The raindrops beat about them as they started off. The horses, clearly uneasy, began their slithering and slipping on the glutinous surface. They snorted and curveted, their heads lifted, their eyeballs rolling, their breath rising on the damp air.

They were always conscious of the sound and the movement of the river and the splash and stutter of the rain, sometimes a downpour, occasionally a cloudburst. The swash of the water against the softened banks was sinister since the soil was becoming softened to the point of complete dispersal. The horses' hooves churned up a mixture of treacle and muddy water. Jade's body was swung from one side to the other of the too-large saddle. The trees, though in the main unseen, reminded her of their presences. A branch would strike at her head or shoulder, throwing her off balance, her skin would be perforated by a spike or a notch in a leaf, the sharp tip of a twig. Nothing was safe or familiar. But there was no sound of the rest of the convicts.

She had a terror of being separated from Heriot and Johnnie but she could not continually be crying out for reassurance. Logan would lose all respect for her. Her stomach muscles were clamped tight as springs.

Occasionally, a dim light would penetrate the cloud and deluge and she would see the wet outlines of trunk or sapling, the dark spray of a cluster of leaves, all sharp and elongated, a wrack of dark sky moving.

Johnnie and Heriot said nothing. All their senses seemed concentrated on finding the path that was lost in a tempest of rain and wind.

Jade was soon wetter by far than on the first part of the journey. Cold water ran over her breasts as though they were uncovered. Her crotch was sore and chafed, her thighs and calves uncomfortable in the extreme. She was saddle-sore, longing for a bath and a quiet bed though they were as far away as the unseen moon. She compressed her lips to hold in the complaints that cried out for expression. At least they must be far away from the Davieses' convicts who could not have gone far on foot. They'd be shuddering under a wilga or a thorn tree, cold and hungry, waiting for the dawn.

Her knees clamped the streaming flanks of her mount. The horses were tired from dragging the laden buckboard from Elsrickle to Bess and George's house and hers was more weary, apparently, than Logan's or Dart's. They came to a shallow ford, an offspring of the Hawkesworth that soared softly but dangerously, only feet away A fig tree loomed up, innocuous but frightening for the horse which reared and slipped sideways so that, for a moment, she hung over swollen and racing waters.

She was vaguely conscious of screaming, of being precipitated from the wet saddle that had been such purgatory. Water closed over her, not fresh and clean but smelling of putrescence and death. Something cold and hairy bumped against her. She thrust it away, appalled, and felt the shoes sucked from her feet. The long skirts hampered her struggles. Somehow, she shot upwards and her head broke water. 'Heriot!' she screeched. 'Heriot! The river –'

And then she sank again, aware that her body was being carried on the surging current, spewed from side to side of channels where boulders grazed her flanks and hurt her shoulders. Each time her head surfaced she gulped in deep breaths but the emergence happened less frequently and she was afraid as she never had been. But she was too busy struggling to think that she may be destined to drown.

Her head broke through the polluted surface for what must be the last time. She sobbed with frustration that her energetic attempts had brought her no closer to the dimly discerned bank. A floating branch tore at her long hair.

'Jane! Jane!' It was Heriot calling her, tantalizingly close. 'Grab hold of something.'

But what! Anything close at hand raced in the same direction as herself and there was the horrid sound of a fall not too far away. The soaked skirts pulled at her tired legs, inching her down through a mess of drowned birds and rats or scratching twigs. A dead sheep bobbed beside her, its eyes only cavities, reminding her of the tethered crow. A great cry burst from her throat and this time she thought she saw Heriot on the other side of the maelstrom, his arms flailing strongly, then a floating bush came between them and attached itself to her buoyant hair. Her scalp seemed about to come adrift and she called out helplessly, unable to disentangle herself from the great encumbrance.

A picture came to her of a painting she had seen of a drowned girl but the corpse had been beautiful and calm, floating in a welter of water lilies and scattered flowers, the dark lashes curved on cheeks that showed no pain or stress. Its unreality was borne upon her as she gasped and floundered, her fingers outstretched to grasp anything that was stable. But she was in mid-stream, anchored to a harsh mass of vegetation that hid her from Heriot's searching.

Water poured into her mouth as she cried out for what must surely be the last time. Daniel! Who would care for her baby now?

A body collided with her own and she pushed it away in revulsion. It would be someone dead long since and she could not bear to be reminded of mortality.

She was calling out for Daniel but he would be asleep and safe. Only not so protected if she died. Jade struck out strongly, restored by the thought of the boy who depended on her for everything. The dark bulk in the river was some way off.

'Jane! Jane. Let me help you. Don't push me aside a second time.'

She found herself laughing, choking on her own hysteria. Heriot could not possibly be there. It was the voice of the Devil, trying to claim her by making her give up too easily. But her throat was raw and painful and she had lost power in her arms. Floundering and pulled down as though by unseen fingers by the weighted gown, she threw up one hand in a last effort of will.

The hand was seized by something cold and very strong.

Her head was under water and her lungs and eyeballs bursting. Water rushed into her protesting mouth. Spluttering and shrieking, she was impelled to the tainted surface. The sour stink of rotting things turned her stomach, but she was above the river's coursing bosom, free of the great bush but attached to something living that took her with it.

Her limbs turned flaccid and useless but even in her last conscious moment she was no longer afraid. Her senses rushed away with the sound of a water-wheel caught in her brain, splaying, creaking, turning to eternity.

She struggled feebly and was lost.

She returned to consciousness in a shivering pinkness that bathed a stained ceiling and several faces. A damp blanket, exuding steam, was wrapped about her. She coughed miserably and a wooden cup full of water was pressed into her hand. All she could see were Bess Davies's eyes and a hand she knew instinctively was Heriot's.

The blanket fell away, revealing an old-fashioned calico nightdress that enveloped her from throat to ankles. 'It's not mine,' she heard herself muttering. 'It's not mine.'

'It's mine,' Freda Symons said out of the pink gloom.

Jade, raising her eyes, saw that the room had only half a ceiling. The rest was collapsed in the far end of the room, showing a gap through which the stars pricked the sky.

'I came to help,' Jade insisted, 'to help.'

'You can help tomorrow.'

The walls bore great patches of slime and darkness. She knew they could do nothing here. The Symonses' house was ready to fall.

'My – throat hurts.'

'So it should with all the yelling you did from the Hawkesbury,' Heriot said a little grimly.

'I remember now. My hair was caught in a floating tree. It wouldn't let go.'

'It held you up, more or less, until I reached you.'

'I was drowning.'

'Come here,' Heriot ordered.

She obeyed, every step an effort she did not wish to repeat. Heriot pulled her to his knee and settled her head on his shoulder. People spoke in low voices but in a moment the murmuring drifted away like the current in the river and she fell asleep again.

She was perfectly well when she awoke a second time, apart from a stiffness of the body and a raw throat. But it was true that it was due to all the screaming she had done. Heriot had saved her. She owed him her life. The bush had not really held her up, only entangled itself in the ends of her long hair. She had been a prisoner, doomed to drown but for him. She no longer owed him her gratitude for caring for those she loved most, but for the essence of her being. It was a burden of debt that would not be easily repaid.

The Symonses must rebuild and had nowhere to stay in the meantime and no labour since they had also released their half a dozen convicts.

'You must come to Elsrickle,' Heriot told them, 'all of you.'

'Yes,' Jade said. 'There is plenty of room.' She knew he was pleased with her reaction.

They set off in the afternoon towards the Davieses' house. The Symonses were to follow when they had recovered any treasures that the flood had not carried away. The skies had emptied themselves and there was no more danger.

All the way along the water-logged track, Jade remembered being thrown into the river. It was something she would never properly forget. It was strange how quickly they came back to Bess's house.

The men went to look for firewood so that the house could be dried out a little but Bess stared around her with an angry desperation. To think that all the days, weeks and years of endeavour should result in such havoc! She felt she could not bear it. It was so unfair.

Jane Benson, in spite of her narrow escape, was unsparing in her efforts to bring back order. Bess had seen the evidences of the girl's devotion to Heriot whom she liked. That lingering clasp of his hand with hers had not gone unnoticed. Perhaps rumour had been distorted and Denver *was* bad.

Johnnie came in with some sticks that had miraculously escaped the water. He cleaned out the stove and coaxed a sulky fire inside the black-leaded iron. Jade filled a large pot and while she waited for it to boil she went round the house seeing what needed doing first. Water still slopped around the floors so she found a broom and swept as much out as she could. Any rugs, she picked up and took to the porch where she hung them over the rail to dry off. The rain had stopped and she made her way up to the buckboard and took out a dry gown for Bess and some tea and bread and butter, then covered up the rest.

The water had boiled by the time she came back, but Bess, white and shocked, still sat without moving. It seemed she had lost all will to do anything for herself.

Johnnie said he should go up to the bunkhouse where the convicts had been in case any had stayed.

Gently, Jade coaxed Bess to allow her to remove the spongy clothing, then washed and dried her body by the growing warmth of the fire and squeezed her into the gown. Then she found a teapot and, washing out the sediment of mud, prepared tea.

Bess stared at the cup and the bread and butter on the plate. Her face crumpled. Jade caught her in her arms. 'It'll be all right,' she said. 'It will, you'll see.'

She waited till Bess had recovered herself and made her drink tea and eat a piece of bread, then she heated more water and began to clean the kitchen. One place that was reasonably presentable would work wonders for Bess's morale.

The bedrooms were unusable. Coverlets and mattresses needed many days of washing and thorough baking in the sun. Jade left them alone and went to the sitting-room where she was surprised to see Bess busy with a bucket and cloth.

'You should have stayed by the fire,' Jade said. 'I could do this.'

'You made me ashamed.' Bess would not look at her. 'I'd marked you down as – '

'A wanton? Bent only on getting all she could from a man?'

'Something like that. But I see I was wrong. And so was I for giving up hope. We're all alive. There's nothing that won't be improved by a bit of striving. Don't stay away in the future, Miss Benson – Heriot told us about the convicts coming back.'

'Jane.'

'Miss Jane. You'll always be welcome at our house. Freda must have got you wrong. I knew those transports were bad places and I've heard tales since you were here that made me think. Now that I've seen you do have proper feelings for Logan, I can't pretend I'm proud I was so stiff-necked. That Denver's pure evil all the way through and that beating's made him worse. Any trouble with the men's because of him. They've been treated fairly but he makes them dissatisfied. That's why George didn't want to let them out in spite of the danger. It's a pity Denver's got some of them on his side.

I always felt they were waiting for an opportunity to get hold of the keys and unlock his chains, and now he's free. It's like loosing a plague on the world. Anyway, that's beside the point. All I'm trying to say is that if Logan comes in the future, you must come too. I won't take no for an answer. Now, let's see what more we can do. It takes your mind off worrying about the menfolks, doesn't it? Never one to sit idle, I wasn't. Can't think what came over me.'

Together, they tackled the business of cleaning the aftermath of the worst flood for a decade.

The bed-chamber was the only place where Jade and Heriot could be alone since the Davieses and Symonses had come to stay. It was only for a few days but already it seemed like years and helped to show Heriot and Jade just how pleasant their lives had been. Nan was discreet and Daniel asleep by six or thereabouts. Johnnie was available for any emergency after tea-time. They had had all evening to themselves before the rains and had not really appreciated the freedom.

Now it was a snatched hour or so between supper and sleep and both had come to realize their cosanguineness. They were friends now as well as lovers.

'What other poor souls was George meaning?' she asked and leaned over to blow out the candle, but Heriot shielded the flame. 'I want to see you. I realize, selfishly, that I'm disinclined to share you,' he told her. 'We were talking of the convicts who are at liberty. They won't come here but may trouble other people.'

'At least one good thing's come out of the flood. I am accepted by women who thought very little of me before this. But there's nowhere for those convicts to go except to double back on their tracks. There's only the bush beyond the Symonses' land and the bush is a killer.'

'Nevertheless, the bush has always been the sanctuary. They'll crawl out one day, those who are left, and give themselves up to the devil they know. It always wins in the end. Familiarity. Safety.'

'Just as you will always do the same. With you I am safe.'

'You make me sound dull.' But he smiled as he said it.

'I don't find you in the least unexciting.'

'You need not have troubled to put on that nightgown for I am going to take it off again.' He cupped her breasts with his hands.

'I'm afraid you are not,' she said. 'It's the time of month I can't oblige you.'

'Damnation,' he answered, vexed. 'You know, Jane. I had thought to see you with child long before this. We've not lived what you'd call chaste lives.'

'How can we have a child and not able to marry? You want an heir, not a bastard, surely? One day you'll want to wed – and it may not be to me.'

'So long as you are alive, I'll want no one else.'

'It will be five years before we can marry. You could change in your feelings and I'd not tie you with an infant. Not until we are both absolutely certain. You'd not be forgiven by your other friends as you have by Bess and George or Freda Symons. I don't want to cut you off from their society. You need them – and I'd rather not blackmail you –'

'I need you more and always will.'

'You think you will. But men change –'

'And so do women!' he cried.

'Then, that's your answer.'

He allowed her to put her arms around him but the conversation had given him much food for thought. It seemed that it might not be any disability of his that was to blame for Jane's childlessness. Those visits to the apothecary – he had never questioned what was in the bottles. If she had a child by him it would be the lever to make her become his wife. He could always approach Governor Macquarie – explain the situation. And if she did not become pregnant?

He refused to think of the possibility.

Henry Lambert had looked forward to Jade's visit more than usual. She had consented to sit for him while he attempted a portrait of her.

Jade, in turn, could not wait to go there because he had promised her some painting materials which Heriot had still not been able to purchase in Sydney. Anyone who had come provided with such things wanted them to produce pictures of Australia's flora and fauna or seascapes of Port Jackson Heads, or views of Sydney and Parramatta. Artists earned good money executing scenes for sale to departing emigrants. This had become an increasingly lucrative business.

Meanwhile, the artists' brushes and pots of paint Heriot had ordered were still somewhere on the ocean and he fretted because Jade must do without them.

Escorted like some lady of quality into Henry's Spanish drawing-room, Jade accepted a drink flavoured with mint and relaxed elegantly in a handsome carved chair made comfortable with red cushions. Her eyes half-closed, she thought suddenly and incongruously of Jack Flynn and the citadel, of Nick Caspar's brothel. Images of leprous buildings, of cold, filth and what seemed like nothing more than the darkest nightmare. Unpleasant odours, dirty clothing, want, poverty, the hanging at Newgate, Eliza, Bella Scrivener, she could not believe that they had ever existed.

And then the unwelcome thought of Denver obtruded. He had the power to make it all real again, for his pale, cruel eyes and shaven head seemed the essence of the past. Henry's world was the dream and Denver's was reality.

Heriot and Lambert were such agreeable contrast that she was impelled to go and kiss them both, and Logan, of course, pretended jealousy. 'You can't have her,' he said again, 'not unless –'

But Jade would not let him joke about dying. Life was too good. There was only the memory of Masson that gnawed at her like a maggot in the heart of an apple. But Gabriel was gone. She must forget him.

Henry showed her where she must sit for greatest effect and set up an easel. The sunlight struck through the long window and the white drapes behind her, outlining her slender body and firing the edges of her wood-brown hair. The green gown Henry had requested she wear was a mystery of gold and lime, of thin emerald stripes. Heriot's black gaze made her feel wanted and secure. She divorced her thoughts from the present and let them roam where they would.

She was walking in a copse at Ayas Bywaters and the old damp trees were covered with emerald velvet. It was darkening and the grey thorns scribbled queer, hostile shapes against the sky. The quiet house awakening to the music and lights of one of Mama's routs. Jade too young to be part of the drinking and flirting, Papa enjoying the rare taste of company. Mama had kept him in a golden cage, the fetters forged with Jardine money. Papa liked expensive things and being waited upon. Life – There was the fun of watching through the slats of the balustrade. She was riding in the snow towards the house with the stag gate-posts –

She no longer regretted what was irrevocably lost. Heriot had welcomed her into another and more satisfying relationship. She thought they had grown closer together of late and she was conscious of a sense of even greater well-being in the last few days. A kind of fulfilment she could not explain.

Henry put away his work without allowing her a sight of it. 'It must be finished first. I hope you are ready for supper.'

She was. She was ravenously hungry though she had never had a large appetite. Australia's usual heat had always quelled it. Yet, once she had eaten and drunk she was unaccountably squeamish though it passed off quite soon. She had seldom felt better. Heriot had looked almost guilty when she referred to the passing indisposition and then his eyes had gleamed suddenly as though he were pleased about something.

Henry regaled them with more reminiscences of the opal-mining, how the jewel was not a precious stone in the sense that rubies, diamonds and sapphires were. Opal was formed of hydrous silica, produced under extreme pressure in which sudden great heat and water were the chief agents. There seemed some tenuous connection with opal and lime deposits, fishbones and other such theories, but the finding of the meteorite boulders with opal at their centres seemed to point to the first suggestion being the most tenable.

'Of course, one always finds a great deal of potch—'

'Whatever is that?'

'Inferior opal. Lacking the wonderful fires and "life" of the real stone.'

'So it's all a great lottery.'

'You're far safer with your sheep and horses,' Henry told Logan.

'But you have the superiority where the romantic aspect matters. You can bestow your seductive gems, whereas all I can give is a ewe or a ram.'

'That's *not* all!' Jade defended and surprised a look in Henry's eyes that put her on her guard. He must not be allowed to become too fond of her. That would spoil the whole relationship. Constraint crept into the ensuing chatter. Henry noticed, being perceptive, but Logan carried on especially cheerfully as though he'd been given a bonus.

He carried her to bed that night and treated her like a piece of porcelain. She could not understand his behaviour and would have preferred him to be his normal quite passionate self. Yet she was a little tired though she had done less than usual and it was undeniably comforting to be held in his arms, knowing that she need never lose such a refuge.

She had passed the stage where Heriot's attraction lay in the fact that he resembled the man she loved. Her feelings for him were real and soundly based even if they did fall short of what Logan required. But there was a lifetime in which to change them.

Henry was quiet next morning and she did not feel at ease as she took up her position by the window. But she was comfortable leaning against the red cushions, her body lapped with a content that was part lassitude and a thankfulness that nothing more strenuous was required of her. The geraniums on the sills glowed like fire. She and Heriot had Elsrickle to themselves again but the invasion of neighbours had gone on for longer than anticipated. Both Davieses and Symonses had decided to rebuild their houses on higher ground and, whereas Bess and George could return to the original building when it was dried out, and superintend the making of the new structure, the Symonses had had nowhere to live but Elsrickle.

It was good to be back to the normal routine with plenty of time for Daniel and the women of the house, yet, strangely, Jade had found even the little boy's romping more tiring than usual. A vague sensation of disquiet permeated her peace of mind. She hoped she was not going to be ill.

'You've changed,' Henry said abruptly. 'Between your last visit and this one, you've altered.'

'How?'

'I thought I was going to paint a girl. But you've become a woman.'

'Is that so bad?'

'No. It's not bad.' Henry obviously wanted to say more but contented himself with scowling ferociously at the easel and plying the brush more energetically.

Jade returned to her reflections. She'd written to Ma Lee, posting the letter to the address in Lavender Street. Lily Stalker would see that it was delivered. The evocation of Ma's stout, satin-clad shape had the power to make Jade feel, for a moment, acutely homesick. Ma Lee had been like a mother. She could never be sufficiently grateful to her and poor Jack, dead trying to protect her! It was terrible to think that a man could disappear in a city like London, almost without question. But she had paid her debt to Flynn by doing her best for Nan. Johnnie Dart was truly in love with the girl and Jade thought that Flynn would have approved of him. She'd get Governor Macquarie to arrange a special dispensation so that they could marry. There were always a limited number of such concessions on the occasion of the King's birthday or that of some other member of the Royal Family, and Heriot was seeing the Governor tomorrow while Henry escorted her back to Elsrickle. Her eyes gleamed. She'd speak to Logan later.

'What schemes are you involved with now?' Henry asked curiously, noting every fleeting expression.

She smiled. 'Oh, just a little plan that will give me the greatest pleasure and to two other persons I love.'

'Surely you can tell me? After all, we are friends.'

'I will, once it's settled.'

'You can be a maddening creature.'

'You said that with great feeling.'

'I should have paid Jeffers to send *me* the most beautiful and spirited girl from the *Caroline*. Then –'

'Don't!' she said, suddenly disturbed. 'We're happy as we are – We can't be – if –'

'If I speak out?'

'I want things to stay as they are. I'd be desolate if we couldn't meet comfortably – You see, I could never pretend – Not to Logan.'

'I've pretended for some time.' Henry stood closer to the easel and put a delicate stroke into the shadowing of Jade's hair, then touched a spot of light into one eye.

'Then, you must continue to do so,' she replied steadily. 'I could never give Heriot cause for distress. I owe him far too much. You can't know what went before –'

'I'm not a fool,' Henry told her, standing back to look at the portrait through narrowed lids. It was not a detailed painting, more an impression, diffused and fragile as a dream. That was how he saw her, of course. Far off and beyond his reach.

'Then you must know that I'm no man's ideal,' she said crisply. 'Not at all the sort of woman you should be seeking. Take one of your ships and go to London or to America. Find a proper wife, one you'll never need feel ashamed of and who'll never drag you down to her own level.'

'Don't speak so!' he retorted angrily. 'What level!' He defended her as strenuously as Heriot. Throwing down the brush he said, 'That's the best I can do. There's something about you that slips away the more I try to grasp it. Come and look.'

She went to him, taking hold of his arm in the old, friendly way, but he remained stiff and stubborn of expression. She had always known Henry had this stronger side.

Her eyes went from him to the painting. Against the white-hot light that came through the filmy drapes, he had presented her as an enigma. Nothing at first sight seemed quite finished, then, mysteriously, became complete. Once recognized as a whole, the shadowed face remained so. Henry's touch was subtle, indeed.

'It's more than good,' she said. 'But Heriot would not understand it. He'd expect something more – in his own words – straightforward.' This set her off laughing in a way that Henry recognized as a secret joke between the two people he thought he loved most. He felt excluded. Unhappy – Hating Logan.

'It's not for Heriot,' he replied a little brusquely. 'That's for myself. I'll do one that's more conventional if you can bear to sit for longer.'

'All I seem to want to do at present is to loll about like some emperor's concubine.'

'Then, go back and loll. Pretend you are part of Solomon's court. Sheba – '

'And you won't forget my recompense?' she asked.

Henry frowned.

'You were to give me some painting materials. Enough to do two or three miniatures.'

'Oh, that. Of course. I'll have them made up into a little parcel and left in your room.'

'Thank you.'

He removed the portrait and set another prepared board in its place.

So Heriot found them when he returned from his riding. Unable to resist a look at the new painting he watched Henry for a moment, the fine, swift movements of wrist and brush. 'You have her features quite well.'

'So I should,' Henry answered evenly. 'I've stared my fill of her.'

Heriot stood still for a moment, then laughed. 'There's no charge for looking. You're not the first to envy me and you won't be the last. I know my good fortune.'

'Do you?' Henry attacked the portrait like an enemy.

'I know that I'll not be satisfied until she's my wife.'

'You'd have to get on Macquarie's right side for that.'

'Why do you think I'm seeing him tomorrow?'

The paint-brush ceased its sure movements.

Jade sat up straight in the chair. A red cushion tumbled to the floor.

Heriot laughed. 'I seem to have put the cat among the pigeons.' The black eyes danced with triumph and a happiness that seemed not altogether connected with herself. 'You said that given time you'd be able to reciprocate my feelings?'

'I said I might –'

'Then, that's sufficient for me. Leave off that portrait, Henry. I need no reminder of Jane Benson, now or ever. Wasn't it Mary – Henry's daughter – who had the word Calais imprinted on her heart? Well, I have one embedded on mine.'

And it's not even my own, Jade thought wryly. It's a sham, like most of the things I am. He should have waited until she was sure. But she would never have been that. Masson stood in the way like a great rock. Perhaps Heriot had been wise not to wait too long for what he sensed might never happen. Gabriel hated her and would never want her now. Most women made do with second best.

'Go, get some wine, Henry, and wish us well.'

The paint-brush clattered to the floor.

'Make it your best,' Heriot said grandly.

'Of course.'

Jade was the only one who noticed Lambert's lifelessness.

It had been easy to persuade Heriot that Johnnie and Nan deserved the same happiness as themselves. He had stroked her, kissed her, loved her with a passion that had seduced her body. But not her heart.

'If the Governor grants us permission, we can wait until we make proper preparations. Let Nan and Johnnie marry first. We are lovers already and the matter has not the same urgency. Let them enjoy their ceremony, their jubilation, without being overshadowed by our own marriage.'

'How unselfish you are.'

But she was not. It was her own sense of uncertainty about the rightness of marrying a man she did not love wholeheartedly that troubled her. It did not seem fair to Heriot. But the new perplexing calm overrode her mental reservations. Her body accepted the prospect of safe harbour even if her spirit was not totally reconciled. Because Masson had cast her off, that was no reason why she should not become a good wife and, eventually, a mother. Daniel had aroused such pleasant feelings of motherhood. If it had not been that she'd sworn she would never entrap a man by bearing his child so that his love would become an obligation, she might have neglected to order Ma Lee's nostrums long ago. Such was the strength of her regard for Logan Heriot.

Henry was silent over breakfast. Jade affected not to notice.

She kissed Heriot on his departure, then found herself alone with a Henry made brave by the knowledge that time ran out.

'You're set on going through with this farce?' he demanded, his gaze devouring the ravishing picture she made by the sunlit window, her body perfectly visible through folds of diaphanous greens, the crown of her hair brown satin.

'What farce?'

'You don't love him.'

'I don't love you, either. But I have the strongest feelings of friendship –'

'Blast friendship. I want you. All of you. I'd make as good a husband.'

'There is – loyalty.'

'And damn loyalty!'

'Oh, Henry, if the boot had been on the other foot, you'd have welcomed it.'

'I'd better take you back to Elsrickle before I forget myself.'

'If you continue to talk so, I'll not come back. I mean it,' then, softened by his unhappy look, she continued more gently. 'I'll not forget you were the first to cherish me. Even Heriot had his reservations –'

'I've never had those.'

'And I love you for it.'

'Jane!'

'As a sister.' Her voice was firm.

'Come, then.' He was pale. 'And don't forget the parcel I made up for you.'

'I won't forget.'

Just before they settled themselves in the carriage – Heriot had borrowed a horse from Lambert to ride to Sydney – she was again conscious of an unaccountable nausea that did not last long but which perturbed her. She was usually so strong. Jade hoped it was nothing that would affect Daniel. All those flies! They must carry disease.

She sat back among the cushions, her body so relaxed that it was almost fluid. They set off in silence. The Blue Mountains shimmered in shades between harebell and indigo, the deep chasms between their outcroppings making it a miracle that any road should have been built through them.

The grey-green foliage swayed gently. Crows cawed monotonously. The journey should have been peaceful but the calm was marred by Henry's tight-lipped quiet.

Half-way to Elsrickle, he pulled the horses to a standstill.

'I cannot let the matter go without making some last stand – '

'No, Henry. I would lose both of you. You'd despise me eventually for deserting a man who has been good and kind.' If a little pompous. Jade smiled as she looked back on some of Logan's little pretensions.

Henry took this for encouragement. His slim, strong hands, browned with the years of Australian sun, were plucking at the buttons of her gown, dipping inside the top of the white, be-ribboned shift.

Jade wanted to push him away but the weakness of her body betrayed her. Disquiet fought with the sense of outrage. The image of that subtle portrait almost overcame her determination to keep him at a safe distance, and, recognizing her change of mood, Henry pulled down the shift and kissed the smooth white flesh he had exposed. His knee pressed against the inside of one thigh.

'No,' Jade said quite loudly. 'I should never forgive you and neither would he.'

For a moment he did nothing, then raised his head from her breast and began to restore her garments to decency. Then he took up the small switch and flicked it over the black horse hides.

The carriage proceeded on its way to Elsrickle.

She did not have her usual woman's bleeding but perhaps her indisposition was the cause of the upset. It still had not come when Heriot arrived back, and by this time she realized what had happened. Logan had his dearest wish. She was pregnant, or was almost certain she was. It was too soon to be positive but it explained the weariness, the sense of fulfilment.

Governor Macquarie had been pleased to grant the two dispensations. She was free to marry Heriot. It seemed odd that her pregnancy coincided with his determination to make her position legal and she wondered what arguments he had put forward. Perhaps he had mentioned her part in the restoration after the flooding. Not that she had done a great deal.

Heriot had brought her a locket from Sydney, to house the miniatures she'd planned to paint. She showed him first the tiny portrait of Daniel. He stared at it in silence then pushed it across the table. 'Where's the other?'

The other was Gabriel's pictured face. It was an excellent likeness and sufficiently like Heriot to pass as his own portrait.

'You've made me look anaemic,' he complained, but she could see he approved.

'It's how you look when you are sleeping in the moonlight.' That was true at least.

'I'd no idea you were so talented. And how have you been in my absence?'

Was it her imagination or did he watch her too keenly? Almost as though he knew her secret. He couldn't, of course.

'Quite well.'

'You are sure?'

'Perfectly. At least –'

How brilliantly black his eyes were. And how like Masson he looked under stress of excitement. She began to tremble.

'At least?' he prompted.

'It's too early to be certain but I think I might be with child. I should have waited before telling you – Raising your hopes –'

He gave a great shout of delight. 'Of course you shouldn't. It's what I've wanted to hear for a long time.' And he swept her up into his arms and kissed any portion of her that was not covered.

Lizzie, who had come in with cool drinks to refresh the returned traveller, coughed and set down the glasses.

'We've all missed you, sir,' Lizzie said.

'Good.' Heriot took a cigar from the silver box on the table and punctured the end of it. 'I admit it's good to be back. Something special to drink at supper tonight, Lizzie.'

'Good news, is it, sir?'

'The best news.' He struck his favourite attitude in front of the hearth, the tail-warming Scots squire surrounded by family and dogs. He was so enchanted and she could not even give him the best. Then the smell of the cigar smoke overcame Jade and she had to rush out of the room, nauseated.

She was very pale when she returned and Logan was contrite. 'It is true,' she told him. 'I know it now. You are really pleased?'

He gave her a glass of wine and kissed her hungrily. 'You know I am.'

'Have you seen Johnnie yet?' she asked.

'No.'

'We must tell them they have no need to wait any longer.'

'I've asked the preacher from Windsor to come next Monday to discuss the arrangements.'

'Well, you seek out Johnnie now and I'll look for Nan. It's time Daniel had his bath anyway.'

'And us?'

'We'll wait until after Nan's wedding. She deserves to have all the attention. And a few weeks later –' She shrugged. 'It will be our turn.'

'I'm all impatience.'

'How can you say that?' she asked, smiling mischievously, 'after all the times you've bedded me? I've lost count.'

'I'm impatient every time I set eyes on you.'

He went unwillingly.

Jade found Nan and Daniel in the kitchen, waiting for the bathwater to heat. Jump was on the grass in the paddock and the sound of the kookaburras, now so familiar, passed almost unnoticed. Mrs Doyle was not there.

'You do want to marry Johnnie, don't you?' Jade asked. 'You still do?'

Nan's face changed. 'We – can – not. Not – for years.'

'You can now. Heriot has arranged everything. There's nothing can stop you.'

The huge blue eyes glittered. At that moment, her eyes filled with tears, Nan was the most beautiful girl Jade had ever seen. She flung her arms around her and was hugged and kissed in turn. Daniel joined them, demanding his share of affection.

Heriot came bursting in with Johnnie Dart and a bottle and glasses, and everyone was involved in a spate of embracing, necessary plans.

Across the room, Heriot's eyes met Jade's. Our turn next, his gaze told her, and somehow all the gladness evaporated as though she were asleep and an especially good dream had turned to nightmare. It was not Heriot she was avid to marry.

The wedding was at Elsrickle. Nan had been too shy to want to go to Windsor. Two or three happy days were spent in making the sky-blue gown and Jade had produced a piece of lace to make a head-covering. Lizzie and Mrs Doyle fashioned silk garters and Johnnie bought blue shoes with heels for the bride and a set of fine underwear. The new bedgown had blue satin ribbons threaded through it. Daniel presented Nan with a posy of flowers.

The Davieses and Symonses were invited and as many of the sheepmen and their women as could be spared.

Elsrickle overflowed. Heriot had been generous with the food and drink and Jade and Mrs Doyle had worked hard to have everything ready and presented as attractively as possible. Everything shone. Jade had allowed her garden to be raided. It had flourished since the rains. Wattle had been picked and arranged in large vases so that every corner seemed filled with sunshine. But the yellow blooms were no brighter than Nan's golden curls.

Johnnie was dressed in his best, looking a little stiff and uncomfortable, but whenever he looked at Nan his expression showed a depth of feeling that reassured Jade. He was bound to find out that Nan was not a virgin but he would know that it was not her fault. He would listen to her halting voice where no one else had bothered. He would pity her efforts to keep herself intact. Johnnie would bear no grudges. Mrs Doyle sang endless songs of Ireland.

Heriot was attentive since his return from visiting the Governor, trying to dissuade Jade from all the work attached to the wedding, simple though it was.

'It won't hurt me,' she protested, pushing away her dampened hair. 'I've no patience with women who languish. Child-bearing is a natural thing and goes on for far too long to allow of over-much indulgence.'

'It's our child. We worked hard for it,' Heriot pointed out.

She laughed then. 'Work? I found it no effort. Did you?'

He laughed too. 'It was the pleasantest work I ever undertook.'

'It will be all right. It's much too soon to play the invalid.'

'I suppose so.'

And then the wedding-day was upon them and the minister spoke the solemn words to a flushed Johnnie and an alabaster pale Nan who had begun to look as if she would never thaw out again.

Bess spoke kindly to Jade and kissed her on the cheek. 'It's your doing, I suspect. But why not yourself?'

'Because I think too much of Heriot. I think, though, that he means to have his way. We are free now to do what we will. He's spoken to Macquarie.'

'I'd like to see him wed you.'

'Then so you shall.'

Freda was equally warm. Between them they had brought

the newly-weds sheets and pillows and a kangaroo-skin bed-spread for winter. It was a generous gift.

Johnnie had his own house as overseer. It was the usual dwelling of cabbage-tree panels and timber, wattle and plaster, clay and cedar wood, but it had stood up to a great deal of bad weather and would, doubtless, withstand anything short of the cyclone – or willy-willy – Henry had so graphically described. The roof was of shingles, the lime for mortar being made from oyster shells collected by female convicts in the coves around Port Jackson. Everything, Henry had told her, was built on slavery, even the ancient Egyptian empire. Henry–

Henry had not accepted an invitation to the nuptials. In fact, he had not come at all since that ill-fated visit and had not asked them to visit him.

Heriot, overjoyed by his own forthcoming wedding and the knowledge that he was not, after all, incapable of fathering his own children, had not had time to notice Lambert's with-drawal. He must, in time, and Jade wondered if he would connect the ensuing coolness with any act of hers and hold it against her.

But once the ceremony was over and Nan was, for always, Mrs Dart, the white stillness left her and she laughed and danced as readily as any of their guests. A fiddler had been hired and the music and the flowing drink loosened everyone's inhibitions. Jade had never been to such a gathering and found it much more agreeable than any of Mama's routs.

She still could not reconcile herself with her own state. Once, during the festivities, she went to her own room and opened the locket that contained the pictures of Daniel and Gabriel, so curiously alike, and willed Masson to think of her, to do something decisive that would prevent her marrying Heriot. But what could he do? He probably never gave her a second's thought. In his book she was a traitress and thief. That night in Newgate had shown her his true estimate of her character. Why did she cling to his memory? She knew there was no future in it. He detested her. Heriot loved her to dis-traction. There was no real choice. Heriot had obtained her freedom so long as she remained in Australia. If she left the country her term would remain as before. Another five years or so of being the sort of convict Denver was –

She hated to think of Denver. As soon as he'd recovered from his flogging, his mind would have gone to the two people he'd consider responsible. Herself and Logan Heriot. All these weeks and months he would be working in his chains, cursing and reviling the man and woman who had brought him such suffering. Always, the memory of his ice-blue eyes and shaven skull would haunt her. Bess Davies said the lack of hair made him recognizable even if he were to acquire clothing other than his convict wear. Denver was dangerous. An animal. Worse, because animals had their own code of conduct. Their loyalties.

Jade went back to the carefree gathering, noting Heriot's boisterous good humour but part rejecting the thought that in a few weeks this hectic gaiety would encompass them. Would Henry come to Heriot's wedding? He must or Logan would demand a reason for that ostracism.

The time came when the Darts disappeared, bound for their little house in the shade of the ghost gums. Daniel had been fast asleep for two hours. Mrs Doyle sniffed into a hand-kerchief and the sheepmen and their mistresses had started off across the paddock, laughing and dancing on the grass, disturbing Jump who leapt for safety, making Heriot snort with amusement.

'I'm glad it's over,' he said as the last carriage and buck-board left. 'It's been too much for you. You look tired.'

'I'll be fine tomorrow. I feel better now that I've seen Nan properly settled.'

'And living so close,' Heriot pointed out, 'you'd never need lose her.'

He was a devil reminding her of her bond with Nan. How cleverly he had enmeshed her in fetters of committal. Flynn's daughter wed to his overseer. His baby. Their mutual obligation to her unborn child. How had it happened? She could not rid herself of the feeling that he'd known before she had.

She was ungrateful.

He was looking at her curiously, as though he followed her train of thought.

'It's all for the best,' he said. 'Isn't it, Jane?'

What else could she say? 'It's for the best.'

'Come to bed, then.'

'There's still work to do.'

'The others can do it in the morning. They aren't pregnant.'

'I'm not supposed to be. Yet –'

'But you are.' His hand came over hers. 'You are and neither of us must forget it.'

It was almost as if he knew that he'd needed this lever to bring her to the point of agreeing to his proposal.

'Happy?' he asked.

She was not totally happy but it was easier to say that she was. Heart-warming too when she saw Heriot's pleasure. This was to be her life, pleasing her husband-to-be. It need not be so difficult. Only a short time ago it had seemed right and desirable but now, so near to the actual date, she wanted to go away where he'd never find her.

It's only natural, she told herself, to be beset by doubts.

But she still did not care for the suggestion of sinking quicksands, the illusion that she'd be putting herself back into captivity.

She would cope with it when the time came.

All she wanted now was to sleep. To forget –

Jade had, some time ago, painted a small picture of Greenway's church at Windsor. Heriot thought it remarkably good. She herself could not tell if it were or not.

'Perhaps,' he had suggested, 'you could send it to Governor Macquarie? A thank you for your freedom.'

She had thought it a good idea and so the painting had been sent to Elizabeth Farm, Parramatta. A letter had come back almost immediately.

'I find the painting irresistible. I think it is high time I met the creator. Can you bring your fiancée to the rout my wife and I are holding in Sydney next Wednesday? I know it is short notice, but few things have pleased me so much since I took office here. Macquarie.'

Jade was exhilarated. Briefly. 'They'll all know who I am. How can I?'

'The Governor has summoned you. And not only because of the painting. You risked your life, remember, to help free settlers? That's the sort of gesture a Scotsman loves *and* makes for good relations! The Davieses and Symonses despised you and yet you were nearly drowned going to their aid. I will not pretend it will be easy, but it *is* what you want, isn't it? To be recognized as an independent person, above the whispers and the sneers?'

'Yes –'

'Then, we must go. It's a summons we really can't ignore. A hand of friendship.'

'It's so close to our wedding – '

'We'll be back before that.'

'Just.'

'I've not demanded anything of you for some time. This, I must.' His face was that of the old, arrogant Logan, expecting his due. It was a face she had almost forgotten. Perhaps the change had been expediency. He was so intent on an heir. His child would not be barely tolerated as Daniel was. The difference between them would be so marked that Daniel was bound to be unhappy. But at least he was assured of a home and a future. He could have died of neglect long since. At Elsrickle he would, at least, be Mrs Heriot's son.

'All right, Logan. We'll go. What shall I wear?'

'Your wedding dress.'

'It'll be unlucky.'

'Nonsense. It's a mere convention that requires the bride to wear something new. Surely a woman of such intelligence pays no attention to old wives' tales?'

'Of course I don't.' He'd obviously despise her if she said she did. All women did.

'There's no problem, then. Had you insisted upon a new gown –'

'I haven't!'

'It would have taken too long, you know that. And I want you to look your best.'

'Yes.' Jade was uncomfortable in her role of sycophant. But Heriot was right. A new dress was imperative but the only one she had was that intended for her marriage. She would be foolish to disappoint him. This was her accolade. If she intended to live out her life in Australia, being accepted by those in authority was a necessity. Logan was pleased and flattered. He'd expect her co-operation. And rightly.

She wondered, later, if Henry would be there. He would, of course. Lambert was the perfect Australian, moneyed, influential, an asset. And unmarried, able to draw some society girl who'd add prestige to the rest.

The thought did not induce a shred of envy. She loved neither of the men who wanted her enough to marry her. Either would be any settler's dream but she was made in the mould of loyalty. And all her fidelity was for Gabriel Masson even if he abhorred her memory. Why couldn't she forget him?

Heriot decided that they would go before the actual day so that she might see Sydney properly. 'We'll stay at the best hotel.'

'Are there any?'

'One or two. Sydney's altered since the first settlers came. And Macquarie's made many changes.'

He did not wait for her agreement. Perhaps he was so sure of her now that he could revert to form.

Jade, unsettled, went to see Nan, taking Daniel with her. It was hot and the grass was drying again. Nan was thrilled to see them and looking so pretty and self-assured that Jade saw in an instant that the marriage was indeed a success.

She shrugged off the unaccustomed envy, had a cup of tea with the beautiful Mrs Dart and noticed that Daniel was not in the room. Jade was not unduly disturbed. The doors were open to allow the maximum airflow in the little house, and the boy could not have gone far.

Nan had gone for replenishments to the teapot so Jade went out to the back of the house since the gate of the front paddock was firmly closed. Daniel could not have gone that way. There was a gap in the fence that bordered the copse of trees where the crow had been tethered. The storm of cawing and carking told her that the replacement was in good voice. It would be this noise, or the sound of the kookaburras that had attracted Daniel.

The ground was dry now, the tempest of growth that had appeared after the heavy rains browned and dwindled to spikes and furze and drifting seeds. More than ever, the trees were bone-like and colourless against the browns and oranges and grey. Only the mountains glimmered blue as harebells, cleft with great gullies of indigo, lifting her spirits momentarily from the everyday.

Disturbed, she realized that there was no sight of the child. There were figures in the paddock near the bunkhouse. Daniel might have run there in search of diversion. He was a friendly boy. And so beautiful —

'Daniel?' Her voice was pitched a little too high. She would frighten him.

Then she saw him and a great wave of relief beat around her. 'Daniel,' she whispered, and began to walk towards him, not too quickly so as not to send him running off where she might lose sight of him. He had grown so quick and agile during these last months.

He was staring up into the tree where the most recent crow was tethered, holding up his hands in a vain endeavour to reach the black, flapping feathers. Close by, the kookaburras laughed in that idiotic, half-clucking way that had always amused them. Today she was not amused. She could not explain why. Perhaps her pregnancy weighed down on her, though it was surely far too soon?

'Daniel!' She was pleased that the note she struck was between fondness and firmness.

The child turned his head to smile at her and she hastened her footsteps, aware of a sense of disquiet she could not explain. Although, Heriot had warned her not to come to this place. It was outside the bounds of safety, he had said, but what harm could come to them so near the bunkhouse and the great noisy paddocks where the merinos surged and bleated, were tended, dipped and sheared as the months progressed?

She remembered that fire was the great Australian hazard. Anything could set off a fire when it was hot enough. A single spark – The sun beating on something that glittered. A buckle –

Daniel, seeing that his brief spell of freedom was almost at an end, began to run towards the kookaburras. Jade, hurrying after him, saw him go behind a large cluster of cabbage palm. 'Mrs Doyle has made some cake for you, my darling,' she called persuasively, knowing that he could perhaps outrun her in her present state of fecund indolence. Heavens! If she were like this in the early stages, whatever would the latter months be like!

Daniel refused to be drawn by promises of cake. Jade rounded the cabbage palm breathlessly. The grey-green clusters cast queer, spiky shadows over the pale dust. She saw the kookaburras nudging one another on the strongest branch of a hollow tree. The sort of tree that would burst into a roaring holocaust if there were cause.

And then she forgot the menace of fire. Daniel was staring at something that lay in his path. Craning her neck, she found herself freezing with the greatest horror of her life. There was a snake lying in the sun. The gleaming coils moved lazily. The shining length undulated, came to rest again.

'Daniel,' Jade whispered. 'Keep still. Keep very still.'

The harsh whisper must have impressed upon the child the knowledge of his danger. His mama never normally used such a voice to him. He obeyed.

Perhaps she should throw a stone? No! That would be the worst possible thing she could do. The snake, disturbed, would strike at the first thing it saw.

The deadly paralysis left her. Inch by inch, she made herself move towards the child. If she could get close enough, she'd pick up the boy quickly and run. Of course it would never work. The snake would strike the minute she moved. But it would only strike once. She could get Daniel back as far as the fence. Someone should have noticed the gap. But it was not in a place that affected the sheep and had not been important until today. If only she had seen the little boy go out of the room.

The snake lay under the hot sun. One tiny black eye glittered. Daniel was like a small, Mediterranean statue with his black curls, olive skin, long, curving lashes. His whole being was riveted on the scaly monster that watched him so inimicably.

Jade stood on a stick. One moment the scene was a tableau, the next the stick exploded with a dry spiteful crack and the snake moved. She opened her mouth to scream but something else was quicker.

The nearest kookaburra, attracted by the movement below, swooped and grabbed the snake. For a moment, Jade saw the portly, top-heavy bird, its scissor-like beak closed around the snake, and then it rose up into the air, the reptile twisting and rippling as it fought for escape.

Daniel, the hypnotic spell broken, ran to Jade, burrowing his head against her thighs. Her whole body was drenched with perspiration and her heart beat irregularly. The bird was quite high now, about forty feet in the air.

She snatched at Daniel fiercely, holding him to her breast. Her legs had begun to tremble with reaction. They should go back to the house but she could not take her eyes from the sky. She screamed as the big, kingfisher-like bird dropped the snake. It fell not far away. It was still alive, she saw with a sick fear and gathered herself to run away from the cabbage palm and the surrealistic shadows on the dust.

The kookaburra was dropping back to earth. It straddled the snake and fastened the cruel beak around it, then flew upwards, not quite as high as before, then released its struggling victim to flop dazedly into the sand.

She ran blindly, aware that Johnnie Dart was coming towards them, his kind face set in lines of concern. He took the crying child from her, then supported her with his other arm. Why couldn't she have met someone like him? Someone without arrogance and hurtfulness. Nan had the sort of shining happiness that seemed to make a mockery of anything else.

Slowly, as they neared the Dart house, the worst of the shock wearing off, Jade admitted to herself that she needed the stimulation of fighting for her own kind of fulfilment. Anything else had no challenge.

'Don't tell Heriot, please,' she asked Johnnie. 'He'd be so angry.'

'He probably knows already.'

'He told me not to go out there. But Daniel got through the fence.' She showed him the gap and he said he'd have it seen to immediately.

Nan made her sit down and pressed more mint tea upon her but Jade could not forget the threat that lay so close to Elsrickle. She had endured the violence of the floods, the terror of the wilderness beyond the thin veneer of civilization. The child she carried must be protected from such incipient fatalities for its entire youth. She wondered if she would have the courage to defend it.

And then she saw that the same thing that told her that only a challenge would suit her in a physical and mental relationship applied just as much to adapting herself to this sometimes brutal life. It was not in her to sit wringing her hands and deploring fate, and, thank God, it never would be.

The journey to Sydney was accomplished far more quickly than when Johnnie had brought them all to Elsrickle in the buckboard. Then, they had stayed at the homes of settlers with whom Heriot had business dealings that required deliberation with his manager.

This time, Jade was very cosseted and ladylike in the carriage, Heriot still intent upon her comfort. He had found out about the business of the snake but his anger diminished when he realized that it was accident and not deliberate disobedience that had resulted in near tragedy. When she had pointed out that the next time it could be his own child, he had set two of the men to going over the entire fence for signs of wear and to replace any gates that required attention, however slight that need might seem.

Secure in her new position and in the excitement of the journey that would lead to rehabilitation and possible favour, she relaxed and put thoughts of dissention out of her head. They saw aborigines in a copse, not the usual drifting shadows but a family conclave. Jade thought them very curious indeed with their kangaroo skin strips and hair ornaments of dog's teeth, bones and lobster claws that Heriot assured her were stuck into place with gum.

'How odd!'

'They think *we* are the returned spirits of the dead,' he pointed out.

'I wish we had been closer. One sees so little –'

'I'm glad we aren't! They never wash. Just smear themselves with fat that goes rancid and to which everything sticks. *Everything.*'

'How gruesome.' She made a face and Heriot, distracted by the contrast between this girl in green and aborigines who stank and thrust bones through their noses, leaned over to kiss her.

'Shall I tell you how they fend off mosquitoes?'

'If you must.'

'They cover themselves in whale oil.'

'Oh.'

'But the women, though you'd never imagine it from their ferocious aspect, seem to suffer very badly when they see the convicts flogged. They are upset for days.'

'Then I don't care about the rest,' Jade told him and waved from the window to the natives who, misunderstanding her gesture of friendliness, melted into the grey-green haze of the copse as if she had been an ogress.

Heriot thought it very funny.

The flickering leaves of the eucalyptus were a waving blueness and the air was perfumed with resin. She found herself wondering what the tropical north would be like with its dark walls of jungle and vine, enormous fan-like leaves and the staghorn ferns like green baskets. The lyre bird lived there, Heriot said, and could mimic anything it heard. They'd go there one day, but Jade still regretted the English seasons.

Her eyes closed on visions of humid splendour.

Heriot smiled as her head slid sideways and came to rest on his shoulder. His gaze, descending, decided that no one would guess that Jane was pregnant. She was still small and slim-waisted, only her breasts more clearly defined. Not that he objected to that. Inside her body was the heir to what he possessed. He was exalted by the thought. A man was intended to breed children and that was what he had done.

They spent the night with friends on the other side of Parramatta when Heriot discovered that Lambert was not at home.

He'll be attending the Governor's rout,' Heriot said as they drove away.

Jade, with memories of that last unhappy meeting, said nothing.

'It's not like him to be so offhand,' Heriot went on. 'I've not wanted to mention it before but now it's obvious. I've lost Henry.'

'It's not because of anything you've done.'

'Why is it, then?' Heriot's voice had turned sharp and unfriendly. 'Is it because of something you or he has done?'

'It's because of something neither of us has done. It's me he can't forgive. I'm sorry, Logan. I knew you'd notice sooner or later.'

'So he tried to take you away!'

'You knew he'd never succeed, didn't you?'

'I'm a plain man and Henry has a good deal of polish. Charm. I do not. That's why I've always admired him. They say contrasts are interesting.'

'Then, doesn't the fact that I rejected all that tell you anything?'

'I can never quite believe that I have you. It was easy in the beginning. You were just another whore. I knew where I stood. Then you became a person and I knew you were better than I was –'

'Logan, that's not true!'

'And I found out I'd grown out of harlots and wanted roots.'

'Well, you have at least one root now. An incipient root.'

'Yet I can't shake off the feeling that it's only a sort of – dream.'

'I'm with child – your child – we are to be married soon. Thanks to you I'm a free woman so long as I remain in Australia. We are to take supper and dance at Government House. How could it be a dream!'

'You're right, of course. But Henry –'

'Don't tell him you know. He accepted my refusal –'

'Like a gentleman, I suppose,' Heriot growled.

'And you must greet him as if you were unaware of what I've just told you. I'd have said nothing if you hadn't suspected the coolness was your fault. You know that.'

'I won't let you dance with him.'

'Oh, yes, you will.' Jade's tone was as violent as his had been earlier. 'Whatever there was, and it was little, stopped before it began. We'll be friends again and I intend to begin at the rout. And, if you've any sense, you'll do as I ask. I could never live happily with a jealous man, particularly when there's nothing to be jealous about.'

They relapsed into a silence that lasted until they reached the home of the Hunts. It was a pleasant enough house and Tim and Amy Hunt were apparently amiable. They had not been able to visit Elsrickle during Jade's time there as they had young children dependent on them and Amy had recently been brought to bed of a fourth.

Jade noticed that husband and wife exchanged glances when she was introduced as Heriot's fiancée. Australian society being what it was, everyone knew about everyone else. Their well-bred faces showed even more surprise when they knew the reason for the trip to Sydney.

'Even we have never been to Government House,' Amy said, not without envy, and, Jade was sure, a trace of anger on Tim's behalf. Heriot seemed not to notice the moment of coolness.

Tim, however, was not going to let his wife put up barriers. 'I'm glad you decided to visit us at last, Logan. And those sheep you sent us are doing well. The merinoes are, indeed, the best.'

He got no further, for the door opened on a nursemaid and a stream of small children dressed in white. There were only three, Jade decided after the first, hectic inrush, but there could have been twice as many, judging by the noise and energy they expended. They were brown with the sun, accentuating the English fairness of hair and brows. Taking, no doubt, but none as beautiful as her own Daniel. And there was to be another. In this moment she accepted the knowledge as reality and a queer happiness twisted in her stomach, forcing itself upwards to burst out of her in a catch of the breath only Amy noticed.

'You like children?' she asked.

'Oh, yes.'

'We intend to have several,' Heriot said, taking up the littlest Hunt and dandling him on his knee.

Jade was shocked to silence. He had never done such a thing with Daniel for all that he believed him hers. And never would. Watching him smile and tease the infant, all the time looking so charming and pleasant, she almost hated him. She could never be happy if he persisted in his neglect and dislike of her boy. That was as clear as the fact that she was to become a mother. Odd how one never quite believed it at first and then was suddenly convinced.

The older children wanted as much attention as their little brother and Jade was too busy for a time to worry much about the future. But she was quiet over the meal, once the children were in bed, not that it mattered for Heriot was ebullient enough for both of them.

'I'm sorry,' Heriot said as they all rose to go their separate ways to bed, 'for the lack of notice. It was a sudden whim to go to Sydney.'

'You need give no notice to us,' Tim told him, but Amy's face told a different story, not that she'd let him see it.

Jade was quite glad to leave after breakfast next morning. No one had been actively disagreeable and yet she was conscious of some degree of censure. They'd be talking together now, saying how Heriot was ruining his life by wedding a girl he'd had often enough already without the benefit of a ring.

Well, let them! She didn't care. Not in the least. How she hated being broody with child. They made their own fetters. One had to consider their well-being first. Heriot would never forgive her if she made his child a bastard. Yet, if she went through with the marriage, Daniel would not be happy. But Nan and Johnnie would always be there. They'd be kind to him.

'Such deep thoughts this morning,' Heriot observed. 'And you were quiet last night.'

'I was thinking,' Jade said clearly, out of her sense of disquiet, 'how kind you are to the little Hunts.'

'Why shouldn't I be?' He frowned.

'And how cruel you can be to Daniel.'

'Are we to quarrel about that brat again?' His face darkened. 'I'll not have it.'

'Oh, but you will, or I'll not give your child his name.'

'Are you threatening me?' His lips were thin with surprised anger.

The carriage bounced over a rut and flung her into his lap. She sat stiff as a marionette, her green skirts disordered. His hands lay quiet on her flesh.

'Yes,' she told him. 'I'm afraid that if you can't relent towards him, I'll have no other choice but to refuse you.'

'And why did you have to wait until now?' He pushed her arm away from him.

'I was optimistic enough to imagine you were the same with all children and that perhaps the birth of your own would bring about a more kindly attitude towards my adopted son. But I saw last night that this wasn't so. You fawned over those children like a fond uncle. You'll *not* change towards him.'

'You said – adopted son.'

'And that's what he is, in spite of the captain's records. He owed me a favour and I wanted the boy. As I want the baby you gave me. I could never ignore and be spiteful to a child as you seem able to do so easily. If we are to remain together, Daniel must be as happy as any other member of the Heriot family. I insisted that he was mine because I was not sure of you or your intention to keep us and I needed that legal hold on him if we weren't to be separated.

'The first child I'll ever bear will be yours. Yours, do you hear!

'I swore I'd never give away the fact that Daniel is an orphan but if there's no other way to change your attitude, I have no choice but to tell you, once and for all, that he's not. mine. Though I wish he were –'

'And this is the truth?' Heriot asked heavily.

'Yes.'

She had frightened him by saying she might not after all marry him. But the thought brought no triumph.

'Whose was he?'

'A poor widow woman who stole bread. She died during the voyage. You need no more have been jealous of him than you need be of Lambert.'

The carriage rattled again, depositing her close to him. They stared at one another as if on opposite sides of a chasm.

The faint scent of her perfume came to him across the narrow gap. For the first time he believed her. The musky smell reminded him of what they had been to one another. Still would be if he were not so stiff-necked and bristling with his own importance.

No other man had impregnated her. He should have known. There wasn't a mark on her body that spoke of previous child-birth. And she'd have been too young.

She saw the struggle behind his eyes, the sudden capitulation.

'I'll try,' was all he said, then reached out a hand to grasp her arm as if even now she might evade him.

*

Jade was tired when they reached Sydney. She had almost forgotten the beauty of the still water with its ring of islands and the great protective headlands that stretched far into the west. The black silhouettes of sailing ships at anchor charmed her. The grey-green woods and aprons of pale sand repudiated the thought that misery and death had landed there.

The town, wide-avenued and tidier, had taken on a prosperous look. Heriot pointed out the Governor's house which was attractive with its central doorway and circular pediment, the steps shining in the sunlight. The windows sparkled and there were sentry boxes at either end of the building. She had a glimpse of military uniforms. Cannon peeped over the walls with deceptive quietude and there were winding paths and round flower-beds bright with colour. Trees cast welcome shade. How she longed to see inside the place.

Up the slopes of Rose Hill the small houses gleamed white and box-like beyond fields sewn with crops. There was smoke from chimneys. The sails of a windmill turned lazily in the light breeze.

But the dreamy pleasure was spoiled by the sound of tramping feet and clinking chains and a long file of grey-clad men made their way past the vehicle. Eyes stared hostilely from dusty faces. Someone spat on the wheel. Jade felt suddenly defiled. She turned away from the sharp crack of the whip. Heriot, more used to the contrast and the presence of chained men, had not noticed her reaction.

'We'll find a room at the Castlereagh,' he told Jade. 'You look weary. Perhaps we shouldn't have come, after all.'

'There's no harm done, nor like to be. I've done nothing but sit.'

'It'll be the last journey until it's all over. But it was necessary. One can't refuse –'

'No, Logan. I agree.'

The hotel was very new and had pretensions towards vying with the Governor's residence. Already bushes of yellow flowers bordered a rectangle of lawn at the back and galahs and parakeets made home in the branches of established trees.

Inside, it was cool and the bed-chamber overlooked the garden so that it was reasonably peaceful. Jade drank mint tea, washed herself and lay down, was instantly asleep. Heriot, seeing that she was likely to remain so for some time, stared down at her. Her near nakedness, for the heat precluded getting beneath the sheets, the artless abandon of her position, roused him to a tumult of feeling. She had put a pistol to his head since they left the Hunts and all was still not as it had been, but Daniel was no longer the vague threat he had at first represented. He'd stomach the boy now that he proved not to be of Jade's flesh. What a strange creature she was, gathering encumbrances along the way of life. Well, the remainder of those dependants would all be Heriots. He'd see to that.

He experienced an acute desire to force himself upon her but she was tired and also pregnant. And he loved her. Heriot took himself off to complete some business matters while he had the opportunity. They could do their sight-seeing tomorrow before they left.

Jade awoke refreshed and excited. There were flowers in the room that had not been there earlier. One of them was the exact shade of the cream-coloured gown she'd had made for her wedding. She still did not want to wear it but none of the others was suitable for so grand an occasion and a second one would have needed to be specially made for her since she was so small and slight. She'd never find a ready-made garment with her measurements.

Heriot arrived back and hard on his heels came a brace of footmen with trays. She did not feel much like eating but the mint tea was always a delight.

'I'll leave room for supper,' she said.

'Don't starve him.'

'Starve whom?'

'My son.'

'We may have nothing but girls.'

'We'll have a boy,' Heriot said confidently. 'I'm sure of it.'

'You mustn't count on it. And there's no exchange system, not with babies.'

'I see my flowers arrived.' He ignored the warning.

'They're lovely. I intend to do up my hair and put the big creamy one in the centre of the swathe.'

'We are having baths sent up in an hour and that doesn't give us time to go out first. I thought – it's a few days since we slept together. What d'you say?'

At the beginning, she had been ordered to bed very summarily. Now Heriot considered her wishes. But only, she suspected, because she carried his child.

'And what if I say no?'

He looked so furious that she couldn't help laughing.

'If only you knew,' she said, 'how I've hated being treated

like porcelain. I'll never be the complete lady, swooning on sofas like a drooping lily, and I wish you wouldn't encourage me. Not ever. Let's live normal lives.'

He took off what little she had on and dropped her right into the centre of the big bed. She had not felt so much like making love for a long time. The change was exciting, the scent of the flowers seductive. And Heriot unclothed was eminently personable. He would not lie over her, but, face to face, they kissed and embraced adequately enough and when he entered her she imagined she felt a keener pleasure though Heriot, she knew, would have preferred her beneath him.

Afterwards they looked out of the window, his arm around her waist, seeing the silver waters of the harbour lap round the darkening islands and the great heads growing first grey and then black in the dusk. The parrot cries grew more and more infrequent. Footsteps and voices grew less and less, but there were snatches of music, some laughter, the occasional discordant shout, the rattle of wheels. Sounds one would connect with any town once day had turned to night.

Baths and soap and towels arrived almost too soon, breaking the sense of content. But, once dried and dressed in the cream gown, the flower a living coronet, Jade powdered her face with a rabbit's foot and reddened her lips, staring into a mirror that showed her as almost a stranger. She looked older, more sophisticated. And Heriot hung over her, kissing her shoulders and the nape of her neck, arousing flickers of sensuality that were the essential part of her nature.

Once ready, she found herself defensive. It would be an ordeal facing the gimlet glares of the Australian autocracy. As much a trial as walking past the settlers' wives on the decks of the *Caroline*. The fact that she had won over the Daviesses and Symonses since then would matter not at all. She'd heard Mama speaking endlessly about which families were acceptable and which not and deplored the snobbishness. It was what people were inside that mattered.

'You look beautiful,' Heriot said and grasped her in the way that told her that he desired her again. His hand slid over her rump possessively. It was the only word she ever connected with him consistently.

'It's almost time to go,' she reminded him.

'Damn!' As usual, Heriot was straightforward.

It was affectation to take the carriage to Government House when she could have hitched up her skirts and walked there.

But it would never have done. Conventions had to be observed. It was absurd and yet it was satisfying to be helped out of the conveyance as if she really were someone of note and to walk inside the building on Heriot's strong arm, knowing that they looked a striking pair.

The brief sense of power faded at the entrance to the ballroom. They were announced so loudly and a kind of silence fell over the big room as Heriot propelled her towards Macquarie and his Scottish wife who looked uncomfortably well bred.

Jade thought she might have preferred Macquarie's little West Indian heiress but she was long dead of the feared lung disease. Elizabeth Campbell of Airds, who now shared his hearth and bed, was very much the Governor's lady. Jade clasped the white-gloved hand and let it go. The room was quite heady with the scent of flowers and candles.

She moved on towards the Governor who stared at her with interest. He had an interesting face, rather hollow-cheeked and fleshless, his eyes deep lidded, the mouth inclined to thinness. 'So this is the lady who painted Greenway's church?'

'It is. And my fiancée,' Heriot said.

'I'd not forgotten.' Macquarie wore his uniform well, his spareness a welcome contrast to the fleshiness of some of his aides. Heriot, fit from all his riding and the energy expended on his range and flocks, looked very handsome. She was proud of him. Elizabeth Macquarie thawed visibly as he chatted with her.

The Governor understood Jade's discomfort. His eyes approved her, sympathized. 'It's a pleasing picture and I'd like it if there were another to hang beside it one of these days.'

'Surely,' Jade replied. 'Have you any favourite scene?'

'The harbour and the heads.'

'I will certainly try.' She was conscious that most of the undoubtedly cynical eyes in the room were on them both and lifted her head higher.

The Governor saw the swinging lights of the chandelier reflected in green eyes of great beauty. The girl had spirit and her voice was charming. None of that London whine that infiltrated Australian conversation and would not be eradicated. And the flower that sat on top of the mound of brown hair was the colour of her skin. He pushed away the memory of his own dead girl-wife. It was not a night for sadness.

'Mr and Mrs James Wengate!'

This was their signal to move on. 'Thank you,' Jade said in a low voice. 'I do thank you for everything.'

'We'll see you again, doubtless.' Macquarie smiled with real pleasure and this approval did not go by unnoticed. Jade, moving away to make room for the Wengates, could read the passing expressions quite accurately. If the Governor thinks fit to welcome this woman, perhaps we should unbend a little? After all, Logan Heriot is going to marry her. Not that it isn't before time!

A dozen pairs of shrewd eyes descended from Jade's proudly borne head to the region of her waist. They'd see nothing. Even without the little French stays there was nothing to see.

The touch of Heriot's hand on her elbow was the greatest comfort. Jade smiled at him brilliantly and became the target for male eyes that assessed her quite differently. Several officers stared quite openly, their uniforms lending them a probably spurious grandeur. Husbands were more discreet but equally appreciative.

Heriot nodded to right and to left and accepted glasses of wine from a passing flunkey. They stood close by the long windows that overlooked the bay, seeing the risen moon reflected in black water. The sound of the sea crashed on to the shore below.

Jade, warm and uncomfortable in the cream silk, was over-poweringly conscious of all the little gossiping groups. The women would be unkind except directly to her face, now that the Governor had shown his approval. She did not need to be told what the men were thinking. They envied Heriot and wanted to take her to bed. Her lack of innocence excited them. She was 'available'. Wanton –

Sipping the light wine with apparent enjoyment, Jade's reflections were shattered by Henry Lambert's name being called. Heriot turned sharply, his expression not friendly. She saw his fists clench.

'Logan. You'll start something that could dash all your hopes of further visits,' she whispered urgently. 'We are the cynosure of all eyes, anyway, and everything you and I do or say is going to be noted. You know that's true. Be careful.'

She saw Lambert taking Elizabeth Macquarie's hand. The smattering of young girls in the room were aware of him too. One or two bridled and she felt sorry for them. Even if they had expectations of money, they were too plain to attract any but fortune-hunters and their mothers had not done the best for them. If she had them to take in hand she thought she could improve their looks and style. Some women, of course, did not like competition, particularly from their own daughters.

She finished the wine quickly, needing some bravery from it, half her mind admiring some of the confections of silk and satin, brocade and tussore, the designs on the fine Chinese shawls, ivory-handled fans and paste shoe-buckles, the men's coats which were either dark and severe or gay and much embroidered, like the waistcoats beneath them. There seemed a preponderance of wigs.

The conversation had risen to a crescendo just at the moment Lambert saw them. Jade wanted to suggest to Heriot that they go out into the garden as some of the other guests were doing, but that would only postpone the inevitable.

Henry smiled a little disbelievingly, caught the remnants of a languishing look from the plainest of the girls nearby, then came forward purposefully, weaving his way around little family gatherings, studiously unaware of Heriot's lowering glare and the timid smiles of unattached daughters.

He was very attractive tonight, Jade thought, wondering if it might not after all be a good thing if Heriot and Lambert descended to a bout of fisticuffs, thereby precluding them from any further Government House occasion. She did not think she could face these hard-eyed harpies again. But she must, for Heriot's sake. Everything connected with this visit had been entered into for his benefit, not hers.

Lambert reached them, impeccably dressed, his fair hair shining under the light of a hundred candles. 'Logan. Jane. How good that you are here.'

'I don't suppose you expected us.' Heriot was stiff as a hedgehog.

'Honestly, no.' Henry took out an exquisite snuff-box and sniffed at a pinch of the contents. The grey eyes took in Heriot's sullen displeasure. 'I see you are aware of the reason for my non-appearance at Elsrickle. I could not help admiring Jane. We do have some things in common, you and I. But she was perfectly honest and utterly faithful. If I recall, she slapped my face extremely hard on the one occasion I tried to kiss her. That was the day I was detailed into driving her home to Elsrickle. She ticked me off very roundly for my not

315

too damaging presumption. Sore pride kept me away, Logan. It was silly and unnecessary.'

He made it all sound very innocent. Jade had the feeling he had rehearsed the speech many a time. Painting and acting were closely akin.

'I see.' Heriot did not look quite so angry. He wanted to believe it.

'I admit I've suffered by my own folly. Friendship is not so lightly discarded. I've missed you. Both of you.' And Henry was persuasive.

'As we have done,' Heriot was driven to admit.

Henry seized a glass from the nearest silver tray. Jade was not sure how much of the facile explanation was sincere but it was perfectly executed. 'Do you want another, Jane? There. Logan?'

They all took the fresh glasses and Jade saw that Heriot was unbending. Only a little, but it was a start. She encountered the suddenly hostile gaze of a very young girl who stood close by with a perfect dragon of a mother or aunt. The clear young eyes filled her with an unexpected sense of loss. This girl's past would not be littered with the debris of relationships such as her own with Nick Caspar, Captain Joel, Collin and Heriot. Nor with those sordid fumblings in Newgate. The violence of her own feelings for Masson. She was not very much older than the child who condemned her but the past two years had been crammed with enough incident for a lifetime. It was hard to be so well known as a fallen woman.

The musicians on the dais beside the potted palms were tuning up. The dancing was to begin. Jade wondered how many business deals were taking place under cover of the chatter and the tuneless sounds, how many affairs flourished, how many young hearts were quickened or downcast by the predilection of some man of their choice when he turned to another. How many marriages were about to be arranged as her own once was. She was unexpectedly diverted. Henry and Logan had not come anywhere near exchanging blows. Apart from some sour or disapproving looks from the matrons, there had been no real unpleasantness. Macquarie had been generous. It could have been much worse. Optimism returned.

'Will you dance with me?' Henry asked.

'When I have danced with Logan.'

'Of course. His is the right,' Henry said smoothly, and Jade knew now that he only pretended cordiality towards his former friend. Without meaning to she had indeed driven a wedge between them.

Heriot was not a good dancer but none of those who watched them was concerned about the way he performed the steps. Mothers who had once entertained hopes that he might take one of their daughters impaled him on jealous glances. A second look told them that his convict wife-to-be had exquisite taste. Her slight body, wrapped so beautifully in pale silk, the elegant line of her neck revealed by the upswept hair. The cool loveliness of the huge flower that gave her an almost Oriental appearance. And underneath, badness and a sorcery that drew Heriot towards his inevitable doom and bewitched even the Governor. Lips were tightened. The barrier would be insuperable.

Jade closed her eyes and let the music sink into her bones, responding as she always did to the suggestion of hedonism. If her body was not entirely in accord with his it did not matter. This was only the smallest part of their lives.

Dancing with Lambert was vastly different. For one thing the dance was the new and rather daring valse and he performed it admirably. There was not an eye in the room that was not on the tall, blond man and his partner. The fact that they seemed oblivious of everyone else pleased few. A hard-necked little bitch she was to flaunt her sexuality before the gaze of the man she'd entrapped in marriage!

But Jade saw none of this, though Henry did. Her eyes were shut again as they revolved so fluidly and excitingly around the room that was hazed with the scent of perfumed candles and with flowers, the music sensuous and interspersed with little icy chinkings from the chandelier that was nearest the french windows open to the gardens and the view of the bay, the evening breeze.

Macquarie stifled a sigh as he saw her drift by. She *did* remind him of his first love.

Heriot, standing by the door, could not fail to see their pleasure in the valse. The dance had been damned for its familiarity and he could see why. It enabled a stranger to hold a woman as closely as though they were lovers. He did not think he could bear to see them twined together for much longer. His doubts reawakened, Heriot stepped out into the garden to wait for the music to end.

Several couples stood silhouetted against the rail that bordered the garden. The moon was brilliant now, casting a shivering pathway across the sea. He stood silent and alone, detesting the envy that gnawed at him.

Jade, held close to Lambert's chest, thought she had never enjoyed anything so much. The music finally ending, she laughed and looked around for Heriot but he was not there. 'It's warm,' she said.

'We'll walk in the garden for a minute,' Henry suggested, then drew her to the open door before she could object. Outside, it was much cooler, the air filled with little spicy scents and the rustle of birds. Here and there, she made out the pale shadow of an evening gown, the white of a shirt front. Snatches of conversation travelled through the silence but they were not the romantic whispers one might have expected. They spoke of Napoleon, of the King's lechery, of whale oil and the East India trade. The price of tea and silk. Sheep —

The path they found themselves on was apart from the rest. Jade shivered in the contrast from the heated ballroom and Henry put an arm around her shoulders.

'You'll catch a chill, if I do not,' he murmured as she made an attempt to draw away.

'Henry, I thought we'd decided —'

'How can I decide anything when you look like that?' he told her and twisted her round to face him. 'I can't stand by and let him take you. I'd almost reconciled myself to doing without you until I saw you again tonight.' He leaned forward and kissed the portion of bosom that rose above her neckline. The touch of his mouth was not unpleasant. Jade did not struggle immediately and that was her undoing. 'Oh, God! Jane —'

His arms were around her like boa constrictors. Squeezing the breath from her body. His own body was urgent with desire. 'I made the mistake of listening to you last time. It was weak and foolish. I don't intend to do it twice. You're worth fighting for, my dear.'

'Let her go.'

Neither at first recognized Heriot's voice, it was so harsh and warped with rage. Lambert turned his head, surprised, and Heriot struck out at him. Jade, suddenly released, was hurtled backwards to slam against the trunk of a blue gum.

She cried out and Heriot, forgetting Lambert, ran to her. 'Are you all right?'

'The back of my head hurts a little.'

Everything hurt. All her bones had jarred but she would not add fuel to the fire.

She winced as Heriot touched her shoulder.

'I'm sorry,' Lambert said. Heriot turned on him like a fury. 'Psalm-singing hypocrite! So much for all that cant about friendship. The moment my back's turned, you're up to your old tricks.' He launched a vicious blow at Henry's face, which, if it had landed, would have had him on his back. But Lambert twisted and received only a glancing blow that cut his lip. His head snapped sideways.

The sight of the trickle of blood brought Jade back to full awareness of what they were doing. Heriot had staggered back from an uppercut from Lambert's fist. She ran between them. 'Have you taken leave of your senses? Remember where you are! It's unforgivable to behave so here. I blame you, Henry, I'm afraid. You knew what you were doing. A pity you had to ruin everything.'

The moon lay on both men's faces. There was nothing there but hostility. All conversations in the garden had ceased and the faint strains of music mocked them.

'Come, Logan. We must go inside.' She pulled at his arm, feeling the tenseness and the incipient threat that bound it with hardness.

'We have to,' she whispered.

Heriot moved unwillingly. Jade, taking his arm, walked beside him, aching with every step. She even managed a smile as they re-entered the crowded room. It was as she thought. The whisper had gone around already that Heriot's harlot had caused a rift between good friends. She might as well have been dressed in scarlet. The Governor would hear of the episode eventually.

Outwardly unmoved, inwardly disturbed, she braved the ambuscade of sneers and whispers with a seemingly effortless calm. Heriot's fury gave him a quiet reserve that could pass for detachment. Anxiously, she searched his appearance for some tell-tale scar that might betray the scuffle but he looked much as before.

It was only as she passed the huge gesso-framed mirror that she saw that the flower was gone from her hair.

Henry Lambert was at this moment picking up the big, creamy bloom, holding it, for a moment, to his lips. Then he dabbed at his cut mouth, seeing that blood had disfigured one of the petals. It seemed like an omen.

Slowly, he walked towards the gate that led to the roadway outside.

*

Jade and Heriot quarrelled violently afterwards but his anger was moderated when he discovered that she had suffered physically from the incident. She could hardly move next morning and he was immediately anxious about the well-being of his child and insisted upon calling in the doctor.

That would cause more scandal, Jade thought, past caring. She could imagine the highly-coloured reasons for the bruises on her back and behind. How Heriot had marched her straight here to the Castlereagh and walloped her as she so richly deserved. Her only regret was that she must have fallen in Macquarie's estimation, not because he was Governor, but because he seemed to have liked her for herself. Perhaps he would merely smile over the report.

The doctor prescribed hot baths with an addition of salts and assured Heriot that nothing else ailed her. Relief made Logan apportion the vastly greater blame to Lambert. After all, he had heard Henry say that he'd made the mistake of listening to Jane last time. Not that she had struggled too hard.

But he swallowed his inclination towards remarking on the fact. He'd keep her out of Henry's way, and once they were safely married she'd keep her side of the contract. He'd learnt to recognize her integrity.

There was one way to keep her. Daniel. Her greatest wish was to see him making up to the boy and it would no longer be so impossible.

Jade packed the cream gown carefully but noticed that there was a small blemish on the back of it. The sight of the little mark renewed her conviction that she should not have worn it before the ceremony. And she had lost the flower she had intended to press as a memento of the occasion.

It was two days before they could begin the homeward journey and another two before the spire of Greenway's church rose up out of the roofs of Windsor. Jade was disturbed to realize that she did not want to see Elsrickle appear beyond the paddock, but then she saw Daniel running down the path, Jump close at his heels. She gathered up her skirts and hurried to meet him. He was more beautiful than ever. More like Gabriel.

She was overwhelmed by a torrent of feelings she could not separate. Passion for Masson, love for the dark child she held, a vast tenderness towards the new life inside her. And for Heriot?

She stared at him in surprise as he lifted Daniel from her

and rubbed his stubbled chin against the boy's cheek. 'Hallo, Daniel. We have gifts for you from Sydney. Would you like to see them?'

'Presents. Yes! Yes – Mr Heriot.'

'Papa,' Heriot said. 'Let's try Papa, shall we?'

He continued his way towards the house. Daniel laughing at Jade over his shoulder. She did not believe Logan had changed. Not yet. Only time could decide that, but it was a beginning.

Heriot's wedding was fixed for a week today. Jade lost her appetite, though it was expected. All brides lost their taste for food, Mrs Doyle said, and cackled cheerfully, enjoying the preparations. Jade, more aware now of the coming child, thanked God that Logan was the father. Whenever she felt caged or unhappy she would remind herself that it could have been worse. It might have been Nick's baby.

They never spoke of Lambert now that they were back at home and Jade tried not to think too much of Gabriel Masson. How differently she would have felt if she were wedding Gabriel. The thought of him still had the power to move her.

Her fingers moved towards the sea-horse and she stroked it as though it had the power to change one man into another. Heriot into Masson. A superficial likeness no longer seemed enough to bind her to Logan for a lifetime.

They received an invitation to have supper with the Davieses and Jade welcomed the change in routine.

Supper with Bess and George would be a diversion. Life at Elsrickle could become insular. Jade dressed up for the occasion and Heriot's pride in her was obvious. He wore the dark coat she liked best and his new shirt and cravat.

During the journey he kept his arm round her waist. Protectively or possessively? She was afraid it was both. Used to fighting her own battles, she was not sure if she wished to be taken care of so thoroughly.

Wedding nerves, she told herself. A few more days and she'd be Jane Heriot. Jane Benson and Jade Benedict would disappear into limbo. She touched the jade carving at her throat to reassure herself that the past was not entirely gone.

It was still light and the crows carked desolately. The eucalyptus leaves shivered, showing their pale undersides. Jade pulled the collar of the pelisse closer.

'Cold, my darling?'

'A goose walked over my grave.'

'And you call me superstitious!'

'I want you to know,' she said suddenly, 'that you could not have made me happier.'

'Why now?' But he was more than pleased. His hand reached out and took hold of hers, caressing each finger.

How could she explain that she was afraid to put off saying her thanks, expressing her gratitude?

'I just wanted to.'

'Shall I stop the carriage? Take you home again? I'll have your thanks in privacy.'

'Isn't this private enough?' She gestured to the sky and trees, the dark, ruffled bosom of the river.

'You know the conditions I have in mind.'

'There's tomorrow. A thousand tomorrows.' She made her voice brave and carefree.

'What's that?' Heriot's voice had sharpened and he sat up straight.

She peered ahead. There was a glow in the sky. Somewhere a large fire burned.

'There's trouble,' Heriot said. 'And you mustn't be part of it.'

'But I am part of your life! You made me so. If it's a bush fire, there's always escape in the river. But if it was, the wildlife would be coming towards us. So far there's nothing.'

'It's a building.' Heriot was disturbed. 'George's house.'

'Then we have to help.'

Heriot flicked his switch and the carriage rolled on faster. But they had not gone far before they heard faint cries and screams, the sharp crack of shotgun fire. Heriot cursed and dragged at the reins. The little carriage came to a standstill. The redness in the sky had increased.

'It's a mutiny,' Heriot said roughly. 'George's men must have overpowered Frank, the overseer, that's what must have happened. Not a new story. I told him he should have had more help like Frank and not rely almost solely on the convicts. A sheep farmer near Parramatta had the same trouble the year I arrived. It was a bad business. I'll have to take you back and fetch some of my men. There's nothing I can do unarmed and with a pregnant woman to care for.'

Already, he was turning the carriage. There was a queer bump as though they had hit something. Heriot cursed and whipped at the horses and the next moment the vehicle was bowling along at a breakneck pace. The stars swirled in the sky and all the trees were a blur.

'What happened?' Jade asked, craning for a last look at the fire behind them.

'We hit something. An overhanging branch, probably.'

It had not felt like a branch. Jade felt sick. The Symonses were almost totally unprotected since the floods when most of their work force had escaped and been replaced by a skeleton gang of only half a dozen until more convicts arrived at Port Jackson.

The Davieses would have no chance if their workers had freed themselves. Fortified with rum, of which George always had a plentiful supply, only God knew what they would do if Denver were there to urge them to excesses of cruelty.

Great as was Jade's anxiety for their neighbours, she was even more concerned for the safety of the Darts and the small staff at Elsrickle. A number of Heriot's sheepmen had been given leave to go into Parramatta since the work was well forward, and Heriot, indulgent because of his forthcoming marriage, had relaxed sufficiently to grant a short holiday before the next strenuous cycle began. They were to return on his wedding eve.

The eucalyptus trees that had been so pleasant a background on the way to the Davieses' home became a jungle beyond which lay unseen danger. Every shadow was an enemy on the track. There was the upper road, repaired after the rains, along which escaped felons could proceed almost unnoticed until the final moments when it could be too late. The Davieses' buckboard would get them to Elsrickle in a comparatively short time.

As soon as the carriage came to a halt, Heriot sprang to the ground and seized Jade firmly by the waist, thrusting her towards the house. 'Go inside,' he ordered. 'I must go up to Johnnie's and rouse the rest of the men. We'll let the dogs out. They can help patrol. Bolt the door and let no one in but me or Johnnie.'

'Take care! Please —'

He turned his head and smiled. 'Of course.' He had never looked so handsome, so like Masson. Her breath caught in her throat. Heriot turned away again and was on his way across the paddock, running, shouting to anyone who would listen. The dogs began to bark and lights showed in the bunkhouse windows, pooling the dark grass with splotches of yellow.

Jade banged the door and pushed home the bolt with unsteady fingers. Her heart beat quickly and irregularly. She ran to the kitchen and found Mrs Doyle sitting at the table, her hand covering a glass of rum but not concealing it fast enough.

'I thought you'd be out till all hours. Whatever's amiss?' She looked guilty.

'The convicts have broken out at the Davieses' place. They could have been helped by the gang who ran away from the Symonses. If they've been having a hard time living off kangaroo and cockatoo, they could have come back out of resentment and desperation.' Jade did not repeat the tale she had heard of escapees who had been driven to cannibalism by the harsh conditions of the bush.

'May the good Lord preserve us!' Mrs Doyle tossed back the contents of the glass, forgetting it was something to which she had no real right.

'Daniel,' Jade said. 'You've looked in at him recently?'

'To be sure I have. Ten minutes ago.'

'I'll go to him in case he's wakened by the racket. You tell Lizzie and Dora they must get up and find something to protect themselves with, pokers or firedogs. Anything –'

Jade hurried to the staircase carrying a lighted candle. The treads of the stairs were barred with bands of moonlight. In the distance, she could hear voices, shouts, the frenzied barking of the dogs. The sheep, aroused, bleated dismally. From the hall, the parrot squawked, then stopped with appalling abruptness as though something had been flung over the cage. Or if it had died – She deplored her imagination.

She stopped. She had not told Mrs Doyle to bolt the back door. But surely the woman would think of it for herself? Of course she must, she wasn't a fool.

Pushing open the door of Daniel's room, she looked at the small shape under the bedclothes. The little boy slept soundly. Her hands went instinctively to her stomach. There was still no appreciable change in its gentle roundness. It was far too soon for that.

Reluctantly, she left the child and went into Heriot's room where he kept a small pistol. For a moment she could not remember which drawer he'd put it in and opened first one and then the other, fumbling with the assortment of cravats and 'kerchiefs, dropping small objects to the polished boards.

She got to her knees and felt about in the shadows of drawers and press in order to retrieve them. Something struck her violently in the small of the back and she was flung

324

forward, her face hitting the cold smoothness of cedarwood. She opened her lips to scream, but a tough, sinewy arm was put round her mouth and a body was thrust across hers. She fought and twisted, turned her head sideways to find herself looking into decolorized eyes, so pale that they might have been made of ice. In this frigid setting the pupils looked abnormally black. A tight, bony face, a scrub of short bristly hair. Lips that were compressed into a thin line of bitterness then curled away unpleasantly into the semblance of a smile.

'You don't want to wake the brat, do you?' Denver whispered.

Jade shook her head. Daniel must not be aroused. Denver would have no more feeling for him than if he were a troublesome fly to be swatted. 'What did you do to Mrs Doyle?'

'You mean the old lady in the kitchen? Put a gag on her and tied her up before she woke anyone up.'

'You didn't – hurt her?'

'Only two people are going to get hurt. You and that whoring Heriot.'

She could not take her eyes from him and the threat he represented.

'How – did you get here?'

'Hung on the back of the carriage.'

She remembered the thump Heriot had imagined was the result of hitting an overhanging branch.

'All I needed do was to stay where I was in the dark until he went off. You locked the door too fast but no one touched the one at the back.' He fastened a hand in her hair and dragged it back until she grimaced with pain. Then he hooked his other fingers into the neck of her gown and ripped it to the waist.

'Don't make a sound,' he warned softly, 'or that brat gets hurt. Understand?'

She nodded. The stench of his clothes and body revolted her. He rasped his unshaven chin across her mouth so that it flamed into pain, then tugged at the fine shift so that the buttons flew across the room.

Fancying she heard a sound from Daniel, she struggled to raise her head but, keeping his grip of her hair, Denver hit her savagely just above the eye and then across her cheek. She held back a moan. His mouth was on her breast, biting her painfully so that she was forced to move beneath him. Unable to escape, his fingers still locked in her hair, she was compelled to endure his gropings under her skirts. Not that the delicate undergarment proved any barrier against the hard, vicious fingers that tore and dragged.

'No! No –' she whispered frantically. 'Beat me if you must. But don't make me –'

'He does.'

'We are to marry. In a few days.'

It made no difference to his intention. Strong thighs separated her own, uncaring of her pain. His fingers tore at her maidenhair. Gasping, she recoiled for long enough to allow him entry. He drove into her like a ramrod. She cried silently, flinching under that relentless thrusting, consumed with an endless misery. His teeth fastened upon the round of her shoulder and she cried out.

Intent upon his pleasure, Denver seemed not to notice that involuntary sound. Forcing his hand around her buttock, he lifted her closer, panting as he began to come near fulfilment. She could not bear the thought that he would spend himself inside her. She began to push him away with all of her strength but made no impression on his iron determination to possess her. He was whispering filthy things, bestial encouragement.

Around her the boards creaked. The candle-light bathed their bodies shamefully. Denver's slitted eyes glittered with points of ice or fire, she could not decide which. All she knew was that this ravening act had undone all the striving towards respectability and normality she had made the goal of her life in Australia. She had achieved nothing. Denver had taken her back to the citadel, the Holy Land. The condemned cell. Nick Caspar.

Denver gave a great, whooping catch of the breath and thrust his mouth over hers. Though his body was relaxed, he still covered her, his foot hitched over one ankle, so that she was compelled to lie where she was.

He lifted his head. She still could not quite believe that it had happened.

'Next time,' he said, 'I want you to behave as you would with that whoremonger of yours. You can't tell me you'd lie like a cold fish for him.'

Her eyes blazed. She spat into his face.

It was a mistake. Denver shouted. His fist crashed into her temple and she could feel her senses slipping away. Next time, he had said. Next time. He was standing over her and his foot struck her side. Her head spun like the globe of the world Papa had once had. She thought she called his name but could never be sure.

There were voices downstairs and Denver had sprung away from her. He was pulling at the drawer that held the pistol. The weapon was in his hand and he was staring towards the door, his body quite still.

Jade struggled to rise but could only lean over to vomit on the floor. Wiping her mouth, she tried again to get up but could not. Heriot was in the doorway, his face ashen and his eyes burning with rage and pity. She tried to speak but the horror of the tableau was too great.

Denver, smiling, cocked the pistol deliberately and fired. Heriot rocked for a moment on his feet, then fell forward slowly. His outstretched fingers touched hers.

Denver stepped over his body and pushed his way out of the room.

She heard him thrust open another door and was terrified he'd go into the child's room. Jade crawled across the floor. Heriot's dead face looked up into hers, fixed in its expression of horrified disbelief.

'Logan,' she whispered, then remembered that she could do nothing for him. It was Daniel who needed her. She pushed herself upwards, clinging to the door jamb, hearing Denver pulling open drawers, then the clink of coins. They rattled into his pocket.

Daniel was crying. 'Mama. Mama?'

He would be getting up. Jade took a step and again found herself face to face with Denver. There was blood on her hand where she had touched Heriot. Violently, she wiped it against her skirt. Her head throbbed and her throat felt stiff and sore.

Downstairs, Mrs Doyle was whispering something to Lizzie.

'I'll be coming back for you,' Denver was saying to Jade, 'when I've settled with them. You're going with me.'

Jade heard the pad of the boy's feet against the waxed cedarwood floor. 'Mama.' He came out on to the landing and stared at her with growing fear. She must present a frightening spectacle with her torn and bloodied clothes and blackened face.

'Get out of my way,' Denver said in a hoarse, ugly voice.

Daniel, petrified, did not move. It was like the day of the snake and the kookaburra.

'I told you to get out of the way,' Denver said, almost without emotion, and struck out at him. One moment Daniel's mouth was opened on a scream, then he toppled backwards. She could see his body tumbled from stair to stair, his fingers reaching out vainly towards the banisters. Then the small hand flopped and no longer tried to grasp the bars. The soft, terrible bumping ceased. Daniel lay hunched at the stair foot and there was blood coming from his mouth. His eyes were like Heriot's, frozen into eternal questioning.

Mrs Doyle was shrieking like a banshee.

Jade, blind with rage, leapt at Denver. Grinning coldly, he threw her aside and began to run down the stairs. Her head struck the doorpost. She was momentarily aware of his hurrying footsteps, the dull crump of the pistol butt on something yielding, and the abrupt cessation of Mrs Doyle's voice. Then nothing.

'Here,' Henry said. 'Drink this.'

Jade obeyed passively. It was easier to do as she was told. If she accepted everything it did not hurt so much. But there were times when her thoughts broke out of the cocoon of non-resistance and she was forced to see things as they were. And what she saw was terrible.

This dark, bitter stuff was the colour and taste of that shocked realization, but it brought a temporary forgetfulness. She could sleep. Shut away truth.

Henry smiled at her. If it had not been for Lambert she would have lost her reason. She knew that.

She dreamed, obscenely, of Denver. He had opened the door of an unlighted room and found her there. What he did made her scream. She was fighting him off and somehow the dim place was light and she was pushing against Henry Lambert.

'You had a dream.' His voice was very gentle but she could not help the traitorous thought that it would be better if he were firm with her. She could not be cushioned from life for ever.

They had hidden the locket that contained the miniatures of Gabriel and Daniel. Sometimes she got out of bed and wandered about shakily, looking for it. But she could not discover the hiding-place and her heart was empty. If only they realized that she did not want to forget them completely.

It was winter and she never felt warm. Always she insisted the pelisse was left beside her. Huddled inside the warm folds she could dream herself back in Masson's house, waiting in the green silk room for the sound of his steps on the stair. There was the tart, fresh smell of oranges – snow and church bells.

Henry gave her the set of opals she had most admired. The flashing green, so subtly shot through with colour, was something she never tired of watching. He brought her flowers, rolls of silk, lace, hung her framed portrait on the wall, now that Heriot was no longer there to object.

Heriot. Anguish welled up in her at the thought of his useless death. But apart from that last, sick moment, he had been happy, she told herself. It was only one moment out of all the weeks, months, years of happiness.

She never thought consciously of Daniel. It was as though he had gone out into the night a very long time ago and would, somehow, find his way back.

The doctor from Windsor had come frequently. It was he who had told her there would be no baby. Denver's treatment of her had caused the infant, if one could call it that, to abort. There was little reality about the news.

Today, she wanted to get up. The longer she stayed in bed, the more difficult it would be to adjust to her new life. She had no claim on Heriot's estate. That would go to a distant cousin in Scotland. Not that she minded. Elsrickle had been an oasis but she had never planned to become its mistress. It had seemed like home because of Heriot's presence and need of her. Now it was merely another house.

Nan might miss her but she had Johnnie Dart and there would be her children. She had her place in Johnnie's house and always would.

Soon, Jade thought, she must think of her own future. Henry wanted her to stay here, near Windsor, but that would be too easy. There would be another situation exactly like the one before. Living with a man who loved her but for whom she felt only friendship and deep gratitude for his recent care. It was not enough, not fair to him.

How thin and pale her hands were and they hardly had the strength to fasten her gown. Her eyes looked enormous. But she made herself walk about the bed-chamber until she was stronger, then brushed at her tangled hair.

The view from the window was exquisite, the long avenue, the grass, the flowers. Far off, on a rise, stood Francis Greenway's church. But she did not want to think of God. Her sense of loss was too raw and keen to accept such unnecessary death.

She heard Henry's step on the stair and turned to greet him.

'You shouldn't be up yet.'

'I must some time.' She shrugged. 'Why not today?'

'You still look dreadfully ill.'

'I must get used to things as they are,' she said steadily. 'It will hurt more later if I act the ostrich. You mustn't encourage me to do that. We had a good life, Heriot and I,' and I don't want to push it out of my mind.'

'You need never lack a refuge –'

'I don't really want a refuge. I'm so used, now, to fighting for myself, that I'd never be happy cosseted and protected. I want to go right away from here, accept some challenge. Only I'm tied to Australia and I fear I've grown to hate it. I am free to marry if I choose but I don't want to take that path unless my heart is in it. And it's not.'

'It's too soon, of course. But later – You know I'd be waiting.'

'It could be a long time. Perhaps never.'

'What do you want to do? If it's in my power, I'll help you.'

'I think you mean that.'

'I'd do anything for you.'

'How kind you are.'

'Damn kindness!' he said savagely. 'There's nothing gentle in my feelings so don't imagine there is. But if I can't win you in your present state, it seems I have no recourse but to be patient. For years if necessary.'

'There is something I want to do. You may remember I mentioned having lost track of my parents through no fault of theirs or mine. I imagined, foolishly, that I could never seek them out but since – since Heriot died, I think I must find them. But I'd have to go to London. Begin there. And, of course, I am not free to ask for a passage.'

'I see.'

'How is poor Bess?' Jade asked when the silence became protracted. Bess had been the only one of the quartet to survive the convict uprising, and that only because they imagined her as dead as George and the Symonses.

'On her way to Sydney where a ship is waiting. She has a passage booked and will go back to the village she lived in as a girl. Somewhere in Yorkshire, Mrs Doyle told me. She wished you well.'

'I wish I'd seen her.'

'You were too ill, my dear.' His fair, Viking face expressed concern.

'At least she is free! Free to go where she wills!'

'There is a way you could go. The *Isabelle* will be calling on her way back to London, in a matter of two to three weeks. I'll speak to the captain and explain matters so that you are kept apart. No one need know you've left illegally. I'd take you aboard myself the night before sailing.'

'But what when Governor Macquarie makes enquiries about me? As he must.'

'I will plead ignorance. And you would have stowed away, destination unknown. It would be some time before you were missed. Many ships leave from Port Jackson. They could not prove you left on mine.'

'You'd do that for me?'

'That and more. So long as you promise you'll think of my offer of marriage. If you say you'll regard it as the most serious proposal of my life, I'll help you to reach London. Have papers made out for you under some other name –'

'I always meant to tell Heriot – I do have a real name.'

'Then tell me.'

'It's Jardine Benedict. Jade –'

'How very outlandish. But how well it suits you. Why did you conceal your identity?'

'Because of those roads to Newgate that I can't talk about. If you trusted me last year, why not now?'

'As you say, why not. And you are sure you must go?'

She could have wept for the sadness in his voice. He had shown her the depth of his love by making it possible for her to leave him.

'I am absolutely sure.'

'I – I will do what I can about the papers. Jardine Benedict, you said?'

The name sounded strange after having been so long unused.

'Yes. My father called me Jade.'

'And gave you that little Chinese piece you wear.'

On Anna Masson's chain. Gabriel would be in London. It was not impossible that she might see him. She felt quite faint with anticipation.

'Yes. He gave me the sea-horse.'

'I think there's another reason for going to London, isn't there?'

'How could you tell?'

'I think I always knew. That miniature you painted. It wasn't really Heriot, was it? Superficially, perhaps. You had a lover and he was too like Heriot for comfort. Wasn't that it?

The terrible bond you felt you couldn't break? Well, I'm not in the least like him and I'll not have that fatal hurdle to overcome. When you've seen him again and got him out of your system for good, write and tell me and I'll catch the next boat after you. And don't tell me how kind I am!'

'Very well. I'll only think it.' It was the first time she had smiled in weeks.

'Have you anywhere to go? Any money?'

She shook her head. 'My parents sold the house. They may still be abroad.'

'Then you must stay in my London house. I've not given that up. I'll give you a letter for Mrs Abel – '

'Mrs Abel?'

'My housekeeper. She'll look after you. And I won't let you go unless you accept a loan. No, do not argue! How can you scour the streets of London, looking for two people who may or may not be there, and nothing to keep you in clothes and the paying of solicitors and the like? I take it that's how you'd start?'

'Yes. I did think that might be best.'

'I'll give you the name and address of my own. William Pickersgill.'

'Dear Henry. I feel I must kiss you.'

She made a move towards him but he would not let her approach. 'No, Jane, if I took hold of you I'd not let go and then I'd be worse than Denver. I'll wait.'

Jade shivered. 'Did they catch him? I've never been able to bring myself to ask.'

Henry shook his head. 'Not yet. But they will, and I'll have great pleasure in seeing him hanged. Unless the bush gets him. A snake perhaps, or thirst or hunger. Sunstroke, madness. The aborigines.' He shrugged. 'I don't care which.'

'We may never know.'

'Australia's like that.'

A spasm of pain racked her. 'I feel I never want to see it again.'

'It's a great country. A beautiful country. Things will settle down.'

'Perhaps.'

'Come downstairs if you insist on being up and you shall have mint tea.'

'That will be lovely. I hardly like to ask, but Heriot's cousin – will he want Polly? My mare?'

'He shan't have Polly. She was a personal gift to you and I can vouch for that. No, my dear, Polly will go with you. I'll have her delivered to Tudor Place. You can ride her in Hyde Park. Rotten Row.'

'She will be – something of my own. And you must write and tell me how my Nan progresses. It will be a wrench to leave her.'

They moved slowly down the staircase.

'I promise to tell you everything.'

The stairs negotiated, Jade was glad to sit down and accept the mint-flavoured tea.

'Will you be strong enough to go in three weeks?' Henry asked doubtfully.

'I will have the entire voyage in which to recuperate.'

'Of course. And you'll not put your head in a noose, will you? They won't be looking for Jardine Benedict in London, will they, but someone may recognize Jane Benson.'

'I must make sure that won't happen.'

'Things could go hard with you.'

'I know. But I've made up my mind. I'll be safe enough in your house. Thank you for making it possible for me to start again.'

'Be careful.'

'You're sorry now that you promised, aren't you?' She held out a hand towards the heat of the fire.

'Yes.'

'Only you have and I must hold you to that.'

They sat in silence and a cloud came over the sun, casting the long room into shade. Jade felt as though she had come to the end of a long battle. Her eyes closed gradually and she was dimly aware of Henry taking the glass from her fingers before sleep overcame her.

She was in a pleasant place where deer came up to the fence and rabbits played outside the window. Gabriel was there and Mrs Beddoes. The old lady was holding her hand and saying, 'You've brought your young lady again.'

'My wife,' Masson was replying. 'I'd only bring my wife to Stagshaw.'

'Of course.' Mrs Beddoes's soft voice was dying away. Only the pressure of a hand remained, then that too was lost.

PART THREE

FINALE

CHAPTER TEN

The chaise came to a standstill in front of No. 33 Tudor Place. Jade, still in the black widow's weeds and veil she had worn all during the long voyage on the *Isabelle*, descended from the vehicle and waited for her box to be set on the pavement.

She could not help thinking the tall, dark house was forbidding. London felt cold as charity. Paying off the driver, she climbed the three steps and tugged at the bell-pull. Visions of Rio de Janeiro came to tantalize her with their colour and beauty. Tenerife, a frieze of swaying palms and the mountain behind them, all the hustle and colour of the dock, the fruits and flowers. Vociferous humanity. Life.

This time she had gone ashore. Jardine Benedict had not been barred from leaving the *Isabelle*. She had ridden in a little carriage, had only to reach out her hand to touch the walls of houses, to descend from the vehicle to buy what she would. But it was lonely. Often, during the voyage, she had almost wished that Heriot lay beside her in the quiet cabin. Even though her heart did not require his presence, her body did. There was no one to turn to, to talk to. To care.

The door opened with startling abruptness and a liveried footman stood there, staring at her with unabashed curiosity. The chaise was already several houses away, shadowy now with the onset of dusk. She had left Australia in winter and arrived here in winter. But London was much colder. A spiteful little wind fluttered dead leaves and bits of rubbish blown from the less salubrious areas. The footman, deterred from frivolity by her funereal garb, asked in a hollow voice, 'Who did you wish to see, ma'am?'

'Mrs Abel. I have a letter for her from Mr Lambert.'

'Mr Lambert?' She had obviously startled him.

'Yes. He owns this house, doesn't he?'

'He does. But he's in Windsor, Australia.'

'And I have just come from there. We are friends.'

'Step inside, then, ma'am, and I'll fetch Mrs Abel.'

'There's a box on the pavement.'

'I'll have it brought in.'

She was ushered into a red-papered room with a small fire burning and a preponderance of gilt-framed portraits almost all betraying that Viking streak that was so much Henry's. Blond, bearded and moustached, the faces that were like and yet unlike his stared down at her. None was so refined or gentle-seeming. But Henry was not so mild under that gentlemanly exterior. He was as passionate and desirous as Logan had been. She could understand why they had originally got on so well together.

The long months of the voyage had softened the outlines of Heriot's cruel death. She could even think of Daniel now, without mentally tearing herself to pieces. Lambert had returned the locket before he took her aboard. The mare would arrive tomorrow. She would not be without a friend, memories.

Jade stretched out her fingers to the sullen warmth, then was suddenly aware that she was not alone. She swung round to encounter the blackest pair of eyes she had seen since Gabriel's day. Everything about Mrs Abel echoed Masson's colouring; a white face with high, sculpted cheekbones, thin, arched brows, smooth hair sweeping from a heart-shaped parting, a mouth that was the one wrong note in a mask of asceticism.

'I understand you have a letter for me.' Even the voice might have belonged to a nun, quiet and somehow remote.

'I have.' Jade drew the sealed envelope from her reticule.

Mrs Abel took it in narrow, white fingers. Her waist, inside the black gown, was slender as a child's. Jade had the fancy that they must look like a pair of crows about to squabble over a carcase. Henry's carcase? The thought made her smile involuntarily. Mrs Abel caught the remnants of that reflex but ignored it.

She broke the seal with a finicky correctness. Jade would have ripped it apart, longing to know what news had come from abroad. Mrs Abel contained herself but there was a suggestion of smouldering fires below the veneer of coolness.

The paper crackled. There was a long silence. 'Mr Lambert says you are to be staying here. For a time.'

'For a time. Yes.'

'A room must be prepared.'

'I can wait here.' Jade was aware of her almost unendurable weariness. 'I confess I'll be glad to rest. Recover from the journey.'

'You must be tired,' Mrs Abel agreed unemotionally. 'You'd

better sit down. I'll send you some refreshment, and, when your room is ready, I'll have someone take you there. Mr Lambert made some mention of your mare. It will be stabled in the mews at the back of the house. He says you are to be treated as one of the family.' The white fingers plucked restlessly at the black skirt. The keys at the tiny waist jingled.

'We are great friends,' Jade said. 'I was to marry Lambert's best friend. He – died. I have a list of introductions to some of Mr Lambert's acquaintances. As soon as possible I'll make use of it.'

'I'm sorry, indeed, that your fiancé is dead,' Mrs Abel said formally. 'It must have been a great shock for you.'

'It was. I cannot think what I would have done if it had not been for Mr Lambert. He is a very good person.'

The black eyes devoured what they could of Jade's face beyond the shadow of the delicate veil, the shape of her body under the severe gown. 'I'm sure Mr Lambert would always do what he thought best.'

'How long is it since you saw him?'

'I cannot quite recall,' the precise voice pronounced. 'Eighteen months, perhaps? I hoped we would have seen him before this but he made his discovery of opal and that kept him abroad.' The dark eyes went to Jade's hand and settled on the ring she wore. 'Is that – ?'

Jade held out her hand. 'Yes. That's one of Henry's. I have others. You must see them when I am less tired. It was a notable find. He has been generous.'

'Of course.' The controlled voice had dropped almost to a whisper. Mrs Abel swung on her heel and was gone. Disquiet hung on the air like a cloud.

I should not have said I had several of Henry's opals, Jade thought too late. The woman obviously has a hankering after Henry. The way she held the letter to her breast. Her silences. Her disapproval. How ironic that she, herself, had only a platonic affection for Lambert and how sad that he had apparently no idea that he was the centre of his house-keeper's dreams. Life was such an untidy business. All these loose ends –

She was almost asleep when a diminutive maid returned to leave a tray on which wine and biscuits were set out. Thanking the girl, she nibbled at the Bath Olivers and drank a glass of red wine. The beautiful colour, seen against the firelight, reminded her of waiting for Masson during the time of snow.

Her heart sprang into uncomfortable life. She longed, yet dreaded, the thought of seeing him. But stronger than the impulse that had sent her back to search for news of her father was the necessity of knowing what had happened to Gabriel. For a moment she entertained the thought that Phoebe Lewis's elderly husband might be dead and that Gabriel might, once again, be under her spell. Even married to her!

Common sense told her that Masson would not seek the same trouble twice.

But it was more than three years since they had met. Time had not stood still for either of them. She had been within an ace of being wed even if it had not been out of love. And he? What of Masson? They said time healed most wounds.

Tomorrow she would hire a carriage and wait outside Gabriel's house. She would stay there until she caught a glimpse of him. She pressed her hand to her mouth.

'Your room is ready, Miss Benedict.'

Mrs Abel had not, after all, sent one of the servants to escort Henry's guest upstairs. How silently she moved. Jade followed the straight, slight figure, hardly noticing her surroundings. She saw only the huge, welcoming bed, the box lying at its foot.

Raising the veil, she removed the bonnet and allowed her hair to fall about her shoulders. She ached with weariness.

Mrs Abel was staring at her very intently. 'Will you require food later?'

'Oh, no. All I want is to sleep. Sleep –'

'No one will disturb you. What about your clothes? One of the maids?'

Jade shook her head. 'I can manage. Tomorrow, perhaps.'

'Very well. Good night, Miss Benedict.'

The moment Mrs Abel had gone, Jade almost staggered to the edge of the bed. Something about the big, plumped-up pillows reminded her of Ma Lee. She sat down, smiling, then lay back, watching the firelight on the tester and ceiling. She was in the same city as Masson. Gabriel – That church in the snow.

Ages later, in a queer half-sleep, she opened her eyes a fraction and saw something black and still outlined against the bed-hanging. Like an ebony pillar. Jade made a superhuman effort to struggle out of drowsiness but neither her mind nor her body would respond.

A shadow fell over her face but it became a part of the

night – of oblivion.

She slept for a whole day and awoke refreshed and ravenously hungry to find that someone had covered her with a quilt. It was too late to visit Mr Pickersgill, Henry's lawyer, but she'd go in the morning. She ate as if she had never seen food before and sat up late, burning the candle to its end reading Scott's Romantic Poems and the beginning of one of his Waverley novels. The room became a sort of womb, warm and quiet, reassuring.

Tomorrow she must break out of it, draw her first breath in a changed world. It pleased her that she would be reborn. The black veil would be a barrier between her and the outside because she must never forget that Jane Benson was still a criminal who had served only two years of a sentence before absconding. Widows were left alone, treated with respect, and she was as good as a bereaved wife. Logan had lain with her, given her a child – that died.

She turned the pages rapidly, disliking the trend of thought that led her back. It was imperative that she look forward. Some day, perhaps, she'd learn to think of Heriot and Daniel without bitterness, but that day had not yet come. The images of Lambert were kinder in retrospect. He had wanted her but respected her sufficiently to allow her a breathing space. Henry would wait for a few months at least. The knowledge was a comfort.

As she ate breakfast, the sound of a bell tolling echoed out of the fog.

'What is that?' she enquired of the footman who lingered by the sideboard.

' 'Tis the old King. Dead, he is. Poor old madman that he was. 'Tis only a few days since his son passed away. The Duke of Kent. 'Twill be Prinny now for King, though who'll come after, no one can rightly say since Prinny's daughter's been dead these two years and her baby with her. And he has no truck with that Brunswick wife of his, nor ever will.'

'Oh. Poor old man. The country will see great changes, I expect.'

'And none for the better, ma'am. What with his mistresses and spending, and that great furren edifice he's built at Brighton, 'twon't be a change we can rightly look forward to when we has George the Fourth.'

'Have you everything you want?' Mrs Abel's cold, tinkling

338

voice broke into the footman's gloomy prognostications. The man moved away hastily.

The deep tolling cast a gloom over the morning and the fog-shrouded windows reminded Jade of the night of the rout and the Mandrakes' visit. So long ago.

'I've finished now, thank you. Would it be possible to hire a chaise?'

'Roberts could call one, Miss Benedict. Mr Lambert gave up the coach when he went abroad. He keeps on only his favourite horse and one or two others meantime.'

'I'd be glad if Roberts would. Has Polly arrived yet? My mare?'

'Not yet. But she'll be taken care of when she does.'

'Someone covered me up the first night I came. I fell asleep on top of the bed.'

'I – I looked in, seeing the candle still burning, and went for a quilt.'

'Thank you.' But Jade did not enjoy the realization that Mrs Abel had indeed stood over her while she slept. Yet she could hardly lock her door.

She went to fetch her black garrick cloak with the edging of sable. Henry had insisted she take a generous loan. The bonnet with the delicate veiling and the soft black feather was both attractive and a subtle disguise. She had a pelerine for indoor wear and an assortment of Spanish-style combs that Henry had brought her from Sydney. Two narrow gowns, some underclothes and two pairs of shoes, one of winter boots, Henry's opals, her locket and charm and very little else but a good riding-habit, completed her list of possessions.

Leaving her box open so that someone could hang up the garments and distribute the rest among the drawers in the press, she went downstairs to find the chaise waiting. Ordering the driver to take her to Mr Pickersgill's address, she climbed inside, aware that Mrs Abel watched her from an upstairs window.

There was something very funereal about that journey, she in her mourning, the two horses that drove the chaise both black as night, and the interminable sound of the bells that told the whole of London that George the Third had died. Perhaps he'd been glad to let go of his spirit. His wife gone, Kent dead only a few days, and having suffered so many spells of near-madness when he had been restrained, King yet prisoner.

Figures moved in the fog, voices echoed. It was not the sort of day to spend sitting in a chaise waiting for a man who might never stir from the house. It had been a foolish notion, born of her unchanged love for Masson. They would eventually meet. The conviction grew and she felt happier.

Mr Pickersgill was a small, round man. His silver-rimmed spectacles and tufted hair gave him the look of an owl. It was not easy, at first, to explain her requirements and the lawyer must have noticed how she glossed over her departure from the Benedict household. He did, in fact, ask why she left home and she said merely that the choice was not hers, but now that she was in a position to do so, she wished very much to know where Vera and Mark Benedict were, if that were possible, but that she preferred to make her own approach to them. It would be advisable, she explained, to ascertain she would be welcome.

'Your father must have had a lawyer.'

'I have forgotten his name. I was not interested at the time.'

'I see.'

'Mama always saw him. They would be closeted together, then he'd go. All I ever saw, personally, was the man leaving.'

With great attention to detail, Pickersgill drew out of the girl particulars of her life at Ayas Bywaters.

'It will take time.'

'I expected it would.'

'And I can always contact you at Mr Lambert's?'

'Yes. If for any reason I leave there, I will certainly inform you.'

'Very good.'

She felt lost, once she was shown out. The thought of driving straight back to the Lambert house was vaguely unattractive. Though she saw little of Mrs Abel, she was only too aware of her presence. Common sense took over. There was nowhere else to go. The fog would prevent any kind of excursion. She would return, then go through the list of Henry's acquaintances. One or two particular friends' names had been marked with a star. She could gamble a little. Take her hat-pin and close her eyes while she directed the point towards the paper. Chance had a habit of sending one on the right course.

As she waited to be shown into the presence of Mrs Flora

Earle, designated on Henry's list as his favourite cousin, Jade was aware of a feeling of such inadequacy that she almost rose to her feet in preparation for flight. But the sound of footsteps in the passageway outside kept her still.

The door was opened impatiently and a slim young woman stood there. She was not pretty. Her face was too long for conventional good looks, but the large grey-blue eyes were sympathetic and the mouth betrayed humour.

'Henry has told me about you,' she said without preliminaries. 'He wrote to me while you were so ill and again when you decided to come back to London. It was dreadful, what happened to Heriot. I knew him. Fell in love with him myself years ago, if you must know, but it was a schoolgirl emotion. I met my husband but Logan and I remained friends. I'm glad you came. Actually, I have a friend with me today who is more than interested in hearing you have not only sailed to Australia but have first-hand information about the life over there.'

'What *did* Henry tell you about me?' Jade, disarmed, was curious.

'That your sister was affianced to a settler and that you travelled with her for company on the voyage, met Heriot and were to marry him, until the uprising that bereaved you.

It was a very clever story, Jade conceded, and truthful as far as it went.

'Come into the morning-room. It's warmer and Elizabeth will not forgive me if I do not introduce you. We are just about to drink tea.'

'I hope I've not intruded. It would have been better to send you a note, I see that now. I'm afraid I've behaved foolishly but I find I cannot be comfortable in Mrs Abel's presence and I've no friends left in the city. Henry's offer was so kind – '

'Henry's a darling but he's also shrewd. I think he wants to keep you under his eye even though you couldn't bear to remain in New South Wales. I can't blame him for admiring you. I also know what you mean about Mrs Abel. She always reminds me of a praying-mantis and I confess I had a nightmare once about the possibility of her having devoured Mr Abel!' Flora laughed and Jade could well understand why Henry was fond of her. She was so refreshingly outspoken. And honourable. It would be an effort to deceive her as she must if they were to become friends.

'Elizabeth's husband's family also had connections with the East India Company,' Flora went on, ushering Jade across the hall, 'like Henry's father. That's how we all got to know one another. She won't ask any questions that will hurt you – I explained why you are here. You'll not be reminded of your grief, never fear.'

'Thank you,' Jade answered. 'I'd prefer not to dwell on what's past. I – I had a sudden longing for – companionship, I suppose. I was a recluse on the voyage, by my own choice. Now I think I want to live again.'

The room that opened out before her was small and cheerful. The fire leapt and crackled. Silver winked and candle-light mellowed the velvety shapes of sofas and chairs, picked out the carved edge of a piecrust table that supported a tray and china cups, a graceful teapot.

But Jade hardly noticed the accoutrements of the pretty chamber. It was the woman who rose from the chair nearest the fire who claimed all of her attention. The grey gown was the same and the white cap that was her trade-mark. Mrs Elizabeth Fry. It seemed incredible that the point of a hatpin had drawn her here on this particular morning.

Jade's thoughts whirled. The last time Mrs Fry had been in her thoughts was on the eve of her execution when she had wanted to talk to this woman more than she'd ever wanted to do anything. She remembered her strength and goodness with deepest gratitude. Her kindness to Nan Flynn. She recalled, too, her keen eyes, that impression of noticing everything, however small. She'd be recognized and though Mrs Fry might not remember, at first, where she had seen Jade, she would, in time.

The bravest thing Jade had ever done was to put back her veil and accept the cup of tea. The velvet-covered chair closed around her stiff body.

'Tell me,' Mrs Fry said, 'which ship did you travel in?'

'The *Caroline*.'

'Ah, yes. That was before –'

'Before,' Flora broke in with a stream of excited words, 'before Elizabeth found out what happened when women prisoners left Newgate.' She recited the whole, unsavoury story and Jade re-lived in every detail the ride in the open wagons, the jeering and mud-slinging, the reception at the docks, the chaining, the disgusting conditions aboard. Fever in the hold – bodies wrapped in sailcloth, ready to be tipped over the side.

Perspiration broke out in little beads on her brow. Her hands felt faintly damp.

'I've upset you,' Flora said contritely. 'You must have seen much of this yourself.'

'I did – see it.'

'And what went on once the women were aboard?'

'Yes. It seemed much the same as what happened to the women in Newgate. They were the – perquisites of whatever men were aboard. From the captain down – I saw a woman die and her child left – '

'What happened to the child?' Tea was forgotten.

'He was adopted by one of the convicts.'

'Who treated him well?'

'As her own.' Jade was unaware that her eyes were brilliant with unshed tears.

'Then he was assured of some security.'

Jade could not speak. The locket hung round her neck and she had only to open it. But her fingers could not perform the small task. She had thought her feelings for Daniel were almost entirely subdued but they were not.

'Things are no longer so grim,' Mrs Fry said gently, well aware of the visitor's distress, admiring the dark green eyes that were so beautiful, expressive. She imagined she had seen other eyes that were like these, heard a voice that thanked her. A voice not unlike Miss Benedict's. But she met so many people and Miss Benedict had been abroad for some time. Where had it been?

'The women are taken in closed hackney-carriages nowadays,' Flora said cheerfully. 'No one knows who they are. No one is in irons unless this is unavoidable. And the evening before they are to be transported, Elizabeth, sometimes one of us, reads to the women to comfort them and travels to the ship with them next day. They are all given small possessions – material for making patchwork or other sewing – and there are now schools for the children in the ship's after-part. One of the prisoners to teach them, the one best fitted. Some clerk or forger, usually.'

'And the men?'

'We are still trying to do what we can about the women being abused but it's early days yet. We've achieved one step on a long, dark path.'

'I saw one prisoner in chains,' Mrs Fry said, 'and the fetter was so small that the metal had become embedded in the flesh of her ankle. It had almost to be torn out and the poor woman screamed and swooned. I will press to have chaining made illegal for all women.'

'Flogging,' Jade insisted, 'I would outlaw that. I believe this to be the most iniquitous punishment.' And she went on to describe the second-stage lashing that was callous beyond words and Lambert's story of the boy-poacher beaten so often that he went mad. She could not bring herself to say that this was the castigation that had led almost directly to Heriot's death. The thought of Denver came, rank and evil, sickening her. Her face became pale.

The discerning Mrs Fry changed the subject and an hour passed reasonably pleasantly over Jade's recollections of Australia's vegetation and fauna.

'If you are truly motiveless,' Flora suggested, 'then perhaps we could persuade you to come to Newgate with us?'

'What could I do?' Jade was shaken.

'Read to the women. Help distribute gifts and necessities. There's the school for the children. They have few luxuries, only donated equipment. We need flannel for the babies. Calves' foot jelly for the infirmary. Dozens of things.'

'I would have to think about that.'

'But in the meantime you must visit me. Often.' Flora beamed generously.

'We do need more women who understand the problems of prisoners,' Mrs Fry told Jade as she rose to go. 'You've had a bad experience but memories fade. Just think that any conditions we can improve will stay that way. We have friends in Parliament who will see that they are made law.'

People like Peter Masson, Jade thought, then was visited by a sick urgency to set eyes on Gabriel. She felt she could not go on for a single hour without a sight of him. She would hire a chaise – wait for him.

Schooling her emotions to a pretence of calmness she took her leave.

She did not hire the chaise. But, since Polly had arrived, and in good fettle, Jade put on her habit, the fog having diminished to an almost imperceptible haze, and set off for Rotten Row. The streets were quiet.

It would be madness to go back to Newgate. Only a fool would contemplate it having once escaped. But only a woman who had undergone that ultimate degradation knew best how

344

to improve the lot of those unfortunate enough to end up in Dance's Prison. The Governor would never connect the bereaved Miss Benedict with the ragamuffin Jane Benson who was transported to Australia. There was only one person who might see through her disguise. Dick. The turnkey knew her intimately. He had loved her. He might recognize the turn of her head, the way she walked, the colour of what hair escaped from under the bonnet and veil. The timbre of her voice. But he would remember her with love and regret. He'd never betray her. Henry would not object if she used his all-too-generous loan on clothing for infants who would otherwise die, on food for sick women. Nan had been saved for Johnnie Dart by Dick's gifts of nourishing remedies for which Jade paid unstintingly in the only way possible.

She had a good mind to accompany Mrs Fry and Flora Earle! She must do it. No one need know. The thought filled her head, blotting out the sight of the park with its half-hidden trees and the grey glimmer of water. It would be a challenge. For a moment it seemed as though her life had moved inexorably to this point. To be in a position to help those pawns of fate! The realization became as heady as wine.

The feel of Polly between her thighs obtruded. She saw the whiplash branches twist and turn in the wind that had grown stronger. There was a queer, faint drumming that made her blood hurry.

Jade rode on. The drumming had turned to a purposeful thudding. Out of the vaporous aisle of the track a black horse had appeared. The man rode it like a devil, his black coat-tails flying, his face a chiaroscuro of black and white. Everything the colours of night and moonlight. Masson.

She drew aside, trembling, in case she were run down.

Gabriel had given her no glance. It was as though nothing existed for him but the necessity to pound the earth, to ride against the wintry cold.

She looked after him, gasping, but already he was almost swallowed up in the misty pall.

Her body was riven with futile longing.

'Gabriel!' she called out. 'Gabriel —'

But he did not hear.

The strange episode would not leave her mind. Had she really seen Masson riding in the park? Or had her longing been so great that she had evoked his presence? He had been there but he could not have known her trapped out in black with the fine veil over her face. She shivered suddenly. He had not seemed even to see the mourning figure she represented.

Mrs Abel's cold watchfulness drove her out towards the Earle residence earlier than she'd intended. More than once Jade had wondered about the advisability of writing to Henry about his housekeeper but some instinctive caution prevented her from doing so. Instead, she told him about the old King's death and funeral, of Kent's demise, and of the great steps Mrs Fry, with the aid of women like Flora Earle, was making. She informed him, mischievously, of the fact that she had at last been persuaded into helping the Ladies' Committee with the occasional visit to Newgate, the first of which was today. Poor Lambert would worry himself into nail–biting until he received her next epistle; but, if she did not mention it, Flora would. She liked Mrs Earle very much indeed. Theirs had become a communion of minds whereas her bond with Nan had been one of championship and of obligation to Jack Flynn, a debt she now considered honourably discharged.

The hired chaise set her down into a grey-brown murk out of which trees stretched out extended claws of protest. Nearby, a church spire loomed out of obscurity. It was like the day she had seen Eliza and Paddy in the basement and, at the thought, she was conscious of a deprivation that disturbed her. For a long time she had known that her body was capable of urges that had nothing to do with love or affection. The sight of Masson had brought her to life after the trauma into which the deaths of Logan and Daniel had plunged her so terribly. She could not forget the sight of that powerful body astride the black horse, the distorted face that looked into Hell.

She wanted him. Loved and needed him so violently that she had not been able to sit quietly, reading until it was time to leave Lambert's house. The depth of her renewed dependence on Masson frightened her. If he rejected her she might be forced into some undesirable liaison in order to appease the body-hunger the sight of him had aroused. And then she would hate herself. No! If Gabriel rejected her she would accept Lambert's offer of marriage. She had been honest with him and he still wanted her, with or without her whole-hearted co-operation. It would be as it had been with Heriot. Desire and liking. Not loving – Companionship. Better than loneliness.

Flora received her with every evidence of pleasure. No. It

was not too soon to arrive. Any friend of Henry's could come when they would.

They took sherry and ratafees and talked of Henry from childhood to manhood but Jade saw only the dark avenue of trees in the park, the beat of her pulse became the thud of hooves on the track. The pale, devil-haunted face and virile body dressed in black and white became essential to both soul and body. This time no second-best would do.

'We need friends in high places,' Flora said, her eulogies of Henry having ended. Lambert had probably written to her recently, asking her aid in furthering his suit, Jade thought, only half amused.

'Friends?'

'To aid us in our prison reform. Otherwise everything will progress too slowly.'

'There was a man I heard of who worked against the hanging of minors,' Jade said slowly. 'His name was Peter Masson.'

'Then we must co-opt Adeline!' Flora told her. 'She'll know all about his aims if anyone does.'

'Adeline?'

'Adeline Masson.'

So Gabriel's cousin now had a wife. Most politicians found them quite essential, Jade knew. Hostess, confidante, rock when all had gone wrong.

'I remembered Peter Masson's name from the past,' Jade said quite steadily. 'I believe he had a cousin who wrote tracts.'

'You mean Gabriel.' Flora looked thoughtful. 'I never knew a man change so much. I blame Phoebe Lewis, of course. She let him think he was to be her husband then threw him off for Jerome. Much good it's done her. He's bed-ridden, poor man. Still, Gabriel seems over all that now, and yet, he's so different.'

'You knew him well?'

'Not really, but London is a gossipy place. It's Adeline I know somewhat better. Peter Masson hardly at all. I'll mention his name to Elizabeth and she'll, no doubt, contact Adeline. I think she'd come if she knows I'm implicated. We were quite friends at one time but when one marries one's habits change and Adeline was abroad for a while. Some matter of her health –'

'I see.'

'There was something about Masson that put me in mind of Heriot,' Flora said pensively. 'Nothing obtrusive. They were

347

both dark, of course, but it was more than that. Still, I shouldn't keep mentioning Heriot. You'll never forget him so long as I revive his memory.'

'I won't forget him, never fear. I wouldn't wish to. That doesn't mean that I'll never let another man into my life –'

'So I can reassure Henry, can I, that he can still hope?'

They smiled at one another but Jade did not want to be reminded that Lambert still hankered after her. 'I really cannot make any promises at this stage.'

'No. I suppose not. But I'd love to have you in the family.'

'You know nothing about me,' Jade pointed out.

'But Henry does.'

'He doesn't know everything.'

'You speak as though there were something of which to be ashamed.' Flora was outspoken as ever.

'There is. No, don't ask me. If I think you should know, I'll tell you.'

'In other words, you won't marry my cousin without putting your cards on the table, is that it?'

'Something like that.'

'It can't be very bad, whatever it is.'

'Shall we stop conjecturing and get on our way? Aren't we to meet Mrs Fry outside Newgate?'

'Yes, and we should have gone five minutes ago!'

They hurried into cloaks and bonnets and plunged cold hands into muffs. Jade had a bundle of flannel for the babies and Flora a large basket of calves' foot jellies and some prayer books.

Jade prayed silently for courage as they approached the huge, innocuous-seeming building that was Newgate. It now seemed so stupid to put her head into such a lion's mouth, and the thin veiling over her face a slight disguise.

Once joined by Mrs Fry and her relative Anna Buxton, the quartet was escorted along passages at once horribly familiar yet subtly different. They still smelt. Nothing would prevent that, but they were not so rank. The quality of the sound, too, was not the same. Some of the wildness had gone from it.

The turnkeys were men she did not know. They studied the women curiously and, next to Mrs Fry, Jade was the main target for their stares. She was so slim, so straight, so steeped in her mourning. So contained. Like a narrow black vase one dared not break for fear of what might come out of it. Jade would have laughed if she had known they were a little afraid of her.

She waited for the usual forest of begging hands at the bars but there were none. A tired-looking woman with greying hair peered out and said, ''Tis you, Mrs Fry.'

Mrs Fry replied pleasantly in that queer dialect that was part of her religion. It was so biblical and unnatural, yet one could not imagine her speaking any other way.

The keys turned and the little party was let in. Jade's pulses beat a tattoo. There was the corner where she had looked after Nan. Other things had happened there. Things she would not even think about. Her hands closed tightly over the lengths of flannel she had brought, knuckles stretched white.

The women were cleaner than she'd expected. So far there were no faces she knew. Bella Scrivener had not come into her mind until too late for retreat, but the bane of her existence here was gone and she breathed easily again. Most of the women sat in groups of about a dozen with a woman in charge of each. Some were standing or lying against the walls just as they had always done.

A school-room had been established in the laundry which was white-washed and renovated and partly fitted as work-room. The whole area was still horrible but Jade felt there was little connection between it and the dreadful scenes enacted there more than three years ago.

Mrs Fry went to each group to inspect the patchwork and children's clothes, and Jade, bemused, found herself studying each face to find the depravation and bestiality that had been the order of the day during her own incarceration. She found it still there in part – faces that were mean, shifty, downright unpleasant, but these characteristics seemed held more in check where once they were allowed freedom.

There was to be a small shop soon, Anna Buxton said, noting Jade's interest, where the women could buy small luxuries out of the money they earned by selling the finished patchwork quilts. It would stock tea and sugar. Chocolate perhaps. Comfits. Combs and hair-pins. Ribbons.

Most of the prisoners were garbed in aprons of a reasonable standard of cleanliness but here and there Jade caught the malicious flicker of a smile or a scowl, the glitter of un-converted eyes. There was still ugliness under the apparent order. People did not change so readily.

Gradually, the resentment and tension left Jade: because she had suffered here there was no reason why other persons should. It was a wonderful thing that Elizabeth Fry was doing and she deserved the greatest recognition.

A book was thrust into her hand. 'Here. You read the lesson this time. They'll listen to you. You're new and they all understand grief.'

'No –'

'We all take our turn.' The voice was firm.

She stared at the opened page. It was the story of the Prodigal Son and Jade did not know whether to laugh or to cry. But she did neither. Somehow she gained the courage to read the first line. The rest was easy.

Adeline Masson came to Flora's house a week later. Mrs Fry had allowed no grass to grow under her feet. Anna Buxton was there too and as Jade was shown into the Earle morning-room, she was agreeably surprised to find that she was welcomed sincerely, as someone of value. This was so far removed from her own estimate of herself that the discovery touched her.

She was introduced to Adeline who was not quite what she had expected. A woman in public life must have reserves of strength she did not detect in young Mrs Masson. She was very slender and pale-skinned, the pallor accentuated by dark shadows around the eyes and little colour in her lips. Adeline was shy except with Flora. They had been girlhood friends even if they had lost touch in recent years.

'Peter may not have the necessary influence to help you much as yet,' Adeline told Elizabeth Fry. 'His inclinations are, as you so rightly supposed, on the side of prison reform, but he is rather a buck surrounded by lions in the House. He has a long way to go before his voice is really heard. I told him about your invitation to me to accompany you to the women's prison and he's anxious to have my views on the subject.'

She looked far too frail to be subjected to such an ordeal, Jade thought, then found herself the target of Mrs Masson's clear gaze. Adeline smiled and it was not the hearty approbation of Flora, but something much more delicate and oddly sweet. Jade responded whole-heartedly. Again, her life had taken one of its disconcerting twists for the better. Here she was of some use, liked for herself. Anna, she already knew, approved of her.

Longing to introduce Gabriel's name, she knew she dared not. But Flora brought up the subject. 'How is Gabriel?'

Adeline's smile faltered. 'Well enough,' she said without conviction. 'As well as any of us at this low point of the year,' and she held out her thin, pretty fingers to the blaze. They were almost transparent against the warm glow and Jade was conscious of a sharp unease on the girl's behalf. What was wrong with Adeline? Flora had mentioned a visit abroad for the sake of her health but it had not seemed to bring any success.

The topic of Gabriel was dropped, much to Jade's chagrin. But at least she now moved in circles where it would be possible to encounter him socially. How would he react? Denounce her to the authorities, she decided wryly, once he was over the shock of seeing her. No, she dared not be in his company for even though she was back to being Jardine Benedict, Gabriel would not be fooled for a minute. But she could not help remembering Englefield Green, wanting to see it –

The little meeting over, Jade looked forward to getting to know Adeline Masson better and knew that her own feelings were reciprocated.

She rode in the park each day but had not seen Gabriel again, though she fed on the memory of his momentous appearance out of the long avenue of fog-bound trees, the dark virility that had not changed. Sleep came less readily and it took an hour or two of Scott to put Jade in the right mind for slumber. She dreamed of Masson coming to her bed, could almost feel his warm nakedness under the linen sheet with its smell of lavender.

He was an obsession from which she could not free herself.

Adeline accompanied the quartet of ladies on the next two visits to Newgate, bravely denying her weariness though her poor, pretty face was pinched and white.

'I'm desperately worried about her,' Flora said soberly. 'She was never so fragile before. And so shortly married. A few months only – '

'It is a pity,' Jade agreed, feeling sorry for Peter Masson. 'But she blames the end of winter. It's always a difficult time.'

'She likes you,' Flora ventured.

'And I her.'

'Do you feel any better now? About Heriot?'

'Yes, I do.'

'Sufficiently to – '

'You've heard from Lambert again, haven't you! Trying to influence me!'

Flora flushed guiltily. 'He told me to tread lightly, but I've been obvious, as usual.'

'I wouldn't have you any other way.' Jade kissed Henry's cousin and laughed. 'In a world of dissemblers, you are unique.'

'Henry adores you. He has known young women before, and once I suspected – no, it cannot really be true – '

'What!' Jade's curiosity was aroused. 'What did you suspect?'

'That he and – '

'Oh, Flora! Do get on with it!'

'The praying-mantis. I fancied he'd shared Mrs Abel's bed. There! I've opened my all too loquacious mouth and spoiled his chances for ever.'

Jade laughed even harder. 'That's why you had your night-mare about Mr Abel. If he ever existed! Titles for house-keepers are a convention. It gives them more authority to have at least a titular husband.'

'And women without husbands can be prone to – '

'Lusts of the flesh?' Jade was no longer amused. 'Is that so unnatural?'

'No,' Flora admitted. 'But should they be put aside – '

'You think that Henry enjoyed Mrs Abel's favours, then made off to Australia when she showed signs of possessive-ness?'

'You are very discerning.'

'It was plain as a pikestaff. I knew long before today. I should think twice before eating mushrooms in Henry's house.'

'How disagreeable. Perhaps you should come here!' Flora grimaced.

'I couldn't intrude. Married couples are entitled to their privacy.'

'So, when you and Henry are wed, I'll not be able to fly to you for refuge?' Flora's eyes danced mischievously.

'You've not led him to believe that I'm about to capitulate?'

'No, my dear. I've reported most faithfully anything you've said.'

'Good. I want no relationship built on deceit.'

'And you praise my honesty! He'll be a fool if he doesn't snap you up somehow.'

They embraced fondly on parting.

Jade shared Adeline's carriage after the next Newgate visit. Mrs Fry had to rush back to her children who were smitten with some childhood ailment and Flora had been unable to attend because of the funeral of a distant relative.

'Come back home with me,' Adeline begged, her eyes seeming the only thing alive. She leaned back against the buttoned upholstery and closed them so that Jade saw only the deep lids with their little river-courses of blue veins showing through the paper-thin skin.

There was no mist today and the streets were more cheerful with chestnut-vendors at corners and hurrying men and women with faces reddened with the touch of the frost that whitened cobbles and slates.

'But your husband! Won't he be far too busy to be troubled with stray callers?'

'I'd hardly call you that.' Adeline smiled. 'One of Mrs Fry's angels of mercy?'

'Please don't call me that.'

'I'm sorry, I hadn't thought to offend you.' The girl was surprised.

'It's not that: I feel – I don't deserve the description.'

'You are far too modest. Flora thinks the same. I'm sorry now that I lost touch with her for so long. But it was mainly my own doing.'

'Oh? How?'

'I seemed gradually to be losing my strength. My health obsessed me for a time and there's nothing so pitiable as a hypochondriac.'

'I'm sure Flora had no such thoughts!'

'Probably not, but I'd no wish to lose any real friends because of this preoccupation. One by one my friends married – '

'But you did too.'

'Yes. Little did I think when I was introduced to Peter last year that I'd end up finding a husband.'

'Oh, you had not always known him?'

'No. Peter and I were table companions at dinner one evening. A match-making friend.'

'How romantic. And how soon before he proposed?'

'Peter? He never did. He's more – a man's man, I fear.'

'But, I thought – '

'That I was Mrs Peter Masson?' Adeline opened her blue eyes and smiled faintly. 'No. It's his cousin I wed. Gabriel.'

The day seemed, shockingly, to be split open, revealing secrets of ugliness and wounding pain. This girl she liked so much was Gabriel's wife. His wife. Jade made herself think it several times before the realization made true sense.

'Are you all right?' Adeline's voice was suddenly anxious.

'Perfectly.' No one knew the effort required to give that answer.

'You look – pale.'

'A headache. Perhaps I should not come today. Another time perhaps. Could you deposit me within walking distance of Tudor Place? Plantaganet Terrace, perhaps?'

'Oh,' Adeline sounded genuinely regretful. 'I'd so looked forward to having you visit us. But we are not anywhere near either.'

'I'll take a chaise then, or a sedan chair.'

'Why not come and perhaps tea will take away the headache. Then Gabriel can take you back –'

'Oh, no! No.'

'He is not so terrifying.' Again Adeline smiled wearily, her face drawn into little lines of fatigue.

You did not see him a month ago, Jade thought numbly. He was a fiend, beset by devils. Gabriel – Why didn't you wait? But why should he? Disillusioned, bitter, what could he do but turn to someone gentle and caring? Someone like Adeline.

'Since my unhappy experience I have not been easy in men's company.'

'I understand that. But Gabriel is endlessly kind.'

I don't want to hear about his kindness, Jade protested silently. I don't want you to talk to me about your husband. He is not such a paragon when he goes prison-visiting. But I love him and he's no longer free.

'He did not wish me to go to Newgate but I prevailed against him. I've mentioned you to him. He was interested when I mentioned Windsor and Sydney.'

'Indeed?' Jade made one more attempt to escape. 'I do believe I spy a chaise at the next corner –'

The words died on her lips. Adeline's eyes had turned oddly blank, then they rolled upwards horridly, then closed altogether. Her body swayed then slumped against Jade's.

Jade, panicky, began to chafe the limp hands. She could not leave Adeline now, that was obvious. Perhaps Gabriel would not be at home. Mrs Pratt would hardly connect her with Masson's thieving mistress, nor would Betsy if she still worked there. They would all be far too occupied with Gabriel's wife. As he would be.

She pushed her head out of the window. 'Hurry, please! My friend is taken ill. Is it far?'

'No, ma'am. I'll be quick as I can.'

The measured trot became a gallop over shining cobbles. The carriage swayed. Adeline moaned suddenly and the soft, brown lashes parted. She did not seem to be in pain, only languid and somehow wasted. 'I'm – sorry.'

'It's not your fault.'

Jade found another and terrible reason for Adeline's swoon. What if she were pregnant? Gabriel's child – They were suddenly in the street where Masson lived.

'This happens now and again. It – doesn't worry me now. I am all right again next day. How thankful I am you were with me. Is it naughty of me to be glad you were forced to come after all?' Adeline's eyes closed again. She made no attempt to sit up but smiled that rather pathetic, weary smile.

The girl was still ill. Jade abandoned the faint hope that she could leave Adeline outside her own door. That must draw more attention towards herself than ringing the bell and handing Gabriel's wife over to the first person who came to answer it.

Gently, when the carriage stopped, Jade assisted Adeline to alight. Between them, she and the driver half-carried the girl up the path and on to the step. There was no need to ring. The door was flung open and Gabriel stood before them, his face taut with worry. Jade was struck dumb.

'I told her not to go. I was watching for her. She said she would probably be home at about this time.' Gabriel picked up his wife bodily and stared at Jade.

'I said I'd – bring – Miss Benedict, and I have,' Adeline murmured.

His dark eyes lost some of their certainty. 'Oh, yes. Miss Benedict.' The black gaze tried to penetrate the puckered film of the veil. 'Come inside.'

'Oh, really. You have enough to worry you –'

'I said, come inside. Stay where you are, Maggs. I'll need you in a little while, I expect.'

Jade had not noticed the coachman particularly. If she had, she'd have been warned long ago whose carriage this was.

Silently, she followed them into the hall and upstairs to the green-silk room she had known so well. There, Gabriel deposited Adeline carefully on to the chaise-longue. 'I'll have tea brought. Do sit down, Miss Benedict.' He pulled the bell-cord and straddled the fireplace, all the time staring at the newcomer, his face in shadow. Refreshments were ordered.

That had been Heriot's favourite attitude. The thought still had the power to make Jade sad. But, in spite of the circumstances, there was a heady excitement in being in Masson's brooding presence. He looked older, she thought, but more handsome than ever in spite of the fatigue that etched small lines around his eyes. There was no trace of that violence that had overtaken him during the ride in the park.

The look he gave Adeline, Jade noticed, was not in the least like the ones he had given her when she had lived with him. But whores were different, not entitled to devotion and respect.

'I think I should go – '

'Miss Benedict, I understand you had taken up good works because you had too little to do. Then why the unconscionable hurry?'

'Gabriel! That's rude.' Adeline's face coloured.

'No, my dear, only honest. That's what you told me.'

'Very much exaggerated,' Adeline protested.

'You are beginning to look better,' Gabriel said, pleased. 'An argument always agrees with you. And you, Miss Benedict? How do you find England after your long absence?'

'Changed.'

Tea arrived with little cakes and biscuits. Masson poured out and handed the delicate cups with the green and gold design. The china had not changed. Nothing in the room was altered, almost as though he had wanted it to remain untouched. Or had it been indifference?

'So you've been in Australia?'

'Yes.'

'Sydney, I believe.'

'No. Windsor.'

'Miss Benedict may not wish to be harangued about New South Wales. I did tell you, Gabriel – '

'Harangued?' Masson laughed suddenly. 'What quaint expressions you do have, my sweet. I merely make polite conversation.'

'There's no need,' Jade told him and caught him listening to the echoes of her voice.

'And would you not drink your tea more easily if you removed your bonnet?'

She pushed back the veil a fraction and found his gaze lingering over her mouth. It was as though he had kissed her.

But he did not address her again, having remembered perhaps that she was in mourning and obviously not in a conversational mood.

Adeline flagged and Masson was at her side in an instant. 'You must rest, my dear. Come, I'll take you next door and call Mrs Pratt. Excuse us a minute, Miss Benedict. Please, do not go as soon as my back's turned. There is the matter of the journey home.'

How carefully he supported his wife. Jade was riven with a storm of emotion, a dreadful regret. If only they had met properly long ago. That first evening at the theatre – Her hand slid over the back of the chaise-longue. It seemed that she was back in the past, dressed in green velvet, the room scented with oranges and wine. Snow heaped on the roofs and sills. She had been happy.

Slowly, she went to the window. There was the place where Nan had stood, beaten and terrified. She turned swiftly, dislodging a small photograph that stood on a table close by. She knelt, bending down to search for the object that had clattered into the shadows.

Her fingers reached it, inched it out from under a chair. She did not hear Masson come across the carpet. The first intimation she had of his presence was when he reached down to tear off the veil, removing the bonnet so that her abundant hair fell around her shoulders. They took stock of one another silently.

'How – did you know?' she whispered at last.

He said nothing, only lifted the narrow chain that held the sea-horse which had slipped out from under the neck of her gown as she leaned forward.

Seated on the chaise-longue, sipping wine, Jade said, 'I would not have come if it hadn't been for Adeline.'

'She told me. There's a great deal I want to know. Must know.'

'I didn't know she was married to you until an hour ago. I thought it was Peter.'

'Did you mind?'

'Of course I minded!'

'I could not rid myself of the feeling I knew you. Knew your voice. But the way you shrouded yourself – It was so extraordinary. I had to know why.'

'We can't sit talking so in the room next to your wife's.

And you may be certain Mrs Pratt will soon have her ear to the keyhole!'

'I'll escort you back. We can say all we have to in complete privacy.'

'That will be best.' She was trembling so violently that the wine slopped about in the glass.

'Here,' Masson said very softly. 'Give that to me.'

Their fingers touched. He set down the glass and took hold of her hands. Kissed the wetness on her cheek, the white column of her throat. Her fingers plucked at the back of his coat as though she would tear it from him. Adeline, she thought. Adeline. But the touch of his mouth against her skin banished the attempt at honesty.

'Oh, Gabriel. I love you. That hasn't changed.'

He broke free of her embrace. 'For God's sake put that creation on. I'll tell my wife I'm seeing you safely back to Tudor Place.'

She heard his voice as she replaced the bonnet and picked up the shreds of veiling.

'I'll see you later, my sweet. But I hope you'll be asleep when I return. It will do you good to rest completely. Dr Howard will come tomorrow.' A door closed. He beckoned from the doorway.

They said nothing until they were seated in the carriage and the horses were on the move.

'Where have you come from?' Masson asked, and Jade noticed how he sat as far away from her as possible. So he had remembered he had obligations. She took off the bonnet again and laid it on the seat. The black gaze followed every movement. The sky had become dark again, heavy with snow, and the curtains at the carriage windows were almost drawn. There was a flicker of light from the coach lamps. It lay on the line of his nose, the outline of his mouth, in the pupils of his eyes. On the strong, straight thighs that pressed against the expensive material of his breeches.

'Things went well for me in Australia. I suppose you knew at the time that I was – reprieved.'

He hesitated. 'Yes, I knew.'

'Nick, the man I told you about – I suspect he had a hand in the matter – He had ways of putting people in his debt. But I suppose I must thank him for that.'

'You never mentioned his name. Why don't you tell me everything? It's what you should have done long ago.' He made no attempt to move closer. He was probably ashamed of the weakness he had shown in the silk-walled room.

'Benedict is my real name. Jardine Benedict, the Jardine after my grandfather.' Once started, she could not stop. If her voice faltered over the part of her story that was to do with Caspar and Flynn, he made no sign that he noticed. But he moved sharply when she told him of being forced to witness the hangings and the departure of her parents.

He opened the window once and shouted to Maggs to take his time, to travel the quiet streets or the perimeter of the parks until he was ready to stop.

It was when she came to her incarceration in Newgate that he said harshly, 'Don't speak of that.'

'Why not? Wasn't it the truth you wanted?'

'I know what it must have been like. What you endured. I'm ashamed of my part in it.'

'Oh, Gabriel –'

'Do you think I haven't gone over it a thousand times?' His voice was rough with pain.

'I've forgotten it.'

'Adeline says you met some man in Australia. Were to marry him.'

It was more difficult to speak of Heriot and Daniel. Impossible to bring up the subject of Denver. Easier by far to stress Lambert's kindness and generosity.

'That's all,' she said finally, her throat tight with misery. 'All –'

'All?' he repeated savagely. 'It's a wonder you did not go mad. I can't bear to think of what I've done to you.'

'It wasn't your fault. You begged me to speak and I would not.'

They stared at one another across the gloom.

'You are married now, Gabriel. I can't come again. I like Adeline too much to cause her any grief.'

'Do you think I want to hurt her?'

'No.'

'Then this is the last we shall see of one another?'

It could not really be the last? She reached out towards him, repudiating the suggestion. 'I never stopped thinking of you.'

He pulled her to him, thrusting his hands inside the garrick cloak, closing them over her breasts. She tried to think of his wife but the picture of that tired, pretty face was overlaid with the intoxication of his presence, the smell of his skin and pomade, the lingering traces of tobacco and brandy. None had changed. How warm and strong his chest was through the thicknesses of material.

Masson reached out to close the gap in the curtains, pulled off the cloak and began to unbutton her gown in a fever of impatience. It had begun to snow and the soft flakes brushed the small panes, whispering. His mouth touched the curves above her bodice, sliding from one satiny round to the other. She was pressed against the seat and his thigh flung over her, his fingers moving swiftly, uncovering herself and him. His lips were on her breast and she was clutching his back, dragging her nails across warm flesh and muscle, urging him to enter her.

She had never known such perfect pleasure. He was not gentle and that hard, driving force excited her beyond measure. There was never any man who made the act seem entirely right but Masson.

She murmured his name, kissed his throat, dissolved like some phantom of foam on a river that ran as far as time, was hurtled into a pool where even the resulting calm was filled with fronds and tentacles of sensuous feeling.

They lay together, spent and indolent, their world bounded with content.

CHAPTER ELEVEN

Afterwards, they were quiet for a space. The carriage rocked soothingly like a baby's cradle. Masson pulled the curtain a fraction to show her a world of grey and white, then returned to stroking her body.

'Haven't you had enough of me?'

'What an unnecessary question.'

'I always wondered if it was really done in carriages,' she said.

Masson gave a snort of laughter. 'Now you know.'

'I'd say it took experience. You've done it before.'

'Why pretend otherwise? After you, I used to wait after leaving the theatre, knowing someone would come. And they did. But I never took them home. I became adept at manœuvring. But you are such a little thing, there was no real problem.'

'But your legs are so long!'

'Did you have any complaints?'

'Oh, my darling. None. But we shouldn't have done it, should we?'

'Because of Adeline, you mean?'

'Yes. I've behaved very badly. She's my friend.'

His mouth twisted. 'Being the person she is, I doubt if she'd have minded greatly.'

'But she must! If I had you I'd hate the woman who took you.'

'It's – some little time since we slept together.'

She stared at him. 'Why? Do you not get on?'

'She loves me. A great deal more than I do her, and that's not inconsiderable.'

'You do love her.' Jade sat up and pushed his hands away.

'In a fashion. Because of her sweetness and her dependence on me. Because she was so different from – '

'Me?'

'Those other women. The Haymarket women, Phoebe Jerome. She was clean and doted on me and I was lonely. And I imagined you gone for ever. I wanted to protect her.'

'Then, why – '

'We were man and wife for a short while. An undemanding relationship. Then she became so easily exhausted that I could not bring myself to approach her. She would not have refused, being Adeline, but I could not.'

'No.'

'It gradually became obvious that her health was seriously impaired.' He had resumed his caressing of her breasts. 'I'd have been a beast to force myself on her.'

'So, instead, you took to riding in the park at the devil's pace.'

'You're a witch!'

She shook her head. 'No. You almost ran me down one day. Stared through me as though I didn't exist – '

'Why didn't you call to me?'

'I did. But that black monster of yours just clashed his iron hoofs on the hard ground and breathed out some smoke and fire. Then you both vanished.'

He laughed but there was no humour in the sound.

'I dreamt of you for several nights after that,' she told him.

'Were they good dreams?'

'Tantalizing. You came to my bed but before we did more than a little preliminary skirmishing, there was the maid to light the fire while mine went out, agonizingly slowly – '

'Oh, Jade.'

'But it seemed so real. You were warm to the touch, just as you are now.'

'This is as tantalizing as your dream. You say that once you leave this carriage we will not be together again. That seems infinitely worse than imagining you dead at sea, or working your fingers to the bone at Parramatta.'

'It will be as bad for me. Adeline will think it strange if I repulse all her attempts at friendship. It would hurt her and I can't bear to do that.'

'You always think of someone else,' Masson said roughly.

'Not always. Today I thought only of myself and how much I wanted you. How much I still want you.'

He groaned, then took another look at the swirling landscape. 'We are in limbo,' he whispered. 'Look, my darling. We are accountable to no one. There's not a house in sight. Only trees and sky. People don't exist.'

She stared past his shoulder. They were passing the park and Maggs was driving very slowly as he had been ordered to by Gabriel. The whirling snow was not thick but it created a pall through which no building obtruded.

They could have been the only persons in the world.

'We have a short time before we reach civilization,' Masson whispered.

'And we can only hang once for stealing sheep.' She wished she had not said that. It came too close to home for comfort.

Their hands were about one another and Jade, reflecting that there was something about love-making in a moving carriage that most people would consider indecent, could not help laughing softly. Any carriage for that matter.

He did not ask why she laughed, being much too busy with other more important matters. She could never have too much of him, his mouth, his hands, his warm, muscular back, his strong, insistent thighs.

She said his name and could not stop saying it.

'I love you,' he told her. 'Love you.' He had never said it before and the words were sweet and strange.

There was no one alive but herself and Masson.

She awoke to a sense of doom. The bed-chamber was still

dark and the long rectangle of the window just touched with greyness. Memory flooded back. Gabriel helping her to fasten her clothes, to swathe her hair under the black bonnet, wiping away the unexpected tears with his fingertip. Only they had come faster and faster, silent and agonizing so that her eyes were two little springs that flooded a landscape.

He'd produced his handkerchief then and dried her face very gently. Once more he asked, 'You really mean not to see me again?'

She nodded.

'What if we meet by accident?'

'That – can't be avoided. But don't contrive meetings, will you? That will make it much harder.'

'All this to save Adeline from hurt?'

'There is the matter of self-respect. If I disregard every decent feeling in order to indulge my passion for you, I'm no better than the whore I was trained to be. And you see the road that lies ahead if we are to be thrown into one another's company. We cannot help ourselves. And no matter how right or how wonderful it seems at the time there's a taste of shabbiness afterwards. It's true, isn't it?'

'Yes, it's true,' he admitted. 'But I can't regret our journey in limbo.'

'Nor can I. But now that it's over all I seem to see is Adeline. Needing you.'

'If only – '

'If only?' she prompted.

'If I could see an end to her illness.'

'What does the doctor say is wrong?'

'Some lack in her blood. She's very brave and uncomplaining but I foresee the day she will not rise from her bed and she's very young to live out her life an invalid.'

'And she's too good a person for you to deceive. You will be torn two ways.'

'But now that I've found you again – ' His face was a mask of anger and regret.

'No, Gabriel. We must remain apart. I knew I shouldn't go on with the plan to visit you but it was impossible to abandon Adeline on that occasion.'

'Very well,' he said in a low voice. 'We are almost there. This is the corner of Plantaganet Place.' He pushed his head out of the window and shouted, 'The next street, Maggs. What number is it? Thirty-three!'

He tried to catch hold of Jade's hand but she would not let him, averting her eyes from the pain in his. 'I will doubtless hear news of you from your wife.'

'Doubtless.'

The carriage stopped and Masson opened the door, descending so that he could help her down. Snow crunched under her feet. The face at the upstairs window hung for a moment, wraithlike, then disappeared as though a cloth had been wiped over a slate.

Masson bent over her hand and kissed the back of it. She could not look at him, only hurried up the steps and pulled at the bell several times in her agitation. She heard the slam of the carriage door, the slithering sound of hooves against the soft whiteness. There was nothing inside her but a vast emptiness. She waited until the sounds of departure were almost gone before she looked after the carriage, hardly noticing that the door of Lambert's house had been opened so that she might enter.

She had encountered Mrs Abel on the stairs when her throat had been too tight with grief to do more than merely incline her head. But she knew she must have looked odd with her blurred eyes and the shreds of veiling in her hand like sooty cobwebs.

'Is anything wrong?' Mrs Abel asked.

'A – headache, I'm afraid.'

'What has happened to your veil?'

Jade had a vivid picture of Masson's strong, determined fingers ripping it across, released her hair around her shoulders.

'I – caught it on a projection in the carriage.'

'You are not hurt?' the brittle, echoing voice enquired conventionally.

The question almost made Jade laugh. The hollowness within her was replaced by tiger claws tearing and shredding and Henry's housekeeper-cum-mistress asked if she was hurt! She took a deep breath. 'No. I will go to my room now – No, I don't want anything. There's been no message, I suppose, from Mr Pickersgill?'

'I'm afraid not, Miss Benedict.'

'Nor any letter from Mr Lambert?'

There was a small hesitation. 'No.'

Any sort of message would have been a comfort. Held a sense of direction. 'Thank you, Mrs Abel.'

Jade had gone to bed to lie sleepless, going over every

moment of the meeting with Masson, glad that he now knew the story of her past, reliving the brief ecstasy of the snow-blurred drive with the curtains drawn against the world.

And now she was awake and motiveless, cast upon currents and eddies of despair that only Gabriel's presence could alleviate.

Mrs Abel had sensed her unhappiness as a vulture or a buzzard could scent carrion. Had she really been Henry's mistress for a time? It seemed all too possible. Even Flora had thought so.

Flora Earle seemed the only person Jade could turn to in her present frame of mind. The long window showed traces of pink colour. Morning could not be far away. As soon as was discreet, she would order a chaise and go to Flora's. Young Mrs Earle would put the attack of black dog down to the happenings at Elsrickle and hope again that Jade would turn to Henry.

Henry seemed the real answer to Jade's main problem. She had to put Gabriel out of her thoughts, and some considerable distance between herself and his body. She had sworn never to return to Australia, could not, in fact. But Henry would take her anywhere she wished. She liked and respected him. He wanted her on any terms.

Perhaps she should write to him, accepting his proposal of marriage. He would not appear as quickly as she might want but a promise to Lambert would keep her from committing more folly with another woman's husband. Her promises were binding.

An aching need in her loins drove her from bed. She could not have Gabriel! Wrapping herself in the garrick cloak she took out paper and sat down at the bureau by the window.

Half her attention on the beauty of the snow with the rose tint of dawn covering it, she began to write.

Flora's joy was unbounded when, some time later, Jade told her what she had done.

'I did, of course, say that although I am still not really in love with him, I know that he will do his best to persuade me.'

'Most women would give their eye-teeth for Henry.'

'I realize that. But he seems fixed on the notion of making me Mrs Lambert.'

'He always was unexpectedly single-minded. But you will try

to love him, won't you, Jardine?'

'Of course.' Jade was uncomfortable without the protection of a veil but she had decided she could not wear one permanently.

'I wonder, sometimes, if there is not some other man from the past? Someone you have not mentioned. I know you were to marry Heriot but Henry let slip once that he was sure you hadn't loved him either.'

'I did!'

'But not totally. And you are so obviously capable of love and sacrifice. That's why I feel it must be centred on one person. Is he dead too?'

'As good as.' Jade stared out of the window, wishing her face was hidden.

'Oh, my poor girl.' Flora was too wise and concerned to probe further. She did consider Jardine Benedict too young to have already encountered so many hard lessons but Henry might prove to be her safe harbour. Flora liked to think that all of her friends should be as protected and secure as herself and one could never want a more appealing sister-in-law, or cousin-in-law she supposed was the correct designation, though sister was how she would think of Jardine. And, as Jardine said, Henry was utterly determined to have her and there was that ruthless obstinacy lurking under the pleasant exterior. He would find ways of making his fiancée forget the man she could never have. He'd be married, of course, and Jardine was too honourable to become any man's mistress.

Flora's cogitations were put to flight by the advent of Mrs Fry and Miss Buxton who were to accompany them to Newgate this afternoon.

Mrs Fry, once comfortably seated, said, 'We have lost the fifth member of our little party, I'm afraid.'

For a moment, Jade was aware of a cold fear. Had her continued grief and regret over Gabriel's inaccessibility resulted in Adeline's death? Of course it hadn't! One could not influence the death of any person, especially a woman one liked so much, by abstract thought.

'Poor Adeline Masson is confined to her bed and must stay there until she is stronger.'

The ladies all made sympathetic noises. Jade could think of nothing to say.

'Perhaps when we leave Newgate we might find some flowers to take? Then leave them at the house? Flowers are so cheering when one is ill. She has, I must confess, been extremely low this past month. Mr Masson looked quite pale when he called to tell me the news.'

'He always looks pale,' Flora observed, pouring sherry.

'Never so grim as he does now,' Mrs Fry replied, crossing her feet under the grey skirts. 'And his eyes so red-rimmed as though he'd not slept. Miss Benedict, forgive me for saying so, but you do not look well either.'

'I am well enough.' Jade was aware of Flora's suddenly keen glance.

'You've been so assiduous in your attention to our cause. Take care not to overdo it, that is all.'

'It is work I value because it is so long overdue.'

'I still say you are too thin and white and must not overtax your strength.'

'I'm sure I shall not.'

'Miss Benedict has good news,' Flora said, bursting to share her own enthusiasm. 'She has just consented to become my cousin's wife though poor Henry must remain in ignorance for many weeks yet, the distance being too great for any instant communication. But the letter is a month on its journey so I feel we may wish Jardine all good luck?' Flora raised her glass and the others did likewise.

The die is cast, Jade thought for the first time. For the past month she had not fully realized that something that could not easily be reversed had been put into motion. Now, with those lifted sherry glasses and kind, approving smiles, she felt as shackled as Denver or a chain-gang in the Australian dust.

Forcing herself to smile, she acknowledged their good wishes.

All the way to Newgate she was quiet and oppressed as though some fresh blow was to fall. But engagements were sometimes broken. Not that she could hurt Lambert in that way. She never could break her word. They would undoubtedly marry because she had said so and, in time, they would probably be as happy as she had been with Heriot. So long as there was always an ocean between herself and Gabriel.

Flora was looking at her with a trace of worry and Jade threw off the painful reflections and tried to look happy. It would be pleasant to become related to the Earles. She had been very lucky.

Newgate was not so quiet as last time. A new influx of prisoners, the turnkey told Mrs Fry as they swept along the grey passages. A few troublesome women could speedily disorganize those who had been orderly, inciting them to rebellion and dissatisfaction. Although Elizabeth Fry had succeeded in stopping the practices of begging and drinking, some women found it hard to give up the undeniably pleasant results of spending what money they had on ale from the yard-tap. It was this small nucleus who could be weaned back to their bad ways with incredible ease by some amoral newcomer who could not always be placed under solitary confinement when the prison was full.

Bella Scrivener, Jade thought uneasily. She was the sort of woman who would upset Newgate's hard-won peace. But the Bellas of this world no longer had the power to hurt her. Immediately, she regretted her selfishness. What happened to oneself was of little importance. It was what concerned others that mattered most.

Many of the women were in their groups when the members of the Ladies' Committee were shown in, but little of their past tranquillity was apparent. They looked over their shoulders, the work idle in their laps as one band of about twenty squatted by the wall, talking loudly and screeching with ribald laughter, cursing and swearing with no regard for those around them. Children shrank away, hiding their faces against their mothers' skirts.

It was the first time Jade had seen Mrs Fry look so angry. She drew herself up to her full height and walked across the straw-strewn floor towards the disruptive rabble. After a brief pause, Anna Buxton followed, Flora and Jade going after her.

The prisoners were grouped around one woman and Jade was overpoweringly thankful that the bonnet she wore shaded her face. Molly Connor sat cross-legged, her posture bordering on indecency, her golden-brown face flushed with wine and anger, her lovely mouth twisted, spilling foul words.

An uneasy silence descended.

Jade remained perfectly still. If she moved she would immediately become the cynosure of all eyes and Molly hated her enough to denounce her.

A minute ticked away while Elizabeth Fry and Nick Caspar's mistress tried to outstare one another. It was Molly who looked away first, kicking out at a toothless beldam who clutched at a practically empty gin bottle. The bottle flew across the intervening space, spilling what little remained. The old hag cried out with rage and disappointment and in a moment had launched herself at Molly who fought back strenuously and vituperatively, showing a great deal of leg and thigh, her gown's bosom cut almost as low as her nipples.

Mrs Fry looked on with a weary detachment as a well-built matron in grey hurried across, accompanied by two turnkeys who separated the pair and dragged Molly to her feet. Her furious gaze and Jade's controlled awareness collided.

It was difficult to decide which found the instant more momentous.

Molly gaped unashamedly. Jade turned white.

'Remove this woman,' the matron ordered harshly. 'Solitary confinement.'

Molly struggled against the grasp of her captors, her face a mask of fury and cupidity. 'I ain't done nothing! No more than what *she's* done! She's as much a whore as I am, that Jade Benedict! Knows her, I do. Masson's mistress and others I can mention. Why's she pretendin' to be a lady? Why is she here in the first place? Tell me that! Why? Let go of me, scum. A whore she is. Bad as I am. Bad –'

The ugly voice receded. The old woman clutched at the empty bottle, crying wheezily and rocking herself to and fro. The others, struck dumb, all stared at Jade who was frozen into immobility. Their expressions all showed the same emotions. Shock, speculation.

Mrs Fry recovered herself. 'Perhaps we should go to the work-room, ladies?' and she swept off firmly with Anna hurrying to keep up with her.

Flora, her blue eyes filled with hurt, looked at Jade almost accusingly. Elizabeth Fry had made those observations about Masson's pallor and Jade's own sleeplessness all in the one breath. Jade could not blame Mrs Earle for connecting the two in the light of Molly's disclosures.

'Is it true?' Flora ran true to form. 'Is it, Jardine? Or is it Jane? That's what she called you.'

Jade could not speak.

Flora took the silence for consent. 'She did mean Gabriel, didn't she? Not Peter.'

'Yes. That was what she meant.'

'Oh, Jardine.'

Jade, unable to bear the reproof that was all too plain, turned suddenly and hurried across the room, hardly seeing the aproned women and staring children intimidated by her black garments and distraught expression.

'Please let me out,' she whispered to the turnkey. 'I feel unwell. Hurry.'

It seemed an age before the key turned and the door swung

open to be clanged shut almost immediately, drowning out the sound of the footsteps that hastened after her.

The second guard, curious in his turn, accompanied her towards the outer gate. 'Drink o' water, ma'am?'

'No – no, thank you.'

'It's raining.'

'It doesn't matter.' Jade walked away, her face lifted to the clean cold touch of the quickening drops. She felt so soiled and degraded that only a flood would make her clean again. She could not forget how those decent woman had looked, even Flora who was her closest friend in London.

She experienced a longing to have a shoulder or a bosom to cry against. There was no shoulder but there was a bosom she remembered with an aching gratitude. So far she had not contacted Ma Lee's cousin, Lil Stalker, but she had written from Australia so the woman would recognize her name and would know of her from her cousin Nancy Lee.

The rain, heavier now, wet the shoulders of the garrick cape and dripped from the black bonnet but Jade continued her almost unseeing path, unconscious of the man across the street, aware only that she must hire a chaise or a sedan chair.

Nick Caspar, who had been on his way to see Molly who had recently been arrested after creating a drunken disturbance, saw the black-clad figure from the other side of the street. His eyes narrowed with disbelief. Jade? It couldn't be, but that pale, lovely profile was damned like hers! She turned as she caught sight of a sedan chair and he saw her full face. He stopped, incredulous. It *was* Miss Jade Benedict and she looked as though she were in trouble. Recollection flooded over him, bringing sensuous pictures of the girl he had coveted, raped, taught to please any man who came her way. Killed for, suffered for in his own warped fashion. Loved –

The green eyes, darkened now, passed over him impersonally. She saw only the approaching conveyance, the slanting rain. The cool purity of her bone structure drew him afresh. He'd never got the proud little bitch out of his mind. And he'd give a hundred sovereigns to know how she came to be here, within ten minutes' reach of Newgate.

Forgetting Molly, Nick began to follow the moving sedan chair.

Lil Stalker's room was in a mean little street of houses that leaned over practically to meet one another. As though they meant to hold conversations, Jade thought, still in a daze of numbness and disorientation.

She knocked on two doors before she found Lil's. Mrs Stalker was in no way like Nancy Lee. Ma had been generous and open. Lily Stalker looked thin and miserable, her shoulders hunched under a none too clean shawl and there was a stone gin bottle on the table among the dirty crocks.

'Who are you, dearie?' Lily was understandably confused.

'I wrote some time ago. From Australia.'

'I ain't had no letter.' The woman looked doubtful.

'It was addressed to Mrs Nancy Lee. Care of this address.'

'For Ma! I didn't get no letter. But anyone could have took it knowing this place! How come you knows Ma, though, a lady like you?'

'We were – friends, over two years ago. I wanted to find her again.'

'No one won't find poor Nancy this side o' Heaven,' Lil said lugubriously. 'Died she did, only a few monfs ago. But she did say she wished she'd seen a – Jade – Jade Benedict again. Said she was real sorry she hadn't. Would that be you? Sent you her love should you turn up any time.'

Jade nodded and two tears flew on to the dirty table like jewels.

'I'm sorry I troubled you. I had no idea –'

'Ain't no trouble, dearie. A glass o' mother's ruin?'

'No – no, thanks. It was just a compulsion. I used to go to her when I was in trouble. She – didn't suffer?'

'Not really. Not that she said much. Her heart it was. Went sudden-like, the way she wanted to go. No, I don't believe she felt anything.'

'I'm glad. There's something for your bother.' Jade laid a coin on the table. It would buy more than one bottle of Geneva.

'Ain't no bother! Thanks, miss. Wish I could have done more, really.'

Lily Stalker's gratitude followed Jade down the crude, smelly stair. The rain still hissed across the passage end. She emerged into the street, sorry in a vague way that she'd paid off the chair. Shadows in doorways alerted her to the inadvisability of remaining here. She was full of pain for Ma's end.

She hurried up the narrow alley, her wet shoes clattering and slipping on glistening cobbles. Sounds of children crying and adults shouting came through grimy windows. She was sad for Ma Lee. Unutterably sad. Sad for Flora's disillusion-ment, Mrs Fry's disappointment.

Jade straightened her back. It was no use descending into the depths of self-pity. Distasteful though it may be, she must go back to Lambert's house. No one would visit her but she did not want to speak to anyone as yet. And then she saw fully what she had not done until now. Molly would not be quiet and eventually someone must listen to her.

She herself would be found quite easily at Henry's house. She would bring disgrace on both Henry and the Earles. Lambert did not deserve that.

She wandered to the end of the street, her mind filled suddenly with panic. She had money with her but it could not last for long. Most of it was still at Tudor Place. She had counted so much on finding Ma.

Common sense returned. No one would be waiting for her yet. She had time to go for the rest of her little hoard.

The slanting shadow of a man behind her frightened her. Running, her skirts lifted, she saw a chaise and hailed it, thankful that it stopped immediately. Safe inside the dry dim-ness, she saw the man hail another conveyance. He was tall and well built but the beaver hat concealed his features. He was nobody, a lecher out in search of a drab, but he'd not dare touch her in Tudor Place. She'd ask the driver to wait until the house door was opened for her.

Nick, wet and perspiring in the chaise behind, cursed irritably. He had been so sure of waylaying her but she'd sensed his presence too soon.

He relapsed against the musty interior, scowling.

Jade, once inside Lambert's house, tried to take stock. The footman broke into her still-unformed thoughts.

'Letter came for you today. Took it in, I did.'

'Oh? Where is it?'

''Spect Mrs Abel's got it. Fair snatched it off me, she did.'

She was conscious of a great thankfulness. It must be from Henry. He seemed the only stable thing in her tumbling world. Except that he could not be with her for several months yet and she doubted if the money he had given her would last that long.

'Just like the last letter, it was. Same handwriting,' the foot-man continued.

'Last letter?'

'Yes. Came about three or four weeks ago.' He looked puzzled.

'And did Mrs Abel take that one too?'

'Now you come to mention it, she did. Said she'd put it in your room.'

'Thank you. I'll go now and ask her for it.' She took a coin from her reticule and gave it to him. 'You must tell me if there is ever another.'

'Thank you, Miss Benedict.' He went off, grinning.

Jade, her mind no longer muddled but strong in the grip of a wholesome anger, went to the housekeeper's room and knocked loudly. Confronted by Mrs Abel, she was instantly conscious of her bedraggled appearance. Mrs Abel was so meticulously neat, her mouth so scornful over the wet, limp cloak and bonnet, the strands of sodden hair that had escaped from confinement. But Jade had the advantage of right on her side. Ignoring Mrs Abel's supercilious look she said, directly, 'I want my letter, please.'

'Letter?' The housekeeper was shaken.

'I don't suppose I'll ever see the previous one but I'd like the one that came today.'

'Of course, Miss Benedict,' the soft, dangerous voice promised. 'I'll bring it to you, shall I? Why should you imagine otherwise?'

'Now, if you don't mind!'

Mrs Abel looked as if she did mind, very much, but forbore to say any such thing. Jade, immensely weary after the emotional buffetings of the day, went slowly to her own chamber and took off the wet clothing. Even the shoulders and bodice of her gown were thoroughly wetted, but, before she had time to change that too, there was a tap on the door panels and Mrs Abel was handing her a letter, the seal of which showed obvious signs of having been broken and repaired.

Jade, a little sick at the woman's duplicity, realized the ineffectuality of challenging her. 'Thank you,' she said, staring pointedly at the seal.

A faint, unhealthy colour suffused Mrs Abel's white cheeks. 'That will be all,' Jade said, tight-lipped. Useless to ask for the previous letter.

But after the housekeeper had closed the door behind her, she ripped at the offending red wax and opened the stiff, crackling sheet, then sank on to the side of the big, empty bed to read it by candle-light.

Henry missed her, was desolate without her presence. Hadn't she had enough of London and loneliness yet? Nan Dart was with child and as happy as the day was long. Johnnie was as proud as a dog with two tails. If the baby was a girl it would be called Jane, if a boy, Heriot. This was the one true, fine thing to come out of Jardine Benedict's visit to New South Wales. The Darts were endlessly devoted.

The glow that this pageful of news engendered was put out as though by a bucket of water on page two. Denver had been caught and tried and almost immediately hanged for the killings of Heriot and Daniel. He had shouted defiance right to the end. She could see his shaven skull and ice-cold eyes.

Jade let the missive slip from her fingers, reliving the terror that Denver had brought to Elsrickle, remembering the flogging that preceded it. But Denver had been a rogue before the lashing, cruel and uncaring, prepared to use her and throw her into the flooded river. He had admitted as much. He'd been segregated from the other convicts because of his innate badness. It was not her fault that he'd met such a terrible end, any more than she could excuse Nick Caspar and the rest of the Bluegate Fields gang for what they did. She picked up the letter.

Lambert went on to vow his undying love and to express the hope that he was soon to receive news of her acceptance to his proposal. The sight of her portrait, satisfying though this was, could in no way compare with the original. 'You are beautiful and you are all I want on this earth,' Henry wrote with uncharacteristic freedom. 'Put me out of this misery I find myself in, as soon as may be possible.'

He said nothing about the man he knew she intended to see. It was as though, ostrich-like, he intended to ignore him, knowing that her former lover was decisively out of reach, no threat to his plans for the future.

Jade was overtaken with a fit of shuddering. The wet gown clung to her coldly, reminding her that she should have changed it long ago. Shivering, she took it off and put on the other. It was impossible to stay here now that she was recognized. The garrick cloak was all she had to cover herself for the pelerine was too thin for the coldness of the weather. Recovering the remainder of the money Henry had given her, she thrust it into her bag along with the letter and shrugged her arms into the soaked sleeves.

She would tell Mrs Abel she was to stay with Mrs Earle for a few days. There must be some apparent reason for her departure and Flora could not be hurt any more than she had been already.

The opals she left in a drawer, feeling that they were not properly hers until Henry was acquainted with every detail of her past.

Mrs Abel was in the hall when she went downstairs. 'How is Mr Lambert?' she asked.

The sharp rejoinder died on Jade's tongue. There was nothing to be gained by outwardly antagonizing Mrs Abel. Perhaps there was right on her side if Henry had encouraged her and then taken flight. Besides, she did not feel at all well.

'As usual. I shall be away for a few days at Mrs Earle's.'

'Very well. When will you be back?'

'I don't know for certain.' Jade found that she was trembling uncontrollably.

'Are you all right?' Mrs Abel asked with false concern.

'Just cold, that's all. It will pass. If there are any more letters for me, see that they are put into my room.'

'Of course.' The black eyes glowed with a touch of redness. Jade was repelled. 'Shall I have a chaise come for you?' the housekeeper suggested.

That would have been sensible but Jade felt, suddenly, that she could not stay under this roof a moment longer. 'No. I'm sure I will see one quite quickly.'

Mrs Abel opened the door and Jade went out, aware that the door was shut very firmly after her. But she had already burned her boats. She did not want to go back.

It was still raining and the bag that held her change of clothing felt heavy and cumbersome. But she was in luck! There was a chaise at the kerb only a short distance away. She would go to some small hotel and take stock in the morning.

She waved and the chaise drew alongside.

'Where d'you want to go, lady?' The voice was muffled in a long wide scarf.

'Do you know of an inn? Respectable and not too costly?'

'I think I know exactly what you want.'

'Then take me there, please.'

The man dismounted, opened the door and handed her into the obscurity.

She took a step inside and encountered a pair of outstretched legs, two big grasping hands. Jade was too shocked to make a sound. She was pulled on to a wide, strong lap. 'Hallo, Jade.'

From the first second she had known that it was Nick.

The chaise was bowling along and the gas lamps flickered feebly through the downpour. 'How did you know I was here? At that house?'

'I was about to visit Molly and get her out of Newgate when I saw you on the street.'

'And followed me to Lily Stalker's.'

'Yes. Only you were too quick for me when you left.'

His hands were round her midriff, sliding up and over her breasts in the old, possessive way. 'And how did you come to be back in London?'

'Got someone to give me a free passage. Stowed away from Port Jackson.'

Nick laughed. 'Trust you to manage that! Weren't you afraid you'd be recognized?'

'I suppose I was – too clever.'

'You're trembling.'

'It's not because of you! I was unwell and my clothes became very wet today. I've – taken a chill, I think.' Her thoughts were echoing as though she spoke into a tunnel and she felt very strange. She would like to have struck away Nick's exploring fingers but either strength or will-power had deserted her. Her weakness horrified her. Lack of proper sleep, shame, panic, incipient fever all worked on her, reducing her to a shuddering bundle in his arms.

'Where – are we going?' Not that she greatly cared.

'Surely you know that?' he said softly. 'Up to your room at the top of the house. The one with the red paper and the bars at the window. Remember?'

She remembered. Even through the resonance that invaded her mind she would not forget that room. 'I – don't want to.'

'My dear,' Nick murmured. 'Your wants count for very little.'

He had not changed, she thought helplessly, unresponsive to his intimate caresses, afraid of the dizziness that attacked her. Then her senses diminished and she relapsed against him with a sigh.

He caught her to him fiercely.

Watery sunlight painted a line of bars across the wall. Jade stared at them wonderingly. Red wall and thin black bars.

A large, familiar head blotted out most of the scene. Drogo's beautiful, long-lashed eyes surveyed her. He had the same habit of grinning widely though nothing was amusing.

It surprised her that she was pleased to see him. Nan was gone for ever. Ma Lee had followed Jack Flynn to eternity. She had liked Drogo, was sorry for him.

'Better, are you?'

'Very tired. But better.'

'You must take.' Drogo poured medicine into a silver spoon. It would be stolen, of course. Jade almost smiled. She opened her mouth obediently and made the appropriate face. Drogo jumped up and down laughing. It was almost like old times.

'Has you working here now, does he?' She raised her arm and saw that she was dressed in a night robe of lace and satin.

'The girls like me.'

'I'm sure they do. Where's Nick, Drogo?'

'Downstairs. I must fetch –'

'No.' She reached out and tugged feebly at his sleeve. 'Wait. I must get away from here. I've money if you help –'

Drogo frowned. 'Not good idea. Nick is angry if I do.'

'He need not know.' She tried to sit up, but could not.

'Nick always knows.'

'Think about it. I couldn't run away today. I'm too weak. But soon –'

'I go.' The dwarf went, his little legs working pathetically fast.

Jade closed her eyes. How long had she been here? Her hair was damp and matted and her veins showed bluely on the backs of her hands. But the bed was comfortable and whatever was in the black, bitter potion made her deliciously drowsy.

When she opened her eyes, Nick was there. He was wearing a dark green coat and a gold-embroidered waistcoat. 'Hallo,' he said, his smile crooked.

'Have you seen Molly yet?'

'Yes.' He tilted back his chair, rocking it dangerously. 'She's squawking to get out but I haven't paid up yet.'

'She told you about me, didn't she?'

'Never could keep her mouth buttoned-up. But there's been no one to hear but the turnkey. She's still in solitary.'

'She told everyone in hearing who I was that day I went to Lily Stalker's. Everyone must know.'

'I can't quite get over your sauce! Do-gooding with that

Fry woman and her ladies. I always said you had spirit.' Nick laughed and the light from the window reddened his hair.

'When will you let me go?'

'Got nowhere to go, have you?'

'What makes you think – ?'

'Please take me to some inn. Respectable and cheap,' he mimicked. 'You're safer here.'

'Until Molly gets back,' she told him.

'Why d'you think I haven't paid yet?'

'But you daren't leave her there too long. If she talked about me, she could do the same with you.'

Nick frowned and righted the chair with a mind-splitting crash. 'Just let her try!'

'Please – Let me go.'

Nick smiled slowly. 'Got other plans for you,' he said softly. 'Can't have you wasting yourself on any gentleman from Australia. Oh, yes, I read your letter. Still want you, I do, my girl.' He leaned forward and traced the line of her throat then continued down the pale green satin until his finger-tip was on her nipple. He teased at it gently. Jade closed her eyes only it was too late.

'Liked that, didn't you? Being starved of it makes it all the better. God, I'd like you now only it's not much fun prodding at a corpse and that's what it would be like. Take your medicine, did you?'

'Yes.'

'I'll leave you to get better then. Only don't be too long about it.'

'I'm – very tired.'

'And don't go pretending, neither! That won't save you when I think the time's right.' He drew himself up to his full height, seeming to fill the room. 'I'm not usually so patient with a woman. But so far as you're concerned I'm ready to start again. Don't have much choice, do you, if you stop to think about it?'

He was gone.

She did think. It would be better to sleep now and eat whatever was brought later. Then she'd be strong enough to approach Drogo again. Nick wouldn't wait for ever.

By the following afternoon she was sitting up and Drogo washed her hair for her and dried it with a big green towel. She took the black draught without making a face, then fell asleep half-way through a bowl of broth.

'Molly will be getting desperate,' she said next morning when Nick came again.

'Blast Molly.'

'She'll think you mean to leave her there.'

Jade could see that Nick thought the same. It might take his mind off herself. But she had no sooner got the words out of her mouth, when there was an uproar on the stairs and Molly came thrusting her way into the room. She looked quite distraught. 'You left me to rot!' she screamed, launching herself at Nick who caught her wrists with practised ease. 'If it hadn't been for Porter who'd heard where I was and paid my fine for me, I'd be there still! And all because of her. Didn't you have enough of her last time? Came looking for you, did she, when all her fine friends turned their backs?'

'No,' Nick said, 'I went looking for her.'

Molly's big brown eyes blazed. 'Just like last time! But I got rid of her then and I'll do it again, you'll see. I won't let her have you.'

'We must have a talk,' Nick told her. 'Come along, Moll. You're upsetting the invalid. Well, not so much of the invalid now, are you?' He smiled at Jade and she knew what that remark meant.

He marshalled Molly from the bed-chamber, her cries and shrieks lingering on the stairs, then diminishing as they went into another room and shut the door.

Drogo came with a glass of wine, his customary smile absent.

'Bad, she is!'

'That's why you must help me. She still wants to kill me. Drogo?'

The dwarf padded about the room, his eyes frightened.

Jade sipped the wine. She did feel stronger but she had no idea where she would go if she did manage to get out of this house. All she knew was that she couldn't betray Masson with Nick Caspar.

Every instinct urged her to go to Gabriel but that refuge was barred for her by Adeline's presence. And then she knew where she might find help. Why hadn't she thought of Mr Pickersgill before? He must know some quiet, respectable house where she could wait for news of her parents. He might even have news of them by now. Papa would help her to escape. Her fingers touched the sea-horse on its delicate chain. She had always believed it to be lucky. Even the darkest moments of her life had been offset by others of beauty and splendour. Hope.

She got out of bed, conscious that Molly had began to scream in the room below, but this time they were not cries of anger and jealousy but those of pain and fear.

Weakness attacked Jade immediately. She swayed and clung to the bedpole, her senses swimming. But, as she gritted her teeth, forcing herself to remain upright, a little strength returned, enough to make her way, shakily, around the bed to the chair where her clothes were lying.

Sitting down, she began, with infinite slowness, to put on each garment. At last, she managed even the gown and started to fasten the little jet buttons on the bodice. She had had to leave off her stockings for the effort of bending down made her too dizzy, but she had slipped her feet into her shoes.

The door opened suddenly and Nick was there, frowning. 'What do you think you're doing?'

'I realized I must get up if I mean to recover –'

'I wanted you in bed.'

'Please, Nick! Another day. Tomorrow, I'll be stronger. I'm weak as a kitten –'

He came across the room, ruthless and arrogant as ever, his mouth set in lines of purpose. 'If you are well enough to get up and dress, you're capable of lying down again to pleasure me.'

'What did you do to Molly?'

'Gave her a beating she'll never forget. But I don't want to talk about her. You know what I want. What I've waited for some days now.' He took her fingers away from the task of fastening the small black buttons. Her eyes were fixed on his hands, large and predatory, the backs covered with fine, reddish hairs that caught threads of light from the burning candle. The strong fingers began to undo what she had just done, each unfastened button revealing a little more of the lace-threaded shift and the smooth scallops of breast that came above its low neckline.

She looked about her for some weapon but there was nothing that would keep him away from what he intended. Cruel grey eyes locked with hers. She would not give him the satisfaction of begging.

Slowly, and with obvious relish, Nick went on with the task of undressing her.

CHAPTER TWELVE

Gabriel Masson stared at Flora Earle almost unseeingly. She was secretly afraid of the violence behind those penetratingly dark eyes while admitting to herself the all-too-potent fascination of the man.

'And, after this Molly Connor had divulged these – unsavoury facts – what did Miss Benedict do?'

'She – ran off towards the women's door and asked to be let out. I hurried after her but was too late to stop her from leaving alone.'

'You were her friend. She told me.'

'Yes. I feel she may have thought that I condemned her –'

'And did you?' Masson's black gaze was very direct.

'Perhaps – in the first moment. I thought of your wife –'

'As she did. She refused to be in my company in case Adeline was hurt.'

'But I could not keep up the censure. She seemed too good a person for shabby behaviour.'

'Her own word for any further contact between us. The taste of shabbiness was how she described it.'

Flora was greatly moved. 'Oh, poor Jardine.'

'It's ironic that, on that same morning, Miss Benedict was absolved from all blame in a dreadful business that resulted in her being transported to New South Wales. She was quite guiltless, being forced to do what she did.'

'Then Henry must have suspected this,' Flora said, deeply disturbed.

'Henry?'

'Mr Lambert, my cousin. Though he did make out, for appearance's sake, I suppose, that she was a settler.'

'Oh, yes. Lambert. She said he'd helped get her out of Australia on one of his vessels.'

'And is now to marry her,' Flora told him. 'She accepted his proposal a month or more ago. As soon as he receives her letter, he'll be on his way. It's his dearest wish. And now that she is legally innocent –'

'The Home Secretary himself has made it so,' Masson said, and his voice was now heavy and lifeless. But Flora could not regret having put Jade out of his reach. Masson was married, with responsibilities to his wife. No good could come of it.

'How is Adeline?'

If Masson saw the drift of her confidences and questions, he gave no sign. But even his lips were white. She had certainly dealt him a body blow.

'Much as usual.'

'Give her my regards. I'd like to visit her, if I may.'

'Of course. But I am concerned for Miss Benedict. She goes away, upset and frightened, fearing re-arrest, and only Mrs Abel has seen her since. She came back to Tudor Place, soaking wet, and went off half an hour later, still in her dripping cloak, according to the footman. I suppose she could not bring herself to involve Lambert in what she imagined would be the sordid business of being sought by the Bow Street Runners.'

'That does seem more than possible,' Flora agreed, her heart sore for Jade.

'And said she was to come here for a few days.'

'But she never came. I had not asked, though she'd have been welcome.'

They stared at one another in silence until the maid came in with the tea Flora had ordered.

'If she does,' Masson said, taking up his cup, 'I would want to be told immediately.'

'What if she does not want to see you? In the circumstances.'

'She must at least be told that her fears are groundless. She may see my cousin Peter, should she shy away from my presence.' He sounded bitter now and Flora was half sorry she had interfered by telling him of the engagement. But surely it was fairer to both him and Jardine? Not to mention Adeline. Flora wanted very much to ask what it was that Jardine had been forced to do but, of course, she could not.

Masson finished his tea and rose to his feet. 'Be kind to her, should she return.'

'Oh, I will. I'm very fond of Jardine. I wonder where she could have gone?'

'I wish to God I knew,' Masson said in a low voice, then took his leave.

He drove next to Mr Pickersgill's office and was told that Miss Benedict had not gone there either.

'I have news for her, too,' the little solicitor said, rumpling his hair even more wildly. 'News that is not altogether good.'

'Oh. What news is that?'

'Her mother, Mrs Vera Benedict, unfortunately has departed this world. In Italy. She seemed to have lost the will to live. I made enquiries, you see, at the former Benedict house, now occupied by a Mr and Mrs Hill. Mr Benedict did call just in case Miss Jardine might have gone there. He'd never given up hope entirely and this visit took place last summer, after Mrs Jardine was laid to rest. He left a forwarding address to which I have written, expecting Miss Benedict to be at Tudor Place. I felt it more sensible to be in touch with her father before raising her hopes.'

'She may go back to Lambert's house,' Gabriel said without much conviction.

'And what if Mr Benedict arrives post haste and Miss Jardine still away?'

'If he comes to me I can tell him everything he wishes to know.'

'Except her whereabouts.'

'As you say, except for that.' Gabriel left his card.

Outside, in the carriage, Masson admitted defeat for the moment. And he owed it to Adeline to return home. She saw little enough of him and time hung heavily on her hands when he was out of the house.

He found her lying listlessly, the room seeming over-warm after the cold of the streets. Her cheeks were flushed, giving Adeline the appearance of health, but her eyelids were heavy. 'What have you been doing?' he asked gently.

'I had a visit from Mrs Fry and Miss Buxton. They brought flowers.' She indicated the vase on the bureau.

'That was kind of them.' He stroked her fingers and she clung to him.

'They told me some tale of Jardine Benedict. How she was denounced by some woman at Newgate and went off without explanation. I'd asked after her.'

'I heard the same tale today. The pity of it was that she need not have taken fright.' He realized that the ladies would take good care not to mention his part in Molly Connor's outburst.

'Why not?'

'It's a long, sad story.'

'You must tell me.'

He told Adeline, glossing over some of the worst aspects of the business for she had a sensitive heart and would lie sleepless on Jade's account in any case. As he had expected, she was horrified. 'To think that one cannot look at a servant without wondering if they are some cuckoo in the nest!'

'You need not worry about mine.'

'That poor girl. And what agonies her parents must have endured. We should ask her to come here more often. I liked her.'

'We must find her first. She's disappeared and is not with any acquaintances she's so far made.'

'Oh, Gabriel! What if she's been seen by anyone besides the Connor woman? That maid, Eliza, for instance? Or one of the others?'

Gabriel clenched his hands. As if he had not thought of that already! But the Connor woman was still at Newgate until someone paid her fine, and the most likely person to do so was her whoremaster.

Masson did not want to think about Nick Caspar. The thought of the man made him feel murderous. And Molly Connor was the woman who had been responsible for Jade's apprehension. She would never give away Caspar's address. The Runners would demand one but it would turn out to be some hovel with no connection at all with the real house. Peter had told him all the dodges.

But Peter might have heard of Caspar. He had his contacts in London's underworld. There was no use in calling on him this evening for Peter was out of town for two days on some constituency matter and had not said where he was to be staying. And the Connor woman was confined for disorderly behaviour.

Masson told himself he must contain his impatience. Jade might not, in any case, be there. She could have gone to earth in almost any inn in the city or out of it. He wanted her violently, so much that he could not bear the thought of inaction, of separation, the frustration that eroded like an acid.

'Play to me,' Adeline asked, seeing his torment, regretting her part in it.

'What shall I play?'

'Anything. It doesn't matter.'

Tiredly, he crossed over to the spinet in the corner. It had been brought up here now that Adeline was confined to bed, a bed he suspected she was never to leave.

The only tune he could think of that suited his mood was Für Elise. He played it over and over again, the notes dropping into an unbroken silence. Beethoven had understood nostalgia perfectly.

He was waiting at Peter's chambers with a burning impatience long before his cousin arrived. Peter's man had let him in and he paced the room, unable to rest, studying the names on the spines of the tooled leather books without really seeing them, drinking more than one glass of brandy, then cutting the end of one of Peter's best cigars and puffing the fragrant aroma around the room.

The black coat hung a shade looser than it had a month ago and the little lines round Masson's eyes were a fraction deeper. But he was just as good-looking in his chequered fashion, the waistcoat and stock immaculate, his boots polished.

Jade was not back at Tudor Place for he had gone there first, drawn by a desire to see the dwelling that had last housed her. The strange housekeeper had drawn him in like some dark insect, all legs and elongated head. He'd found her repulsive, but her eyes were fine, if hungry. He was all too well acquainted with body lust. She'd given him wine and a biscuit but he could not wait to get out of the place. Her expression as he questioned her showed him that she did not want Jade to return in spite of her supposed concern.

Peter arrived, cold and hungry, demanding supper before they talked business. But, mellowed by oysters and beef and apple pudding, he listened attentively over the port and brandy.

'There's one man would know,' he said at the end of Masson's recital. 'A Runner, Jeremy Bowles. He was another Jonathan Wilde, running with both hare and hounds. You must have seen him at the Benson girls' trial. Sorry, Miss Benedict's! He was hand in glove with Molly Connor there but Caspar resented the whole affair most bitterly, particularly as Isaac, the fence, was lost to him. He swore vengeance on Bowles and had him so cruelly beaten by some Colossus from Bluegate Fields that the man's left a cripple. He'll never walk again, poor devil. The question is, will Bowles be too frightened to speak out? Or will he be so burnt-up with the need to have his revenge that he'll tell us what we want to find out?'

'Where does he live?'

'Some cess-pool up by Seven Dials.'

'I want to see him.'

Peter Masson looked at his cousin keenly. 'You've never been able to dismiss that girl from your mind, have you?'

'No.'

'But it won't do, will it? Granted, none of this was Miss Benedict's fault, but you've Addy to think of –'

'And do you think I don't! I tell myself a dozen times a day that she must always come first, especially now, but it seems that I was intended to love only one person in the truest sense of the word. And, in spite of my abominable treatment of her, she loves me. But she's put herself beyond my reach. Promised herself to a man I wake up at night hating for his good fortune.

'You needn't worry, Peter, I know where my duty – and much affection – lies. I'll give Adeline no cause for unhappiness, however long she lives. And I can't expect Jade to grow old – waiting for something that might never happen. She deserves some security. It's just that I cannot bear the thought that she's lost and unhappy. And possibly in danger. No more than I can stand the knowledge that Adeline is cheated out of what should have been her happiest years.'

'She's not unhappy,' Peter told him. 'I think she's happier than you realize, just because of your devotion in spite of –'

'In spite of the fact that we are precluded a normal marriage? I confess I find it hard to subjugate certain desires.'

'Quite natural ones. Addy told me in confidence that she would never blame you for taking a mistress. She thinks she has failed you miserably. Poor child.'

Gabriel helped himself to more brandy. 'She's an angel. But since I found Jade again, I've no taste for other women. And she will not resume a liaison of the kind you envisage, so there's no more to be said.' He tossed off the generous measure of brandy as if it had been water and rose to his feet.

'Bowles,' he said firmly. 'You've had time to restore yourself, Peter.'

'The night is the worst time to go to Seven Dials,' his cousin warned.

'I'm in a mood for danger,' Masson said savagely. 'You've a pistol, have you not?'

'I have –'

'Then we'll take it. And I seem to recall a swordstick. It

would give me the greatest pleasure to slit Caspar's weazand from ear to ear.'

'We may never get into the house. Bars, bolts, bodyguards. That's what it will be like.'

'Damn bars and men who cripple others.'

'She may not be there.'

'I have to know. Don't you see? I must.'

'Yes, Gabriel. I do see. If she is – she may come here afterwards. I've no objection. She'll be her father's business when he arrives. There's nothing here that would remind her of anything she may wish to forget.'

'Only your name.'

'Well, I can't change that and she does not sound the sort of person to expect it. Which will you have? Swordstick or pistol?' Peter forced himself to bravery.

'Swordstick, I think.' Gabriel laughed and his eyes glittered.

Peter was suddenly sorry for anyone who stood in his way tonight.

They left carriage and driver some distance from the Dials. It would be safer. Gabriel thought he would never forget the walk through those abominable streets. The smells, the sounds, the sights were so nightmarish that it was brought home to him what Jade must have suffered. Women screamed and tore at one another. Dark figures writhed and entwined in stinking corners in horrid travesties of intercourse. Faceless shapes loomed in doorways. Ragged children darted from shadow to shadow, snatching at anything that was momentarily unprotected, then running like hares into obscurity, their feet echoing in alleys no wider than an adult form could encompass.

More than once, Masson was bumped into quite deliberately, but he turned such a face of devilish rage upon the would-be thief or assassin, drawing the sword from its scabbard to glint in the moonlight or gaslight, that he remained unmolested.

Bowles's room was on the ground floor of a dwelling that shook when one entered it. Everything creaked, boards, plaster, the very stones with which it was built. Bowles himself, hunched and pale as a colourless spider, sat in a rotting chair. Bitterness corroded the lines of his mouth and there seemed nothing under the folds of the dirty blanket that hung from his lap.

Gabriel's stomach muscles clamped tightly. Caspar had ordered this abominable punishment, had probably watched and gloated over it as he had over Jade's last sight of her departing parents.

All the time Peter explained the whys and wherefores of Jardine Benedict's unjust sentence for crimes she had not committed, Bowles sat iron-hard and still. It was as though the loss of his legs had strengthened everything else about him, his long simian arms, his neck, his self-control, the wide shoulders that seemed the greatest part of him.

When Peter asked for Caspar's address, Bowles did not answer.

'For God's sake, man. *He* did this to you! Here's your chance to see he suffers.'

'Only if this girl is found there. She could be anywhere.' The voice was harsh and rusted with hate. 'If you storm the house and the exercise is all for nothing, he'll think of who might have opened their lips and I couldn't run. Could you?' He tore off the blanket, shockingly, revealing only his thighs lying on the frayed cushion.

Gabriel felt sick and Peter looked away. The blanket was replaced. 'It was Maul who got me but no one was there to be witness.'

Jade had mentioned Maul. She'd been terrified of him.

'He might get her this time,' Masson said. 'You remember her, don't you? You helped have her sent to Newgate. A child not quite seventeen.'

'It all fitted in with what Molly said. You yourself were not guiltless.'

'No,' Gabriel admitted. 'I must take my share of blame. But she was visiting Newgate and Molly Connor saw her. She could have told Caspar, or some visitor to the prison might have. I'll kill him if I get my hands on him! I swear I will!'

Something approaching a smile showed briefly in Bowles's sick eyes. 'Don't do it too quickly, will you!'

'You mean you will?'

'I see you mean business,' Bowles said. 'Include Molly if you can, the bad bitch. If it hadn't been for her –' He sat brooding while Masson watched, afraid that he would change his mind.

'I'll send Runners to protect you,' Peter Masson offered.

Bowles laughed and the sound was terrible. 'D'you think yourselves invisible? There'll be a hundred witnesses to say you were here. But I find, suddenly, I don't care very much to keep this carcase of mine alive. I'll take my chance.'

'Where?' Gabriel asked.

'Tumbril Street. Nineteen.'

'You'll be all right?'

'Fine,' Bowles laughed crazily. 'Why shouldn't I be?'

'Is there anything you want before we go?' Gabriel put two gold pieces on the table. The candle guttered, spilling wax over them.

'You'll see a boy in the doorway of the next house. Send him in. Say I need him to go to the grog shop.'

'Very well.' Only drink could blur this man's thoughts and make his life bearable. Nick Caspar became very real and Jade's danger hideously so. She had escaped him once but he'd take good care she didn't do it a second time. If she was there –

Peter had to draw his pistol on the way back to the coach to scare off a slinking pack of jackal-like creatures who seemed entirely grey. Gabriel flicked the sword point at them while he and Peter slid past the group, their backs to the wall. It was difficult to believe they were human. Even their thin, glinting teeth looked like steel. A leaden finger-nail glanced off Masson's cheek, tearing away a sliver of skin. The hurt was out of all proportion. A thin trickle of blood ran down to stain the white shirt front.

The moon came out as they retreated, the tip of the thin sword pinking one of the dodging figures. It emitted a sound like a rat's, shrill and inhuman.

Sweating, the two men made good their escape, elbowing aside a pair of harridans bent on plucking out one another's eyes. A shawled child passed a doorway and vanished soundlessly.

They reached the carriage and fell into it, half-exhausted.

Gabriel shouted instructions. 'It's in the neighbourhood of Drury Lane!'

The vehicle entered more salubrious streets but there was a constant traffic of women towards Drury Lane, all shapes and sizes, all ages. They were thick round the side doors, just out of range of the gaslights, and as they shifted, the yellow radiance showed up a made-up face, a shag of hennaed hair, a foot perhaps, a bosom encased too tightly, a tawdry feather or battered bonnet, glinting buckles, a rash of beauty spots, the folds of a skirt splashed with mud, high-bosomed, tight-waisted silhouettes, shawled anonymity. Here and there, a child –

Gabriel knew some of the women, had grappled with them in his own carriage. Neither the acts nor the remembrance of them had brought him pleasure. Jade had led a far cleaner life than his. She had submitted out of necessity though she had not tried to excuse herself, had, indeed, given the impression that not all her encounters had been bad. Lambert had been gentlemanly, had helped her to go off to a new and hopefully better life. She was right to take him. But damn Lambert, anyway!

Tumbril Street was filled with narrow, secretive houses with pitch-black basements and glimmers of feeble light. There was a total absence of humanity, a sharp contrast to the rat-pit that was the Dials.

Number nineteen was not quite so dark as most of the others. There were lights on most of the floors and even the attics seemed occupied. Of course, one could expect plenty of activity in a bawdy-house.

'How do we get in?' Peter whispered, his thin, dark face creased into a frown.

'I've just remembered. Jade told me how she arrived here. Caspar knocked on the middle panel. Four deliberate knocks, I think she said. Then a window was opened. There's a wrestler-turned-doorkeeper. Now what did she say his name was? Ten thousand damnations! Wait while I think. Oh, Christ Jesus! It's a name that somehow lends itself to battery.'

Peter waited, obviously uncomfortable. 'Look here, Gabriel. I am a Member of the House. Doesn't look too well, stationed outside Caspar's.'

Gabriel laughed unexpectedly. 'There's nothing unusual about Members outside whorehouses, I assure you!'

'What's the doorkeeper's name? Hurry up, Gabriel, for God's sake.'

Gabriel sobered. 'I must remember! Thomas? Tobias? Toby! That's it. She says he has a flattened nose and shoulders like a bull.'

'And how do you propose to get him to let us in?'

'I will be a prospective client – rather tipsy, I think. I have had dealings with Molly and she has invited me to call on her, giving me the code for entry. I will call the man by his name. When he opens the door you will menace him with your pistol and shoot him if necessary –'

'Gabriel! That girl may not be there at all. I'll have killed a man for nothing.'

'It won't be for nothing. I feel it in my bones.' Gabriel's heart was unaccountably lighter. 'Fire at his legs then. That should suffice. But keep him downstairs.'

'God!' Peter muttered and got out on to the pavement. 'Wait at the end of the road,' he told the driver, 'and if we do not come out in a very few minutes, fetch the Runners.' His complexion, under the gaslight, was greenish. 'How will you find her?' he asked Masson, indicating the lit windows, some with plush curtains pulled over them, allowing only a crack of light to escape.

'She was taken up to the top of the house last time.'

'You can't guarantee – '

'Of course I can't,' Gabriel snapped. 'I'm sorry, Peter, but it must be done.'

'I was not made in the mould of champions,' Peter groaned. 'I'll strike any blow with my pen or my tongue but I've never been a physical person. You know that. As if the Dials at night weren't bad enough.'

'Only you will, this once,' Gabriel insisted softly, reaching forward to strike on the door, 'do just what I ask. You were adequate when we encountered those juvenile assassins earlier.'

'That was not planned as this is. I knew that we'd keep them off. But this – this fortress – '

His words were cut off sharply as the window in the door was opened.'

'Wot is it?' The nose was just as Jade had said, flattened by some crushing blow.

'Toby, is it?' Masson asked, his voice slurred. 'Molly said to ask for her. She gave me her favour recently. Molly Connor. I'd a mind to repeat the experience. And my friend – wantsh – wantsh – somebody too. Let's in, there's a good fellow.' Gabriel jingled the coins in his pocket. He was safe enough since Molly was in Newgate. Toby would offer him some sleazy alternative. A key to one of those rooms. Which he would ignore.

'Molly? She's in 'er room but I don't know. She's – not feeling well.'

'Well – anyone, then.' Gabriel shrugged. 'I'm not particular.' But he was jolted.

Toby, disarmed by the correct signal and Masson's knowledge of their names, slid the bolt. The two gentleman looked suitably drunk and money makes a good noise however you look at it. He yawned self-indulgently.

He was astonished, then alarmed, to be thrust aside as soon

as the door was open. The thin, dark gentleman pointed a pistol towards his chest, halting him in his instinctive rush forward. The broad dark man, no longer drunk, was asking him where the Benedict girl was. 'Ain't no girl like that here.' His voice rose on the denial, but his eyes shifted uncomfortably.

'She is!' Gabriel said with a good deal of satisfaction. 'In the same room as last time, is she?'

The shot went home as he had intended.

Toby opened his mouth to shout but Gabriel forestalled him. 'I'll have no compunction in running you through.' The thin steel blade glittered. The man subsided prudently.

'Do as I said,' Gabriel told Peter quietly. 'Don't bother to aim for his legs if he gives trouble. And keep your wits about you.'

Gabriel set off up the staircase, his footfalls muffled by the thick, red carpet. Gilded cupids postured at each turn of the banisters. Voices issued from every room but they were mostly the soft, amused voices of persons pleasurably occupied. A woman laughed vulgarly. There were sounds that required no explanation. He grimaced.

He was half-way up the twisting stairs when he saw the shadow begin on the wall. Gabriel stopped involuntarily. The moving darkness expanded and became the figure of the biggest man he had ever seen. The gross body was covered in a soiled white shirt and breeches. The waxen head was bald and shining.

Maul smiled. Masson's mouth was suddenly dry.

Jade was spreadeagled on the bed. Nick's eyes gloated as he looked down at her. 'You've grown into a woman since last time. What I don't understand is that man in Australia helping you to get away from him.' He laughed.

'Because he was decent,' she told him, trying to stave off the inevitable. 'And that's a quality you've never had any dealings with.'

'Don't act the lady with me. You know and I know what we've done together and not all of it unwillingly.'

'Only because you're a good teacher.'

'And you were the best pupil I ever had.'

'Oh? I thought Molly was that?'

'In her own way she's an artist.'

'Strange. That's exactly what someone once said about you.'

'I thought,' Nick said, his voice suddenly ugly, 'that you'd never mentioned me to a living soul?'

She shrank a little from the cruelty in his expression. His hands slid to her throat and encircled it lightly. 'Who'd you squawk to?'

'It wasn't like that—'

'What was it like then?'

'That man I picked up at the theatre—'

'Masson, you mean? The swell cove who got all uppity when you went off with his sister's trinkets?' The hands pressed warningly into her soft flesh.

She shook her head from side to side, eyes wide. 'No, Nick. Don't—'

'What did he say?' He relaxed his hold a fraction.

'We—we had lain together—'

His eyes showed anger.

'Well, that was what you sent me out to do! We were not meant to sit and twiddle our thumbs, were we?'

'Tell me. How did he come to mention me?'

'He had no idea who you are! But he knew that I was not a virgin. He said that whoever had taught me my tricks had been an artist in his own fashion. Nothing too gross—' Her voice caught at the recollection.

'So, there we are,' he said in a better temper. 'Molly and me. Both artists.' Then he switched again to displeasure, grasping her upper arms so hard that she closed her eyes in pain. 'Was that all?'

'Yes. You asked me in Newgate, remember? Wouldn't I have told you then?'

'Perhaps you would.' The ruthless fingers were taken away but agony pumped through the bruised flesh. She cried out in spite of herself.

She must keep him off her, Jade thought desperately, only she couldn't fend off a butterfly. Her illness had drained her of strength and resources. But Nick, having disposed of his suspicions to his own satisfaction, was not to be put off any longer.

His mouth came over hers, stifling protest, his great weight overlay her like some enormous cat that, through some grotesque quirk of nature, desired a helpless young rabbit. She pushed against his chest but he thrust against her the harder, his face suddenly sensuous.

'I—warned you, Nick. You—should have listened.'

Nick raised his head, incredulous. 'My God, Molly. You'll wish I'd killed you when I've finished with you! Get out. You're mad.'

Jade, twisting her head sideways, saw Molly leaning against the bedpole. One eye was closed and puffy, almost purple, and there was a cut on her cheekbone that still oozed blood. Her lips were a travesty of a mouth, only the lovely golden-brown body was recognizable and the cloud of dusky hair. She had something in her hand but it was impossible, from this angle, to see what it was.

'What's that you've got?' Nick, suddenly uneasy, prepared to rise from his victim.

'I always saw her as the one that was really bad,' Molly said in a queer, lifeless voice, 'but now I see it was always you. Always you, Nick. Jack Flynn was decent to me when he took me off the moor. But there's no particle of good in you an' I've only just seen it. Taken me a long time, it has.' She stood up as she said this and Jade saw at last what she held.

'Get off, you mad bitch! You're crazy!' Nick said roughly and started to roll away from his discarded mistress. But he was not fast enough. Molly, with one final spurt of strength, almost fell forward and drove in the knife almost to the hilt. For a moment, he hung half over Jade, then began to slide off the side of the bed, making queer, stifled noises that seemed worse than screams. All the colour had ebbed out of his face.

Molly gave a great sob of fright, realizing what she had done. Nick got up infinitely slowly, then staggered towards the door. His fingers closed briefly over the jamb, leaving crimson streaks, then he took another step that hid him from Jade's view. There was blood on her, she noticed for the first time, and she lifted the sheet in a spasm of revulsion and wiped it over her body as she struggled to sit up against the pillow. It was like the episode with Denver, all over again.

Molly came towards her.

Gabriel heard Jade cry out. He would have known the timbre of her voice anywhere. He began to mount the next flight, never taking his eyes off the man in the dirty white clothes. The huge shadow crouched, a separate entity, taking up most of the curved wall. Masson had a sickening recollection of Bowles whipping off the blanket to disclose legs severed above the knee.

Jade had not screamed again but he heard a mutter of voices, one of them a man's. It would be Caspar.

Maul grinned again and lifted distended fingers derisively.

There was nothing to do but go on. Gabriel wondered how Peter felt downstairs with Toby and a pistol he was loath to use, but all the time his gaze was on Maul's stupendous bulk, his small, dark-ringed eyes. He wanted to smash away the grin of triumph that decorated the fleshy lips but the thin sword seemed a puny weapon. He gathered himself for the encounter that seemed unavoidable.

Another shadow encroached on the edge of his vision. Diverted momentarily, Gabriel stared beyond Maul. Another figure had appeared on the stairhead, an almost naked man, ashen-faced and walking only with difficulty. A big, bloodless hand caught at the banister and missed. The red head slipped sideways.

Both man and shadow pitched forward. A cry echoed in the hollow spiral and Maul's attention was briefly distracted. Caspar struck Maul with all the force of a charging bull. The big man shot forward and was impaled upon the long spike of the sword. It was odd how surprised men always were when they died.

Gabriel, flung aside in the death collision, picked himself up, his coat bloodied, and ran upstairs to arrive, breathless, at an open doorway. He saw Molly immediately, making her way towards the bed, and rushed forward to grab at her arm. She turned her battered face almost uncomprehendingly. 'He's not dead, is he? Didn't mean to kill him. Shouldn't have been so cruel.'

But Masson scarcely heard. *She* was there, sitting up with a reddened sheet around her, her green eyes strangely calm, almost as though she'd expected him. The commotion downstairs as the Runners burst in went almost unnoticed.

Molly slid to the floor and crouched against the valance, looking at nothing in particular.

'Gabriel.' Jade stared at him until her eyes swam, but the white handsome face and contrasting darkness ebbed away into a kind of mist. She was only conscious that her fingers were taken into some comforting warmth, that her body was lifted, encircled with something that was protective. 'Gabriel?'

Dimly she knew that she was safe.

The dwarf told the whole story. Jade, recovered now but dreadfully pale, could not keep her eyes from Masson. Vaguely, she realized that the man with him was the hitherto unknown Peter who was not in the least like the man she loved. He was nice, though. He'd smiled at her twice and shown that he was on her side. Drogo. She would like to do something for Drogo if it were possible.

The house, for a time, had been noisy with screams and oaths, for the prostitutes and their clients had been disturbed by the crashings on the stairs and the Robin Redbreasts' pounding feet. And Peter had, involuntarily, fired the pistol which had decapitated a gilded cupid in the hall.

Toby had been almost glad to be arrested.

Drogo had seen everything. His small body went practically everywhere unnoticed. He could squeeze into almost any corner. Molly had been removed in the sinister black van Jade remembered all too well and was off to Bow Street with almost indecent haste. It was a clear-cut case of murder.

The bodies of Caspar and Maul were laid out in a bed-chamber. Jade tried to remember how many were left of Flynn's gang. There was Eliza. Hateful Eliza! Tom. Paddy. The old woman with the slop bucket didn't count. All she wanted was a roof over her poor head. It was only Eliza who was really wicked.

Then she forgot the treacherous maidservant. The Elizas of the world never really succeeded. They made their own unhappiness.

Masson was there, his face cut but still impossibly good-looking, his eyes filled with something only she was meant to recognize. She returned the message silently. The hubbub went on but for them it did not exist. His love for her was as plain as hers for him.

Slowly, the pale ghost of Adeline materialized between them, a piece at a time. A hand, an eyelash, a cheek without any trace of colour, the soft, sweet voice.

The unlooked-for happiness faded. Ghosts did not make for comfort.

Jade declined Peter's offer of refuge. Now that she was freed in every sense, she must go back to Tudor Place. Both Massons drove her there. Mrs Abel brought them refreshments in the drawing-room, exclaiming over Jade's pallor. 'You said you were going to Mrs Earle's,' she said mock-reproachfully.

'I changed my mind. Would you please leave us, Mrs Abel? I wish to speak privately.'

'Very well.' The housekeeper went huffily.

'There's something you should know,' Gabriel said. 'I

couldn't tell you in that place. But I saw Mr Pickersgill – '

'He has news!' Jade was injected with spurious energy.

'Part good. Part bad.'

'Mama is dead. I knew. That evening of the rout she seemed to go away from me quite decisively. It's not really a shock.'

'But your father had left an accommodation address on his last visit to London, a visit connected with you. He never really believed you dead.'

'Papa – ' A look of great happiness transformed her face.

'I think he'll be here soon. There will be someone to protect you. And you do, of course, have your fiancé.'

Jade could not hide her surprise or her regret.

'Mrs Earle told me,' Gabriel said.

'Oh, I see.' The brief strength had gone and she was pale and listless. 'I shall be perfectly all right with Papa until Henry arrives. They'll – like one another. Papa likes beautiful things, pleasant surroundings. So does Henry.'

Masson's eyes conveyed the message that the only lovely thing that concerned him was Jade Benedict. She smiled suddenly and Peter, caught in the backwash of that smile, saw only too plainly why his cousin had never been able to put the girl he had imagined to be a thief and prostitute, out of his mind. He was sorry for them both, but not too sorry not to remember Adeline.

'Adeline will be worrying,' he said, unconsciously adopting Flora Earle's tactics. 'She won't sleep until you go back, Gabriel.'

'No. I'm afraid that's true. I'm glad we were able to be of service to you.'

'God knows what would have become of me if you'd not broken in. I'd seen murder committed. I knew many secrets. They'd never have let me go. I should have been killed or sent to another brothel which would have been worse.'

Jade was annoyed to find that her voice had grown high with a kind of hysteria she deplored. She had never broken under anything that had happened to her. But her rescue, just in the nick of time, and by the man she loved beyond reason – she admitted it all too frankly – had almost unnerved her. She could not bear to see him go. On the other hand, she could not bear to think of Adeline deserted.

'Don't distress yourself needlessly,' Peter advised since Gabriel seemed incapable of words. But it was only a temporary malaise.

'Take care of yourself, Jade. If you should ever be in trouble, I should like to know.'

'Thank you, but I will almost certainly have Papa.' She could not bring herself to say Lambert's name a second time and Gabriel would not wish to hear it anyway. All of a sudden, she had a surfeit of champions, but, ironically, the only person she really wanted and needed with her whole being could make only a conventional bid to help her through what would prove to be the most traumatic period of her life. Heriot and her lost baby still had the power to hurt but the second loss of Gabriel would be infinitely worse than the first, when at least there had been hope. Neither had then been committed to anyone else.

Papa returned at about the same time that Henry received Jade's letter saying that she had considered all the ramifications carefully and had decided she'd accept his proposal of marriage if he could overlook the fact that she was still not sure that she loved him but was prepared to allow him to teach her how to be a good wife. So long as he understood this, her promise was binding.

Henry, exalted, dashed off a letter of agreement and said that he'd be following in a matter of weeks, once all the tiresome legalities of selling his house and transferring his business obligations to London could be arranged. Once there, he would consider best how to protect Jade. They would have to go somewhere she would be safe. The rest of the world was at their disposal. He would sail in the *Temptress* which was due to arrive at Port Jackson from the Spice Islands in July, all going well. If she kept an eye on the arrivals board at Lloyd's of London, she would know exactly when to expect him. Having bound Jade to him irrevocably, Henry Lambert settled down to performing his last duties in a country that had seemed empty without the woman with whom he knew he would always be in love, even if she felt nothing but affection. But he'd alter that!

In the middle of these far off and happy plans, Mark Benedict came back from Italy to arrive in a late English spring. London was golden, fair with cherry trees and candelabra of chestnuts, the soft green of limes.

Jade received Mark in the drawing-room of Henry's house, Lambert having insisted that she remain there until his arrival. It seemed not to have occurred to him that there could be awkwardness resulting from his liaison with Mrs Abel. Sometimes the most sensitive men could be obtuse.

Mark was affected by the reunion with his daughter. To him she seemed so womanly. She had gone out of his life a pretty child, but the Jade who faced him across this typically Regency room was almost a stranger.

Her green eyes brilliant with tears, Jade ran to him, conscious of the gulf that lay between them, but still charmed by Benedict's good looks and obvious emotion. She recognized his weakness, almost with indulgence. The fact that she would be more a prop to him did not deter her. She only thanked her stars that she was intended to be strong.

Masson, to whom Mark had been directed by Mr Pickersgill, had given Benedict a watered-down version of Jade's sojourn in Bluegate Fields and Newgate, laying subtle stress on her happy conditions in New South Wales until the convict uprising.

Jade was glad her father knew only a part of her experience in captivity and was able to reconcile himself with those chapters with which he'd been acquainted.

Happily, almost disbelievingly, they sat in the May sunshine, more like brother and sister than father and daughter, seizing on little points of difference, exclaiming over Jade's changed looks and Mark's more static ones, skating away from any direct reference to the Holy Land or its inhabitants; talking about the foreignness of New South Wales while avoiding mention of chain-gangs and rebellion. Mark was always an escapist.

Of Vera they said little beyond establishing the fact of her death and burial near Florence. Jade saw that her father had suffered no lasting loss. The Jardine money had been left to herself should she return but she would see to it that her father had his share. Old Grandfather Jardine had sewn up the inheritance very thoroughly in favour of daughter and granddaughter. But Mark, in spite of this, had sought for her, knowing well that if she reappeared, the fortune was lost to him. The realization of his love was balm to her.

Mark took some rooms close by and they embarked on an exploration of London that delighted them both. The Tower of London, Buckingham Palace, the British Museum and its Harleian Manuscripts and Royal Library, not to mention the Elgin Marbles, Somerset House, the Royal Hospital, Chelsea, the Embankment, the Garrick Club, the Longacre which was the centre of horse and harness dealers and coach-builders, the Drury Lane Theatre with its painted pillared colonnade, St Clement Dane's Church, so reminiscent of Jade's favourite nursery rhyme, 'Oranges and Lemons', Prince Harry's Room in No. 17 Fleet Street, the Temple, with its grave of Oliver Goldsmith, St Paul's Cathedral, the Bridewell, the Mansion House, the Guildhall, Milk Street where Sir Thomas More was born, Carlton House and other famous Regency buildings constructed under the auspices of the Prince Regent, now King of England, all were targets of satisfaction and pleasure in the weeks to come.

Jade visited her father and he visited her at Tudor Place, but there was an unspoken recognition of the fact that they would, in future, lead their separate lives. He was endlessly interested in Lambert and in what Jade and he would make of their future.

'He'll be good to you, won't he?'

'Of course he will, Papa. How many times do I have to tell you?'

'You deserve twice as much happiness as anyone else.'

'Papa – '

'When I think of that abominable girl!'

'Let's not talk about Eliza again.' Jade grimaced. 'There must be pleasanter topics. What will you do, Papa, once – once Henry and I are wed?'

'I thought I'd take rooms in the Albany.'

'You didn't – consider marrying again yourself?'

'Great Heaven, no!' Mark looked amazed.

'Were you so unhappy with Mama?'

'Not always.'

'There should be someone to see to your comfort.'

'I'll be like Peter Masson, have a man to see to my needs.'

And keep a mistress, Jade thought, not surprised but regretful. It would be pleasant if Papa were to meet a woman who could fill all his requirements, an unpossessive woman who preferred to give rather than to receive, someone witty and intelligent, not too intense. Attractive. But she had conjured up a paragon and there were not many cast in that mould.

They went to Astley's Circus and Vauxhall Gardens, to the opera and the theatre. The visit to the theatre was painful because Peter had, unknowingly, taken Gabriel there and their boxes were cheek by jowl. Every time Jade looked sideways, Gabriel was looking at her with a brooding torment that was hard to bear, and Mark insisted that they all meet in the interval, not realizing her distress.

Jade, out of mourning, wore a silver-green gown that reminded her of the eucalyptus tree near Elsrickle. Gabriel could not keep his eyes from her, so slim and small-waisted, her hair piled in a huge swathe in which a green ornament was fastened. She plied a fan of soft, green feathers, using it frequently to hide the emotion that overcame her as the subject of Adeline was brought up.

Adeline, it seemed, was neither progressing nor regressing. Tied to her bed, she relied on the visits of friends for news of the world beyond her bed-chamber. She wondered why Jade had not come and Gabriel had been obliged to give her a promise to bring Miss Benedict to visit. She already knew of the business of Jade's pardon – and of her visit to the Home Secretary who had implemented the verbal account already related by Masson. He had been kind, apologizing for the miscarriage of justice that was more than half her own fault, Jade reflected, remembering her own silences. He had been impressed with her work with Mrs Fry.

'You must go,' Mark told his daughter, and Jade agreed unwillingly.

Gabriel was out when she called and was ushered into Adeline's presence.

Adeline looked better than Jade expected and her smile was warm. She expressed her distress over Jade's sorrows and trials of the past and swore she'd not mention them again. Then she buried her nose in the bunch of roses Jade had brought and spoke of the garden she'd known as a girl, that was filled with snowdrops and daffodils in spring, lily of the valley, cornflowers, honeysuckle, and peonies in summer, Mary and Joseph and big, brown, velvety daisies later, and Michaelmas daisies and chrysanthemums in the autumn. In the winter it had been laden with snow that dropped down the well and increased the stream until it overflowed its banks. She had fed the innumerable birds from a high table out of reach of her white, black-spotted cat, and wondered if the shingles of the roof would still show their patterns of orange lichen when the ice and snow were gone. There had been hills, a robin who became tame and came into the kitchen when the cat was out on his deadly errands. The town had seemed the strangest place in the world after the peace of her country life.

It was so much the contrast of London with Ayas Bywaters that Jade was astonished, then punished with sympathy and memories. They were not unlike, Gabriel's wife and herself. She had a heightened awareness of their separate problems. But she, at least, had strength in her body while Adeline could no longer rise from her bed. Pity became a kind of love. She promised to come again, hoping that Masson would follow the same rule and be out on business when she arrived. If she were thrown into his company she could not vouch for the consequences.

Adeline mentioned the fact that Jade's appearances coincided with her husband's disappearances but seemed to notice no connection between the events. True or false? Jade wondered. She thought she would have known had Adeline been aware.

She became close to her father in a sisterly way since Mark was such a fraternal figure. They giggled and exchanged jokes that were quite juvenile by adult standards. Jade was in the odd position of feeling older than her own father. But he had been feather-bedded while she had grown up in a society that brooked no weaklings.

One of the worst aspects was that her body was denied gratification. Jade knew that, to many, this would be reprehensible, but Nick had been a good tutor and she had come to understand that a body was like a good violin, requiring to be played and kept in tune, otherwise it would deteriorate. And only one person would alleviate those desires and longings and he was the husband of this poor, devoted friend. That seemed far more cruel than the beastliness of Denver.

Jade saw Gabriel once, riding in the park. Long before the hoofbeats reached her, she had known it was Masson, all black and white and savage, and she had taken Polly behind the sanctuary of the trees to watch him thunder past, expending all the energy he would have used up in her body, had he the chance. And she, in turn, had ridden the mare until she was exhausted. Certain impulses required sublimation of a kind.

Jade had told Mrs Abel that Lambert was on his way. It seemed more sensible than allowing the forthcoming event to remain a mirage. The housekeeper had received the news of the incipient marriage calmly, whereas Jade's own feelings were that she had acted too hastily. But she remembered her promise that was quite binding and she would not bring any man half across the world only to disappoint him. Henry had left Australia and that meant she was under an obligation to him. Try as she may, she could not evoke his looks however much she studied the portraits of his ancestors. The image of Gabriel overlaid every memory, burying the Viking fairness under his own, strong, night-hued attraction.

She dreamed of Masson, yearned for him. But knew that when she called at his house she would see only Adeline and sometimes members of Newgate Ladies' Committee.

The summer passed and the autumn came with its yellowing leaves and the fog that curled about basement and chimney. Jade and her father took the carriage out to Windsor.

They had, of course, to go by Englefield Green and she saw the cottages again all lapped in Michaelmas daisies and copper beech, then the gate-posts that led to Stagshaw. She even had a glimpse of the Tudor house, shining white and black beyond the orange foliage, a twist of blue smoke over it like a pennant.

She craned her neck out of the window until Mark asked her what she was about and she was evasive in her replies, then relapsed into a daydream in which she went up that drive and was admitted by Masson's nurse, who told her she must go upstairs to the master bedroom where Gabriel awaited her. The house enveloped her in a kind of skin as though she'd never belonged anywhere else.

But when she pushed open the door of the bed-chamber, Adeline was in the carved oak four-poster, her face the colour of whey.

Jade thrust away the fancy and took stock of her real surroundings, her eyes gladdened by the woods that sprawled around the foot of the castle that seemed pure gold with the low sunlight on it. The King's flag flew and they were later treated to the spectacle of King George the Fourth riding in company with a fair, bosomy lady, a replica of the Mrs Fitzherbert he was reported to have wed morganatically so many years ago. It seemed men did prefer the same type throughout their lives. Adelaine Masson had long, brown hair and a slender figure. She was not unlike Jade superficially.

Mark took his daughter to the best coffee-shop in the village and distracted her with gossip about the theatre and politics. A man called Cobbett was riding the countryside, arousing the yokels to rebel against their masters. The King's pavilion at Brighton had been completed a few months ago.

It was like some Arabian Sultan's seraglio. George Stephenson was making railroads. Nash's Regent Street must be explored. Newgate remained tamed.

Jade did not want to think of things of iron and stone and glass. Soon she would be required to be a wife with all the changes and responsibility that involved, and her heart was not in it. Perhaps her father sensed this, for he insisted on carrying her off to see the Pavilion at Brighton for herself and they marvelled at its domes and minarets and paddled in the sea, much to the astonishment of the more staid residents who promenaded sedately well out of range of the beach. Jade felt that she had been given back a taste of her lost childhood. What pleasure it would have been to have had a small boy or girl to join in the fun. Her heart ached afresh for the child she had lost and she fingered the locket that held Daniel's portrait. But it was disquieting how far off Daniel seemed. Only Papa and Gabriel had any true dimension.

There was a woman staying at the hotel who looked like Molly. Jade did not think of Molly Connor with any bitterness. She had gone to see Nick's mistress in the death cell, not knowing what reception she would receive. But Molly had grown quiet and curiously childlike, accepting the fate that was in store for her because she had destroyed the thing she loved.

Jade had spoken words of comfort and left her money for luxuries to ease the final days. Molly, it seemed, did not mind dying. Jade had never really wanted to die. She would always fight strenuously to go on existing, loving, being needed – hoping.

She had noticed another woman, both in the hotel and walking on the sands. They had exchanged tentative smiles and good mornings and Jade had come to look for her appearance with a definite pleasure. The woman's name was Mrs Carlisle and it seemed she was a childless widow holidaying with an elderly aunt who stayed much in her room.

Mrs Carlisle had an inborn elegance and attraction of a gentle kind that had not gone unnoticed by Jade's father. When he mentioned this one evening, Jane decided it would do no harm to contrive a meeting that would put them all on a more intimate footing. She went to the beach alone at a time Mrs Carlisle was wont to walk there and struck up a conversation they both enjoyed. It was a pity, Jade remarked, that her aunt's disability meant that she had to eat alone in the dining-room. Mrs Carlisle said it would indeed be pleasurable to have someone to talk to. She missed discourse more than anything.

Mark, surprised but intrigued, found himself studying this woman with the fine, aristocratic features and sympathetic grey eyes with more than a passing interest. She wore her clothes with a discreet distinction. Her voice was unaffected and charming. One would never tire of it. Best of all, she had a sense of fun. He enjoyed being diverted. They took to sitting for hours over the evening meal, regretful when they could stay at table no longer.

Mrs Carlisle's husband, an army officer of good rank, had been killed at Waterloo when she had been not quite thirty. Having no children, she had lived quietly since, having met no other man in whom she was interested.

Jade, watching their relationship blossom, thought that they might be happy together and, when Greta Carlisle went off with the old lady, addresses were exchanged and fond glances on parting.

Mark said no more about having a man to look after him and Jade smiled to herself secretly.

Back home in London, another letter awaited her. Mrs Abel could hardly conceal any others after the affair of the first, and the footman had been bribed to keep his eye on any that arrived and were not handed over.

'Soon,' Henry penned exultantly, 'see that you go to Lloyd's. I confess I am so excited now that I pace the deck like a love-sick schoolboy. Time to make your wedding-gown, my sweet. You've made me the happiest man on earth.'

Jade thrust the letter into a drawer and called for the carriage that Mark had at their disposal so that she could go to Lloyd's. The *Temptress* was due to arrive in three weeks.

Now that the time was almost upon her, Jade found herself riven with a tempest of conflicting emotions. Mark had set his sights on a second try for happiness and her own future was shortly to take its quite pleasant course, so she should be grateful. Henry would be kind, sensitive, in all probability a good lover. They were young and healthy and there would be children. Blonde little Vikings –

She did not want to go straight back to Tudor place. Mark was having luncheon with Peter Masson with whom he had struck up a friendship. They were much of an age and not unlike in many ways.

Jade decided to visit Adeline. What was needed was to be in the company of someone worse off than herself. Arming herself with some expensive flowers, she sat back in the carriage and tried to school herself to calmness. Her life was mapped out for her. She could not change it now.

Arriving at Masson's house, she descended and went towards the door. There was something different about it but she could not, at first, decide what it was. She pulled the bell and heard it clang inside.

It was Gabriel who answered. He was very pale and his eyes were red-rimmed almost as though he had been crying! Masson crying. It seemed ridiculous. And then Jade knew what was not as usual. The blinds had been down.

She stared at him, her fingers digging into the hot-house flowers, the tips pierced by thorns that drew blood. She scarcely felt the physical pain.

'Adeline – ?'

'She is dead.'

'Oh, Gabriel!'

Her cry tormented him.

'She – just faded away. It was all over quite quickly.'

'Oh, I'm so sorry!'

'I believe you are. Come in, please.' His voice seduced her.

'No. I mustn't. I'll leave these.' She held out the roses and he took them almost unseeingly. Jade remembered the Haymarket all those years ago. Even then she had fantasized over Masson, wanted him for her own. And now he was free. But she was not. Never would be – '

'Please, Jade – ' She could not bear the look in his eyes.

'No. I mustn't. Henry's ship comes in quite soon.' Her tone was bright.

'I see.' The black eyes lost their brief fire.

'I promised, Gabriel.'

'Yes. Of course you did. Thank you for calling.' He was all impersonality.

She turned away, unseeingly. If she had not been so impulsive, so honourable. The thought made her want to both laugh and cry. But she could do neither.

'Jade!'

She had only to look back. But she didn't. Slowly, she got back into the carriage and drove away without a backward look.

*

Jade had driven about for hours, her gaze fixed on the winter trees. The driver would be cursing her but she could not help herself. Poor Adeline. The slow, painful tears would not be shed, only squeezed out from below hot eyelids.

She was sorry Gabriel's wife was dead. Adeline had been so young. She wondered what this fatal disease of the blood was, but even the doctors did not seem to know. Adeline had been brave and uncomplaining and Jade was glad she had been strong enough to see that she could not give her cause for sorrow. She would never regret her strength of mind.

It was her hastiness in accepting Lambert that was her real stupidity. It was her intention of putting Gabriel decisively out of reach that had resulted in this intolerable situation.

But Lambert would soon be here. She'd tell him she could not live in England after the affair of being taken a second time by Caspar, that she'd prefer to live abroad. He would do as she asked. It was for his sake, after all. Another month and she'd be gone from these shores. Away from temptation –

She decided she was resolute enough to return.

Tudor Place was wreathed in city fog when she got there. It was almost dark. The footman let her in, exclaiming over the change in the weather. She went upstairs slowly, the evening stretching ahead of her like a penance. Papa might come but she could not count on it. It disturbed her that she had no one, on this particular evening, to talk to.

The fire was lit in her room. She put a light to the candle, not wanting to ask the maid to do so small a thing, and hung up her winter coat and bonnet. She must put Masson out of her mind and prepare to welcome the man she was to marry. Jade shrugged her arms into the pelerine.

Opening the drawer to re-read Lambert's letter, she saw immediately that it had been shifted. Anger overcame her desolation. She really could not allow this interference into what should be private!

There was not far to look for the culprit. Jade swept along the dim passage and rapped on Mrs Abel's door. The door swung open revealing the attenuated figure of the housekeeper standing beside the open window. The woman turned and Jade saw at once that she was far from being herself.

She went towards her, half-annoyed, half-disturbed. 'You've gone too far into what should concern only me,' she said. 'You must stop it.'

'It was meant for me,' Mrs Abel said, and her long bony

fingers pulled at the folds of material in her bunched skirts. The keys on the chatelaine clinked like pieces of ice. 'It was my letter.'

'No. It was mine,' Jade reiterated. 'Henry will be here quite soon and then we will be married. It is all arranged. You must have understood.'

She would never forget Mrs Abel's howl. It reverberated through the room and out on to the hall and landing. 'Not you!' she screamed. 'Me! It's me he writes to and will come back to.'

'Mrs Abel—'

Jade got no further. The woman sprang towards her, all blazing eyes and drawn-out pallor. 'I'll not be set aside. Henry has been seduced—'

'No! It is his own wish.' It was the wrong thing to say, of course.

Mrs Abel ripped at the front of her prim dress. The strong material was split as if it had been cheesecloth, disclosing small high breasts and a narrow rib-cage. She wore no shift. There was something obscurely unpleasant about being forced to look at another woman's unclothed body.

'See?' Mrs Abel whispered harshly. 'It's this he wants. This! This!' The strong hand flashed forward and grabbed at Jade's bodice, tearing it open to the waist. 'He didn't like me to cover myself as you do.' She seized the neck of the white shift and twisted her fingers into the lacing of ribbon, dragging at it like a fury.

Jade cried out with the pain.

'Why are you so different? Why can he contemplate putting a ring on your finger and not on mine? It should be mine. He came to my bed and lay with me.' The grating voice went on to describe what Henry Lambert had done. The details sickened the girl.

'I don't want to hear—'

'But you shall!'

The long, cruel nails tore at Jade's cheek and throat. The strong, remorseless fingers were round her neck, compressing, shutting off breath. Jade kicked out strongly and seized Mrs Abel's forearms in an attempt to break her hold. Together, they thrust and turned beside the open window through which tendrils of fog twisted inquisitively.

Jade's hand slid to Mrs Abel's wrists but she could not prise her grasp away. She was becoming weak and her head was near to bursting. It could only be imagination but she thought she heard Mark's voice. The thought lent strength to her struggle.

And then it was all over. Mrs Abel, surprised, let her go and Jade, stumbling heavily, heard the woman shriek and disappear into the fog. There was a thick crump, then silence.

Her father came towards her, appalled. Jade sank to her knees.

'What a catalyst you are,' Mark whispered, but she never knew if he spoke to himself or whether it was meant for her.

She stayed where she was, feeling the strength come slowly back.

The wedding-dress was all but ready. The dressmaker had been asked to make the neck as high as possible to hide the marks of the bruises. Not that Henry could miss them once they were in bed together.

The wind roaring and tearing down the chimneys echoed the violence of her thoughts. She could remember nothing of Henry but his kindness and the red and white and black of his Spanish room. The pelargoniums. Nothing of him.

Flora was to be her matron-of-honour. They had not seen a great deal of one another in the last months since Papa had arrived to take up so much of her time. Earle was to be best man. It would be a quiet affair, particularly after the scandal of Mrs Abel's murderous attack and accidental fall. A shadow had been lifted from the house since that evening.

Jade could not help wondering what Henry's reaction would be. But his intentions had been good. His own home should have been the refuge he envisaged but his past had betrayed him.

There was a great clatter on the roof and a shifting of slates, a mushroom of soot from the fireplace that all but drowned the glowing coals. It was the worst gale she could remember.

Maids scurried round, repairing the damage, while the footman went out into the street to inspect the roof and chimneys, only narrowly escaping a hurling slate.

Mark arrived and as they sat sipping chocolate, he said, 'Greta and I are going to follow your example. I have proposed marriage and she has accepted.'

'Oh, I am pleased. So happy for you both.' Jade went to him and put her arms around him.

'I wish you were as content.'

'Oh? What makes you think I'm not?' She went to the

window and watched the falling slates and tossed leaves.

'I'm not blind. You don't want Lambert for a husband, do you?'

'I have promised –'

'That's not what I asked.'

'You're quite right, Papa. But I shall do it just the same.'

'It's Masson, isn't it?'

She could not answer for the bitter-sweet lump that sealed her throat.

'I've suspected for some time. It was Peter who confirmed my suspicion.'

'He shouldn't have.'

'If it hadn't been for Adeline Masson's death, he would have kept quiet.'

'I owe Henry my honesty –'

'And what of the love you've cheated him out of?'

'He – thinks it will come right afterwards.'

'I suppose it might if you were not already so besotted with another man.'

'Papa –'

'I think you should tell Lambert the truth. If he is the person I take him to be, he'll release you from your promise.'

'You don't know the depth of his –'

'Obsession?'

'Yes. His letters have told me a great deal more about him. He says he wants no one else.'

'I still say he should be told.'

'It won't be easy.'

'When did you ever shy away from what's difficult?'

It was such an uncharacteristically frank talk for her father that Jade saw how important he considered the step. Normally, he skirted around anything potentially unpleasant or controversial. Greta Carlisle had wrought great changes in him.

'When will you marry Mrs Carlisle?'

'She thinks early spring.' He smiled and looked content. So different from her own turbulent misgivings! Papa was right. She must tell Henry everything.

It was calmer next day. Mark told her he would call at Lloyd's for imminent news of the *Temptress*.

Unable to rest, Jade saddled Polly and went to the Row. It was strewn with torn foliage and shattered branches but she picked her way around without too much difficulty. The wind had dispersed the fog but the recesses of the trees were filled with smoky shadow. Riding enforcedly slowly, she wondered if Rupert Mandrake had found a bride and, if he had, was she forced to share a bed with his high-nosed father? Perhaps she would not mind. People were not very moral nowadays and the Royal Family set no good example. For the hundredth time she congratulated herself on her escape from the Mandrakes. She could not think why she was harking back to the past.

He was coming. Always, she recognized his horse's hoofbeats as though they were the pulse of blood in his veins or the pumping of his heart.

This time she did not hide, only smoothed the neat black habit and set the hard hat straight, letting the curled feather spring back more becomingly. The colours of the day seemed soft and unreal. They were two pale, black-clad figures in a dove-coloured wilderness.

She was unable to see herself as Masson did. How brilliantly beautiful her eyes were and her hair was burnished. A faint colour suffused the whiteness of her cheeks. The habit concealed nothing of the slender curves he knew so intimately. Her tentative smile charmed him anew.

'How are you, Gabriel?'

'Well. And you?'

'Quite well.'

'You mustn't take honour too far,' Masson said, toying with a black glove. 'You've behaved impeccably –'

'Apart from a certain journey into limbo.'

'Oh, God,' he said. 'Don't remind me. But couldn't you be selfish now?'

'You sound like Papa and your cousin Peter.'

'They are being sensible. Tell Lambert about us.'

'I have already decided that I will.'

'And – ?'

'If he releases me – and you still want me –'

'Want you?' His voice and his face were filled with a passion at once frightening yet satisfying. He did love her still. Gabriel reined alongside and picked her from Polly's back as though she'd been a child. Seating her in front of him, he kissed her and stroked her body, knowing where and how to pleasure her most. Even buttoned and fastened against the cold as she was, his fingertips found small entrances, brought her to a pitch of longing that left her gasping and breathless.

'Now say you are going to marry another man.' He put her back on Polly, all her senses clamouring, her hands reaching out for him vainly.

'You know where to find me, when you have made up your mind.' Gabriel set off again without another look.

'Damn you,' she whispered, dazzled, and staring about her in disbelief, saw that the wood was full of colour.

Jade could not forget the encounter, the expert arousing of her body, the knowledge that without Masson her life was incomplete. She could not marry Lambert. She thought she had known all along that she must disappoint him. How would he take it? He had sailed all this way at the same sort of pitch of excitement as herself this afternoon, exalted, trusting, feverishly happy. And she was going to kill all that.

She moaned suddenly. He would get over it. Forget her. But she had not forgotten her first love. Her only love. Even Heriot had been only a shadow of Gabriel.

Masson had sought her out today as she had gone to look for him. He had made it impossible for her to carry out her intention. But she still must face Henry.

Slowly, she stopped her trembling and composed herself. The wind had risen again as though repenting of its meekness. Its mocking laughter pursued her down the chimney-stack, fluttering the carpets and disturbing the hems of the curtains and hangings.

She heard the carriage stop and the door bell ring. That would be Papa back from Lloyd's. It could even be Henry. She stood her ground, biting her lips to restore the vanished redness.

Mark was alone. He looked tired and dispirited.

'Well?'

'Lambert won't be coming.'

She stiffened with disbelief – mistrust. 'Why?'

'The *Temptress* foundered with all hands. The gales were a hundred times worse at sea. She was clogged with cargo. Too heavy.'

'You mean – Henry's dead?'

Mark nodded.

She could see Lambert at last, tall and fair, kind and yet ruthless, painting that portrait Heriot had never understood. He would not have wanted to let her go. Jade sank on to the sofa and covered her face with her hands.

The streets were very quiet. The snow had not melted and

every steeply sloping roof was covered with sparkling whiteness. The sky was a cold, sharp blue. Children threw snowballs in gardens and at street corners. The chestnut vendor clapped his hands together and held them out to the glowing brazier whose redness matched his nose.

It seemed that all the ugliness in London was covered in this sparkling blanket, that there was a truce with Heaven.

The carriage stopped at Masson's house. Her boot heels sank into the snow and her skirt hem was powdered with it. The white on black reminded her of Masson's colouring. How she had always responded to that queer moonscape quality of his looks! He was so striking. She loved him. Loved him —

Perhaps he would not be at home?

Her heartbeats quickened as she tugged at the bell. The sandy maid opened the door, peering slyly up at Jade from under her short, fair lashes.

'Mr Masson, ma'am? Is he expecting you?'

'No. But he would, I'm sure, wish to see me.' Jade lifted her dampened skirt purposefully and waited for admittance. 'He said I should come when I was ready.'

She was shown into the green-silk room where the fire burned cosily and cast its pink reflections. It was so long since she had been mistress of this chamber and in exactly these wintry conditions. And now she would be again – but as Mrs Gabriel Masson. Slowly she savoured its sweet familiarity. Her fingers trailed over the back of the chaise-longue.

She had purged herself of sadness over Henry as Gabriel had exorcized Adeline's memory. The ghosts remained but they were surely kindly ones.

Jade found herself in a fever of impatience for Gabriel to come. She stood by the window, looking out at the late snow. She would always love winter most because of those earlier associations with Gabriel. The past could not be exorcized, but the future mattered more.

She was never sure when the door opened. The first she knew of Masson's presence was when his arms came around her waist and his lips came down on the nape of her neck. He smelt of pomade, of expensive cigars and good soap. She did not have to see him to know that it was Gabriel who held her. Would always hold her. There was no need for words.